The
Collioure Concealment

by

Lita-Luise Chappell

Published by
Templar Media
24881 Alicia Parkway #E-144
Laguna Hills, California 92653
www.templar-media.com

First Edition

ISBN 978-0-9966272-1-4

Front and back cover art by Kristina Belanger

Printed in the United States of America

Visit the author at www.LitaChappell.com

Dedication

This book is dedicated to

Vere Chappell

My love and my partner in everything that I do.

His consistent support and abounding love

have allowed me the freedom to write

whatever and whenever I want.

Such a gift is beyond what anyone

could possibly ask for.

Thank you, my love!

Your Lita-Luise

XOXO

Acknowledgements

There are several people to acknowledge who were instrumental in getting this book completed and published.

First, I would like to thank all of my readers, who have followed my writing career.

My first book was *From the Mundane to the Magical: A Lifetime of Poetic Moments*. There wasn't a poem about Collioure in that book, as I was just getting a chance to discover the town when it was published, so I have included one in this book. For those who have enjoyed my second book, *The Thelemic Cookbook*, I have included many foods specific to southern France. I am now pleased to offer a work in the genre of romantic suspense.

The male lead in this story was inspired by the soldiers of the National Center for Commando Training (CNEC) based in Collioure. For years I watched these young men training in the town harbor, and was impressed by their determination, unselfishness, courage, and cheerfulness.

The Tourist Information Office of Collioure was kind enough to provide me with information about their beautiful church, Notre-Dame-des-Anges.

I would also like to thank my cover artist, Kristina Belanger. From only a few photographs she was able to render my favorite view of Collioure.

Finally, I would like to express my gratitude to my editor, Vere Chappell, who made sure that everything was as it should be. He is also responsible for the layout of the book. Thank you for all your help in getting this book released.

Vere and I first discovered Collioure in 1999. In all our subsequent travels around the globe it was this town which most captured our attention with its history, and then won our hearts with its people and surroundings. In 2013, we rented an apartment there and learned more about the history of the area, which eventually seeped into my imagination to produce this story. I got the idea for this story on a starlit evening when Vere and I stood at the viewpoint in front of the gazebo looking down upon Collioure, where Chante and Lucien are standing on the front cover. I hope you enjoy my first murder mystery come to print.

Thank you!

Lita-Luise Chappell

Collioure

Collioure, your ancient land calls out to me
On the Côte Vermeille of France's south shore
A coastal jewel that looks out to the sea
With soaring Pyrenees at your back door

The church of the Lady of Angels old
With each morning's ringing of her small bell
Inside the dust falls in layers of gold
Weaving a wonderful magical spell

Across from the church with high climbing walls
The Château Royal stands always on guard
Its old soldier spirits still walk the halls
As the men that once held her all died hard

There is Port d'Amont and there's Port d'Aval
The first gives tourists all that they may want
The next a beach with its protecting wall
It is the side of our favorite haunt

The first port has narrow medieval streets
The cemetery and artisan shops
The chocolate lady who gives out treats
And the charcuterie with meaty chops

D'Aval's more peaceful with a better view
From the windmill that is atop the hill
Where there the sea lulls with a brilliant blue
That warms the heart and the soul with a thrill

There is the colorful merry-go-round
The pathway frames of Fauvist painters past
Like Innes, Matisse and Picasso found
And Maillol's large sculptures that were bronze cast

The soil and the sea are this land's treasure
The world's best anchovies are here for sale
And Banyuls' sweet wines that give such pleasure
Produced all locally on a small scale

My favorite time of every day
Is breakfast on a bench facing the sea
With my Jésuit and café au lait
Under the shade of a shady palm tree

And every night when the breezes blow
That Mediterranean air so sweet
I know it is here that I want to be
For Collioure's the place where I feel complete

The Collioure Concealment

Prologue

Monsieur Beaux Falchan stared at the calm but stern look upon his friend's face and then he saw the gun. He had shared his secret with someone he thought he could trust. They had become such close friends that this turnabout stunned him. They had agreed to be partners so why hold him at gunpoint? At least he had held back one very significant detail. These were the only thoughts that were able to race through his mind before the bullet hit him and he blacked out.

The night before, he had met his friend at the Chapelle St. Vincent at the far end of Collioure's small bay. They sat and shared a bottle of wine facing the Gulf of Lyon along France's southern shore. Their backs rested against the tiny chapel dedicated to the Saint who protected sailors. According to legend it was on this rocky site that St. Vincent suffered martyrdom. The bright stars held the only light that reflected upon the cold and dark surging waters beyond the rocks below.

Falchan had finished out the end of the tourist season at the highest point of his diving career, with a lifetime's discovery. He had not even told his wife, with whom he was not getting along anyway. Now with her gone to visit her sister for two weeks and the autumn season upon him, he could call his time his own with no interruptions. Normally a season's profit from his diving business would carry him through the winter, but this find might support him for the rest of his life. The places he took the tourists for diving bored him. With more free time and no need to report home for any responsibilities, he had gone diving in the more difficult and dangerous places along the coast.

Three days before, he and a diving buddy had decided to explore a part of the coast that they normally motor right past due to the rocks and currents. While exploring below, they had gotten closer than expected to the rocky shore. The tide was coming in, the surge was strong, and the current was forcing them toward the rocks. His partner signaled that he was turning back, but something made Beaux go just a little closer. That's when he saw the darkening gap of a cave below the waterline. He had heard about old pirate caves, but never found one. His heart beat faster with the possibility of getting a glimpse. But he quickly turned back toward the boat and didn't say anything to his diving partner.

The next day he took his boat back to the same spot. He had broken the cardinal rule of never diving alone, but he was an expert diver and the lure was too great. He thought he knew every inlet, every breakwater, and every rocky extension along the coast even better than his predecessor, who had run the local diving business before him. When he made the treacherous decision to make directly toward the rocks he was not surprised that he could negotiate them. He was a strong swimmer so he pushed ahead to explore the rocky underwater opening. It was rough fighting the current, but he finally made it to the mouth of the cave and went in. Holding his powerful diving light, he saw that the ground had a rock and sand base that rose up at an angle. He was surprised when his head broke the top of the waterline to emerge inside a large cave. He took off his fins and walked out to find the cave high and broad. How could he have never seen this in the last four years of working this coastline?

He dropped his tanks and fins on the wet sand and went to explore. That's when he found a narrow tunnel behind a pointed rock at the back of the cave. He used his flashlight to follow the tunnel for a short while, and then a moment of panic came over him when the floor beneath him gave way. He had slipped into a hollow space below the tunnel he was in. He used his bright light to see where he had landed. He was on soft sand just six feet down, in a passage that opened up into a smaller twisted underground tunnel. He coughed and made his way forward and discovered a small room with something extraordinary. His heart was beating so hard that he had to sit and think long and hard about what he would do with what he had found. In the end, he realized he could not do it alone, so he carefully covered his tracks with the extra dirt and sand around him. He would be back with someone he could trust.

Beaux could not contain his excitement. He guessed that with an extra low tide the cave might be more accessible. He was an expert under water, but on dry land he was not a climber. It would take someone he knew and trusted to climb from the high cliffs above down into the cave entrance. It had to be taken out by land, as it could not be extracted by water. So he let his friend in on his secret.

At first his friend had shown great enthusiasm and willingness to help, but the next day when Beaux had agreed to show his friend the spot, he noticed that he was unusually quiet. Something was not right. He could feel it. It was as if he had seen greed grow in his friend's eyes overnight. He had learned to pay attention to that feeling. He had developed a sixth sense for potential danger and it had helped him to avoid near death experiences several times in his career.

They had taken his boat out and gently motored along the coast heading north. As they got closer to the spot, his friend retrieved a small bag he had brought on board. That odd feeling came back to him. In a split-second decision he decided to go past where the cave was and would simply say that it was difficult to know the exact place because the changing tides made the coastline look different. A few minutes later he cut the engine and stared toward large boulders that were tumbled at the water's edge of a rocky cliff base. That might work. He pointed to the shore where the cliff was high. The entrance was behind those boulders, he told him.

Then the man, whom he thought was his friend, pulled out a gun and told him to stand back. Beaux was shocked. His thoughts had been confirmed, but he was shaken all the same. Before he could say one word he heard the gun go off and then the realization that he had been shot severely registered. The bullet went into the upper part of his left chest, above his heart and below the shoulder. The force pushed his shoulder back and his knees buckled. He fell onto the tarp where the scuba gear was laid out for the planned dive. The pain was so intense that he could not speak or move. He went into shock and blacked out.

The gunman thought he was dead. He took Beaux's wet suit gloves, hood, snorkel, mask and regulator, and stuffed them into the legs of the wet suit. He rolled up the gear, looped the buckle of the scuba tanks around the wet suit and flippers and tied it off. It was a good thing that the tanks were full. They would make the load heavy. He watched as the bundle quickly sank into the water. He rolled up the tarp around the body, folding over the ends, and secured Beaux's weight belt around the middle. The shooter looked once more at the shore to get his bearings, then turned south, heading past Collioure. He cut the engine just out of site of the shore, then rolled the body overboard and dropped it into the sea. He cleaned the boat and made sure all was in its proper place. Then he waited until late that night to motor back to Collioure. As he entered the small bay he cut the engine to its lowest gear and gently glided the boat to its usual slot along the dock. As it was now 1:15 in the morning, no one saw him come in.

Chapter 1

Chante Morgan was very tired from her twelve-hour flight from Los Angeles to Paris and the five-hour train-ride south to Perpignan. She picked up her car from long storage at the train station and drove the half-hour to Collioure. Chante parked in the private lot and climbed the double set of stairs to her apartment dragging her suitcase behind her. The last time she had put the key into the door was ten months earlier with her now ex-husband. He would no longer be making the trip with her to their vacation apartment. Her home in Los Angeles seemed a world away, and her happiness with the man she thought she would live out the rest of her life with seemed a lifetime ago. Her heart continually reminded her that the pain was fresh with only two months since the divorce was final.

The apartment was her consolation prize while another woman had won her husband. This would be her retreat to heal, regroup her thoughts, and determine what she would do next with her life. For now, she had a familiar place in which to rest her mind and heal her heart. The furniture they had inherited two years ago when they bought the apartment was still there. The blue couch and chairs, the small balcony, and the whitewashed walls were just as she'd left them, now the only unchanged and solacing aspect in her life. She dropped her suitcase just inside the door and opened the windows to her bedroom and the French doors off the living room to the balcony. It had been a warm day in mid-September. The sun was already hanging low in the western sky, casting a warm orange hue over the hillside before her. Chante stood on the small balcony and took in a deep breath of the slightly briny smell of the sea just a block away behind a hill of trees. The olive trees scattered and fanned out across the hillside beyond her east window gently fluttered their gray-green leaves, shimmering in the golden light. She watched a lone seagull fly in from the shore, its cry mimicking her own feelings of sadness.

There was nothing in the apartment to eat but a few canned goods, and she was too tired to go out to eat. She would shop tomorrow, but for tonight all she had the strength to do was to shower and sleep. Before getting into the white-tiled shower stall she stood naked looking at herself in the mirror. She was still a slender woman for her thirty-six years of age. She cupped her breasts that warmly rested in her hands. She liked her 34Cs and slender hips. She combed out her long dark-brown wavy hair. Her large brown eyes were a little red from not sleeping. Her oval face, light skin, and petite stature had been inherited from her French mother, along with her love for life and cooking. Even though it had been a good ten years since her mother's death, she still missed her. Chante's naturally reddish lips and few freckles high on her cheeks were the only physical things she seemed to have inherited from her Welsh and English father. She knew she had also gotten stubbornness, competitiveness, and inquisitiveness from him, as well.

Chante's father had asked her to come to London and stay with him after her divorce, but she told him she first needed some time alone and then she would let him know. She stepped into the shower to rinse off the day, and as the warm water soothed her, a few tears brought the opposite effect. At last she stepped out, dried off, blew dry her hair, and then walked to the French doors with the towel draped around her. With a heavy sigh she closed the doors, walked back down the hall and stretched out on the bed she had once shared with her husband. It would now be all hers. She lay in bed staring out the window still questioning her life. The sky slowly changed from a fading orange dusk to the darkening blues of evening, with a glimmer of silvery stars offering hope for a fresh start.

The next morning Chante was woken by the sound of voices. The elderly couple that lived in the apartment above hers was up and enjoying breakfast on their balcony. She blinked away the sleep and slowly sat up. She glanced around the small room and realized her suitcase was still in the hall, so she unpacked it, dressed, and placed her belongings where she always did when arriving. Her clothes were hung up in the closet, her shoes on the floor, and her toiletries on the bathroom shelf, but this would be no vacation. The placement of these items would be quite possibly permanent. This was a new reality being born and she walked through the small apartment and began to look at it with fresh eyes. She took down the four photos of her and her ex-husband together on various trips, walked out her front door into the hallway and dropped them unceremoniously down the garbage chute. Closing that heavy metal door made it feel as if she were finalizing an old chapter in her life.

Then Chante realized she was hungry, so she went back inside, but only to grab her shopping bag, wallet, and keys to walk to town. She walked downstairs to the building's entry and checked her mail. There was a postcard from her father, which cheered her up a little, the first piece of mail since she had last been there. She walked down the paved drive along the narrow side street toward the main coast road. Monsieur Pérusse, a *bouquiniste*, opened the shutters to his used bookstore near the corner and was sitting at his small desk sipping his morning coffee. He did not look up, which was fine with her, as she did not want to disturb his morning peace, or hers for that matter.

At the end of a side street she came to the main road that ran along the coast. On her right was the Dominican Winery with its old bell tower. Across the street was a line of restaurants that followed the south side of the small bay. Also following the curve of the bay before her, a small public parking lot was there for local residents and tourists, if they got there early enough. Next to it was the colorful carousel, and the wide boardwalk that followed the long curving beach going north. To her left, on her side of the street, stretched the southern portion of Collioure with its shops and cafés. It was good to once again see the small town she had fallen in love with five years before.

Chante stopped in at the local patisserie and ordered her favorite three-sided Jésuit pastry filled with almond paste. She remembered asking her husband why they called it a Jésuit, and with his astounding and maddening knowledge for facts, he let her know that its name was due to the triangle shape of the Jésuit priest's hat. A few doors down Chante got a café au lait, and just like so many times before, she went to their bench on the boardwalk next to the carousel. This early in the morning it was thankfully not operating, but the main reason she liked to sit there was because it offered a perfect angle facing Collioure's small bay. The walkway followed the curve of the beach, but sat fifteen feet higher in case of storms. Along it, a small strip of a grassy park was popular with picnickers and playing children. A curving stretch of yellowish sandy beach fanned out to a graceful curve below the boardwalk. The coastline had golden sand and the red rocks that met the sea garnering its name, *la Côte Vermeille*. The small bay joined a narrow inlet at the northern half of Collioure, before joining the Gulf of Lyon as part of the Balearic Sea that eventually opened up to the greater Mediterranean.

It was from this bench, looking out to this blue world and beyond, where she had always found a small piece of heaven. The light that illuminated the sea and sand, and the gentle sway of the palm trees put her at ease. And even though she did not want children yet, their gleeful laughing carried from the small play yard at the end of the walkway, and was a reassurance that life does go on. All of it gave her a familiar sense of belonging. Somehow, everything about the place was able to reach inside of her and allow for a deeper breath. This small park, this bench, this entire village, was well away from their busy Los Angeles business of his art gallery and the hubbub of a big city. Quiet is what had attracted them to buy their apartment in Collioure.

Collioure is both picturesque and quaint, still holding on to its historic anchovy trade, but now making tourism a larger draw than the town's tiny fish. For centuries, vineyards have covered the steep rising hillsides above the town, producing the luscious grapes of the famous Banyuls wine. The wine is for sale from one end of the town to the other and is widely exported. The special wine, the town's fifty or so restaurants, the twenty or so hotels, and its bonus location near the Spanish border, all hold an appeal for tourists from around the world that flood the town in the high summer season. But now in September the tourists are mostly gone, the French are back from their holidays, and children are back in school, leaving the town in its natural state; calm, quiet, and beautiful for its 3,000 residents who mostly live along its shore.

Collioure has two ports, which were originally named Port d'Amont, the busier tourist side at the northern end, and Port d'Aval, where Chante sat now at its southern end. Sitting stalwart between them was the Grand Chateau Royal, which had been there in one form or another since the Visigoths in 673. Of course it had gone through several expansions under various rulers from different countries. Chante studied the castle's steep gray-curtained stonewall rising high above the water with its crenellated rim. It was just as imposing now as it must have been over a thousand years before. She wondered what intrigues had gone on undiscovered, how many battles had come to its walls, the different flags that must have flown from its great height, and the treasures the traders brought and pirates had taken. More times than she could count she had walked the broad stone walkway that hugged the base of the castle and greeted the bay linking both ends of Collioure. She would be walking there again in her annual explorations. Besides, she was going to be looking for some new art to hang on the apartment walls to take the place of those pictures, and the shops along the old town's medieval streets offered plenty of local artist's work.

Chante sat looking out to sea breathing in the solace she had always found there. Her eyes eventually wandered to her right where the land curved a bit out to sea and then turned south to Spain just fifteen minutes away on a windy coastal road. She looked up the hill that rose to that curved road above, unseen. There were hotels and restaurants, one after the other, from the bay's edge all the way to the point and up to a bluff where an old gazebo still stood. From the gazebo one has a northerly breath-taking panorama of Collioure. Above the gazebo, higher on the hill, sits a reconstructed grain windmill. From the windmill one can look west to the foothills full of vineyards, all the way to the magnificent Pyrenees mountain range.

Buying the apartment had been a good decision, and now until she decided otherwise, this little town would be her home. She had some settlement money to hold her for a while, but after that she wasn't sure. Up to then she had followed in her father's footsteps as a writer of investigative articles for travel magazines, employing her love of history and research. It was interesting work and she enjoyed it, but right now all she could think of writing was a depressing love story that comes to a sad end. It was better not to write at all rather than sink to that. She would need to figure out an alternative.

Her pastry and coffee finished, Chante walked to the small local grocer for supplies. When she finished shopping she heaved two full bags up to her apartment, put things away, and decided to go to the winery to stock up her wine rack. She detested beer and really did not drink much wine either, but when some of the best wine in the world was at her door, how could she not be coaxed into enjoying the local beverage of choice? At least she would have something excellent to drink while she cried into it.

On the way back she stopped to say hi to Monsieur Pérusse. He was emptying a box of donated books and placing them on a shelf. Many tourists dropped off their completed books from summer stays when they left at the end of the season. He lifted his glasses off his long nose, suspended by a chain around his neck, and let them gently drop to his chest. He smiled when he saw her. Monsieur Pérusse was charming as usual and greeted her in his favorite way, "Enchanté Chante!" She doubted that he ever remembered her husband's name, but he was always quick with his greetings to her. They exchanged pleasantries and she picked out three books to occupy her mind. One was a romance to lift her heart. Another was a cookbook on anchovies, which she loved, but in all her time spent in

Collioure had not really delved into their culinary diversity. The third was a general history book on the region. She had read plenty on southern France when she and her husband had first come to the area, but a review was due. They had driven all over the south and north exploring the countryside. This time she would be exploring it all on her own, so it was time to read again about the Catalan area and its mixture of Spanish and French history. Maybe she would become inspired to write a new article. She spent the afternoon and evening curled up on the couch, escaping from her past and delving into her new books. Then she had a simple meal before falling asleep.

The next day Chante went across town. She took her time walking along the stone pathway at the base of the castle. Her heartbeat seemed to be in syncopation with the surf that rhythmically rolled up and over the rocks. The small bit of spray was refreshing on the sunny day and the light sparkling off the water in the shallows among the rocks was lovely. As she rounded the eastern point of the castle pathway, she watched a colorful tourist boat come chugging into the small inlet to the docks at the north side of the castle. In high season three times as many boats shuttled along the coast north and south, overflowing with camera-laden, children-pointing, and wine-inebriated tourists. Now, only a couple boats went out and returned in the day with their partially filled sedate loads of the retired.

She also noticed that the young men from the National Center for Commando Training (CNEC) were engaged in exercises along the far side of the port dock. She knew the CNEC was a branch of the army, headquartered on the bluff of the hillside overlooking Collioure at Fort Miradou. Today the men were in their wet suits being timed with stopwatches to see how long they could hold their breath under water. Chante had seen the men once in a while walking the town in their beige fatigues, but they were rarely en masse. Every summer they held competitions among them and now and then were seen in the water with their boats, training in rescue techniques. Chante paused for a couple of minutes to watch, admiring their strong physiques and bright young faces, and then she went on her way.

She crossed the small footbridge just north of the castle. It was not more than twenty feet long, with a gentle upward curve over the dry quay. When it rained, the cemented waterway underneath turned into the Douy River, flowing directly out and into the sea. Most of the year, however, the water was at such a trickle from the hillside run-off that its wide channel served as additional parking for the flood of tourists and market venders. The two ports had taken on new names in recent years. This northern side was now simply referred to as *la ville*, the city, which was more like a small village with its narrow walkways where most of the town's commerce and tourist shops were located; and *le faubourg*, meaning a suburb or quarter outside a town's old wall, south of the castle where her apartment was.

Along the quay on the north side ran the Avenue Camille Pelleta with restaurants lining its pavement. In the village behind this busy boardwalk were alleyways mostly for pedestrians and delivery vehicles. Many tiny streets, alleyways, and paths crisscrossed back and forth along the rising hillside up to the fort, but eventually their irregular pathways angled down toward the shore. One could walk every path around the hill in less than an hour. There are a good many galleries specializing in the works of local painters and photographers. All year long, but especially in summer, painters set up their easels, and photographers worked with their models, in the special light that fills the air; hailed by Matisse, Derain, and Picasso as among the world's finest. Often the modern artists sell their works in the local shops. One hotel, the Hôtel des Templiers, has its walls full of artists' works from floor to ceiling. At one time artists were allowed to trade their works for sleeping and eating there. When the walls were filled, that practice came to an end.

There are also a wide variety of other tourist items available. There are shops with French and Spanish ceramics, leather goods, soaps, knives, clothes, and knick-knacks, along with wine shops that offer tastings, and several places that sell ice cream and pizza, as well as finer restaurants. Chante had probably been in every shop at one time or another over the years, and she recognized many of the venders and shop owners as she walked along. In one shop she finally found a two by three foot multi-tiled view of Collioure that struck her as colorful and charming. Its colors were bold and it made her smile to see the Dominican church and winery at the far left side, the castle in the middle and the church on the right, so she bought it and had it boxed up to carry.

Happy with her purchase, she stopped and got an ice cream cone with her favorite flavor, pistachio, to celebrate. She sat in the shade of a tree along the Boulevard du Boramar, watching the soldiers in their wet suits now departing in rubber skiffs out into the bay, and the thinning autumn crowds walking by. Several colorful little fishing boats in red, blue, green and yellow, were tied up along the small dock. In fact, they were the same four boats that had been there for years, which never seemed to leave the dock and were most likely left there simply for the tourists to take pictures of. Chante listened to the light rhythmic clang and slap of the metal lines hitting the masts on the boats as a breeze continually kept the passersby cooled and refreshed. She watched the bustle of the waiters, running back and forth between the tables scattered with chatty tourists, and heard some light guitar music coming from one of the cafes. The day was sunny and the light blue of the sky matched the same tone of the dark blue sea. Chante closed her eyes for a few moments to drink in the sounds and the feel of the place around her. She remembered sitting there in the same spot with her husband less than a year ago. Not being able to share her favorite place in the world with someone she loved, she had to push away that saddening thought.

Chante reopened her eyes to look past the cafés along the Boramar beach to the church at the end. The old Église Notre-Dame-des-Anges (Church of our Lady of the Angels) stood resilient and proud. Its grey stone walls, slanted red tiled roof, and tall pink conical tower with its white clock seemed rather plain, considering the church contained multiple chapels and one of the most beautiful golden high altars that southern France had to offer. Sitting at the water's edge, it looked more like a fortress than a church. She had not been in it for years. She was not religious by nature and admired the inside of churches only for their art.

Beyond the church, although she could not see it from her vantage point, she knew the Chapelle St. Vincent sat on a rocky promontory facing the sea. At the top of the rocky bluff, it was nothing more than a one-room chapel that was always locked, supposedly housing the saint's relics. In a strong wind its one bell was heard ringing forlornly across the entire bay. Splitting off at an angle from the chapel and running parallel to Collioure's shore, ran a high-walled cement walkway curving out into the bay. Its narrow walkway was protected by guardrails on either side, and ended at a sealed casement with a pulsing radiant light, which had replaced the old lighthouse long ago. Its brightness aided the many boats entering the small harbor at night. From this extended walkway, one could look back on the town to enjoy its lovely curves and historical buildings. In fact, it was a view similar to the one her new tiled art displayed. Collioure was indeed a town of many faces: royal and communal, religious and secular, bustling in summer and relaxing in winter. For years she had been a tourist, but for the first time, thankfully with dual citizenship, she would now be a resident. With this revelation she at once felt a sense of ownership and pride, and her thoughts of Los Angeles faded away.

On her way back to the apartment she walked around the back of the castle along the Avenue du General de Gaulle. She skirted the central square where the outdoor markets were held twice a week, past the police station with its blue shutters, past the town's Mairie, and then past the small street that led to the town cemetery. It was a small village, which could be walked from one end to the other in about fifteen minutes. The avenue turned down with the slope of the hill that led into the southern side of town. She walked past the small library on her right, which she had never ventured into. Perhaps now that she was going to live here she should check it out.

Chante returned back to the apartment and set about mounting her new artwork. She centered the heavy tiles centrally on the living room wall so that she would immediately see it every time she entered the apartment. Sitting on the couch she looked at it for the longest time. The harbor, castle, and church were the quintessence of the town. Smiling to herself, she was suddenly struck with the realization that it was only the second time she had smiled in months.

She had her dinner on the balcony and nearly drank half a bottle of white Banyuls wine by herself. Every time she started to get depressed or remembered something she and her ex had done together, she would glance up at the new tiled art on the wall and her mood would change. She was surprised that something so simple could make such a difference in the apartment and in her life. She was starting to get a settled feeling.

That night though, she dreamt that she was in a long dark hallway, at the end of which was a large door. She could not figure out where she was or why she was there, but she was left with a feeling of frustration.

Chapter 2

When Chante awoke the next day she still had visages of the dream, but brushed it off as something her subconscious was still processing since she had come through a particularly dark time in her life. Beyond those feelings and that door she didn't know what her future might hold, but she was ready for it. She had slept in late and was feeling a little lazy, but today she told herself she would approach life differently. Instead of going to the pastry shop which, at 11:00, was now closing, she just felt like some tea, and instead of moping about the apartment, she was going to the library to check it out. Who knows what she might find that would interest her? Perhaps she would get an idea for an article on local history, maybe find a good mystery story, or just explore the shelves to get to know her local library. It was not as though she had a pressing schedule. After Chante finished her tea she walked the few blocks to it.

The small one-story yellow building was down a few steps and set back from the street on an angle. She noted the opening and closing times on the door. It had shorter hours in the off-season and was closed on Mondays, but for now it was open all day until 5:00. Great, she had hours to meander the shelves, get registered to check out books, and get completely lost in the land of words, one of her favorite things to do. She walked in and up to the desk on her immediate right where a small wispy woman in her mid-fifties wearing glasses was on her computer. She wore her dark hair with graying streaks up in a bun. She had a pleasing face with a wide brow and sharp grey eyes. The nameplate on her desk read Mimi Severin.

"Bonjour, Madame Severin. I have recently moved to Collioure and I would like to get to know your library and register to check out books."

Madame Severin tucked in her chin and looked over her glasses at Chante. "Bonjour. I detect an American accent. Is that where you are from?"

"I am American and have been a tourist to Collioure for several years, but now I am living here. My name is Chante Nicolina Morgan."

Madame Severin nodded her head in a greeting and then reached to a pile of cards on her desk. "Fill this out with your name and address and I will place you on file."

As Chante was filling out the card she commented, "I'm surprised you don't register new members on that computer."

A side smile seemed to slowly develop in the corner of Madame Severin's mouth. "Oh I do and I will. We keep both a paper copy and a computer file. Sometimes this old computer has problems, so having that information on cardstock is our back up, and it makes it easier to have you write your information down first."

"That does make sense," replied Chante. "Can you give me an idea of how your library is laid out?"

"Madame Morgan, it is a very small library. The shelves are marked. I think you can find your way around." She bent her head down and went back to her work.

Chante was a little put off by her dismissing comment.

"It's Mademoiselle. I am no longer married."

Madame Severin looked up briefly and simply said, "Mademoiselle," and resumed looking down.

Chante had just tried to make conversation. When she looked around the room it seemed smaller inside than what it looked like on the outside. She certainly could find her way around in any library. Then, Madame Severin did add some additional information in a slightly kinder manner.

"You are allowed to check out three books on your first visit, and if you bring them back on time, you will be able to check out up to six."

Chante thanked her and went off exploring. In the center of the room there were low tables and short shelves with children's books, but taller rows surrounded three walls of the room. Placards on the top of the shelves showed each topic. Beginning on her left, past the front door, the first held general works and computer science, then philosophy and psychology. The next row had religion and social sciences. Languages and pure sciences were down the next aisle, followed by art and recreation in another row. It certainly seemed to be laid out according to the Dewy Decimal System. Next was literature, which caught her attention, so she went down that aisle and stopped to scan the shelves. While looking for titles that would call out to her, she overheard Madame Severin quietly speaking to someone on the other side of the high shelf.

"Monsieur Reynard, here is a book you might find of interest. It has a chapter on early Collioure, but there are no architectural plans for the fort when it was built. Those would be secured somewhere at the fort, I imagine. However, you would do well to check at the Mairie. They house some records of the town."

A masculine but gentle voice softly answered, "Thank you, Madame Severin. I appreciate your help."

Whoever she was speaking to had certainly won the librarian over. She practically purred to the guy. When

Chante heard her walk away, she had to go to the other end of the aisle and peer around the shelves to get a look. All she could see was the back of the man's head. He had dark straight hair cut short and he was wearing a light blue long-sleeved shirt. A dark jacket hung over the back of the chair. She was about to turn back when she noticed that on that side of the shelf were books on history. That interested her even more. She slowly made her way down the row scanning the shelves and found two books that caught her eye. One was on the Albigensian Crusade and another on Sebastien de Vauban, a famous architect of France. She took them with her to the same table where the soft-spoken man was seated. She seated herself on the opposite side of the table at the other end and stole a glance to see what he looked like.

The first thing she noticed was his tanned face with strong cheekbones and an aquiline nose. He had a slight wave to his hair on his crown with a lone curl of dark hair that turned the other way on his forehead. His brow was smooth despite the obvious look of concentration about him. He looked to be in his mid-thirties. His shoulders were wide and squared, most likely due to his good posture. He glanced up at her and nodded, but went right back to his reading. His eyes were aquamarine blue and well spaced with thick black lashes. Then she looked down at the two books in front of him, and to the one he had open. The edge of the closed one was *The Roman Remains of Southern France*, but she could not see the title of the one he was reading. She took a guess and whispered to him.

"Pardon me, but I could not help but notice that we seem to be interested in the same thing." He slowly raised his head and then his brow furrowed. His face showed surprise as well as concern, so she explained herself. "Local history." Then his look changed completely and became discernibly relieved.

"Oh?" He said almost as an afterthought and then he looked at the two books she had before her. He had an immediate surprised look on his face. "Vauban? Where did you find that book?"

She was amazed at his interest. "Right there on the shelf behind you, just a meter away," she whispered back.

"I must have looked right past it. What is your interest in Vauban?" His eyes narrowed and he finally looked earnestly at her.

"I'm a writer and I'm searching for something to write about. I thought perhaps, I would start with the history of the castle. Vauban was its architect, was he not?" His shoulders seemed to relax, and he finally saw past the question and noticed her lovely face.

"Yes, but he was not the original architect. There was an older building on the site, the Templars added to it, and its structure was enlarged and fortified with its star shape in the mid-1600s." While he spoke, something in his eyes seemed to awaken. They gained a sparkle of interest. History was obviously a passion for him. "Are you visiting Collioure?"

"I discovered Collioure about five years ago and have returned year after year, because it holds something very special for me. There is a light and a history here that has me entranced. My husband and I bought an apartment a couple of years ago, but now we are divorced and I've come to live here alone." She needed to change the subject and leaned in toward him conspiratorially whispering lower. "Madame Severin seems to like you."

"I've only recently come to know her. She is actually not so stern as her name implies."

"You could have fooled me. She was almost rude to me when I just registered, but she practically purred at you." He laughed louder than he had intended to, and she added. "I assume you live here."

"I grew up in Perpignan, but now I am attached to the fort."

"Oh, I probably saw you at the north harbor. So how long can you hold your breath?" He smiled broadly at that.

"Long enough." He responded.

She could not help but smile back at him. Something was happening inside of her that she hadn't felt in many years. Was she actually feeling excited?

"What's your name?" he asked smiling, now curious.

Wow, what a smile, she thought. She stretched out her hand to introduce herself.

"Chante, Chante Morgan. It's nice to meet you. What is yours?"

He took her hand firmly but gently, just like his voice. "It is very nice to meet you Chante Morgan. My name is Lucien Reynard."

Madame Severin rounded the corner and saw them. Her eyes were focused, and her demeanor had turned a 180 since she last stood before him. She glared at his hand touching Chante's and then at her.

"Keep your voices down. No laughing. This is a library."

Lucien responded by standing and gave her a slight bow, being sure to lower his voice. "My deepest apologies, Madame Severin. I seem to have met someone with an equal interest in history. We promise to keep our voices down. Better yet, we could take this outside." He turned to Chante hoping for her agreement. Chante was still considering the question. After all, she had just arrived, but there was something about him she couldn't quite figure out. She seemed to be under his spell, like Madame Severin was, and that was confirmed when the madame reacted to the broad smile he gave her. All Chante could manage was a slight nod.

He took both of their books, made two piles and set them before Madame Severin "Would you be so kind as to register these books for us to check out?"

Madame Severin looked from one to the other and then reached forward, putting the books into one pile. "Of course, Monsieur Reynard. Right away." She actually smiled as she took the four books into her arms and walked back to her desk.

Lucien turned to Chante. "I hope that was all right with you. Is it?" The confident look suddenly turned to one of concern.

"Well, you definitely know how to pour on the charm with her, but what makes you so sure that it will work on me?" He did look a little crestfallen at that remark.

Chante looked directly at him, still considering what it was that seemed so attractive. Lucien thought she was about to say no.

"I realize you just arrived to explore our top library facilities," he said sarcastically, "but perhaps we can discuss our interests elsewhere? Perhaps we could go for some coffee? Would you so permit me?"

He was pretty quick with his pick-up line. "I just got here, and I'm not sure I like having a man sweep me out the door so quickly."

She could see his whole body slump in disappointment, and at once she could see what remained of the boy in the man. Then he gave it another try.

"I assure you Mademoiselle, my intentions are honorable. It's just that when you spoke to me, it was like a breath of fresh air. Sometimes I get so focused I don't see the beauty of the world, even when it comes to sit at my table."

No doubt about it, whether he was practiced or not, he seemed honest and charming. Not a bad combination, and there was that adorable curl on his forehead that seemed to beckon her on.

"I suppose I can always come back later, and any other day in the weeks to come." She was entranced now. Had he just asked her out after just meeting her five minutes ago? It had been too many years to discern the difference between a man's pick-up line and real interest. She was definitely out of practice in rebuffing a man's persuasive charms. Perhaps, she rationalized; she could interview him on the history of the town.

Lucien smiled a wide winning smile and reached for his jacket over his chair. They both walked to Madame Severin's desk where she had just finished scanning the books and had placed them into two piles. They each took their books, cradled them in their arms and walked out the door to the bricked flower boxes in front of the library's entrance.

Once outside he turned to her. "You know it is nearly lunch and I did not have breakfast. Could I persuade you with a small repast? I know it seems presumptuous of me, but I have been here for several years, and I have no real friends in town outside of the fort. Frankly, I have hardly spoken to any woman since I was stationed here. That is, besides Madame Severin here at the library, and Madame Clöet, who owns the *magasin de chocolat*. But I would hardly call them anything but acquaintances. Admittedly, I have used Madame Severin solely for the purpose of obtaining a library card and Madame Clöet solely to obtain chocolate." They both laughed at that.

"You do seem a bit desperate, but I have to admit your charms seem to be diversifying beyond librarians. Perhaps I can get a local history lesson out of you."

He smiled and led her to the large outdoor café along the boardwalk near the carousel. An outdoor café did seem less intimate, and besides the day was sunny, clear, and bright with a gentle breeze. They ordered some sandwiches and a glass of wine, and then Chante needed to know more about this handsome man.

"So how long have you been at the fort?"

"I was transferred here after my training as a staff sergeant in the executive branch. I actually went through the commando training a few years before that, but when my father had a heart attack I requested to be transferred here to be near him. When you were watching the men in wet suits at the north port yesterday, I was not there. My duties lie elsewhere with the fort."

"Which you probably cannot tell me about."

"There is nothing really secretive about what I do. You could say I am really just a glorified secretary. It is not the long objective I had when I joined the unit, but perhaps I will advance my career when I am not so worried about my father. I don't want to be too far from him in case he needs me."

"He is ill then? I'm sorry. I take it your mother is no longer with you?"

"My father is now actually doing fine. My mother died when I was seven. I barely remember her. My father was in the military years ago, but he turned his interests toward history and now he is a history professor at the University of Perpignan Via Domitia. And you? Did you leave your parents in America?"

"My mother died about ten years ago. She was French and I was born in Paris, but I've lived most of my life in America and I have dual citizenship. My father is still alive. When my mother died he moved back to his own country and lives in London. He works for a newspaper there as a journalist. I guess that is where I got the interest to write, from him."

"So have I read anything you've written?"

"Not unless you happen to read travel magazines and enjoy desert housing in New Mexico, or need a good restaurant in London or Los Angeles. My real passion is European history. I like to think I am capable of turning over a historical stone that no one else has turned over. "

"Ah, so you are stubborn and headstrong." He replied. They both laughed.

"You sound like my father, who has always said those things to me, but he doesn't realize I got them from him."

"So, you think you will be writing about the history of the castle? I'm not sure that anyone has done that yet. At least I've not seen anything on any bookstands for sale, besides the posters and puzzles of it. But I would not hold my breath trying to get much information about it, beyond what the castle itself publishes."

"Maybe, but you don't know me very well. I'm very resourceful. Though I guess you are in the same boat, as it seems you are trying to get more history about the fort."

His eyes froze on her and he pulled back, but recovered, thinking quickly about how to respond. "Oh, that, . . . I'm trying to piece together information for a write-up about the fort for the soldiers that come in and out of there. They are always full of questions about the area."

"Oh, then perhaps you can give me the same description that you give your men. I'd love to hear about the fort's history."

"All I can tell you right now is that the fort's modern buildings were built in 2007 and occupy three levels of 25,000 square feet. There are offices, a medical unit, a kitchen, mess hall, and barracks for the men. It also houses the local fire department. I've never been told much about the fort's history. When I finish getting the information and writing up my description, I will share it with you."

She sensed a dodge, but she didn't really care. As long as he kept talking and she could watch his handsome face, especially his mouth, she would listen. His top lip was a little thin, and his bottom lip was fuller, but they made a winning combination when he smiled. Even if he were describing gutting a fish, she would be enraptured.

"I'm curious though, how come you are wandering the streets of Collioure without your fatigues? Aren't you required to wear them?"

"Technically yes, when on duty and on the base, but on my day off it's the last thing I choose to wear. I'm a staff sergeant who helps coordinate personnel that come and go, but my work feels more civilian as most of my work is done in an office and not in the field."

"Are there many men at the fort that are in your similar situation?"

"There are a few of us."

"Is that the whole of your work, checking in commandos?"

"No, once each year the training center offers journalists and reporters a chance to be trained in the field for writing when they need to go into war zones. I also plan their activities and coordinate their encounter with us. It's a very short course that teaches first aid, how to identify weaponry, even how to defend themselves in case they need to in a battlefield. But can we talk about something else? My life is all about the fort, morning, noon and night. It's nice to get away from it when I can. And it is a lovely Saturday afternoon."

When their food arrived, they talked about Collioure and its local sights. He made her tell him where she had gone and what she had done on her various trips in the region. Most of her previous escapades had been to places more north. Almost two hours seemed to pass before they knew it, until he looked at his watch and realized that the Mairie would be closing at 4:00 on Saturday and now he had only an hour to do some research.

Chante noticed that he looked a bit preoccupied. He seemed open and honest, but at the same time also guarded. There was something he was not telling her. Though it could be a million things; they had just met, after all.

"Mademoiselle Morgan, I have been enjoying your company so much today that I had no idea we had been speaking for so long. I need to get somewhere before they close. May I call you by your first name, by Chante?"

"Only if I can do the same and call you, Lucien?"

"Yes, of course. I would like that very much. May I call you? I hope you've seen that I can act like a gentleman, and that I may be permitted to see you again. Could I?"

She had to admit she was warming to his old European charm. She responded without really thinking things through. She wrote down her cell number on a napkin and handed it to him. "You can reach me on my cell. I live just around the corner." She nodded toward the winery in the old Dominican church.

He stood and she looked up at him. A good long three seconds elapsed with their eyes still engaged. He reached for her hand on the table, bent down and kissed it.

"It has been a great pleasure. On my next day off I would like to take you to dinner. Would that be possible?"

She stood to meet his gaze. "Yes, that would be lovely. I look forward to your call." He smiled and his whole face lit up. He placed some money on the table for their lunch, and as he turned away he was smiling broadly. She watched him walk with his determined long legs striding away on top of narrow hips, until he disappeared at the top of the street. Wow, did she just have a lunch date with practically a stranger and then agree to a second date? Is this what it feels like to be single, to take a chance? It was pretty foreign, pretty scary, and oh so nice.

Chante rose from the table and walked over to her bench. She couldn't call it "our bench" anymore, since she knew she would never be sitting on it again with her ex, so she sat with a new sense of ownership and wondered if she would sometime soon be sharing the bench with Lucien. Or maybe they would inaugurate the next bench over? She was beginning to feel less unhappy already and more at home in Collioure than she expected.

Chapter 3

Lucien pulled open the door to the local municipal council of the town's Mairie. Its heavy front door swung out to reveal a bright space with a large wall on the left full of colorful posters of Collioure's main sites. A large painting of the Chateau Royal hung in the middle, while around it were posters: one of a local tour boat full of people smiling and taking pictures, a poster of the town's clock tower and church, divers in and out of the water, fishing boats with nets pulling tiny silvery fish from the sea, and wagons full of Collioure's pride of pick, its grapes for wine.

A wide white counter spanned the far end of the room and behind it stood a fairly young man in his mid-twenties with dark hair and a broad smile. It almost seemed more like a tourist office than a town hall.

"Can I help you?" The man smoothed down the front of his shirt and stood as tall as he could for his small stature.

"Yes, I would like some information."

The man was quick to reply with a litany of his responsibilities, in which he obviously took great pride, although it had the note of a well-rehearsed speech.

"I'm happy to help. This office serves the town in several capacities. This is the town's Mairie or city hall and the main tourist bureau, although there is a second tourist office for bookings across the quay. This office is in charge of the registration of all new businesses, import and export paperwork, and fishing licenses. There is also the

Protection Complète Insurance Company upstairs. I think you will find Collioure has much to offer. We even have a small gallery of art in the next room with examples from our local artists."

Lucien glanced down the hall to his right and could just see the opening of the room that the man had spoken about. In all his time in Collioure he had never entered the town hall and had no idea there was anything here but a basement full of old records and a mayor's office that was probably rarely occupied. The man obviously thought he was a tourist fresh into town. He decided to play the professional approach.

"I am not a tourist. I live here. I am Staff Sergeant Lucien Reynard and I am attached to Fort Miradou. I'm doing some research on the history of the fort, the chateau, and the town, for the Journalists and Reporters Abbreviated Field Combat Encounter next month. If you could direct me to your historical files, I'll stay out of your way."

The man nodded his head in greeting, but did not extend his hand. "Bonjour Staff Sergeant Reynard, my name is Alexis Moniqua. Do you have some identification? We don't open our records to just anyone, and you are out of uniform," he said as he gazed at Lucien up and down.

Lucien took out his wallet to show his military I.D. "Of course. I completely understand. It's my day off and I was walking by, so that's why I am out of uniform."

Moniqua looked closely at the I.D. and up at Lucien. "We actually have a procedure. If you will let me know what you are specifically looking for I can get it for you. Are you interested in Collioure's history of administration, demographics, taxation, trade, activities, or accommodations?"

"None of those, actually. I was hoping to put together an architectural historical summation. You know how reporters can get. They ask pointed questions and I'm hoping to give them at least some general information without too much detail. So perhaps I can look through the historical files and find some information that will satisfy them. Are there any historical architectural maps of the area, perhaps of the chateau or the fort?"

Moniqua squinted his small dark eyes and tilted his head slightly to think about what Lucien had said. "I'm afraid the historical files kept here go back only to 1944 after the Germans were defeated. Anything before the Second World War is housed at the prefecture building of the Pyrénées-Orientales department in Perpignan."

The disappointment on Lucien's face must have been obvious, but he decided to make the best of the situation. He would check in at the prefecture building the next time he was in Perpignan. "Then I will start with what you have here and see what I can find."

Monique nodded again. "Then please come this way and I will show you what we have."

He led Lucien past the display room and into a small room with two computers. First Moniqua sat down at one of the computers and opened the electronic files that had to do with the town's history. Then he got up and gestured for Lucien to have a seat.

"Here are the files that we have for viewing electronically, and I will bring you some additional files that have not yet made it into our digital files."

Lucien politely thanked him and sat down to see what was there. He scanned through the electronic files, which ran only from 1953 to a statement that ended in 1970. He saw general files relating to each President's term. There was a list of all the different Prime Ministers, and the names of those who held regional offices through the years. There was a file on France's possessions and colonies, a list of political and economic agreements, and an alphabetized list of secessions from France that had occurred. Something Lucien did not know was that France was the third country to enter the space program and the fifth to explode a hydrogen bomb. And of course, true to the resolute spirit of the French people and their love for bicycling, through it all, the Tour de France continued to be held. He read the files up to 1970, but there was nothing there that he wanted.

After ten minutes Moniqua returned with two thin folders on the intervening years between 1944 and 1952. Lucien looked through these files, but there seemed to be only summations for each year, and again only on France in general, but at least these files began with earlier dates. The information was appropriate for any Mairie as a broad overview of its town's modern history, but was lacking on events in Collioure, specifically.

When Lucien put the folders aside he noticed that the folds on the back of the folders had once been larger and were now creased to a smaller size to hold the thin stack of papers within them. He wondered if that was because some of the older files had been transferred digitally to computer files leaving the remaining summation files, or because materials had been purposely removed before being handed to him. He smiled at his suspicious nature. He really could not be sure.

His time there had pretty much been futile, and he was thinking he could have spent more time with Chante. As time ran out, he did take a couple of minutes to look at the art in the small room adjacent to the computer room. Only one thing caught his eye, an artist's interpretation of how Collioure might have looked before the fort was built on the hill. The village was small and crowded around the chateau, which was portrayed as a simple castle of pre-Vauban construction. What surprised him the most was that the castle was angled differently than he thought it presently was. The front of the castle was facing more toward the west instead of the present entrance on the north side. He took a picture with his phone and noted the artist's name in his breast-pocket notebook. Perhaps the artist had early maps that gave him an idea of how to portray the town without the fort.

On Monday morning, Lucien quickly changed into his military fatigues and went to his office at the fort. He worked on the second floor with a wide eastern window supported by modern metal beams, offering an amazing view of Collioure and the coast below. Most of the offices on this level had large glass sections along the hallway, so each office could be looked into. Those on the east side of the hall had a view and those rooms were always bright. Those across the hall received light through the hall glass, but they lacked the view. Lucien waved to his assistant across the hall, Private Alerion Bellamy, as he approached his own office and unlocked it. Alerion was coming out of his office toward him.

"Bonjour Alerion, what is new with you?" Alerion stood at attention in his beige fatigues and saluted. Knowing he could be more himself with Lucien, as they had also become friends, he brushed back his short curly blond hair and his body relaxed. He did have a worried look on his face and Lucien could tell from his penetrating brown eyes that he had something important to tell him. Lucien was always surprised at how expressive those small eyes could be. Alerion had exceptional eyesight and had earned himself the name "young eagle" due to this. He looked young for his thirty-two years, but when he was worried, as he was now, his wrinkled brow made him look older.

"Sir, Colonel Grosvenor wants the basement cleared and ready for occupation in only two weeks' time instead of the month that he told us about earlier. He has already informed Colonel Bastion at Mont-Louis that the office will be ready for his two men to occupy. What are we going to do? I haven't even seen the room yet."

"Alerion, we will figure something out. Let's go there now and make a list of what needs to be done. If that is the new time schedule then we will need to move quickly."

Lucien opened his desk to retrieve the key that he had received from the colonel only a few days previously in preparation for the task. He had already seen the room below, had moved some boxes and made an interesting discovery. It seems as though he would be showing what he discovered to Alerion sooner rather than later.

They left that floor of offices and walked down a flight of stairs. On the ground floor were the mess hall and a wing that led to the soldier's quarters. Lucien led Alerion down a long hall to the stairs that went down further to the basement. Alerion had never been in the basement before. When they arrived and Lucien unlocked the basement door, Alerion's eyes greatly enlarged as they swept the packed room. The room was fairly large, approximately eighteen by thirty feet with a normal ceiling height, but it seemed much smaller because the room was filled with boxes that went nearly to the ceiling. The number of boxes, filled with old files before them, seemed daunting. Alerion opened the nearest box and checked the date on one of the files, which read 1989. All files older than twenty years came down to this room. It had been the deep storage for the fort; slowly filling up with more boxes every few years, and like all repositories nothing was thrown away. There was a cleared straight line about two boxes wide down the center of the room all the way to the back wall. Six feet in from the back wall was the only light source in the room, a foot-wide round lamp with circa-1945 metal shade, which hung down from the ceiling. It lit up a card table directly below it. There were also packing materials and odd pieces of electrical parts from old radios.

Alerion was aghast. "Look at all these boxes! My back hurts just looking at them. Where are we moving them to anyway?"

"Just down the hall," and Lucien led him to the room that was to hold all the inventory of boxes. It was a longer, narrower and darker room that had long running electric lights. Then they went back to the first room and looked at the piled up boxes again. It was time to tell him.

"Alerion, there is more here than meets the eye. I have a small confession to make to you. I have already been down here, and I was the one who set up that table on the other side of the room."

"Well thank you, Lucien," he said politely, but then changed to sarcasm. "I don't know how to repay you," and then feeling the task, "but at least it is a start."

"No Alerion, I mean I discovered something unusual about the room."

Alerion cocked his head in question. He could not help but look around and then make his way down the aisle to the table. It was a normal card-table, army green, and surrounded by boxes. There was only sawdust and rubbish under and around the table.

"What? What's so unusual, besides the fact that you were able to actually get a space cleared for this table?"

"It's not the table itself, but what's under the table." Lucien folded up the table and leaned it against the boxes, then used his foot to clear away the debris and push it to the side. The edge of a metal door was revealed.

"What is that?"

"Alerion, that is a trapdoor."

"Going where? I thought that the fort was built on bedrock?"

"So did I. I only just discovered the trapdoor a few days ago and I have no idea where it goes, but I would like to know."

"Well, we haven't got time to even guess, because we have way too much work to do moving all these boxes."

"True," said Lucien, but Alerion could see that there was a longing look in Lucien's expression. "But I cannot help but feel that we have a mystery before us, or rather underneath us. I've been speculating and I think that it must be quite old. I think these boxes were placed here on purpose to cover it up."

"But it is just a storage room, and who knows how long these boxes have been in here." Alerion looked at the few boxes next to him. "We know at least some of these boxes have been here since 1951, but look, this one says 1942, and wow, this one says 1936! That's before the Second World War. I had no idea these went back that far. Are we going to have to divide them up into years?"

"Probably, but Alerion forget the boxes for one moment will you? I want to know what is on the other side of this trapdoor!"

Alerion was feeling a little exasperated with Lucien, but Lucien was his higher-ranking officer. "It looks pretty impenetrable. What do you propose we do?"

"Let me think. We are trained to think and act under pressure. Think of this as nothing more or less than any other military challenge."

"I know, but this is different. This trapdoor was not made by one of our enemies. The French Army probably put this door here. Do you think the colonel knows that it is here?"

"I don't think so. The colonel has been here less than six years, and when I first unlocked the storage door, there were cobwebs across the entrance. No one had entered before me in years. For the last four years I have not moved any boxes down here. I think we have the only key, as the colonel asked me to return it to him when we were done. Besides, he could not be bothered with something so trivial. That is why he had us take on the job of clearing the room. If he'd known about it, he probably would have mentioned it to me."

"This might be a large room, but it is packed. With so many boxes and old junk we will need help to clear it."

"I'd rather no one else was in here but you and me."

"No one else? You must be kidding."

"I know it sounds crazy, but I don't think we should alert anyone else to it."

They both looked down at the old square metal door, and Alerion was the first to comment. "The door looks welded shut on the latch side. What good would it do to force it? I think our best course of action is to clear the room, cover it, and forget it exists. Maybe there are architectural plans somewhere upstairs?"

"The first place I looked was in our own military library off of the mess hall, but there was nothing there. Then I went to the Collioure library. The only reference was to Vauban, the architect, with little else. The librarian felt that the fort must have something in our archives, but then she did recommend the records in the basement of the Mairie. They have next to nothing there that dates before 1944. Any older records are kept in Perpignan, at least what they showed to me."

"Do you think that means the plans might be in this very room, in one of these boxes?"

"It is possible. It would not hurt to go through what is here to try and find them. But what good would finding the plans do us? We still would not know what is below us, if anything of interest. That's why we should forget the plans and get through that trapdoor as soon as possible."

"We? This is your idea Lucien, and it isn't a very good one. Besides, how would you do it anyway?"

"Let's look closer and make that determination."

As they did, Alerion was surprised by all of the sawdust. "Why is there so much sawdust in here?"

"I guess whoever filled the room used it to soak up any moisture that might seep in. This room is one floor down into the hill, and it is pretty chilly in here. It might even get damp in the winter."

They cleaned the sawdust away from the trapdoor as best they could with their hands. The embedded door was two feet by two feet. Its recessed handle and the edge of the door had been welded shut.

"It's no good Lucien. Look how secure that is."

"I see that Alerion, but what I did not notice before was how rusted the hinges are on the one side. If we can break them, we might be able to wedge a crowbar in on that side and pry it up. How old do you think these welds are? The door looks quite old. "

"That's hard to say, but it might be at least fifty years old."

"Really? I think they look older. Old enough for rust to weaken the hinges. Let's try it. We have nothing to lose."

"Without getting permission to dig in a secure government building? Only our jobs! But then it might also be seen as an act of treason."

Lucien looked over at Alerion and smiled. "No, I don't think so. Not if what we discover brings newsworthy attention to the fort."

"Lucien, why do I get a bad feeling about this?"

"Nonsense, we need a sledge hammer, a crowbar, and more light."

"And how are we going to get those things into the fort and down here without seeming suspicious?"

"My friend, you are one of the smartest men I know. You'll think of something."

Alerion was stunned, but Lucien could see the wheels already starting to turn in his head. A characteristic rolling up of Alerion's eyes, another one of his traits, made it look as if he was looking up at his brain. Lucien had grown rather fond of his friend's facial reactions. It amused him at how expressive and emotional his assistant could be. It did not take long for a response.

"Okay, you can hang a sledgehammer at your belt and place the handle down the side of your fatigues. Your jacket should cover anything that might show the bulk. I will slip the crowbar under my fatigues in the same way. As for the lights, that's easy. Since the time frame has been moved up, we can say that we need to work late and need the extra light to see with. Plus we'll need strong flashlights."

"But we can easily work in standing lights. Flashlights might look suspicious."

"Not if we move them in together in the same box. The room needs more lighting anyway. We'll just be purchasing the light for the room sooner. Who would question us? We know Ricardo and Marcello at the gate. They'll just wave us through, as usual."

"Okay, Alerion. Tomorrow, purchase what we need during our lunch break and meet me at my apartment. We will bring the tools in on our person, and bring in a box with flashlights packed with standing work lights. I'll give you the cash, but go to Port Vendres or Banyuls instead of Collioure. There is so much junk in here, we will easily be able to hide everything until we need the tools tomorrow night."

"Tomorrow night? So soon?"

"Yes, Alerion. We have no time to lose. Assure the colonel tomorrow that this room will be ready on time, but we will need to work late past our work schedule to accomplish that goal. He will think nothing of it and even be happy that we are putting in extra time for his request."

They swept the sawdust back over the door, piled up the extra packing material to hide what was there, and moved the table back into place. They made a list of what was needed to be done, locked the door, and left.

Chapter 4

On Tuesday, Alerion drove to a hardware store in Banyuls-sur-mer, a few minutes south of Collioure. He barely had enough time to meet up with Lucien and get back to the fort before their hour lunch was up. Alerion was very nervous. Lucien, on the other hand, was all smiles. Not only would he soon be able to discover what lay under the trapdoor, but Chante's beautiful face and the feel of the back of her hand on his lips still resided in his memory. Those two things made Lucien feel positively giddy. A feeling he wasn't sure he had felt since getting ready to make his first jump from a plane.

Lucien hid the sledgehammer under his desk, and Alerion hid the crowbar under his. Alerion went to inform the colonel that the new office would be ready in time, but the colonel was not in his office. Alerion left a message with the colonel's secretary, requesting permission to work an additional 2-3 hours every day after 5:00, this and next week, to make sure that the job was completed on time, beginning tomorrow tonight.

By 4:00 Alerion and Lucien were able to get into the basement with everything they needed and hide things away. All personnel would be leaving the building an hour later. They had actually managed to go through quite a few boxes searching for fort plans, but found nothing. At least those boxes were now out and in the auxiliary room down the hall to the new storage space. They even marked out spaces for the span of years where the boxes would go. Their nervous and excited energy had helped fuel their work, and by 5:30, when they were sure that the building was empty, they could see progress in the room, although there was still a long way to go before it was empty.

Lucien made Alerion search the floor above to make sure no one was about, and to grab some food for dinner. He returned carrying a tray with cups of coffee and bags of food.

"No one is upstairs that I could see, but I took the liberty of having the cafeteria leave us some sandwiches before it closed. I also got us some coffee. We can hardly expend our energy this evening without having something to eat."

They ate their sandwiches, downed their coffee, and then pulled out the two boxes of lights that they had packed. The boxes were heavy because they contained large hand-held flashlights with two extra hefty batteries. Lucien was surprised and turned to Alerion to ask why.

"Well, what if it takes us several evenings and the batteries are faulty? It's better to bring everything in at one time. Besides, we can donate them to the officers down here when we are done. In case the fort loses electricity in a storm, they'll have battery power."

"Alerion, good thinking."

Their first task was to lock the storage room door and place packing material at the top and base of the door to block out any residual noise. Then they placed a thick old rag over the hinges of the trap door so when the sledgehammer hit the metal it would not have a metal-to-metal clang, and would sound more like a thud. The hinges were more secure than they thought they would be. It took awhile before they were able to chip some of them away. Lucien was thankful that they were underground. Even when Alerion performed a sound check by standing in the hallway on the floor above, he could only hear a distant thud. With no one above, they were unheard by anyone.

"Okay," Lucien breathed heavily, "let me wedge the crowbar in between the hinges." But there was too little room to wedge it in so they had to pound away on the hinges for a while longer. Then they placed the open forked end of the crowbar between the two hinges and hit it with the sledgehammer. A few large pieces of rusted metal chips flew up, but the door held secure.

"Lucien, I'm tired and it is getting late. If we stay much longer it might look suspicious."

"We are so close Alerion, but you are right. I don't suppose you could smuggle in a torch kit tomorrow?"

"Are you crazy? An oxyacetylene torch kit with tanks? No way. We will just have to bang at it the old fashioned way."

Lucien agreed, so they repacked and hid their equipment, covered up the trapdoor once again, replaced the table, and headed out of the building, exhausted. Lucien gave a fond hello to Marcello who was on duty at the exit, letting him know that he and Alerion were going to be working late for the next two weeks on a project for the colonel.

When Lucien came in Wednesday morning and sat down, a pile of paperwork was placed on his desk, meaning he would be busy most of the day. At 3:30 the two were able to head downstairs and resume with their work, going through the boxes and moving them to the room down the hall. A quick look of panic crossed their faces when the colonel himself made an appearance in the hall, on their way back from moving two more boxes to the new storage room. They stood at attention and saluted.

"Sir!" they responded.

The colonel stood in his tan dress uniform with red epaulets and rows of colored bars upon his chest. He wore his blue and red cap about as smartly as any colonel could. He was of medium build but with wide, rounded shoulders and a broad chest. His face was rather pale as he spent most of his time indoors these days. His jowls were slightly bagged below his cheeks and his lips were thin. His longish mustache had a tendency to bounce when he spoke, but woe to the man who smirked at it. His only other obvious physical trait was his belly, which was rounding out a little more each year. It must be nice to approach retirement.

"At ease, men. I see you are hard at work. I got your message Private Bellamy. Let's see how you are doing." Alerion dared not speak, but Lucien took the lead.

"Yes, sir, right this way," and Lucien led the colonel into the room. "As you can see colonel, we've made some good headway. This far right wall should be cleared by tonight and within a few days we should have the rest of the room completed."

"Excellent. Then next week I want to have the walls painted, a carpet put in, and an air-conditioning vent extended from the hall into this room. I see you have already set up some lighting in here, very good."

Lucien swallowed. "Yes, sir. You can count on us. All will be ready."

"Very good. Carry on." They all saluted, and the colonel turned and walked out the door.

Alerion rolled his eyes back and took in a deep breath. He waited for a good ten seconds to speak while Lucien held up his hand to keep him from saying anything, until the colonel was sure to have exited all the way down the hall and up the stairs, and only then did he lower his hand.

"One week? How are we going to accomplish all this in that time?"

Lucien smiled. "I guess we will just have to step up our time frame, just as the colonel has. This means that we cannot take the time to look in any of the boxes for plans. We will need that time to just move the boxes." Not only did they need to get the trapdoor open sooner, they also had to move more boxes quicker. "I hope you packed us some dinner, my friend. We are going to need it."

Alerion said he had and it was in his office. When Alerion did his search for personnel on the floor above at 5:30, there were still two people working. He made the pretense of working in his own office and then checked again 15 minutes later. Both soldiers had finally gone and he returned to the basement with his and Lucien's dinner, which they ate first, but then Lucien lost no time.

"Okay Alerion, let's get started."

They prepped the door for noise as before, brushed away the sawdust and extra packing materials and set to work. The prongs of the crowbar could now be wedged in the gap where the hinges once were, but the door did not move one millimeter.

"Lucien, it's no good, it is not moving at all. What are we going to do?"

"There is only one thing we can do. Beat the hell out of the cement surrounding the door next to the hinges. At least then we will be able to shine a light into the hole and see what is below."

Lucien was more determined than ever. He used the crowbar and the sledgehammer to chip out chunks of cement closest to the hinges. He was amazed at how thin the flooring of cement actually was, less than two-inches thick. In less than fifteen minutes he had made a hole that was about eight-inches wide and big enough to put his arm in with the flashlight at the hole and peer in.

"Lucien, what do you see?"

"Not much. All I can see is a metal ladder that seems to go down to a platform less than three meters down. It looks like we will need to make our hole larger."

"St. Vincent," Alerion prayed for strength and patience. "You want to go down that ladder don't you?"

Lucien got up and turned to look to Alerion with a broad smile on his face. "Yes, I would. But St. Vincent won't help us. He only protected sailors, and besides he got caught and burned to death, remember?"

Lucien immediately took up the sledgehammer and the crowbar and once again set to work. They took turns swinging the sledgehammer, feeling the reverberations all the way to their teeth. Twenty-five minutes later the hole was enlarged to almost two feet wide in a jagged circle, when the last chunk of cement fell into the hole.

"Lucien, it is just after 2000 hours. We have to go."

"Alerion, I am so surprised at you. At last we have a hole big enough to get into and you want to leave? I'm going down right now. But there is no telling how strong these old metal bars on the ladder will be. I may have to jump down. Hold on to the flashlight and when I am down, toss it to me."

Lucien carefully backed into the hole and felt for the first rung of the ladder with his feet. It held, and in fact the entire ladder still seemed strong. Having been closed up from the elements must have kept the rust from forming. When he got to the bottom, Alerion tossed one of the flashlights down to him.

"What's in there? What do you see?" He got the second flashlight and shined it down into the hole.

"I am in a small room about three meters by three meters. It is empty, but one very interesting thing is here."

"What Lucien? You are driving me crazy. What is it?"

"A door, my friend. A big, heavy metal door." There was a pause while he went over to it. He tried the handle but it was locked, or rusted in place. He couldn't tell. "I'm coming up Alerion." When he reached the top and crawled out, he stood over the trapdoor and looked down.

"Now what do you want to do?" asked Alerion.

"Now we move all of our tools down into the hole to hide them, we cover the hole and we break into that door tomorrow night."

"Lucien, you just don't give up. We just spent two hours getting into a room that goes nowhere, and we still have to move more boxes tomorrow to look like we've actually been moving them tonight."

"Alerion, you are as smart as you are good-looking. That is precisely what we need to do." They spent fifteen more minutes moving their tools down the ladder, moving a large piece of cardboard over the hole, covering it with sawdust, and centering the table over the area. They tried their best to brush off the dust from their clothes and exit past the guard without looking as exhausted as they felt.

Thursday morning Lucien gave Chante a call from his office.

"Lucien, I was beginning to think that the fort had swallowed you up."

"That's why I am calling. It has." Lucien could not help but realize that was a fair estimate of what had happened. "The colonel has us working extra detail this and next week, and by the time we get done at night we are exhausted. He is expecting some personnel to arrive in a week and we need to prepare for their arrival by clearing out a room and making it into an office. Believe me, I've been thinking about you a lot. I just can't get any time free until Saturday. Would you be willing to wait two more days and then join me for dinner? I should have the majority of what has to be done completed by then. Then, I promise you my full attention."

"I think I can wait until then. I guess I will just have to go back to the library and find more books. I've been reading the books I checked out, and some books I got from Monsieur Pérusse's bookstore. Do you know the shop?"

"No. I guess you will have to take me there. I told you, I have pretty much stayed on the north end of town. So much of my time is taken up with work. I will call you on Saturday morning and I'll let you know when I will be there to pick you up. There is a restaurant I would like to take you to."

"That is very nice of you. Is it in town?"

"No, it is south of town, but I think you will really enjoy it. So I'll speak to you on Saturday. Is that okay?"

"Thank you for calling Lucien. I appreciate it. I look forward to seeing you."

They said their goodbyes just as Alerion poked his head into his office.

"Lucien, I'm free. Can you get away for more work downstairs?"

Lucien rose from his chair and turned off his computer. "Yes, let's go now. I came in early this morning and did a lot of paperwork in order to get done early. If we start downstairs by 1400 hours today, we should be able to get a lot done." He locked his office and they left down the hall.

They moved boxes for several hours and saw a great improvement in the room. Of course the auxiliary room was filling up fast, and the room that needed clearing was getting leaner as they worked. They hoped they would finish in time and not make it look as if they had been lagging, all because they actually had been occupied with something else. Of course they could always say their normal workload and duties upstairs had caused some delays, but they could only use that excuse for so long.

When 5:30 arrived they were already tired, but nothing would stop them from exploring what was to be their next challenge. Their routine was now set. Alerion scanned the upstairs. Today they were lucky. No one had stayed. They locked and blocked the door, and moved the table, sawdust, and cardboard away. They turned on their flashlights, went down the ladder, and closely examined the metal door.

"Well the bad news," said Lucien, "is that this door is also welded shut, and the hinges do look quite rusted."

"I don't get it," said Alerion. "How can the ladder have little rust, but this door have more rust? And how come there isn't a lock on the door, but it is sealed?"

"The answer to the ladder is obvious. It was replaced at some time. As for the rust on the door, there must be more moisture on the other side of it.

"Lucien, with the door welded closed, that could mean that no one should be entering. I guess our investigation stops here.

"Alerion, hand me the sledgehammer."

"Lucien, you're not listening to me. You can't get through that!"

Lucien tapped the handle of the sledgehammer to the right of the door along the wall. He heard a hollow sound and smiled.

"I don't think we need to go through it. I think we can go around it, just like the trapdoor above."

"Whoa, wait Lucien. We don't have the time or strength to break through a wall."

"Sure we do," replied Lucien. "Watch me. Stand back."

He pulled back the sledgehammer and swung with a wide, strong swing. The head of the hammer actually went right through the wall. The plastered wall, the plasterboard within the wall, and the dirt behind it all spilled onto the ground on the other side.

"Well at least it isn't cement," smiled Lucien. "All we have to do is clear the plaster and dirt behind it and angle our way in next to the door.

"Wait Lucien, remove your shirt. If it gets covered in dirt, the guard will know something is up."

"Alerion, you are right. Between the two of us, we make a good team!" Alerion gave him a nervous smile, half because he really liked having Lucien think of them as a good team, and the other, because he was nervous about what they were doing.

"Great, I'll remind you of that when we are both court-martialed for destroying military property and together in jail."

Lucien smiled at him and took off his shirt placing it across the room. It only took ten minutes to smash through the wall using the sledgehammer to break holes into the soft dirt and have it crumble away. When they broke through to clear space, the smell of dank stale air filled the room.

A few minutes later the hole was big enough to get through. They grabbed their flashlights and went in. Alerion gave a low whistle.

"It's a tunnel! And it is heading downhill."

"Of course it is," responded Lucien. "Where else would it go? The fort is on a hill. Hey, do you still have your compass on you? I left mine on my desk."

"Yeah, here." He pulled it out of his pocket and gave it to Lucien.

Lucien waited for the dial to stop swaying. "Okay, it looks like the tunnel is heading pretty much due south."

Lucien focused the light down the tunnel, but Alerion was the first to speak.

"We can't even see the end of it. Where do you suppose it goes?"

"Most likely straight to the castle. Didn't most castles have an underground escape plan in case of invasion?"

"Yeah, that's probably it, but I've been in the tunnels under the castle and there is nothing there. You're not thinking of going into this tunnel are you? It looks like it is all soil, and the wooden beams look rotten and much older than fifty years. I'll bet no one has been in this tunnel for at least a hundred years."

"That's probably true, maybe even longer. All the more reason to go exploring." And Lucien turned to him and grinned, but Alerion was more cautious.

"Okay, but let's take it really slow."

"Alerion, you sound like a mother hen. We are trained to go into unstable areas, remember?"

"I prefer to know my enemy. This is a dark hole in the ground."

"Honestly Alerion, you've stepped through mine fields before. This is a walk in the park. Just stay close behind me. I promise that I'll be very careful. Just don't touch the walls. That could cause a cave-in." Alerion just batted his eyes peering into the dark and held his flashlight tighter.

The ground was mostly packed, and at various places they passed under rotten beams with fat posts holding up the sides, but also here and there, parts of the walls and ceiling had partially collapsed, leaving deposits of soil and fallen beams. Old roots hung from the ceiling, and in a couple of places they could see that groundwater had seeped in and run downhill, most likely during a heavy rain. They took it slow. Lucien focused his light on their foot placement and the tunnel up ahead, and Alerion focused his light on examining the walls and ceiling above them. There was plenty of room above their heads, about two feet, and the tunnel was about five feet across. If the way had been completely clear they could have walked beside each other, but caution told them to walk single file. Old spider webs here and there still clung along some portions of the walls, but it was pretty much insect free. After ten minutes, the earth below their feet became softer and had some sandy areas.

"Look up ahead, I think we've come to the end." A minute later they came to what looked like a solid cement wall blocking the tunnel."

"Lucien, I honestly don't think you will be able to sledgehammer or crowbar yourself past this. This is a solid wall. And don't say we can dig around it. We would cause a cave-in for sure."

Lucien stood quiet and thought. "You're right. Let's go back and talk about this."

Alerion was never so thankful for a blockade. They turned and slowly began their way back up the steep tunnel. About half way back, Alerion tripped over a root he had not noticed and without thinking reached to the side of the wall to catch his balance. All at once the dirt beneath his hand gave way and the wall crumbled, dropping away, covering his legs and pinning him down.

Chapter 5

Lucien heard Alerion call out and had just enough time to grab his arm and pull him forward before the rest of the dirt fell over and covered him. Lucien got him to his feet while Alerion coughed from the centuries-old dust and dirt that had been stirred up.

"Come on Alerion. Let's get you out of here."

When they reached the cement room and got through the hole in the wall they sat and rested to catch their breath. They had moved as quickly and as carefully as they could, in case the vibration of their movements might have loosened more of the walls.

"Alerion, I think we are done with our investigation of the tunnel. I'm glad you are all right. I am so sorry that happened, and all on a whim of mine. You are all right, aren't you?"

"Yes, yes, I'm all right, but let's get out of here."

They got the tools up the ladder and made their way up as well, squeezing through the cement hole. Alerion's lower half was covered in dirt.

"You better go upstairs and clean up. I have an extra set of fatigues in my office in my storage locker. I'll put everything back as it should be down here and lock up."

"Are you sure? You need to wash up a bit, as well."

"I will Alerion, go on. I'll be able to cover up the dirt on my undershirt with the shirt you had me take off." He handed him his office key to get in.

Lucien hid the tools behind some boxes, and once more covered the hole with the cardboard and sawdust, replaced the table and locked up. When he was done he met Alerion at his office. They agreed to meet back at his apartment to talk over a bottle of wine. They exited the fort, more haggard than even the night before.

When they reached his apartment a few blocks away and each had a drink in their hand, Alerion at last felt he could talk about it.

"I guess when the fort was built the builders decided to close off the old tunnel to the castle. It simply was not needed any more."

Lucien nodded. "You're probably right. The wall at the end of the tunnel must be the side of the quay's channel that got cemented in for the river's outflow. I wonder when that was built? That might be the last time anyone was in there."

"Thank goodness we have made progress with the storage room, but how are we going to cover up the hole in the floor? I mean, when they go to place a carpet down in that room they are going to see not only the hole but the partially destroyed trapdoor."

"Good question, Alerion. I've been thinking about that and I think I have the answer. When I got the keys to the storage room I poked around in the basement and found another room with some building materials left over from the 2007 construction. I think I saw a large piece of heavy sheet metal that we can place over both the hole and the trapdoor. All we need to do is seal it with some special glue, so the workers cannot remove it. If anyone asks we will say that there was once an old drain and the floor looked weak, so the plating is there to secure the floor."

"That's a good idea. I think there is sealant in the WC off the dining room. I believe it is elastomeric caulk. It must have once been used for sealing around the sink and toilets. I happen to see two tubes of it in one of the storage cabinets."

"And what were you doing," asked Lucien, "in the janitor's storage cabinets?"

"I periodically check all storage for inventory. It's part of my job."

"You do get around, don't you? That is exactly what we need. Tomorrow if you can put one each into the deep thigh pockets of your fatigues we will be able to seal it up tomorrow night. I want that sealant completely dry by the time the painter, carpet, and duct people arrive."

Alerion looked hopeful at Lucien. "So, has your inquisitive mind been appeased now, and we can finally get back to our normal life at the fort?" Lucien gave him one of those smiles and a sparkle to the eyes. "Oh no, Lucien, I know that look. What on earth are you thinking?"

"We've learned one very important thing, that a tunnel exists — or rather existed — connecting the fort with the castle. Even if the tunnel was cut off on this side of the river, somewhere under the castle the other end of the tunnel has to be there."

"Lucien I've been there. The tunnels don't go anywhere. They dead-end and unlike this side, there are no doors or even cement walls to indicate that there ever was a connection."

"One may not be able to see anything now. All I'm saying is that it could be hidden and we have just never seen it."

"If you are going to go poking around the castle, count me out. I've had enough. In fact, I'm going home and to bed. I'm exhausted." He drained his second glass of wine and put it down. "Lucien, thank you for saving me. I might have gotten buried. You're a good friend."

"If it wasn't for me you wouldn't have had such a life-risking adventure!"

"True, but thanks all the same. I'm sticking to desk work if you don't mind."

They smiled at one another. Alerion liked it when they had moments of true friendship like this. It was much appreciated.

"You're welcome. Good night Alerion."

Early the next morning they were able to move the remaining boxes out of the room. They did find a large piece of sheet metal in the building supply storage and moved it in. Then they closed and locked the door, removed the cardboard and swept the storage floor clear. Alerion brought in the sealant and they used it in thick swaths around the metal's edges, and then placed the sheet over the trapdoor and hole they had made. The smell was very strong. The directions said it needed twelve hours to completely dry. No problem, it was Friday, and it had all weekend to harden for the painter on Monday.

Saturday morning Lucien called Chante. "Hello Chante, it's Lucien. Are you still available for dinner tonight?"

"Hello. Lucien. Yes, I am. I've got some things to share. When will you be free?" She could feel herself flush at the sound of his voice.

"I will pick you up at 1900 hours, but I don't know where you live."

"I'm sorry, I'm not used to military time. That is at what time?"

"Of course, sorry, it is 7:00 pm. I'll try to remember to refer to civilian time for you. We have reservations for 7:30."

"I should have realized that military time is what you go by. By the way, I live in a gated community. You won't be able to get in, so let's meet at the carousel."

"All right. See you then. I'm very much looking forward to seeing you."

Chante was all smiles when she hung up. She immediately went to her closet to decide what she would wear. She was surprised that she had not packed anything date-worthy. That had to have been due to her depressive mood when she had packed leaving L.A. If she left now, she could walk to town and find something new to wear and be back in plenty of time. She grabbed her bag and went out the door.

It was another beautiful day. She was convinced that the best weather was not in the summer, but in the fall. The air seemed to be cleaner. Of course there were fewer cars filling the air with fumes. September and October were her favorite months of the year. There were a few wispy clouds in the sky, but the breezes that blew were mild. Come November though, the Tramontane wind was sure to blow through, bringing the cold from the northwest of the Pyrenees toward the Gulf of Lyon.

She scanned a few shops in town, looking past the racks of clothes that the shopkeepers pull out in front of their stores. Those clothes were cheaply made for the tourists, placed there in hopes of luring them in with the lower prices. She'd learn to walk past these into the shops to see their higher-quality offerings. She finally found a white handkerchief dress with a crocheted bust line that showed off her new tan. She had managed to relax in the sun on the beach reading her books the last couple of days and was pleased with the difference in her skin tone. When was the last time she had actually laid on a beach? She could not remember. She certainly never had the time or interest to go to any beach in Los Angeles. She did remember long ago enjoying the beach off La Jolla shores in San Diego, but she had rarely made it that far south. Chante also found a lovely white shell and pearl necklace and couldn't resist its simple and natural appeal. This was weird to be shopping for a man. No, she caught herself.

She was shopping for herself now, for a new look, something different and well, almost virginal for a fresh start. And yes, okay, she had to be honest with herself, for a man too.

Chante spent the rest of the afternoon finishing her paperback novel. There is nothing like a fictional romance to get one in the mood for a dinner date. By 6:30 she had already dressed and applied her makeup. She left a bit early and walked the short distance to the parking lot at the beach. She was surprised to see Lucien already there and sitting at her bench. He doesn't waste any time, she thought to herself. Then he got up and turned, almost as if sensing her approach. He saw her and smiled the entire time that it took for her to cross the street and meet him in the parking lot.

"I so enjoyed you just now walking toward me. Chante you look breathtaking. Is this a new dress?" She nodded and his eyes were dancing all over her.

Whoa, was that a ripple of excitement that just went through her body or the shock of having someone compliment her after so long not hearing such things? He bent and reached down to her left hand, meeting it halfway to his lips, and lingered for a long pause, his eyes never leaving hers. She had to be blushing. Was this guy for real?

"How did you manage to become twice as beautiful since the last time I saw you, only a few days ago?"

"Lucien, you have been busy. It's been a full week. I've read two books since then and gotten a good start on a tan."

"I do apologize. I have been working day and night to finish my task, but it is coming to a close, and I am looking forward to spending some time with you."

Now that line, she was sure she had not heard since she was engaged to her husband eight years ago.

"Thank you Lucien. And your charm might just have doubled since we last met at the library. So where are we going?"

"Ah, I have a surprise for you. We are headed south along the coast road to Banyuls-sur-mer, to a wonderful restaurant there facing the water." He ushered her into his black Citroen DS3 sitting in the lot. He opened the door to let her in and soon they had exited onto the D114.

A minute or so passed before they spoke as he climbed the hill out of Collioure and headed south.

"So then, what have you read this week? What did you discover about our wonderful country?" asked Lucien, trying to keep his mind focused.

"Well, first I read my book from the library on the Albigensian Crusade. It certainly did not take long for the French crown to eliminate the Cathars! I found it fascinating that so harmless a small religious group could be so threatening to a King. I mean they were still Christian."

"Ah yes, but not Catholic," added Lucien.

"True, and it was all for naught with the quick rise of the Dominican Order, which might not have been so bad, but it was also the beginning of the Medieval Inquisition. I read about their military campaigns: the massacre at Béziers, the fall of Carcassonne, and the battles at Lastours, Toulouse, and of course the most tragic at Montségur."

They drove through Port Vendres and up the hill again onto the D914, the Citroen humming quietly along and the vibrations of the engine not helping to calm Chante's nervousness.

"Now it is your turn. What did you have to do this week that kept you so busy?"

Lucien checked his rear-view mirror, pausing to contemplate his response. "I had a mountain of paperwork. With the summer so busy we get backlogged and have to catch up all autumn, but I also had to oversee the clearing of a large storage area and its conversion into more offices."

"Your hands look like you did the construction yourself." Lucien stole a look at his hands. She was observant. There were still a few healing blisters from swinging the sledgehammer.

"Oh, these" he opened his right hand. "I worked one day to enlarge a wall. Remember I'm pretty much a paper pusher. The chance to actually do some labor is a welcome change."

Thankful for the short distance they needed to go and the quick arrival at their destination, he shifted his attention toward the curves in the road and the descent into the port town of Banyuls. He pulled into the lot of the restaurant and they walked in. Inside was a sleek black and white entry with blue lighting. They were lead through the reception area into an enclosed patio lined with a wall of clear glass that gave an expansive view to the sandy beach and blue water beyond. The waiter sat them next to the glass for a great, unobstructed view.

"This is lovely, Lucien. What a treat. I've eaten at home for my first week here and you've made me feel like an indulgent tourist again."

"What do you like to eat? Is there anything you don't like?"

"I love all kinds of food. Would you like to order for us?"

"We've known each other for only a week and you already trust me to order for you? I am a fortunate man. All right. I am happy to do so." He scanned the food and wine menus, listened to the specials the waiter had to offer, and ordered their dinner and wine.

They made small talk about the coastline and the beauty of the Mediterranean islands.

"You know," added Lucien, "Next weekend this very small village will be crowded with locals and tourists. The Grape Harvest Festival is one of this town's biggest celebrations with concerts, food and wine tastings, music, dancing, and a lot more."

"Really? That sounds wonderful."

"Would you like to attend? The beach fills with people having picnics, lots of wine is drunk, and fishing boats bring in the grape harvest."

"Grapes from the sea? Now that is unusual. It sounds like a lot of fun."

"Great, then let's pack a picnic, and all we have to do is just wait with an open glass," and he raised his glass already filled with wine, "because soon the glasses get filled. A brass band sits in the center square and plays all afternoon, and excellent food is also available. I can pick you up in the morning, we can go shopping for a few things to eat, and I'll grab a blanket for us to sit on."

"Thank you so much for inviting me to enjoy it with you. I've never been here this late in the season to enjoy the fall festivities."

Their first course of two plates arrived. One dish was anchovies marinated with lemon, served on Mesclun leaves with candied garlic bread, along with a plate of duck foie gras, roasted smoked duck slices, and Iberian ham.

"I hope you don't mind. Both offerings sounded so tempting, I had to order them both. We will be enjoying a bit of Catalan food with that wonderful mix of French and Spanish flavors."

"On the contrary, this is my favorite way to share a meal." She smiled and they lit into their dishes commenting about the food. He even offered a bite to her on his fork. It was a bit intimate for her, but then it also seemed like the most natural thing to do. He sensed her hesitation and immediately offered a response, that it was the French way to share food. When the appetizers were cleared, he remembered something she had said in the car and wanted to hear more.

"That was an excellent beginning to our meal." He dabbed his mouth with his napkin. "You mentioned in the car that you had something to share. Was it from one of your books?" He hoped if she kept speaking he could spend more time looking directly at her lovely face.

"Oh yes, the book on Sébastien Le Prestre de Vauban, to be exact. What an impressive man. Besides being the Marshal of France and the most important military engineer of his time, he was also an advisor to Louis XIV. I didn't know that he'd been wounded nearly a dozen times in various sieges. His fortification system was brilliant, and he even improved his own designs three times to make them better."

Lucien was already getting lost in her eyes and in watching her lips move.

"And he wrote several practical manuals on his methods of fortification. His method of ricochet firing to break down defenses of other fortresses was unique, along with instituting a company of miners for military mining, no doubt to build tunnels and collapse fort walls."

All of a sudden Lucien sat upright. "He did?" She was a bit taken aback by his reaction, but at least she was sure he was listening. She thought she had rattled on a bit too much and might be boring him. Obviously she was not.

"Yes, he wrote a book about it called *Traité des Mines*, which was reprinted several times. He improved the fortifications in nearly 300 cities, Collioure among them of course, when the urban wall of the castle was reinforced into a citadel. That's when the engineer Saint-Hilaire, operating under Vauban's direction, rebuilt the upper part of the town and your fort."

"I assure you, it is not my fort, but that is fascinating."

"Is it? I thought it was interesting, but there is not much more about Collioure in the book on Vauban."

"I would have thought that was enough to at least start on an article. Have you finally decided to write about the castle?"

"I'm still not sure yet. I need more information. You know, I haven't been back to the castle since the first time I was here as a tourist." Lucien was fast to pick up on that lead.

"Then we should go. It will give you the opportunity to ask more about its history, and we can explore the castle and its underground tunnel, together."

Chante was beginning to catch on. "So you like mining and tunnels?"

"Well no, not particularly. I mean I find all history fascinating, and it might help with my overview of the fort and the area's history."

Chante got the feeling that there was something he was not telling her. His eyes had left her and were looking out to sea. Then the main course arrived. He had ordered the fish with saffron potatoes, and the pigeon breasts with fried artichokes. They both picked up their forks at the same time and looked at each other like excited children.

He suggested, "Shall we?" He then cut a portion of the fish and fed it to her.

"Wow, that is really good, what is it?"

"It is Scorpion fish. The barbs on the end of its fins are very poisonous, but the fish itself is delicious, yes?" She nodded with enjoyment.

The candles on the tables cast a warm glow on their faces, and the outdoor floodlights lit up the waves not far away to reveal a constant rolling and churning of nature. The wine had put Chante in a giggly mood, and Lucien became more charming as the dinner wore on. They enjoyed the rest of their meal, finishing it off sharing a lavender pudding with honey. On all accounts, they looked like a happy couple sharing their food and enjoying the romantic view.

Chapter 6

When it came time to leave the restaurant, Lucien did not want the evening to end, so Chante suggested a short after-dinner walk back in Collioure. They left the restaurant and drove back a little quieter this time. It gave Chante time to think about this whirlwind feeling she was having for someone she barely knew or knew anything about. Lucien's thoughts were focused on getting underneath the castle and exploring the tunnels, but when he glanced at her in the soft reflected light of the car's dash lights, she was so radiant looking, the view made him change his thoughts.

They parked in the same lot from which they left.

"Lucien, follow me. I know right where we can go."

She led him past the Dominican Winery, past the Peske Museum and its cloister, and into the hillside park full of olive trees. There was a dirt path with stone steps up the north side of the park. They climbed slowly for a couple of minutes and at the top of the stairs came to a level area. The old gazebo was to the right and to the left ran a low wall of stone. They stood behind it and looked down upon the town.

"Collioure looks so beautiful from up here." He admired the view for a few moments and then she turned to him and held out her hand to bring him near.

"Lucien, I know we just met, and we don't know each other very well, but this is a special place for me."

"You came up here with your husband, didn't you?"

"Yes, but that was in the past. Now I'm ready to put that behind me."

Lucien came and stood close to her. The lights that circled the bay below shown like a row of pearls on a curved neckline. He turned to her and looked into her eyes.

"Chante, I cannot begin to tell you how good you have made me feel and how much I have been thinking about you since the day we met. When I can see the stars reflected in your eyes as I do now, they make me feel like I am seeing the world in an entirely new way. You are so beautiful and just standing here with you is so special for me, so unexpected."

Chante was entranced. How could something feel so good so quickly with someone? Why doesn't he kiss me, she thought. It was a fantastic dinner and I've brought him to a very romantic place. Damn it, Lucien, kiss me. But he placed his arm around her and he turned them toward the view of the town and the sea.

"Chante, you haven't said anything. Am I acting like a fool? Do you even like me?"

She made him turn toward her again and she slowly wrapped both her arms around his neck, and gently pulled him toward her as she whispered. "Here is my answer, Lucien." She brought him down to her lips and kissed him. Then he embraced her and returned the kiss. As he held her and their kiss filled their senses, waves of excitement rolled through her body. She must have felt this way when she had met her husband, but she did not remember ever feeling quite like this. This was beyond what she had ever felt before. After those intimate moments, she could finally bring herself to speak.

"Lucien, believe me. I like you a lot. I know we just met. I know that we hardly know anything about each other, but I can't ignore these feelings either. I will tell you something about me. I may have inherited the romantic and impulsive heart of my French mother, but I also have the inquisitiveness and practicality of my English father. My father's voice tells me to get to know you better before we take this further, but my mother's voice says to keep kissing you and let my heart lead the way."

"I like your mother." They both laughed at that and stayed close.

"What I was going to say is that I would like to follow both of their voices. To continue to see you and get to know you better, and to allow my heart to experience something new and frankly, exciting."

"Chante, are all American women so rational?" He smiled. "I think both of your parents are wise, and you are wise to listen to both of them." He looked around, "Even though neither of them is here right now. But I agree. We have plenty of time to get to know each other." His fingers played with her hair, feeling its wavy softness. Let me walk you home, we will say goodnight, and we can share things about ourselves when we have our picnic next weekend. I promise to tell you about the time I broke one of my fingers and how my cousin used to tease me. The first time I fell in love, and where I've traveled. Whatever you want to know."

"I'd like that, although I'm not sure I want to hear about your past romances, but I am curious what your cousin would tease you about."

"Ah, well that will have to wait until next week."

Their arms were still around each other. This time Chante did not have to lead. He kissed her passionately. Then she took his arm and they turned to walk back down the park path. She led him behind the winery, past the boules court and through a swinging gate. They walked up to her apartment and stood before her door. Chante got her keys out and then turned back toward Lucien.

"Here we are, but I will invite you in some other time. Now you know where I live, so you can pick me up on Saturday."

"I'm looking forward to that. See you at what, 10:30?"

"Perfect," she said. They embraced, kissed one more time, and then he turned and walked down the stairs.

Chante did not remember even turning the key in the door or feeling the floor under her feet. She went straight to her French doors, opened them, and relived every moment of the evening while looking up at the stars.

That night she had the same dream of being in a dark hallway. This time she was holding up a light to see the door. She reached for the handle, which she had never seen before, but the door would not open. Then the dream ended. Maybe when she finally opened that door to her heart all the way, she would see what was on the other side.

On Monday morning, Lucien completely covered the old storage room floor with several tarps in preparation for the painter, though it was really to cover the metal plate. The room still smelled of glue, but with the door left open while waiting for the painter, it aired out fairly well by the time he arrived. The painter was happy to see the room already prepped. All he had to do was cover the switch plates. When he left, one could not tell the smell of the glue from the smell of the paint.

Tuesday morning the air conditioning people arrived and Lucien showed them to the room. Lucien discussed with them where the air duct would be installed. A vent from the ceiling in the hall just had to be extended through the top of the wall into the new office, and a thermostat installed on the wall inside by the door. He had left the tarpaulin down to catch the debris. It only took them a couple of hours to complete the job. They even touched up the wall with the leftover paint.

On Wednesday morning Lucien prepared for the carpet people to arrive. He lifted away the tarps, rolled them up, and placed them in the building storage room.

When the carpet people arrived he showed them to the room. He ushered the two men in and the metal plate was the first thing they noticed.

"Monsieur, why is that metal plate there? Is it removable?"

Lucien was ready for his response. "No, I'm sorry it cannot be removed. Part of this fort is very old. At one time there was a drain in the floor, but after years of water draining it weakened, so it had to be reinforced to keep the floor solid. I'm afraid you will have to just cover it as best you can."

The worker shook his head a little and considered the task. He bent down to examine the plate more closely and then stood.

"I guess we don't have a choice. We will need to use some extra padded foam below the carpet, but it should be okay, and no one should notice the slight rise at this end of the room."

Lucien breathed a sigh of relief. "Very well then, I will leave you to your work."

The carpet took less than two hours to be laid. Then Lucien grabbed Alerion and they went downstairs together to inspect the room. They could not believe the change that had taken place. From a week before, when it was hardly visible with boxes nearly reaching the ceiling, the room had been transformed into a clean, white-walled space with a new beige carpet. The metal plate on the far side of the room was nearly imperceptible. The carpet people had done a great job.

"Now Alerion, your turn is next. Get some furniture in here to make it look like an office and we are done."

"I have two men ready to move some furniture down this afternoon. The office will be ready for the colonel's new men right on time on Monday."

They smiled at each other. Lucien gave him the key and told him to have it done as soon as possible. Alerion had a deep block of file cabinets set against the far wall by the trapdoor. He had to place a small strip of thin wood against the back edge of the wall to make sure the cabinets sat evenly, which worked well. He divided the room in half with separate desks, one on the left and one on the right. He added shelving, bookcases, office chairs, and standing lamps over each desk. The one central ceiling light that was already there, hung perfectly centered directly over the filing cabinets. All that was needed was to have phones installed and they were going in the next day. When the room was ready he showed it to Lucien. They shook hands on a mission well done and both heaved a sigh of relief.

That night Alerion came to Lucien's apartment and they toasted to the final completion of hiding their secret. Lucien told Alerion what he had told the carpet people, and they both had a good laugh.

"Now I have something else to share with you."

"Please Lucien, don't tell me you have another plan for underground explorations. I don't think my nerves could take it."

"No Alerion, something much more pleasant. I wanted to let you know that I met someone, someone very special."

"And here I thought that smile was for a successful operation. When in the world did you have time to be an investigator and a lover?"

"I'm not a lover yet, but I think I will be sometime in the near future."

"You are not only mysterious, but maddening. Who is she?"

"She is actually an American, a writer who has come to Collioure, and she is beautiful!"

"Oh-oh, I know that look. You are already falling in love, aren't you, with an American no less! You do know that most visitors eventually leave. American women like to play, but then it is home to their boyfriends and husbands."

"No, my friend. She has moved here to an apartment on the south end of town behind the Dominican winery, and she is divorced." He did not tell him how recently. "She has dark wavy hair, dark brown eyes, a slender figure, and the most beautiful face."

"You have left out one important detail."

Lucien looked perplexed. "What""

Alerion smiled, "her name my friend, her name."

"Oh, her name is Chante Morgan."

"So you have been enchanted by an American songstress. You know that makes her a siren, and you know very well to beware of sirens. Remember when we were going through the Kick Program together? You saw that woman at the harbor and followed her for hours, and she didn't even have to say one word to you."

"Yes I know, but I stopped when I saw her sneak off with her tour director."

"All right, I will let you be, but be careful. So how did you meet her and how in the world have you fallen so quickly?"

Lucien described meeting her at the library, and their lunch and dinner together.

"Did she see what books you were looking at in the library?"

"Well yes, that's how we met. She is interested in the castle and is thinking of writing about its history. She's checked out the book I had been looking for, on Vauban."

"Lucien, Lucien, this is not good. What if her inquiries interfere with yours? Then what will you do?"

"I don't know. She has already found out something I did not know."

"And what is that?"

"At dinner she was telling me about Vauban. Did you know that he developed a specialized mining team to dig tunnels? He even published a book about it. I have to find that book. Maybe the librarian can locate it for me."

"Really? No, no, I don't want to know anything more. It will only excite you further telling me about it. We barely got out of the last adventure you put us through."

"Alerion, my dear friend, you know I would never place you in danger on purpose." Then he remembered that Alerion had nearly been buried by the tunnel cave-in. "Except for that minor mishap, which I had not counted on." At which point Alerion rolled back his eyes in remembrance. "I am simply doing some research. Besides, I have a cover story for anything that comes up that she might ask about."

"Oh really, and what would that be?"

"I am doing research on the history of the fort for a short overview of the area. I told her it was for the new men that get sent here for training. You know, we always get questions from them about the history of the fort and town."

"No, I wasn't aware of that. I'm not aware that anyone has asked about the fort's history. They only want to know where the good cafés and bars are in town. But I can see how that might be a good cover."

"Trust me, Alerion. I promise not to involve you."

"So, how will this romance be conducted? And when will I be meeting this siren?"

"This coming Saturday I am taking her to the Grape Harvest Festival in Banyuls."

"That should be fun, if not a little crazy. That beach gets crowded with a couple thousand people. You certainly will not be able to get romantic there."

"Oh I know, Alerion. After a day in the sun, surrounded by that many people, she should be ready for a quiet and intimate evening."

"Ah, as usual Lucien, you are way ahead of me. Then what, an evening stroll?"

"Of course, and maybe sometime soon a visit to the castle so she can check out its history for her research."

"You mean so you can check out the castle tunnel."

"And why not? We are both interested in the history of the town and the tunnel is open to the public."

"Just be careful and don't go knocking any walls down at the castle. That castle already has a long history of being stormed enough times. We don't need another soldier coming to harm and being added to the long list of felled men associated with it."

"Alerion, I do believe you are worried about me."

"Always, my friend, always."

Friday at lunchtime Lucien went back to the library. Madame Severin was there as usual. She greeted him with a wide smile.

"Monsieur Reynard, how nice to see you again. And what can I help you with today? More history?"

"Madame, you are too kind and as gracious as ever." It never hurt to pour on the charm when it might garner him some quality help. "I'm wondering if you can locate a book for me. It is rather old, so I'm not even sure that it is available anymore, but I'm hoping you might be able to locate the book or perhaps an electronic copy of it."

"And what would that be?"

"It is called *Traité des Mines*, written by Sebastien Vauban. I understand that it was first printed in Paris in 1740, reprinted in The Hague in 1744, and then again in Paris in 1799, but there are probably later printings I don't know about." Thank goodness he had taken the time to get those dates from Chante's book on Vauban.

Madame Severin wrote down the author, title, and dates he had given. "If you care to wait I will do a search for them and see what I can find. They are quite old, and by now most likely in private libraries, but we shall see. An author of such notoriety should have his works listed somewhere."

He thanked her and took a seat to wait. She took some time on her computer and he could see her making notes to the side. After about ten minutes she motioned him to return to her desk.

"I found several references. A book with the title *The Attack and the Defense of Places* was published in combination with another writing, titled, *A Practical Treatise on Mines*. I'm afraid it is not in any library system, but is for sale through Bauman Rare Books. It is listed in American dollars for $2,800. "

"*Mon dieu! C'est trop cher!* Were you able to find a more recent reprint?"

"No. I found one more listing for three of his books: *Traite de l'Attaque des Places*, *Traite de la Defense des Places*, and *Traite de Mines*, which were available from Fortress Books, but have already been sold. There are numerous libraries that have works on his life, but the book you are looking for is not available within our library system or on the open market, as far as I can see. However, if you are interested in reading about tunnel warfare, we do have a book describing its history. Would you like to see it?"

"Yes, I would, please."

Madame Severin consulted her computer to search for the title and author. Then she went off to the shelves to locate it. She returned a minute later and showed it to him.

"Would you like to check it out?"

"Yes, Madame, please." She scanned it and handed it to him with another smile.

"Happy history hunting." But he was already halfway out the door when he turned to say his thanks.

That night he read all he could. He knew about the siege method of mining techniques as they had been employed since antiquity. The Greeks, Persians, Chinese, Romans, Russians, Koreans, and Germans, had all used tunnels to dig under fortress walls and had even employed the use of poisonous gasses and smoke to suffocate intruders. Tunnels were also used during the middle ages, but they could be dug only when the fortification was not built upon solid rock. The tunnels were used to excavate an outer defense or to collapse a wall. As the miners dug, they supported the walls with wooden posts, and when the tunnel ran under a wall, they would set the wood on fire so that the wall or tower above would collapse. Sometimes explosives were used to quickly drop the structure above. He also read that tunnels could be used to further defend a fortress by transferring more troops from one end of a battleground into the fortress, to transfer food, water, supplies and weaponry, and to move inhabitants out of a fortress or castle in case of an imminent breach.

All Lucien could think of that night was of the tunnel he and Alerion had been in. He wondered what function it had served over the centuries, and how it was now permanently sealed for all time, at least that section of it.

Chapter 7

On Saturday morning at 10:30 Lucien was knocking on Chante's door. When she opened it he could feel his heart speed up. Maybe it was the two flights of stairs he had raced up, or the fact that he was just physically standing close to her again. She greeted him with a hug.

"Hi, right on time. Come on in. I will quickly show you my apartment, grab my things, and we will be on our way."

The apartment was small but neat and well furnished. He saw the layout of the apartment with bathroom to the right, the bedroom and kitchen to the left and the dining and living room at the end of the hall. Lucien noticed the tiled art on the wall and the French doors that led to a small balcony. She noticed he was quiet and wondered if he had expected something more exotic for a woman who came from California.

"I know it's not much to look at, but for now it is home."

"I like it. Small, neat, and I especially like your tiled art of Collioure. I don't usually see too many renderings of the town that I actually like, but I like this one."

Chante looked at it. "Me too. It was the first thing I changed in the apartment when I got back here." She grabbed her things and noticed that he looked closer into her bedroom before walking out the front door. She smiled but refocused his attention.

"I took the liberty of picking up an insulated bag at the store to keep our food cold at the beach," she said as she turned to lock the door.

"That's great, and I brought my grill for grilling anything we might want to cook. Seafood is traditional."

They walked to his car, which was parked just outside the apartment entry gate. He put her things in and they walked to the winery to get two bottles of wine. Then they drove down the coast to Port Vendres and found a market selling fresh seafood, and a local grocer for most of their other picnic needs. They were able to get some fresh lobster, corn, and artichokes.

When they got to Banyuls the beach was already filling with people and there was a long line of cars trying to get into town. Lucien pulled briefly to the side of the road and quickly unloaded their things. He left her there temporarily so that he could go park the car on a side street at the home of one of the guards from the fort. He was back within ten minutes. Then they picked up their things and walked down the sandy hillside. Chante let Lucien choose the spot, as he seemed to know where the best vantage point would be.

"This is a good place. The bigger crowds gather next to the boardwalk and the band sets up in the square, but it is less crowded here and we will be able to hear each other talk." They settled at a place on the north end of the beach. The town's bay curved out before them.

"Wow, I can see this is going to be quite a beach party. What's going to happen?"

"A lot. All the restaurants along the boardwalk carry trays of food out to sell to those that did not bring food. You can see there are tents and tables getting set up all along the boulevard where the wineries give wine tastings. But instead of me telling you about it, we will walk around later and I'll show you."

They spread out the blanket, set up the grill, and began by opening the wine. They raised their glasses to toast. "To the harvest!" They were quite entertained watching the crowd fill in along the beach and the air fill with smoke from people lighting their grills and cooking lunch. They decided they might as well do the same, so when the grill was hot they put on their split artichokes and corn in their husk, and when they were done they put on the lobsters. By then the beach was full, and crowds were filling the boardwalk and spilling into the street. Bands were playing at different ends of the beach. It was getting very celebratory with people en mass on the beach and sidewalks and pouring wine for whoever lifted their glass. Fortunately, since they were at the far north end it was not quite as crazy or noisy, but they did have a great view of the festivities. At last they filled their plates from the grill and enjoyed their lunch.

"This is so much fun. A little crazy, but I'm loving it." He poured her more wine. "Reminds me of Venice Beach in the summer," she mused.

"There is also a fancy ball that is held tonight, but tickets sell out weeks ahead. Picnicking on the beach I think is more fun. So tell me a little about yourself. When did your family move to Los Angeles?"

"This must be share time. All right, I'll begin. In order to answer that question, I have to back up before we arrived in the U.S. My father was traveling from London to Paris on a newspaper assignment and he met my mother there. She was working at the hotel where he was staying. She says she didn't like him at first, just because he was British, but his assignment got extended and during that time they got to know each other better. Before they knew it they had fallen in love. Then he had to go back to London and he wanted to take her, but she had to stay because my grandmother's health was failing. In the meantime, she realized that she was pregnant with me. My father flew back to Paris as soon as she told him and they married in Paris. Then he went on assignment and several months later had to fly to Los Angeles. At the same time my grandmamma died and my mother ended up having me in Paris; but as soon as we could, my father flew us to Los Angeles. He ended up leaving the paper in London and working for a paper in L.A., and all three of us eventually got dual citizenship. There, now it is your turn. So how did you break your finger and which finger was it, by the way?"

He held up the little finger of his left hand.

"It was this one. One day we were visiting my cousin Mateo at his house. I was nine and he was eleven. I was playing solitaire and he was shooting hoops. He was taller than me so he was much better at throwing balls into the hoop. Besides I wasn't into basketball. I was more into soccer. Every time he called my name to bug me to play with him, I had to close one eye to look up at him because the sun was behind him and in my eyes. He kept calling me one-eyed jack, because I kept closing one eye, and I was playing with cards. Finally, he got me so mad I stood up to fight him, but he threw the basketball at me. I didn't expect him to do that so at the last minute I tried to catch it, but I dropped it when the ball hit my finger so hard the impact broke it."

"Ouch, that must have hurt."

"Oh it hurt a lot, but I didn't know I had broken it. I got even madder at him for hurting me, so I picked up the ball to hit him with it. I couldn't hold the ball as firmly as I wanted to because of my broken finger. But the ball didn't go anywhere near him. Instead it went up high and actually fell through the hoop. We were both so in shock that I had made the basket, it took a minute for me to realize that I had actually really hurt myself. After that I was one-eyed-hoop Jack."

"That's a great story. Now it's your turn to ask me a question."

"Okay, why did your marriage end?"

"Ooh, that's a hard question, but I have a quick answer. He fell in love with someone else. Don't ask me how. These things just happen, I guess. At least that's what he kept telling me."

"I am sorry. I was just curious. I should not have asked."

"No that's perfectly fine. I was in shock for a while after he told me. We were married for about six years. If he wasn't in love with me anymore, I wasn't going to force him, so we divorced. Why haven't you met someone special? A great-looking guy like you who's so smart."

"I don't have a quick answer for that one. My father raised me after my mother died when someone hit her car. After that my father and I became very close. He'd been in the military and was stationed just north of here. I didn't see him a lot in those early days, but he became my hero. Then something about my mother's death made him change his life, probably because he then needed to raise me. He went back to school and became a teacher and eventually a professor of history. I kept remembering the stories he had told me about his time in the military so when I became old enough I joined. I guess I wanted to be just like him. Then I had stories I could tell him, and I became his hero. I trained to become a commando, but then he had a heart attack and had to pull back on his teaching. I guess with all the time I spent in the service and taking care of him, I just never had time to develop any lasting relationships."

"Do you get to see him much?"

"Yes, fairly often, at least once a month. Maybe some time we can take a drive together to Perpignan and you can meet him. He's a smart guy and very likeable."

"Sounds nice. I would be happy to meet him."

Lucien looked around and at the crowd. "Okay, the afternoon is getting on and pretty soon the boats will be coming in. I'm going to pack up our things and take them to the car. When I get back we will watch the boats come in and then we will be free to walk around a bit."

The grill had cooled off enough to carry it, and he grabbed the bag of picnic items, bagged up the trash, and went to load the car. It took him a little longer to get back, simply because the crowds were so thick. He returned just in time to see the first fishing boats, the *barques de Catalane*, coming around the curve of the rocky point at the opening of the bay. The boats seemed to be motoring perpendicular to the shore all in a line, and then all of a sudden half of them turned right and the other half went left. Some began to zigzag back and forth and some even did circles, but eventually they all came in to the shore. It was like a water ballet. When they landed, their hulls were full of containers of grapes, and everyone cheered them on. Unloading the large oval metal containers full of purple and green grapes was a heavy task. The copper containers had brass handles at either end so men could carry them off the boats and up the beach. As the men wove through the crowd the attendees went crazy and cheered even more. People were on their feet, pouring from wine bottles and toasting to the fishermen bringing in the grape harvest.

Lucien and Chante also stood. Lucien told her to grab her things and they wove through the crowd to follow the wine caskets. He kept hold of her so he wouldn't lose her in the crowd, and they wound their way to the boulevard. Everyone was in the street. It was reminiscent of a carnival. Tall men on stilts walked through the crowd. To one side some people were stomping grapes in a large vat, their clothes completely covered with blue and purple stains. They were falling down in the vats, but laughing and having a great time. A musical group was playing outside a café, and jugglers were drawing crowds at street corners. She could not remember ever being in a crowd this large and feeling so much joy.

They hung out at the main square and watched the brass band play a wild horn-filled number. The remainder of the square filled with people dancing the *Sardane*, a circle dance of the region. They even joined in for a few minutes once Chante saw how to step along. As the afternoon turned to early evening and they had wound through the crowd from one end of the town and back again, he asked her if she had had enough. She nodded that she had, so they made their way back to the car and slowly drove through the crowds to finally depart from Banyuls-sur-mer. It had been another great celebration of the harvest.

They returned to Collioure and parked in the same lot by the carousel. They had decided to take a walk along the water. Lucien opened her side of the car and took her hand to help her out.

"Do you mind if I keep hold of you? Earlier I held on to you getting through the crowd because I did not want to lose you, but now I want to hold on to you because I want to stay closer to you." Lucien gave her one of his biggest smiles, but it was because of the sparkle in his eye and the longing in her chest that she kept hold. He bent his elbow for her to hold on to and they began their stroll, stepping together with their bodies close. The air was still, the moon was full, and the sky was filling with stars.

Chante looked at him with real affection. "I really enjoyed the festival today. Thank you for taking me. I've never been here this late in the season so I could attend. I'd read about it, but it is much more fun to be there when it is happening."

"Thank you for coming. This has been one of the best days in a very long time for me."

Having the trapdoor covered and done also provided him with a sense of relief, and because of Chante he had not had to think about it all day. They walked around the base of the castle, crossed the quay, and rounded the sandy curve of the Plage Boramar. Then they circled behind the church, walked the path to the chapel, and proceeded halfway out to the light beacon. They spoke very little but she felt as though they were speaking volumes, holding on to one another. They leaned on the railing looking back at Collioure. Its boardwalk was all lit up and the floodlights at the castle walls cast a golden glow.

"It looks so magical," said Chante. "No wonder most people that come here fall in love with the place."

"And fall in love," he added, and turned fully toward her.

She held on to both of his arms. "Lucien, I don't know if that is what I am feeling right now, but you have certainly changed my outlook on the world. You are so gentle and gentlemanly. I do love the sound of your voice and your thoughtfulness. I like when you order dinner for us, that we can share in the books that we read, how we both like history, the fun we can have together in a crowd, and the way we can be alone and silent, but share so much in that silence."

Lucien could not stop looking into her eyes. They held him, possessed him, and they fed him with something he didn't know that he was hungry for. He pulled her close and kissed her softly and tenderly, and she returned his kisses with more strength, heat, and desire.

"Chante, Chante, I love your name, and if this town holds magic it is because you are in it. I become both lost and found in your eyes. I like the sweet smell of you and your soft touch. I even like those cute freckles on your cheeks. That day when we first met, and I took your hand and kissed it, I think I have never kissed anything so wonderful in all my life. They say in American films that a man can sweep a woman off her feet, but that is what you have done to me, Chante. Now I know what that means."

Chante shivered, but she wasn't sure if it was the sea air or the shock of recognizing a driving desire inside of her.

"Walk me home, Lucien. I want to get closer to you." Again, the silence that falls over all those who carry love within them accompanied them, as they took each step closer to their next embrace.

They stopped at the car so she could get her things and when they reached her apartment she invited him in. She set the second bottle of wine that they had bought that morning on the dining table. There had been so much free wine at the festival that they had not needed to open it. Chante opened the French doors and went and stood on the balcony. She leaned against the railing looking at the stars, and Lucien encircled behind her. He kissed the back of her neck and behind her ear, her shoulder, and the back of her head. She turned, smiled, and led him to her bedroom. The wine could wait until tomorrow.

*   *   *

On the Rue Julien high above Collioure, another couple was in an embrace. Her glasses were off, her hair was down and in disarray, and her negligee was raised to her thighs. Émile stroked her breasts and kissed her fingers.

"Do that again, Mimi. Your touch is so wonderful."

Mimi slid her hands down his body and kissed his wide chest with curling grey hair. His head bent back to concentrate as he held on to her shoulders. His moustache rose and fell with his deep breaths. Within a short time they were again in an embrace and they lay quietly side-by-side. A cooling breeze from the balcony of his bedroom refreshed them. He raised himself to lean back against the backrest, reached over for his snifter of cognac, and took a sip. Mimi adjusted herself next to him and lifted the second snifter.

"Ah, finally some time to ourselves. You'd think that in my position and as many years as I've put into the military I would have more free time. At least we have this evening." He paused to take another sip and realized Mimi was very quiet. "So how is your life at the library going? You are going to shorter hours for the season. You know, you don't have to keep working there."

"I like it there. It's quiet and I will never run out of reading material. I like the work, and while you are off traveling around all I have to do is open a book to that place and I can be with you in my own way. Besides, why would I want to miss the handsome soldiers that come in?'

"Life as a colonel is not as romantic as you think. I don't really travel around that much anymore." Then it finally registered what she had just said. "What do you mean my men are coming in to your library? They are more likely to be in bars or combing the beach for women instead of reading books."

"I don't see too many of them, but your Sergeant Lucien Reynard has been in a few times."

"Really, and what kind of books is he interested in?"

"He asked for books and maps of the fort, and he is searching for Vauban's book on tunnel warfare. We don't carry such maps or rare books by Vauban, but his interest was clear."

The colonel sat up more. "Hmm, I wonder what he is up to? He's been clearing a room in the basement and turning it into more offices. I wonder if his imagination was piqued or if he actually found something?"

"Are there tunnels under the fort?"

Émile turned toward her with a wry smile. "Not to my knowledge. Besides even if there were, they would have caved in and been sealed up long ago. If the sergeant comes in again, I'd like to know what he does check out."

"Of course, Émile. Whatever you want."

He turned to her and smiled, "Whatever I want?" She set her glass down and once more stretched out alongside him.

Chapter 8

When the colonel arrived at his office on Monday morning he saw a note from his secretary that the carpet people had called. The colonel had his secretary call them back. The owner, Monsieur Bodier, who had supervised the laying of the carpet, answered the phone.

"Hello Colonel Grosvenor, this is Monsieur Bodier. Thank you for returning my call. I just wanted to check in with you to find out if the carpet met with your approval. It was a little bit of a challenge to cover the metal plate, but with some extra foam padding, I think it came out well."

"The metal plate?" he asked, raising his bushy grey eyebrows.

"Yes, sir. Sergeant Raynard said there had once been a drain in the floor and that the metal plate had to remain to strengthen the floor."

The colonel smiled, and nodded. "Yes, fine. Good job. Thank you."

"Thank you, colonel." He hung up the phone, and leaned back in his chair. He didn't know there had once been a drain in that floor. Could Sergeant Reynard be letting his curiosity get away from him? The colonel had his secretary call Private Bellamy to his office, since Lucien was on an errand to obtain some specialty office equipment for the new offices. When Alerion arrived the colonel asked him to close the door behind him.

Private Ballamy saluted. "Sir, you called for me?"

"Yes. Are the new offices completed and ready?"

"Yes, sir!"

"Very good, although I guess we had better stop calling that room the basement. The new officers, Privates Rousseau and Duran, might think we have consigned them to a dungeon. From now on we will call it Level A."

"Yes, sir, Level A. Very good, sir."

"Private Bellamy, let me ask you something. When you moved the boxes out, did you or Sergeant Reynard find anything unusual in the old storeroom?"

Alerion could not help but swallow and think about what he would say. "Unusual sir, what do you mean? It was just a lot of old boxes, sir."

"Really, no files with unusual names, odd equipment, or hidden doorways?"

Alerion was very nervous now. "No, sir, we did not have time to go through the boxes. We had to move them too quickly, sir."

The colonel eyed him carefully. "Very well then. The new officers will be arriving later today. Make sure each receives a copy of the key to the room. That will be all, Bellamy."

Alerion saluted, turned and left, his brow beginning to form small beads of sweat.

Then another call came in for the colonel, from Madame Severin. Émile picked up the phone with a smile.

"Mimi, how are you?"

"Good morning Émile. I thought I should let you know that a young woman I saw Sergeant Reynard with a week ago, brought back a book on Vauban, and she told me to hold it for him, that he had asked for it."

"That's fine Mimi, let me know if he picks it up. Thank you for telling me." He hung up and thought about the three interesting conversations he had just had.

Alerion sent a text to Lucien and asked if he would meet him for lunch in town. They decided to meet for pizza at L'Arcade. Lucien was already there when Alerion arrived. He saw Lucien through the window staring off into space and smiling. Seeing Alerion brought Lucien back to earth. Alerion had hardly seated before he began.

"Sir, the colonel wants me to make copies of the key for the new officers for their offices downstairs, and that level is now to be called Level A." Then he bent forward and with a controlled whisper to Lucien, "He knows Lucien. He knows something."

Lucien responded with a whisper. "He knows what Alerion?"

Alerion looked nervously around the sparsely filled pizzeria. "The colonel knows about the . . ." He mouthed the word for "tunnel". "He asked if we had found any unusual files, equipment, or hidden doorways."

"He did? But there is no way he could know anything. We were the only ones in there and the only ones with the key. The painter and air conditioning people never saw the floor. The tarp was laid out over everything. The only people that saw the metal plate were the men who laid the carpet. They seemed quite fine with the explanation I gave, and did not ask any further questions. No, Alerion. I just don't see how he could know that we found anything of consequence."

"Unless, of course, he already knew the trapdoor was there."

"Maybe, but then, wouldn't he have asked if we had found a trapdoor instead of a hidden doorway?" They both stared at each other. "Alerion, even if he does know that there is a room below and a tunnel, he also knows it doesn't go anywhere, and surely he would not think for a moment that we would have actually gotten through that welded trapdoor. He would know it couldn't be opened."

"Still, Lucien, it makes me nervous, the way he asked me."

"Alerion, please don't worry. Nothing is going to happen."

"But what if he gets curious, pulls up the carpet, and sees the metal plate? If he knows there is a trap door he's also going to know the metal plate was not there."

"Alerion, you had better have a glass of wine to calm your nerves. There is nothing that will come of it. If he had known about a trapdoor, he would have told us, so we would be aware of it. No he doesn't know." He watched Alerion take a large swig from his own glass of wine. Then he signaled the waiter to bring another. "I'll tell you what. If the colonel ever does pull up the carpet to look and questions us further, you will know nothing about it, all right? I will simply say that there seemed to be an old drain and the floor seemed weak, so I placed the metal plate there myself. Okay? So let's order pizza. I'm very hungry."

"How can you be hungry at a time like this?"

"Because Alerion..." and he gave him that broad flashing smile indicating something much more pleasant was to be revealed. A radiant smile was on his face.

Alerion seemed to catch on. "You didn't. You did? Well, how nice for you. Was it good?"

"Beyond good, she was perfect, amazing, superb..."

"Okay, okay, I get it. It was good. Let's order."

They were able to finish their lunch without bringing the subject up again. When Lucien got back to his office he called Chante.

"Hello Chante, it's Lucien. How are you?"

"I'm feeling wonderful." He had stayed Saturday night at her apartment and only begrudgingly had left her Sunday afternoon. "Lucien, I want to thank you so much for this entire weekend. I had a great time at the Harvest Festival, and you were amazing. I am so happy."

"I'm very happy too, Chante. I can hardly concentrate today. I want to let you know that as much as I would like to see you tonight I have to play host to those new officers arriving this afternoon. It is also part of my duty to take them to dinner and give them a tour of the town. I hope you understand. I'm afraid you'll have to get used to my crazy schedule. So I would like to make it up to you. On Wednesday, I think I'll be able to take a partial day off. How would you like to play tourist and go to the castle?"

"That sounds great. By the way, I took my books back to the library today, so if you want to check out the book on Vauban it will be there. I told Madame Severin to hold it for you. She did not have anything on the castle, so I will want to see what is available in the castle bookstore. Don't you think it is strange that there is nothing on the castle in the library? It just makes me want to dig even deeper."

"I can very much understand that feeling," he said, as he could hardly wait to get under the castle himself. "I'll call you tomorrow and we'll set a time for Wednesday."

"Of course, Lucien. I understand. You do whatever you need to do. I'll either be here, at the library, shopping, or lying on the beach, but I'll have my cell."

"Chante, I..." but he seemed at a loss for words. "Thank you for opening up your heart to me. You won't regret it, I promise."

She was smiling so hard she couldn't respond, but they did say goodbye with the promise of another phone call the next day.

That evening Lucien and Alerion did their best to play welcoming hosts. Rousseau and Duran were smart guys, and would prove to be of great help with the upcoming winter training. They were fine with their office, although they had hoped for one with a window. All

Lucien could do was apologize and tell them that once they were settled and had gotten to know the peace of Level A, they would enjoy it, and if not, no doubt an office upstairs would become available.

On Tuesday morning Alerion had a message from the colonel to come to his office. When Alerion arrived the colonel had him come in and close the door. He had some concerns and was placing him on special assignment. He was not to tell anyone, and was to report to him first thing every Monday morning. When the colonel had finished outlining the assignment, and Alerion had left his office, a frown was on Alerion's face. Then he met up with Lucien, Rousseau and Duran for meetings, which helped calm him and keep him busy. At a short break, Lucien got a chance to call Chante and they made arrangements to meet the next day in front of the castle at 1:00 pm.

Chante's heart was beating quickly in anticipation of seeing Lucien. She had been so nervous that she could not eat lunch, and hoped they could go for an early dinner together. He waved to her as he walked up the Quay de l'Amirauté, the walkway that followed along the north side of the castle. It was the first time she had seen him in his fatigues, as he was coming straight from work. Soon they were in an embrace and he gave her a long-awaited kiss.

"I think the last twelve hours have been the hardest not seeing you," he said.

"Me too. You've been continually on my mind."

"I hope I stay there. What did you do yesterday afternoon?"

"I went back to the library and got a couple of new books on other nearby castles that Vauban had enlarged. I bought myself some clothes for winter, since I had only packed summer clothes, and I called and spoke to my father. I let him know I was okay, and in fact, better than okay. I told him I had met someone who was a perfect gentleman and I was now seeing him."

"And what did he say to that?"

"He was glad that I was moving past the divorce, but he was his usual skeptical self and cautioned me to not move too quickly. He is still hoping that I will consider this a holiday and move to England to be with him. I told him that I still needed some time and that I would keep in touch."

Lucien hugged her again and they proceeded to walk up the steps to the castle entrance. They entered through the large wooden doors that led into a reception and ticket office. Chante took the opportunity to ask the attendant if there was any history on the castle that she could look at. The woman handed her a sheet of paper with a map and numbered guide to the castle and told her that she was welcome to look on the shelves for information. Chante looked through a couple of books, but did not see anything more than the perfunctory basics she already knew. There was a display case that had posters, puzzles, coffee mugs, and patches with the castle on them, toy knights, and a few children's books on castles, but nothing specifically written about the history of the chateau. She was disappointed, but thought she might be able to query a guard or guide within.

They walked through the entry and emerged onto a wide stone walkway that gently sloped up eastward alongside the north wall, and then turned right to further walk the wall that faced the sea. A plaque told her things she already knew, even though it had been some years since she had been within the castle. It was a pleasant entrance with plants lining the walkway. A wall was to the left that they could just see over, of the bay. They turned right and passed through a large arched entrance that rose steeply upward. A full wing of the castle spanned above them. Ahead they could see light that opened up into the central castle courtyard.

Lucien knew that they had passed a darker entrance into the underground tunnel on their right, but he wanted Chante to go where *she* wanted to go first. As much as he wanted to go into that tunnel immediately, he knew that they would eventually enter and explore it at her pace. It was like eating the plain side of the pastry first, so the last bites could be the sweetest. In some strange way, he liked building up this anticipation. It excited him. That, and walking next to Chante on a beautiful day, filled him with pleasure.

They emerged into the bright sunlight of the castle's central courtyard. Signs indicated several ways to go and several rooms had exhibits to explore. She wanted to look at it all, so they took their time. There did not seem to be any guides anywhere. It was off-season, so she realized that the employers were probably trying to save money. They explored everywhere that they could go on the upper ramparts overlooking the town on three sides and the sea to the east. Then they descended back to the courtyard level and went through several wings of the castle. Most rooms were empty, but some had items that had been found on the grounds like old cannonballs, and some had art exhibits. Lucien had forgotten how big and impressive the place was. At last they had seen the fortified castle and were headed out the same way they had come in.

Chante consulted her map of the castle and then remembered they had not gone into the tunnel. "We have one more place to explore," she said and looked at Lucien who had a big smile on his face. "You've probably been patiently waiting for us to get there, haven't you?"

"I won't deny that it holds a certain fascination for me," and he led the way.

They followed the curtain wall that they had walked along before entering the castle. Here the right wall of stone was fairly upright, but then the roof arched up and curved over their heads to the left wall. The stone path slowly slanted down as they walked. There were small foot lights along the bottom of the walls that guided them down and a string of bulbs hung from the ceiling to light the way. The tunnel was wide and tall enough for men to travel on horseback, and had descended to stables that were once on a lower level that no longer existed. The tunnel itself was pretty plain with little to see. Eventually the stone walkway became uneven and became soft dirt. They came to a dead end with a solid earth wall before them. Chante turned around and began to head back.

"Wait a minute, Chante, I want to look at something." He pulled a flashlight out of his pocket, turned it on, and examined the wall at the end of the tunnel more closely.

"A flashlight? Do you usually carry one around with you?"

"I am a trained soldier, I am always prepared." With that he also pulled out a compass and used his flashlight to read it. "Hmm, that's interesting,"

"What is?"

"I was just curious which way the tunnel was running."

"And why would that be of interest?"

Good question. What was he going to tell her? "I just thought that it would be running directly north."

"And that is because?"

Why indeed? Maybe if he just walked around the castle and found the exact coordinate that matched the other tunnel, he would find the connecting tunnel. "Because of the coastline," he replied. Chante eyed him with a look waiting for him to say more on the subject.

"Chante, do you mind if we go back into the castle? I want to check something out."

"Sure," she said with a glint in her eye. "But I'm curious. Are we doing it because it is a matter of personal interest, part of some assignment, or for the write-up for your soldiers?"

He looked at her and laughed. "I'm just curious about something. Will you humor me?"

She smiled, "Of course."

They turned around and started to walk back up the partially-lit tunnel. Halfway back Lucien flashed his light up to the wall on the right to see something he hadn't noticed on the way in. It was a recessed ledge about head-high. He paused and gave it a closer look, but he had to stand back against the opposite wall to see into its shadow better. It definitely looked like a collapsed intersecting tunnel, which had been partially filled in and partially repaired. He didn't say anything, but led them back to the central courtyard. He checked his compass again and they moved along the north wall of the courtyard until the angle was the same as when he had been in the tunnel on the north side of the river. At that point, they were standing below the northwest tower in the central courtyard. In that corner was an exhibition room containing prints and sketches by a local artist.

"Let's go back in here for a minute. I want to check something out." They entered the room they had been in twenty minutes before. His eyes cast a close look at all the walls and floors. To his surprise there was a door on the other side of the room. It was probably used to access the tower above, but if it went up, it might just as well go down. He quickly crossed the room and tried the handle on the door, but it was, of course, locked.

Chante had watched him with interest. His excited energy was palpable. She was even getting excited just watching him, but she had no idea why. At the door he turned and looked up at her watching him. Then he looked above her and all around the ceiling of the room. He broke into a broad smile as if he had the answer to a puzzle. He returned to her side. "Okay, I've seen enough. Let's go have a drink." Chante was going to get it out of him, whatever it was. This was no military assignment. This was definitely something else.

He wanted to get a glass of wine across the quay at an outdoor restaurant. Chante noticed that he sat in a chair that gave him a direct view of that northwest tower that was barely visible behind some tall trees below the castle wall. They ordered their wine and the waiter brought a basket of bread. She watched as Lucien kept looking up at the tower, while she nibbled on the bread. Chante gave him some time, but then she could not stand it any longer.

"Okay, I give up. What in the world are you doing? You are like a cat with a bird in its mouth. I'm pretty sure you have looked over at that tower a dozen times already, and I'll bet it has nothing to do with your job. Soldier or not, someone just doesn't pull out a compass when they know where they are. What's going on?"

Lucien looked at her sheepishly. In all his enthusiasm, he knew he had failed to hold back his excitement traipsing all over the castle. Like water in a dam about to spill over, his pent up anticipation was about to break its dyke. He knew he had not safeguarded his true interest close enough. He looked around to the other tables, and because it was low season no one else was seated nearby. How could he tell her what was really going on? How could he possibly go on with this new relationship without telling her? He leaned in toward her to speak.

"Chante, what I am about to tell you must stay between us." She leaned in toward him conspiratorially and nodded, their eyes locked. "With many castles built during the middle ages, tunnels were often dug connecting a castle with a fort for many reasons. Collioure has never had documentation of any such tunnels, yet Vauban utilized them in a great many other castles that he did rebuild. When you mentioned at dinner last week that he had formed a mining company and even written a book about it, that seemed like a confirmation."

She leaned in closer with a whisper. "A confirmation of what?"

He took a deep breath before answering. "Last week I found a tunnel underneath the fort, which I think once connected to the castle."

Chante's eyes grew large. "You did? Do they connect?"

"I think they might have at one time, but no longer. It dead-ends at the Douy River at the quay. I thought that the coordinates I took at the fort would match the coordinates to the underground tunnels under the chateau, but they don't. They do point directly to that northwest tower." They both turned their heads and looked intently at the tower and then back at each other.

"Wow, that is amazing. What was the tunnel like?"

"It was just a dirt channel with old beams, partially caved in. Now it is closed off forever, because I had to seal the floor of the room I was working in so no one else would find out about it."

"Lucien, why didn't you tell someone, like one of your superiors? Wouldn't they have found it just as interesting?"

"Yes, but I could also be court-martialed for destroying military property and gone to jail instead."

"What do you mean, you destroyed military property?"

"I mean I had to sledgehammer through a cement floor next to the welded trapdoor that was there, and then seal it so a carpet could be put over it for the new office."

"So that's why you were in the library searching for blueprints of the fort, why your hands were blistered, and why you wanted to come to the castle."

"I confess, yes. All of it."

"You did this all on your own?"

"Well, no actually. My assistant, Private Alerion Bellamy, helped me the entire time. But he would have a fit if he knew that I told anyone. So when you finally meet him, don't say anything."

Chante stared at him in near disbelief. He did have a serious look on his face and he seemed nervous, so it must be true.

"Okay, so now what do you purpose we do?"

"We? Not you. I'm going to open that locked door in that northwest tower, get underneath the castle and see if the tunnel is still on that side of the river."

"But Lucien, even if it is, it is sure to be just an empty tunnel partially fallen in, like it was on the other side."

"Maybe it is, and maybe it isn't. But I've got one good question. If there is a tunnel that once linked the castle with the fort, how come no one else knows about it?"

"How do you know no one else knows about it?"

At that Lucien had to pause. "I don't, but no historian has ever written about it."

"Are you sure? We are fond of history, but we are not historians. We need someone that knows southern France's history well and knows Collioure, someone we can trust, and who can get us some answers."

Lucien got that eager look in his eyes again. "And I know just the person, Chante, my father. Would you like to meet him? He is only about a half hour away. I can call him now and we could ask him in person."

Chante could not resist his excitement, but a look of worry was still on her face as she wondered what it would all lead to. "Okay, we can do that."

He pulled out his cell phone, called his father, and was able to reach him. He mentioned that he had someone he wanted him to meet, and that he had a history topic that he hoped he might get some help with. His father was happy to hear from him and invited them over for dinner.

Just as Lucien was finishing his conversation, he saw Alerion walking by, heading west past the restaurant. Alerion kept looking behind him as if he was searching for someone, but walked past without seeing Chante and Lucien. They were tucked away in a corner behind a white canvas awning that the restaurant used to keep the sun off of its patrons. There was something about his glances that sent up a red flag for Lucien, but he did not say anything. Lucien downed his wine, put cash on the table and rose to go. Chante hadn't realized that he wanted to leave right away, so she grabbed a chunk of bread to hold her over and quickly followed him.

Chapter 9

Lucien drove the D114 to the D914 to Perpignan and then took the Route d'Elme into the Sant-Vicens district just south of the city. His father lived in a house just off Rue Alexandre Ansaldi. The house was white with tall cypress trees in front. He must have heard them drive up, because he met them on the porch.

Lucien met his father first and gave him a hug while Chante hung back.

"Papa, it's good to see you." Lucien greeted his father with kisses on both cheeks and then stepped back to make introductions. "Chante, this is my father, Gervais Reynard. And Papa, this is Chante Morgan. She is very special to me Papa, so please be nice to her."

His father was graying at the temples, but for his mid-fifties he looked the professor type, with sparkling blue eyes. He wore grey wide-wale corduroy pants and a long-sleeved blue sweater. His longish crowning dark hair partially fell from his temple as he stepped toward her and extended his soft warm hand.

"Mademoiselle Chante, it is a pleasure to meet you. You must be pretty special to have been brought here. Lucien has rarely introduced me to his friends. My, you are lovely. Please come in." He opened the front door for both of them. "Please forgive the mess. I've been a bachelor for a long time, but I'm afraid my talents don't extend to housekeeping." He had already cleared the beige couch for them to sit on, but then he also realized that he had better remove more books from the coffee table in front of the couch. He walked the pile to the bookshelf against a nearby wall and placed them on the floor. They were then able to see the small dish of olives and some *Pélardon* goat's cheese with cut bread on the table. They sat on the couch.

"Please help yourself. You're lucky. I just went shopping yesterday. I only had a half-day at the university today and had just gotten home when you called. I have some fresh Camargue rice with ham and a lemon tart for dinner." Then he noticed his son was quiet and Chante even quieter. "Son, I can see you both have something on your mind. What is it?"

Gervais sat down in his large brown leather armchair that had a small rip on the right arm where it curved down to meet the seat. He prepared himself by interlocking the fingers of both his hands between his legs and leaned forward. Chante thought his high forehead gave him a distinguished look. His eyes were lovingly focused on his son, as she imagined they must have been throughout Lucien's childhood.

"Papa, what I am going to tell you, you must keep between us. I've only told Chante today, so it is new to her too, but I need your help with some research for me," he looked at Chante, "for us. I know you are going to think that I'm acting like a romantic student full of crazy ideas, but I need you to tell us what you know about the Chateau Royal and any connection with Fort Miradou."

"In what way? Of course they are connected. They are both in Collioure and a castle and fort have been there for centuries."

"I know that Papa, what I mean is, we want to know if there is an underground connection."

"Do you mean as in the black market or really under the ground?"

"Papa, while I was clearing a room in the basement of the fort for new offices, Alerion and I found a trapdoor. Do you remember Alerion? You met him last year."

"Of course son, a fine young man, but what about the trapdoor? Were you able to open it?"

"No Papa, it was welded shut, but with a sledgehammer I was able to break up the cement floor next to it and we discovered a small room below it. The room was empty, but there was a metal door in one wall. It was sealed as well, but we broke through the wall to one side and discovered a long tunnel that runs down to the river. At the end there was a cement wall so we couldn't go any further. We had to retreat, and on the way back up the hill Alerion nearly got buried. We got out and sealed the floor with a metal plate to hide what we had done. Thick padding and a carpet were laid over the trap door and now it is a double office on what we call Level A."

His father let out a low soft whistle and sat back in his chair. "I suppose you already realize that you could go to jail for destroying military property?"

"Yes, Papa, I know, but to see a trapdoor where there should not have been one was a mystery just begging to be explored. I don't think anyone knows anything about it except for us. We were very careful. Chante and I have been doing some research, but there is no mention of a tunnel linking the two fortifications. Why not, Papa? Why would something so historically important not be written about?"

"Maybe it's so old no one knows about it."

"Maybe, maybe not, but that's what we need your help with. As a history professor, do you have access to some historical reference books that aren't available on the market or in a private library? Perhaps in the special collections at the university?"

Chante finally spoke up, "Monsieur Reynard, I found out that the architect Vauban, who rebuilt the chateau, created a special company of miners for military mining and wrote a book about it called *Traite' des Mines*. We are wondering if either a copy or photocopy of it might be available at the university. Lucien already searched for it in the library computer system, but it was not available. Also, it has become pretty obvious that there is very little historical information on the chateau itself, aside from the one-sheet descriptions that they hand out to tourists and a threadbare historical description online."

Lucien added, "Chante is a writer and thought an article on the castle's history would be of interest to her, but there is precious little to write about. Why is there only a perfunctory outline of its history available to us? There are no historian's notes, no logs, or anecdotes. And there seem to be no architectural diagrams or layouts of either the fort or the castle, or of Collioure itself. Why do you think that is? And who do you think made that tunnel?"

"I can see your curiosity is running ahead of your patience. But you do ask some good questions. I'm not sure I can do too much for you, but I will try. Why don't you let me finish making our dinner, and in the meantime I will think about what books I might have that could help you. Tomorrow I will do a little investigation at the university library, and we will see what we can come up with. If there is anything at the university, I will find it. But I think there is a bigger question here."

"What's that, Papa?"

"What do you intend to do with the information when you have it?"

Lucien and Chante looked at each other in silence, but Lucien finally answered.

"We don't know yet."

"While I am getting our dinner, I suggest you think about that." Gervais got up and headed for the kitchen down the hall.

"He's right Lucien, you've been so intent on your explorations, and as much as I am curious, what would we do if indeed there isn't written information on the tunnels? Prove they exist? And to what end? Do you really think that the General Council of the Pyrénées-Orientales would give you permission to dig up the foundations of one of their most popular tourist attractions?"

"I doubt very seriously that the Military would allow me to expose a tunnel under one of their forts, either. In fact, it is precisely the kind of thing they would not want the public to know about."

"You know what happened when the rumor got started about the possibility of a treasure at Rennes-les-Château, right? People from all over the world came digging holes on that small hillside village. I don't think you want people searching for tunnels in Collioure, do you?"

"No, of course not. But if we find anything of historical value, even something that might change what we believe to be part of our history, isn't it worth sharing?"

"So you fully intend to get under the castle, don't you?"

"I've been giving that some thought, but I need a little time to work out the details."

Lucien's father called from the kitchen that dinner was nearly ready. They all sat down at the small table in a corner of the dated but orderly kitchen and began to eat.

"Monsieur Reynard, this is delicious. The rice is so fresh and nutty tasting. I love it. I'd never heard of Camargue rice before this evening."

"Gervais, please," he corrected her. "If I'm going to be a co-conspirator, we should probably be on a first name basis. But first we eat and then we talk business."

Chante and Lucien glanced at one another. "You are right, please call me Chante."

"Anyway, to answer your question, Chante. At one time the Camargue salt marshes were desalinated to grow white rice after World War II, but the wild variety cross-pollinated and within only twenty years, voilà, we now have a special variety of red rice that we can call our own."

Their dinner conversation mainly consisted of Gervais asking questions of Chante and Lucien about how they met, how they've gotten to know each other, and what Lucien had been up to aside from his underground investigations. When the last crumb of the lemon tart had been picked off their plates, Gervais stood and cleared their dishes.

"Wait right here and I'll be back with some information for you." Within a few minutes he was back with two books. "Here is a pretty good book on Roussillon history, and I found one description of Collioure which might help. I'm sure you've read the usual information printed up for the tourists, but let's talk about that history a little more in depth. Sometimes the truth is hidden right before us. Lucien, forgive me, but perhaps for Chante's sake I will give a brief historical overview of the Roussillon area."

Lucien gave a slight grimace, having heard so much history from his father in the last couple dozen years, but now he was ready to really listen, and Chante agreed.

"Please, Gervais, my history on the area is only rudimentary."

He began. "We know that the Languedoc region was occupied during the Iron Age probably by the Celts. The Greeks and Phoenicians were here from 600 BCE and then the Romans came, we think as early as 121 BCE. We know that the Romans settled in 60 BCE when they established themselves in Narbonne. They called the entire Languedoc and Roussillon province Gallia Narbonensis. They built the Via Domitia, the famous Roman road, as a passageway from Italy through France and down into Spain. We have reason to believe they built something in Collioure, referred to as Caucoliberis, because the Romans used the port as a delivery point. So there must have been some kind of fortification there to protect their goods. It was probably where the castle is now, and the only fortification that was built at the time. There was nothing where the fort presently is except a lookout tower.

"When the Roman Empire began to fall in the 5th century, the entire Languedoc and Roussillon area became part of the Visigoth Empire under Theodoric II, sometime between 300 and 500 in our common era. They held it for about 200 years, and then the western region of the Roman province became part of what was then called Septimania, as there were seven major cities included in its territories. Again, we don't have accurate dates for the Visigoth occupation as few archeological finds exist from that period. However, we do have a record that dates to 673 when they turned Collioure into a commercial harbor. Again, the only fortification we know of is where the castle is now.

"In 843 Louis the Fair's three sons signed the Treaty of Verdun. This agreement divided the Carolingian empire into three kingdoms, which swept all across Europe to the present eastern European nations. The most western portion was called West Francia, which was inherited by the youngest son, known as Charles the Bald, the grandson of Charlemagne. This territory marks the beginning of what was to become the boundaries of France. In 893, Sunyer II became the first hereditary Count of Roussillon.

The Counts of Roussillon that followed were allied to their cousins, the Counts of Empúries, in a centuries-long conflict with the surrounding nobles. At the beginning of the 12th century, the power of the Counts of Barcelona began to rise to such a height that the Counts of Roussillon had no choice but to swear allegiance to them. Louis's illegitimate brothers challenged the possession of Roussillon. To ensure that his half-brothers would not inherit his territories, he left all his lands to Alfonso II of Aragon, who took possession in 1172. Under the Aragonese monarchs of northeastern Spain, the growth of the region continued, and ports in Collioure and Perpignan became important for Mediterranean trade.

"You will recall that by this time there was already the Third Crusade, and by the early 1200s the Cathars came into popularity. They were denounced as heretics by the Catholic Church, which led to the Albigensian Crusade, followed by the Inquisition in 1229. There are some that say the castle in Collioure was expanded sometime between 1242 and 1280, possibly by the Templars, but historians now believe additions were made over the next few hundred years.

"As the French and Spanish crowns grew in power, the region of Roussillon, forming part of the border between them, was frequently the site of military conflict. With the Treaty of Corbeil in 1258, Louis IX of France formally surrendered sovereignty over Roussillon to the Crown of Aragon. James of Aragon took the Balearic isles from the Moors and joined these islands with Roussillon making it the Kingdom of Majorca. In 1276, James I granted this kingdom to his son James II. But James III, his successor, refused to do homage to Philip VI of France and asked Peter IV of Aragon for aid. Peter refused, declared war and seized Majorca and Roussillon, including Collioure, in 1344. This is when the fortifications of Fort St.

Elme were built. The province once again returned to the Crown of Aragon and it enjoyed peace until 1462. That year the French took over the boundary and Louis XI had the Collioure ramparts around the castle built to shelter a large French garrison.

"Disputes between John II and his son over the ruling of Navaronne caused Louis XI of France to support John against his subjects, who had risen in revolt. The province was occupied by French troops until 1493 when Charles VIII evacuated the region as part of a settlement with the Spanish Catholic Monarchs Isabel I of Castile and Ferdinand II of Aragon. Two years later the kingdoms of Castile and Aragon combined to form the Kingdom of Spain. The kingdom of Majorca, which included Roussillon, continued to be contested by the French and Spanish and they fought over it from 1496 to 1498." Gervais patted the second book. "During this time, according to this book on Collioure, the urban wall was modernized and a horn work was added to the castle on its north and west side."

Lucien turned to Chante. "Hear that, the northwest corner."

Chante was distracted. "I'm sorry Gervais, what is horn work?"

"It's a type of fortification that is made up of two demi-bastions with a curtain wall connecting them, and long side walls that sweep back. Think of a big fat letter "M" with its legs seated back against the castle.

Lucien added, "It was built to fortify an area in front of a fortification so the enemy could not occupy the front grounds."

Gervais smiled at his son. "I'll continue. At the same time two star-shaped forts were also constructed on the outside to reinforce the defense: Fort Sainte-Thérèse was built to the north, which is nearly where Fort Miradou stands today, and Fort Saint-Elme to the south, which can still be seen on the hill above Collioure. This implies that the urban wall was already in place sometime between 1462 and 1493.

"In 1542 Henry Dauphin of France took Perpignan by force from the Aragonese. When the Catalans rose against the Spanish Crown in 1641, Louis XIII of France entered the conflict on the side of the Catalans. In 1659 the Treaty of the Pyrenees was signed, securing Roussillon and part of the Cerdagne to the French crown, creating the French province of Roussillon as it is today. For the next fifty years Louis XIV worked to ensure the political allegiance of his new subjects. Beginning in 1669, other forms of construction were realized on Collioure's urban wall, and the castle was transformed into a citadel. The engineer Saint-Hilaire, following Vauban's instructions, forced the peasants to leave their homes. He then had the former upper town of Collioure burned so he could create a fanned slope down toward the citadel where he built on to the urban wall. Fort Saint-Elme was preserved, but fort Sainte-Thérèse was demolished and replaced by Fort du Mirador, situated a little further to the south. He protected the high ground to the north of the town by building Fort Miradou on the site of the old medieval tower. The landward side of the castle was further protected by the construction of a large demilune and a ditch."

Chante got a puzzled look on her face again. Lucien added, "A demilune is another type of fortification in the shape of a crescent moon. We stood on a small demilune on top of the castle today, facing the hillside." Chante thought for a couple seconds and then nodded her head in remembrance.

Gervais continued. "The wall was protected by a ditch which ran from Fort Miradou to the Château Royal, thus enclosing the town." Gervais could see their eyes start to brighten. "Although there were fortifications in Collioure for well over 1500 years, this is the first time that a ditch is mentioned. Not a tunnel, but a ditch. The earliest that there may have been construction linking the castle with the fort would be 1462, but then the same book also mentions that the designs and work for the defense of Roussillon only started after the spring of 1679, so it is probably the later date.

"The Spanish again occupied Collioure in 1793, but only for a year or so, and then the French retook it. We know that the urban wall that linking the fort with the castle was demolished sometime in the 1800s, but I don't know the exact date. Now we jump ahead in time to the Spanish Civil War in the late 1930s. The castle was used as a prison to hold Spanish refugees. I suppose prisoners could have dug an escape tunnel, but then they would have ended up at the fort, which would not have worked out well for them, either."

At this point Gervais took a break and decided he needed some coffee. Chante and Lucien considered what they had heard, but they still needed more answers.

Chapter 10

When Gervais returned with a tray of coffee cups, Lucien focused on a new angle.

"Papa, what about the Templars? You barely mentioned the crusades."

"Is that what you want to know about? You can look them up online, but just know there are conflicting historical reports about them. I've got lots of students who ask about them all the time. I'll give you the best historical information that I have, but it's unlikely the Templars have anything to do with your question about a tunnel.

"I mentioned the crusades, but the Templars were not involved in the early years of the first three crusades. The first crusade ran from 1095 to 1101 with four different movements: the People's Crusade, the German Crusade, the Princes' Crusade, and the Crusade of 1101, all to secure the city of Jerusalem. King Baldwin I was the first Christian King crowned in the new crusader state in Jerusalem. His son, King Baldwin II, was crowned King of Jerusalem in 1118, the same year the Knights Templar were founded. King Baldwin allowed their leader Hugues de Payens, to set up quarters in a wing of the royal palace in Jerusalem, which had been the Al Aqsa Mosque on the Temple Mount.

At that time it was believed that the mosque had been built on the ruins of an older Temple, the Temple of Solomon. That's why the Templars took the name they did, Knights of the Temple. Officially, the mission of the Templars was to protect pilgrims on their journey to visit the holy places in Jerusalem. Some believe the Templars also had an unofficial mission to find proof of Solomon's Temple below the mount. Newer historians now believe Solomon might be a myth, and they may be right, because to this day no proof has ever been found of the first temple, but others claim that the Templars found a treasure below the mount and they took it out of the country. However, nothing has ever been confirmed about what they may or may not have found, though there are about as many theories as there are stones on that mount.

"The Templars were all over Europe and the Middle East. We know they set up foundations in Champagne, where Hughes de Payens was from. They were in Portugal as early as 1122 because there are records affirming land holdings. In 1126 they established foundations in Spain, and in 1128 they had holdings in Toulouse, Douzens, and Carcassone. In 1129 the Templars were fully endorsed by the Roman Catholic Church, with the Pope as their religious leader. A year later, Alfonso I, who was then King of Navarre, gave them more land in Spain. Also in 1132 a Templar Commandery was built called Mas Déu. That's located only a little to the west of Collioure, but it is deserted now. In 1136, Hugh of Bourbouton gave the Knights Templar land at Richerenches, just north of us.

"Three years later, Pope Innocent II issued a papal bull saying that the Templars could cross any border, owed no taxes, and were answerable only to him. By 1150 the Templars were issuing letters of credit to pilgrims who signed over goods, money, and their properties, in order to finance their journeys to the Holy Land, and thereby their wealth grew. Let me give you an idea of what it cost to support a knight. In 1180 a Burgundian noble required three square kilometers of estate to support himself as a knight, but by 1260, just under a hundred years later, this had risen to over fifteen square kilometers. Inflation existed even then. In time the Templars had large land holdings not only in the Middle East, France, and Spain, but also in England, Germany, Hungary, and Scotland, with farms, vineyards, churches, castles, commanderies, and even a few ships. The Templars were greatly involved in the next few crusades, and were able to fund their own efforts.

"In 1187, Saladin, the first sultan of Egypt and Syria, began a major campaign against the Crusader Kingdom of Jerusalem. His troops virtually destroyed the Christian army at the battle of Hattin, and they took back Jerusalem, along with a large amount of territory. Emperor Frederick Barbarossa of Anatolia, King Philip II of France, and King Richard I the Lionhearted of England, formed the Third Crusade to take it back. By 1192 however, King Richard and Saladin had signed a peace treaty, leaving Jerusalem still in Muslim hands. In 1198 Pope Innocent III called for the Fourth Crusade, but the Templars and the rest of the Crusaders instead were to wage battle on Constantinople (today's Istanbul), which ended in the conquest and looting of that Byzantine capital. The Albigensian Crusade began in 1208 and the Baltic Crusades began in 1211. Five years later, Pope Innocent III began the Fifth Crusade by attacking Egypt, but the crusaders were forced to surrender to Muslim defenders ten years later. In 1229, in what became known as the Sixth Crusade, Emperor Frederick II achieved the peaceful transfer of Jerusalem to Crusader control in a treaty, which expired a decade later, and Muslims once again easily regained control of Jerusalem.

"I won't belabor the continuing gains and defeats through the Seventh, Eighth, and Ninth Crusades, and smaller skirmishes. A move against the Templars began with the first arrests in 1307. But the Order of the Knights Templars was not abolished until 1312 by papal decree at the Council of Vienne. Finally, the last Grand Master, Jacques de Molay, and his second-in-command, Geoffroi de Charney, were burned at the stake in 1314, ending the last of their Order. Though some say those knights who escaped arrest went underground in other countries."

"What about the Templars in Collioure?" asked Lucien, "do you know much about them?"

"Sure, son, but there isn't much to know. The Templars were in Collioure. Some say that the Templars built the castle in Collioure in 1207, but we don't believe that is correct. Peter II of Aragon only gave them some land on which was little more than a fortified house. It was the Aragonese that probably built the castle, not the Templars. The Templars did, however, build a small cathedral on the site of an old Moorish settlement, and they established vineyards in the hills above Collioure. Don't forget that the Spanish were there for a long time. The French were there later and longer under the Treaty of the Pyrenees, and the French Kings used the castle as a summer retreat." Gervais paused to let the history lesson sink in.

Lucien looked at Chante, but was still puzzled. "So that's it? No more about the Templars in Collioure?" Lucien looked downhearted. "Then what would be your best guess for who might have dug a tunnel from the Chateau to the Fort?"

Gervais looked from one to the other trying to get a sense of how they were taking it all in, and what he could say that would make any difference. "That's all I know about the Templars in connection with Collioure. Some of it is wishful thinking to bring the tourists in. A lot of it is conflicting guesswork between historians. It is most likely that either the Spanish or the French made the tunnel. Take your pick. And really, would it matter?"

Lucien had to nod his head and agree. Maybe it didn't make any difference. Still, one nagging thought kept whispering to him in the back of his mind. Why had it been kept a secret all these years? Why were there no architectural plans of either the castle or the fort? But his father broke his thought.

"Too bad you didn't get a chip of the wood from the pilings in the tunnel. You could have had it radiocarbon dated."

Lucien wished he had thought of that when he was in the tunnel, but getting Alerion out of the tunnel as soon as possible after the cave-in had been his only concern.

After a short time, Lucien and Chante thanked Gervais for dinner and the information, said their goodbyes, and headed back to Collioure. They were pretty quiet on the way back. There was nothing Chante could think to say to alleviate what she felt was disappointment in Lucien's eyes. Nothing he could hold on to, to verify his find. She reached over and put her hand on his leg. He released one hand from the steering wheel to take her hand in his.

"You're awfully quiet, Lucien. I wish there was something that I could say. I'm not even sure what your father could have said."

"Chante, just being able to share this experience with you has been very comforting. Thank you for coming." Then he smiled and squeezed her hand. "I think my father liked you."

"I liked him too. He is a wonderful man and I can tell he loves you very much." Then she did think of something to cheer him. "Well, at least you have one thing to look forward to." Lucien looked at her with a puzzled look. "The comfort of my arms tonight."

Lucien smiled widely at her invitation, "and the sweetness of your lips." And that smile stayed with him all the way back to her apartment.

Thursday and Friday Lucien had to work, but on Saturday morning he decided to show Chante something not far away that his father had reminded him about in Chante's history lesson. The idea had always captivated his imagination about the Templars. If Chante was game, he thought it would be at least an enjoyable day out. They drove west out of Collioure on the main road via the 612 toward the small town of Trouillas and to its winery. He explained to Chante why their destination was of such interest.

"Remember my father mentioning Mas Déu, one of the first Templar commanderies in southern France? It wasn't just a fort. In its early days the knights raised cattle, grew grapes and olive trees, and ran a salt trade. Mas Déu had its own church, cemetery, and central meetinghouse. It was a place where aged Templars could retire. It was also a repository for Templar documents, and it served as one of their main treasure holdings. When the arrests began, many of the Templars in the area were held as prisoners at Mas Déu. But it is not easy to locate. To discourage trespassers it is not labeled on any map. It is located in the center of some woods, surrounded by vineyards. So yes, before you ask, we will need to sneak on to the land, but I don't think it will be a big deal as no one will be able to see us. There is no telling what state the fort will be in. I've never been there, but I found it on an online aerial map, so I know exactly where to go."

It took less than thirty minutes to get there. They turned on to a small dirt road and followed the sign to the winery, but they continued on between the winery buildings and followed the dirt road. They came to the edge of some overgrown woods as the dirt road curved to the left, and then he parked the car off the road behind the winery. They got out and walked along the wooded area until they came to two old iron bars in a hedge. It appeared to be where an old gate had once marked an entrance for foot traffic. Lucien led the way, trampling over weeds, pushing shrubbery aside, and ducking limbs of old trees.

Finally, a space opened up to a narrow dirt road that crossed their path. Beyond the road, looming up three stories high, were the old red brick and beige plaster walls of the decrepit and crumbling commandery. It was in quite a tumbled state, but had obviously been rebuilt since the 13th century, judging from its mid-1800s architecture. Now, even the newer additions were in ruins. They saw a high arch in one wall that once served as the original entrance, but had been bricked up long ago. A square entrance, which had replaced the ancient entry, now stood before them. Two withered palm trees framed the opening, but they were so old that the only thing left of them were blackened stumps. To the right were overturned boxes with peeling white paint that had once served as beehives. An old sign said to beware of the bees, but even they were long gone now.

"Lucien, why is the building so destroyed?"

"The building was used as an ammo dump by the Germans during the Second World War, but they blew it up when they left. However, you can see one lone tower still stands, out of the original four."

High above on the wall before them was a line of small windows, from which grasses and vines now hung. The roofline of the building was broken up from the bombing and age, and the roof was completely gone. What remained before them was only the shell of a building. They entered under the large square entrance, passing into the interior. A narrow path threaded through the enclosure, overgrown with bushes, fallen trees, weeds, and tall yellow grasses rose to their shoulders. Broken brick and stone, and old burned pieces of wooden beams reduced to splinters lay everywhere making the way rocky and uneven, so that they had to pick each step they took. Arched passageways were half sunken in the fallen debris, which must have once led to various hallways and rooms. Oak trees, thorny bushes, and thick grasses, had taken over the whole of the interior of the site. It was only because previous interlopers had blazed a small narrow trail, that they were able to pick and duck their way through the hollowed out building, which they could see had once been a huge expanse.

They carefully made their way through to the other side of the building. Under an old gnarled oak tree they discovered a broken mound of very old stones, which must have been part of the original structure. These blocks were larger, thicker, darker, and made of coarser stone. Past the stones and a trampled-down wire fence, stood the old church, the church of St. Marie of Mas Déu. It appeared to still have its four sides, squared frontage, and a flat roof, but its double weatherworn wooden doors, which hung askew, were chained and padlocked. Above the door was a high window and across its small expanse were widely spaced iron bars. The beige plaster that partially covered the front of the building was coming off, revealing the irregular stones beneath that were used to build the walls. With this view ahead, they stepped over the fence marking the border of the woods and a farmer's private land, whose home was just beyond a thickly treed border.

It might have been considered trespassing, but there was no sign saying it was private or to keep out. It was an adventurous spirit that led them on. Lucien peeked through the wooden doors of the church but it was too dark to see anything. Instead, he put his camera up to the small gap in the doors, and with the help of his camera flash was able to take a picture. They looked at the camera frame to find out what it looked like inside. Although the building appeared on the outside to be a simple square, the interior was Gothic vaulted with whitewashed walls and had supporting metal struts at the top to keep the structure from falling in. Old tiles were piled on the floor and at the far end was what once must have been the high altar. They circled as far as they could around the church with one side completely covered in green vines, and then wound back and re-entered the destroyed fort.

They tried to make their way toward the west end within the walls, but the ground was so irregular and the brush so thick that despite their best efforts, they had to make their way back the way they had come. They returned to the entrance and went out beyond the entry. They made their way past the beehives to the eastern side and went around the structure with the building on their left. The path was wider there and the walls more intact with high windows. Then Lucien spotted a square hole in the ground, which they nearly stepped into, and might have had it not been for a cement block that someone had placed in it to avoid such an occurrence.

"Here," pointed out Lucien, "is one of the underground passageways."

"I wish we could get into it."

Lucien looked up at her in surprise. "So do I, but there is no point. I seriously doubt anything is left. It would take many years with an archaeological team to unearth its secrets. This site is best left to the imagination for now."

Lucien shined his flashlight down into the hole but all that appeared was a tiny dark square room, fallen in.

Just then Lucien and Chante heard the crack of a branch nearby and both ducked simultaneously. Lucien held his finger over his lips so she would not speak. Lucien thought it was either the farmer who had heard them and was checking out who was there, or someone else was coming to see the fort. After a couple of minutes with no other sounds, Lucien and Chante rose and continued on their way. Chante had a worried look on her face, but Lucien explained that it was probably a branch that had fallen or was a stray animal, as no one had approached them.

Further along the path and in the wall of stone to the left, they saw a huge wrought-iron gate, which had obviously served at one time as the main entry. It had long radiating spokes of iron that filled an arch with beautiful iron scrollwork between the spokes, but all was rusted from age. Opposite the gate and to their right they could see that there had once been a road that gradually sloped up to the fort, but it was now overgrown with underbrush and trees. Lucien tried to get closer to the gate to take a picture, but the thick bushes and trees in front of it made it impossible. They wove around the building further, but the path that continued was filled with low-lying tree limbs and dense brush. Then it opened to the farmer's back yard, so they turned back to the fort entrance where they had begun.

"It must have been quite impressive for the area," said Chante. And with one last look back they tried to visualize what this remarkable commandery had once looked like, with its French and Templar flags flying high. They left, trampling through bushes, squeezing over and through broken tree limbs grey with age, and eventually found their way back to the dirt road and the car. Lucien noticed tire tracks in the dirt where another vehicle had recently been right behind his car. Had someone followed them?

Lucien turned to her as they got in. "Okay, I have one other place to show you."

Back on the main road, they drove just a few minutes to a place between the small towns of Paca and Villemollaque, and then Lucien turned into a gravel parking lot. They got out and could see another imposing beige building on the other side of a wall and gate ahead of them. There was also a more modern home sitting on the front of the property along the main road. Though this site was deemed to be older than Mas Déu, the back building was still intact.

"This is Monestir del Camp. Its origins actually predate anything of a Templar nature. Charlemagne wanted a monastery built upon the spot where a Frankish soldier in his army once struck his sword into a dry lakebed and water began to flow. This much-needed water rewarded his weary troops after the Battle of Panissars in 785. It is only legend, of course, but there is documentation that there had been some kind of temple here dedicated to the Virgin Mary in the ninth century. By 1090 a monastery had already been established. "

"I believe I came here with my husband years ago, but the place was closed."

"It is only open on certain days of the week, and today is one of them."

Lucien rang the bell at the gate and a grey-haired woman with a kind-face, a smile, and wearing a light blue-checkered apron over a dark blue dress, emerged from the front house and waved hello. She unlocked the gate and gestured toward the front door of the old building on their left. They stared up at the three-storied structure that rose further on its left side with a lone tower. The building's front wall facing the small courtyard held a few single and double-arched tall windows. The tower was topped with a curious red roof design that formed a series of pointed zigzag peaks. After walking up three shallow stone steps they passed through a wide arched wooden door and entered into a small dark room. They stood in an entry constructed completely of dark wood walls, floor, and ceiling. When their eyes adjusted to the light, Lucien dropped some Euros in a donation box by the door. Electric lights lit a few photographs of monks that had previously overseen the monastery. A closed and locked door to the left must lead to the tower that they had seen from the front. Against the far wall, on a large wooden table, was a wooden model of the building in its climatic years, but the path to explore lay open past the building model.

The door entered into the convent church, which was rather plain with a single nave, white walls, and a few windows. The altar was a simple wooden table with turned legs covered with a white cloth and several candle sticks. The church was plain and unremarkable. It was the outside that was of more interest.

They exited to a small lovely Gothic cloister that had to have been there before the medieval period. A short wall of stone surrounded the cloister, offering a walkway around the center garden, open to the sky. Slender double stone columns supported the edge of the descending slate roof. At the top of each set of columns were carved capitals, and above them were angled stones to support the vaulted walkway. In the center was a manicured green lawn and around the lawn stood tall pottery vessels with a variety of plants in them. They took a few moments to gaze up at the carved capitals. They were carved with twisted animals, strange figures, and even monsters. One had an angel with long musical horns, and another looked like it showed the Annunciation with a dove and seated maiden with long hair.

"Here, this is what I want to show you. Look at these capitals."

Chante moved closer and looked up at the one he wanted to show her. It showed four soldiers or knights carved at the top with different faces. The next pillar showed four more, all a little different. Then the third column showed one more knight that was holding upright a sword and he was flanked by nine Templar crosses.

"What do they mean?" she asked.

"I believe they represent the nine original Templar knights enlisted to guard the pilgrims on the road to Jerusalem. This cloister is dated to 1307. And why is that date so important?"

"Ah," smiled Chante turning to him with a smile, "because that was the year that the Templars were first arrested throughout France."

"Yes! I believe these three capitals, probably carved by the famous stonemason the Master of Cabestany, were placed here to honor the Knights for their good works. Remember, despite the king wanting the Templars arrested, there was wide support for the Templars among the populace. It is quite possible that some knights took refuge at this very monastery, and that may be why Cabestany decided to honor them."

"They are amazing. One can see so much detail still to this day."

Lucien and Chante sat along one wall and gazed about the cloister, feeling the serenity it was meant to convey. At the same time, the mood was tempered by their knowledge of the darker aspects of the knight's struggles, having both the religious and the royal turn against them. After a time, Chante and Lucien rose and visited the small outdoor museum that rested under the eaves at one end of the cloister, and then left. They stopped at a small winery on the way back for a glass of wine with lunch, and a reflective discussion about the Templars and their struggles.

Chapter 11

On Monday, Lucien invited Alerion to a late lunch as they had a long busy morning. They settled with their glasses of wine and waited for their bowls of *Bouillinade*. Lucien was partial to the fish, and Alerion was partial to the saffron and the potatoes. Lucien decided to test the ground between them. He told Alerion that he had taken Chante to the Chateau Royal the previous Wednesday and that they had looked through the tunnel together. He also told him that he had checked the angle of the tunnel at the castle with the angle of the tunnel at the fort, but they had not aligned to the same degree. He did not tell him about the northwest tower where the coordinates did match, or that he had told Chante about his and Alerion's explorations under the fort. He also did not tell him that he and Chante had gone to his father's house or Mas Déu. Nevertheless, a look of horror came over Alerion's face. He glanced around the room to find no one nearby, and with great reserve but angered strength whispered to him.

"Did she know why you were so interested in the tunnel? Did you tell her why you were studying your compass? She's a writer. She could easily take advantage of you, probe you to get more information and then explode anything you might tell her to the world in some exposé. We could get in deep trouble, not to mention put into jail! You just met her. Hasn't your intelligence training taught you anything? You are trained to resist torture, even the most feminine kind, and not to relay information. Lucien, how could you do this me, to us?"

Lucien was greatly surprised at Alerion's response. He responded in equally hushed and controlled tones, "Alerion, don't get so excited. I expressed a general interest in military operations at old forts. I'm sure she believed that the chateau tunnel was all that I was referring to. Besides, I want her to get to know me, and this is something that might interest any soldier. I think I am falling in love with her and I do see the good in her."

"Oh no! You are not getting me into this any further. I wish you had not told me anything of what you did. You must have known I would be upset, as you waited until now to tell me. You might be the one wanting more adventure added to your stress level, but this could affect my military career, and it's going to be ruined if any of this gets out,"

"Alerion, calm down."

"Calm down? As if I haven't already done enough. As if I don't already know enough. As if that will make any difference when you're caught and I am sent to jail as an accomplice."

A dead silence fell between them as they stared into each other's eyes. Seven seconds later their lunch was delivered. Alerion just stared at his soup bowl, completely distressed, but Lucien took up the first mussel shell and drank its contents right down. Slowly, Alerion picked up his spoon and was scooping out the potatoes and slurping the juices. When he had finally finished his bowl he sat back in his chair. He took one look at Lucien, rolled his eyes in dismay, and shook his head.

"I hope I end up in a seaside prison with *Bouillinade* served on holidays, at least."

That finally made them both laugh and it relieved the tension.

"Alerion, I have an idea that I think you are well suited for."

"No, no, no, no. I'm not doing anything else. No, nothing." He almost got up out of his chair with his arms going for the ceiling as if already arrested.

"Please calm down, Alerion." The only other person nearby was the waitress, who had retreated to the kitchen. "I only want you as a consultant. Besides, if I command you to perform a work function, you still need to follow my orders."

That caught Alerion by surprise. "Like how you wanted me to help you before?"

"I promise, you don't have to go down into any tunnel with me ever again."

"You promise," and he lowered his arms to the table. "Really?" but Alerion was not sure he believed him.

Lucien leaned into him in a matter of fact manner. "You realize, of course, that in our rush to move all those boxes we were not able to take the time to search for any architectural plans of the fort because we had to work too quickly to clear the storage room. Your next assignment is to organize that new storage area by year, create digital files of generally what is in each box, label the boxes, and if you happen to come across any architectural plans of the fort or any of the other forts that previously were in Collioure, you will let me know."

Alerion could not believe his ears. "After everything I just said, you are now going to insist that I be a part of your continuing scheme? You are too much! So I suppose this is an order that I cannot get out of, no matter how much I protest?"

"Correct."

"Unbelievable!"

"There is only one more thing," added Lucien. "I want you to meet Chante."

"Well thank goodness for small favors. I guess I had better, as I should at least know who is probably going to be getting us into trouble. It is always better to know who your enemy is."

"She is not our enemy, she is a lovely woman who I am dating. Besides, you're going to like her."

Alerion just rolled his eyes as Lucien called for the check. When they returned to the fort Lucien ordered him to begin on the new storage room that afternoon. At the end of the day Lucien walked to Chante's apartment, and on the way stopped at the library to pick up the book on Vauban that Madame Severin held for him. As soon as he left she picked up the phone.

Chante greeted Lucien at the door with a hug and a deep kiss. They looked into each other's eyes with renewed excitement.

"Lucien, it is so good to see you. Come in. I've got some dinner going and I thought we would eat on the balcony. I stopped and got some Dominican Banyuls wine, too." She spoke as she broke away and headed to the kitchen. "Why don't you open the wine and I'll finish with dinner."

"*Certainement*," he said with a smile. He set the Vauban book down by the door and headed to the dining room where the wine opener rested next to the wine rack. He glanced to the small balcony table just big enough for two, and noticed that it was already set, but he grabbed the two candles next to the wine rack, went to the table and lit them. He opened the wine, poured two glasses and brought them to the kitchen. He handed her one, they clinked their glasses together, and then he leaned against the doorjamb watching her lithe figure dance around in the small space.

"I picked up the Vauban book today. I'm hoping I can glean some additional information from it. After all, Madame Severin was kind enough to hold it for me. I also had lunch with Alerion today. I told him about our exploration of the tunnel at the chateau, but I did not tell him anything about the tower or us going to see my father. He was pretty upset that I even mentioned liking tunnels to you. Had I shared with him what I had told you about our exploration of the tunnel at the fort he would have completely freaked out." He paused, "I felt lousy for not telling him more. He is my best friend, but there is something in his fear that scares me. Something told me not to tell him more. And what is more surprising, for most of my life I've been trained to keep secrets, but there is something about how I feel, about how I cannot lie to you." Chante looked straight at him. "If you were a spy I would have failed in my task. It's just that when it comes to my personal life I would rather not complicate matters, and I, with you, I . . . I just don't want to keep any secrets from you."

Chante cast a wide smile at him. "Thank you, Lucien, for being so honest with me. Not only do I appreciate it, it speaks volumes for what kind of a man you really are."

Lucien actually began to blush, not only due to what she said, but because he was developing deeper feelings for her. She could see that she had caught him in a vulnerable moment, and purposely turned her attention back to the stove, but hid a secretive smile. "Dinner is almost ready. Bring our plates to the kitchen and I will fill them."

She had made *Poulet Bresse* with caramelized Brussels sprouts and onions in a red Banyuls wine sauce. He set his glass down at the table, grabbed the plates and quickly returned. He breathed in deeply the rich aroma that rose from the plates as he held them. A succulent blend of roasted poultry and wine rushed up at him. Chante removed her apron, grabbed her glass, and they went to the balcony.

Chante lifted her glass for a toast and Lucien followed. "To the adventures we have already shared, and to many more ahead of us, together."

"Together," he repeated and that look of delight once more passed between them. They began, with each bite bringing great satisfaction. He was beginning to really like this little ritual of dining just the two of them on her balcony. It gave him a newfound sense of belonging. When they finished their plates they moved inside, as the evening had turned cool. Chante served them a dessert of poached pears with a white chocolate sauce.

"So," Chante began, "when do you want to break into the tower?"

Lucien almost dropped his fork. "I . . . I'm not sure."

"Well, I've been thinking about it and I have an idea. Today I sat across from the castle entrance and watched the tourists go in and out. Like most tourist entrances and exits they have an electronic infrared beam that counts to keep track of their visitors; partially to have a tally of how many people visit the chateau, partially so they can plan for seasonal staffing, but also to make sure just as many people exit as go in. When we were there I noticed a small red light that ticks off when the beam is broken as each person passes. The pathway is wide so several people can walk abreast and it is also the entrance that the employees use, so I honestly don't think the counter can be very accurate with so many people going in and out, but it might be. Then it occurred to me, if we were to enter in the midst of a crowd of tourists we might be undetected if we accidently drop a few coins and bend down to pick them up, but do not rise up until we pass the counter."

Lucien gave her the funniest look. "Were you in marketing as a crowd analyzer in a past life?"

Chante laughed, "I don't believe in reincarnation. I believe in going all the way and making the most of this life. Something I've recently come to terms with. Besides I told you, I'm a writer. I notice detail. I just thought that if we wanted to go in undetected, that would be a way to do it."

"Wow, I was not thinking past how to get into the tower door itself. I have a lock pick set that I think might work to open the lock."

Chante laughed. "Are you sure you weren't a burglar in a former life?"

"No, but I think I would like the challenge. The truth is the picks actually helped me break into my own apartment when I locked the keys in and the landlord was gone. As for the tower, however, I don't want to place you in danger of getting caught with me. I was thinking that you might act as a lookout, but no more."

"Lucien, what fun is that? I want to go with you."

"But why would you want to get in undetected?"

"Well, if we decided to stay and explore under the castle after it closes, they wouldn't come looking for us. And I thought of two ways to exit."

"You did? There are?"

"Yes. One, we simply stay in the tower until the tourists start coming through the castle the next day and then we just walk out. Of course staying would mean we would need to sleep somewhere in a cold castle. But there is another way. Remember that small garden walkway as one passes the castle along the east side?"

"Yes, why?"

"That wall drops down onto a small grassy slope with benches, near the walkway that goes around the foot of the castle. Most of that wall is too high for climbing over, but right in the middle, the slope rises. Then it's just a simple shimmy down a rope when we are ready to leave."

Lucien laughed. "Chante, you are so much more adventurous and daring than I thought you were. Here you hardly know me, and yet you are willing to risk everything just for a little adventure? One, I might add, that could end us up in jail, or at least a fine."

She simply smiled, and he could not help but bend toward her and kiss that smile.

After the dinner dishes were cleared they set to discussing their plans. It was decided that they would go in the late afternoon on the following Saturday, as more tourists would be there than during the week in off-season.

That week went by slowly, but Lucien and Chante were able to have several dinners together at her apartment and plan more for the weekend. Each day Lucien checked in with Alerion to see if he had found anything of interest in the storage room. Alerion was miffed about his task, but could only confirm that nothing of interest had showed up as yet. Lucien also went to the hardware store in Banyuls for a few tools, some smaller and stronger flashlights, nylon rope, and a spray can of anti-rust. Just when he thought he had everything, he saw the gardening department and picked up a hard plastic trowel. He wasn't exactly sure why he thought they might need it, but he grabbed it anyway.

When Saturday arrived, he packed up everything he thought they might need and placed it all in a backpack. He had arranged to meet Chante at the same café where they met after their last foray into the castle. She was waiting and flagged him down.

"I think I have everything we might need," said Lucien once seated. But Chante was also prepared. She dug around in her large shoulder bag and produced sandwiches, a bag of grapes, two bottles of water and a thermos of hot coffee. "Chante, we're not going on a picnic. Are you sure we will need all that? I'm hoping to be in and out of there within an hour."

"You never know. It's always good to be prepared." She dug again into her bag and pulled out a wide floppy tourist hat for her, and a wide-brimmed American fisherman's hat for him. "I figure we should look like tourists, and if there are cameras where we don't expect them at least most of our faces will be covered."

All Lucien could do was shake his head and smile. "You are amazing. I would never have thought of that."

They stared at the northwestern tower and waited for a group to approach the chateau. At 3:45 a long line of about twenty tourists approached the entrance. Chante and Lucien hurried across the street to mingle with the crowd. Luck was with them, as it happened to be a small tour group of Americans.

Keeping their heads down and saying nothing, they entered with the group and paid their entry fee. They held back a bit, pretending to look at the tourist items in the bookstore, until a crowd headed for the castle walkway. They swung into the group and on Chante's cue, dropped a few coins. They knelt down to pick them up and then remained bent down, still in the crowd, going a couple of yards more and then rejoined the group to stand up again. They winked at each other as they rounded the corner. It was here they let the group go ahead. Then they peered over the stone guardrail and looked over the eastern wall to see what might be their escape route later on. Lucien thought it was a little higher than Chante could handle, but the rope would be more than adequate in strength and length. There was a large strong cypress tree that would hold the rope even doubled, so they could release the rope when they were below. Without seeming too anxious, they slowly walked arm-in-arm toward the northwest tower room. A few tourists were examining the prints on display.

Lucien and Chante had to actually look at the display again, as well, until the room had cleared.

When the last tourist left the room, Chante stood at the entry door and kept a lookout so Lucien could work on the lock. He had slipped his lock picking tools into his jacket pocket to easily reach them. There was no camera in this room, which he had happily noticed the first time they were there. In fact, he had noticed that there were hardly any cameras, anywhere. There were only the ones at the entrance and exit of the castle, one in the central courtyard, and several on the outside scanning the north, west and south walls, but no camera was on the east wall facing the sea. For a supposedly secure castle, it was pretty lax in its security. At one point an elderly couple entered the room. Chante and Lucien had to once again pretend to be engrossed in reading about Jovian Toulard, a local artist who did renditions of the castle and its port. It was pretty similar to the art found already, up and down the old part of town. Chante wondered if the local artists drew lots to see whose art would go on display next at the castle.

At last the couple left and the time was now 4:15. If they were to get into the tower, they would only have about 45 minutes to search for the tunnel, if there even was a tunnel, and then return to exit the castle with the last of the tourists.

Only four minutes later Lucien turned to beam at her. "We're in," he said. She rushed to the other side of the room as he was pulling the door open. They slipped inside, turned on their flashlights and closed the door. "I just hope security does not check all the doors before we are able to leave."

The landing was small but they both fit, and sure enough, there were cement stairs going up and stairs going down. Lucien led the way down, the beam of his flashlight on the stairs ahead. They made two complete circles and then came to the bottom of the stairs where they found another locked door. Chante held her flashlight with the beam focused on the door while Lucien again used his picking tools to work on the lock. There was more moisture on the walls at this level and Lucien suspected that the lock had some internal rust.

"No problem," smiled Lucien and he rifled through his pack to withdraw the small can of anti-rust spray. "I love hardware stores." He gave the door lock a couple of spurts, and then tried his picks again. The lock, which once must have opened with a very old key, finally released after about five minutes, but the door was stuck at the bottom. He pulled at the handle and gave a couple of swift kicks against the base of the door, and it finally gave. Chante was afraid the kicks might echo up the stairs and be heard, but Lucien assured her that it was unlikely. "How's our time?" he asked.

"Thirty-five minutes left."

"We can do a lot in that amount of time." With that he pulled hard on the handle. The door, which had no doubt been tightly sealed, scraped against the cement floor and made a low grating sound. With the door open, they both peered into a vast darkness.

Chapter 12

They raised their flashlights to peer into a tunnel laced with old cobwebs and lined with crumbling grey stone blocks. Chante grabbed Lucien's arm and sucked in air. Lucien sensed some hesitation and apprehension.

"Are you okay?"

Chante recovered herself with a deep breath. "Yes, I'm sorry. It's just that I had a dream about this place, so I'm experiencing a little déjà vu."

"How did it work out in your dream?"

"I don't know. I woke up." Lucien got a look of doubt on his face, but she assured him. "Really, I'm okay."

Lucien was relieved and once again turned to face the tunnel.

"Hmm, I didn't expect to see brick. I expected to see just dirt and maybe some wooden beams for support. But come to think of it they probably had to reinforce this end of the tunnel due to the weight of the castle tower and walls over it."

Chante took a step into the tunnel, but Lucien pulled her back. "You had better let me go first. No telling how unstable this end of the tunnel is. I already had to rescue Alerion. I don't want to have to pull you out from a pile of bricks. They can do a lot more damage than dirt. Don't touch the sides and follow closely behind me."

About a dozen feet in he paused and looked at his compass. "I want to get a fix on the direction down here. It looks like we are heading just as I thought, north by northwest."

The floor of the tunnel was cement and the bricks that made the walls were of a size and shape from a time long ago. A few feet more and they came to two metal doors, one on the left and one on the right.

"Should we try to get into one of these rooms or keep going?" asked Chante.

"Let's keep going and if we have time we can come back and try one of them."

Fifteen feet further and the tunnel ended at a cement wall. "This must be the cement wall on this side of the quay. Okay, we are not going to go through cement, so let's go back to the doors and see what we can find."

When they returned to the doors they consulted their watches and decided to give one of them a try as they still had twenty minutes left. Lucien chose the door to the west and gave the door some anti-rust spray all around the edges and into the lock. After picking for a while the lock clicked opened, but the door was still stuck. This time Lucien did not hesitate to kick at the door and push on its recessed handle. It was pretty stuck, so he gave it another circling with the spray and kicked it some more. At last the door shuddered and he almost fell in.

They shined their flashlights into what appeared to be a small empty room, also with a cement floor and the same grey brick walls.

"This was probably a storage room of some kind, with supplies for when soldiers were sequestered down here. The one across the hall is probably something similar."

They stepped inside and shined their lights into every corner. But what caught Lucien's attention was a metal plate in the floor near the north wall. Chante saw it at the same time. "That's interesting. I wonder what is under that metal plate?" Lucien went to it, bent down and shined his flashlight along the edge to get a closer look.

"I don't think this plate is secured."

Within seconds Lucien was pushing the metal plate over about two feet to one side. He got on his stomach, put his arm down into the hole, and moved his light around the space below. Lucien looked up at her and then he looked down into the hole. He was torn. It looked intriguing.

"It looks like another room, and it is dark at one end. It could be a tunnel. Now I'm not sure what to do. If we leave now we will need to come back another time to find out what is below us and maybe try the other door. We either start back in the next five minutes or we wait until at least midnight before we go over the wall to leave. What do you want to do? "

Chante looked at her watch. "We have only ten minutes left until the chateau closes." There was no hesitation in Chante's voice. "I think we have a mystery before us and we owe it to ourselves to explore it, or we will be staying up all night at the apartment wondering what is here. Besides, we run the risk of trying to get in here again. We shouldn't come back too soon either, as it might seem like we have a big love for castles coming twice in a week, but three times might look suspicious."

"Beautiful and smart. I like the way you think. Okay, so you think we should explore as much as we can tonight to answer our curiosity, and when we are done we make a run for it down a rope over the wall?"

"Yes, that's my vote. You game?"

Lucien could only admire her spirit of adventure even more. "All right, let's explore what is here and satisfy our curiosity."

They both shined their flashlights into the darkness below them. Unlike the tunnel under the fort, there was no ladder to descend into the room below, and there was a distinctly dark space off to one wall to explore. It set Lucien's pulse racing.

"I guess it is a good thing that I brought rope. I wasn't anticipating using it this soon, but it seems it will do double-duty today."

He reached into his backpack for one of the ropes he brought, and with Chante's help they unraveled it. There was little to tie it to in order to secure their descent. It was only about seven feet down, but getting back up would be the challenge without the rope.

"Here," said Chante, "we can tie it to the handle on the outside of the door. It seems to be the only thing we can use. I just hope it is secure enough in the door to hold."

After examining the handle more closely he thought that it was, and began to tie the rope to the handle. Once one end was tied off and the door stood open at a direct angle to the hole in the floor, he pulled at it to test its strength.

"Okay. I'm going to go down first, then you can follow."

With that he pulled on the rope, turned around, and placed his foot on the edge of the cement. Then he took a step down and put his next step against the brick wall below. The wall was somewhat crumbly, but strong enough. Within seconds he was standing on the floor.

"It seems to be another small room and it reminds me of the room Alerion and I found below the storage room at the fort. Now you come down but be careful."

Chante handed down the backpack, her bag, and the flashlights. She sat on the edge of the opening, then took the rope and swung down into the room and into Lucien's arms. He held her tightly and without thinking she released the rope and embraced him. Stimulated by the excitement of what they were doing and their closeness in the semi-darkness, they blocked out all anticipation of the mystery before them. They were too busy encompassing themselves and the power between them with the lingering of a deep kiss. Recovering and realizing their new environment, they scanned the room with their flashlights. It was very similar to the room above, but the brick on the walls was crumbling and powdery all the way around, and there were cracks in the walls. They paused when their lights came to the doorway of darkness. It was a tunnel, but this tunnel was of damp soil and partially obstructed by rotten and broken beams.

Lucien moved toward the opening cautiously. "I was right! There is a tunnel on this side and I'll bet it once met up with the tunnel that Alerion and I found. But I don't like the look of it. It appears to be in just as bad shape as the tunnel on the other side."

"The other side looked similar to this? Then we should take a sample of the wood and have it dated as your father suggested." Just inside the doorway at their feet were splinters from the old wooden doorjamb. She picked up a piece of the wood the size of one of her fingers, wrapped it in a couple of tissues and placed the bundle into her sunglass case to protect it in her bag. "This should do nicely. Well, are we going or not?"

"Experience tells me that we must be more cautious than I was last time. The tunnel cannot go too far, as the quay is somewhere between here and the other side. There is plenty of rope, so let's keep hold of the rope and proceed very carefully. If there should be any kind of collapse we will have the rope to pull on and dig our way out. And please, do not touch the walls. That's how Alerion got in trouble last time."

Lucien gathered the end of the rope into his hands, gave it some slack, and let a portion lay on the ground.

"I'm going to continually lay rope on the ground behind us away from the dirt walls and any old beams.

Stay right behind me, but don't trip on the rope. I can see that there is a small turn in the tunnel up ahead as my flashlight doesn't go any further, so we must be extra careful. Are you ready?"

Chante grinned and her eyes sparkled with excitement. "Absolutely."

They carefully crossed the threshold and timidly stepped onto the dirt. Moving ever so slowly, they eased their way forward, one step at a time, stepping around fallen beams and carefully trailing the rope behind them. Only ten feet later, Lucien paused and flashed his light above him.

"Look, the tunnel is reinforced all around us here. I guess we are right under the riverbed." He ran his beam slowly back and forth to light up the fifteen-foot long metal plating. "Look at the edges. Water has seeped around the metal. When it rains, the water must run through the channel and it probably leaks pretty badly in here. Mold is growing around the edge of the metal. The river must sometimes flow underneath the quay and this shows how much it must get wet down here. I'm guessing we are a meter or more under the cement channel above us." There was dirt underneath their feet, however, so it must have flooded at times and brought the dirt down from the sides to run along the tunnel. When they reached the curve in the tunnel, Lucien paused again.

"How peculiar. I'm surprised that the tunnel changes direction. Hold on a minute. I want to check my compass and get a fix on the direction we are heading." He set his backpack down, handed Chante the rope, and reached into his pocket for his compass. Giving it a moment to settle, he looked up at her. "That is surprising. We seem to be heading east, right toward the coast. But how can that be? If this tunnel originally met up with the one on the other side, we should be going in a northwesterly direction to the fort."

"Lucien, I would not be surprised if there was more than one tunnel underneath this ancient town. Maybe this one goes to the church? After all, several civilizations have held the castle. And we have already gone far enough under the quay."

"I was so sure that this tunnel would meet up with the one from the fort."

"We won't solve the puzzle standing here, so let's continue. How long is the rope that you brought?"

"I brought two 30-meter lengths, so we can at least go that far."

"Lucien, how many feet or yards is that?"

"Oh, sorry. That is about 200 feet or about 67 yards."

"If we have already used, let's say about 20 yards, we have about 140 feet left."

The tunnel did turn toward the northwest and they began to climb at a slight angle. But only about ten minutes later they were nearing the end of the rope and still the tunnel continued uphill.

"Okay" said Lucien, "we don't have much rope left, so we have to stop here, but I have an idea. "

"Are you going to suggest we go further without the rope?" asked Chante.

"No, I would not place us in that danger. However, I think it is important that we check to see where we are." He unhooked the altimeter from his belt.

"I didn't know that an altimeter worked underground," said Chante.

"An altimeter doesn't really measure altitude, it measures atmospheric pressure. It works more like a barometer. Since the weather was good today and there was no sign of a change in weather, the pressure should remain steady. I calibrated it before we entered the castle and since we were at sea level any change will be detected. So measuring the air pressure will tell us where we are in altitude."

"How is that supposed to help us?" asked Chante.

"What we do is walk the old town above us until we find the same GPS coordinates and then compare the elevation with what it registers now. That will tell us where the tunnel runs and how far below the tunnel is." Lucien and Chante both shined their lights ahead. "Our lights only shine maybe twenty more meters. I can't imagine that the tunnel goes too much more because straight ahead has to be the coastline. So let's go back and we can check out the elevation over the city. I'll carefully wind up the rope as we go. Again, be extremely careful. We are literally, at the end of our rope! That's a hell of a long way to tunnel out if there is a cave-in."

They slowly and carefully picked where to step, and made their way back. Ten minutes later they arrived back where they had begun. Lucien boosted Chante up the rope and into the room above. He passed up the backpack and flashlights, then pulled himself up the rope and crawled out.

Chante was beaming. "That was really exciting. We didn't find anything in particular, but I loved it." He watched her eyes grow larger with excitement as she spoke.

"On the contrary, we discovered a second tunnel underneath Collioure. That's very exciting to discover. I'm most puzzled though, where does this second tunnel go?"

"Okay, what's next?" asked Chante.

"That's easy, we have another room to explore. What time is it now?"

Chante checked her watch. "It's almost 5:30, I mean 1730."

"How about we take a break. I need some water, and you probably do too. Also, some of those grapes you brought would be good for more energy."

They settled on the floor of the room with the door still open and the rope attached. They both drank some water and ate the grapes. They ate quickly as both were anxious to get on to the second room. When they had finished, Lucien untied the rope from the door and placed the rope once more into the backpack.

Chante looked back into the room. "Should we push the metal plate back over the hole, or leave it where it is?" asked Chante.

"For now, let's leave it. We may want to come back at some point with a longer rope and explore it more."

They stepped into the hallway and faced the second metal door. Lucien dug into his jacket for his picking tools and took them out with the can of anti-rust spray. Without even trying the lock he went ahead and sprayed the locking mechanism and all around the door. The handle and lock were identical to the one across the hall with one interesting difference. This door opened into the hall rather than into the room. This door seemed to be much more rusted around the hinges as well, and in spite of the anti-rust in the mechanism the pick did not seem to move any small interior tumblers. With more prodding something finally moved, but it was not what he expected. He heard small bits of metal actually break off inside.

"That did not sound good. For some reason this lock is much more rusted than the other door. They look to be the same age, but this one is just falling apart." Lucien used his pocketknife to run along the edges of the door and loosen the rust that had built up around it. With one of the largest Allen wrenches in his case, he rattled the interior of the lock to the point that the inside pieces broke apart. With the last of his anti-rust liquid he again sprayed around the door edges and finished off the can. "I'm not sure this is going to open for us. It's so rusted that the locking mechanism has completed deteriorated inside." As he poked at it, his prodding had actually broken through to the other side of the lock. "Ah, I have an idea. Hand me one end of the rope in the backpack."

Chante got the rope and handed him one end. "What are you going to do?"

"It's possible that I might be able to tie one end of the rope to my largest Allen wrench, push it through, and use it as an anchor to pull the door open, since it is well past the point of being unlocked."

He used his knife to scrape away enough metal on the inside of the lock so that the knot of the rope could fit through the hole. Eventually the knot and metal wrench fit. He set his flashlight on the floor aiming it toward the door for illumination so he could see what he was doing. Gently he pulled it snug so that the tool was held flat against the inside of the door. To get a good bracing with which to pull it open, he carefully pulled the rope taut and stepped back.

"Chante, open the other door all the way and I will step through and brace my feet against both sides of the door jamb. And you better stand to one side in case I bring down the wall instead of the door, if any of it moves at all." She backed into the first room and stood near a wall to one side.

Lucien wrapped the nylon rope around his hand and with all his strength he gave it a strong pull. The door shifted slightly within the frame with a loud crack. He tried it again and before he knew it the door swung open, and he fell flat on his back on to the floor.

Chante ran to him. "Lucien, are you all right?" Both were coughing from the dust.

"Yes, I think so. I actually did not think it would budge let alone open. It was more rusted than I thought."

He dusted himself off and picked up his flashlight. He and Chante stood and waited for the dust to settle before they could approach. While the darkness loomed beyond them a stench assaulted them.

Chapter 13

They immediately brought their hands to cover their noses for a rancid smell engulfed their senses. They had to wait until the dust settled and they could actually see into the space beyond. Lucien approached first, and then they both stood at the open door, shining their flashlights into the space beyond. They were not surprised when they noticed that the room was identical to the one across the hall, but at the far wall a door frame was wide open, and beyond it more darkness. Slowly they entered and crossed the small room, their lights focused on the far side of the wall. Here they stopped and dared not go any further. They lowered their lights across the floor and over the threshold to see a narrow cement stairway descend six steps down and disappear into a shiny blackness. Lucien picked up a pebble from rubble on the floor behind them and tossed it down. The stone dropped into the black brackish water and sent ripples away from them to disappear beyond the floor of darkness.

"No wonder the door was so rusted," Lucien commented. "Years of moisture from this water have obviously made the metal rust and crumble away."

Chante remarked, holding her hand over her nose, "This must either be part of the underground river, or the sea has seeped in underground and been trapped."

"It must be from the port, as this smells like rancid sea water. Obviously we can go no further here. This room was closed off long ago for obvious reasons."

Chante looked up at him. "I guess that is as far as we go tonight. We've explored all we can." She looked at her watch. "It is now almost 6:00 and the sun will be setting soon. We will need to wait several hours before we go over the wall. Let's get out of here."

They backed away from the watery pit and went out into the hall. Lucien untied the rope, retrieved his Allen wrench, wound up the rope and stuffed it back into his bag. It took both of them to push the door closed, but they could still smell the rankness of the water in their nostrils.

Lucien swung the backpack over his shoulder and led the way back. The door at the bottom of the stairwell was still open. They paused, needing to discuss their plan.

"Do you think we should wait here until it gets darker outside? If they have a roving guard he might see us exit the exhibit room."

Chante thought about this for a moment. "True, but the smell of that water was pretty bad and I would love to get some fresh air. We could always pop back in if a guard comes back on a security check."

"Okay, then, we will stay close to the wall under the walkway until we can reach the other side of the courtyard. We can go down the ramp to the tunnel near the entrance to wait, and when the time is right, throw the rope over the side and climb down. Is that plan still good with you?"

"Yeah, that sounds like the best way to go."

They climbed to the landing above them where they came in. They listened for any noise coming from the other side. There was nothing. Lucien put his hand on the door handle and pulled, but it did not open.

"It's locked!" he whispered.

They both turned to each other with surprise in their eyes. If Lucien could unlock it from the other side, surely he could pick it from this side. He directed his flashlight to the door, but there was no lock, only a handle.

"Lucien, if a guard had found the door unlocked he would have opened it and searched for intruders. I'll bet he thought it was kids trying to get into the tower above. But what if he heard us below, came downstairs and found the lower door open?"

"If a guard had done that he would have called the authorities and come searching for us, but he did not."

Chante thought about it for a few seconds. "Maybe he is hoping we panic and call out for help, and he is waiting on the other side of the door to arrest us?"

"Or," Lucien speculated, "someone has been following us and purposely locked us in, and has no intention of calling the authorities to rescue us. That worries me even more."

Chante got a worried look on her face. "Who would do that? Anyone you know?"

He shook his head. "The simplest answer is usually the correct one. The door probably automatically locks as soon as it is closed."

"That makes me feel better, but only a little. Let's say that happened. We are still locked in. Now what do we do?" They both stood there, their flashlights on the wall beside them to avoid the beams in their eyes, but light enough to see each other's faces.

Lucien nodded. "Okay, here's what we do. We climb the turret stairs in the tower and see if there is another way out." Chante nodded her agreement.

With their lights on the steps, they carefully crept up the stairs to a small round wooden platform. There, the tower had four narrow slits equally spaced around it, wide enough to fit an arrow, but certainly not large enough to fit their bodies through. They kept their heads down so they did not appear in the windows. The last vestiges of light were coming through the narrow openings. An orangey glow of dusk was settling over the town and soon the lights would be turned on to light up the chateau.

"We need to stay low so we are not seen." Lucien spoke softly, and then sat down. Chante did likewise. They turned off their flashlights to conserve the batteries and sat with their backs next to each other along the curve of the wall. "I can't remember exactly where the castle lights are on this side."

"I remember," said Chante. "There is a light that shines below each tower facing down to highlight the base of the castle. There are also floodlights that run along the front of the building on the west side, at various places along the wall on the south side, at the tourist entrance on the north side, and at the small boat launch below that. The only place where the lights are low is over the east wall facing the sea. There, the only lights are along the walkway, but at this time of evening that walkway is busy with foot traffic and will be until at least 10:00 later tonight."

Lucien looked at her with amazement. "How do you know all that?"

"I'm . . ."

"Wait, I know. You're a writer, you remember detail."

"Right, and ever since we sat at the café across the quay and you said you wanted to get into this tower, I spent some time looking at the chateau from all angles."

"Okay, that's great, but I'm not sure how any of that will help us right now." Then he thought a moment and looked back at her. "So if you knew this tower had only slits, why did you want to come up here?"

"To get some fresh air."

He couldn't help but smile at her and agree. The stench had been pretty bad on top of all the dust, rotting beams, and dirt for the last hour. He put his arm around her and hugged her to him. At least they had not come to harm and they were on this adventure together. He wondered if he should call Alerion, but he was pretty sure Alerion would not help them, even if Lucien could convince him that something could be done; and he had no idea what that might be.

Within five minutes the floodlights went on and lit up the chateau, which allowed slits of angled light to filter inside the tower. With the light, Chante opened up her bag and pulled out the sandwiches and thermos of coffee. They had a makeshift picnic while sitting on the floor, giving them something to do and more time to think of a plan.

After they ate they rested their eyes to relax, but then once again realized their situation. Lucien thought out loud. "There is only one option I can think of." Chante turned toward him with expectation. "Go back to the long tunnel, stepping as carefully as possible, and find an exit at the other end."

"But what if the tunnel has caved in, or it dead ends?"

"Then we won't be any worse off than we are now. We will have further explored the tunnel, and there is always the possibility that there is an exit. And for some reason, I think there might be or I wouldn't have gotten a good altimeter reading. We can always come back, yell for help, and risk a fine or jail for trespassing after hours."

"Okay, put that way, I guess we could try the tunnel again. We've already gone pretty far and know it to be fairly safe. As long as we don't touch the walls, we should be okay."

"I know it isn't the best or safest plan, but it seems to be the only real option for us. Or we could just sleep here overnight. Chante, I don't like putting your life at risk like this." He took her hand. "Especially now that we've gotten to know each other better, and I am feeling more for you than I expected." He paused and Chante could tell he was trying to say something.

"Lucien, I want you to know that there is nothing you need to feel sorry about. I knew the risks and I chose to come with you in spite of them. The truth is, my feelings are also stronger than I thought they would be in so short of time since meeting you. I am fresh from a divorce and I was not even considering a new relationship. In fact, I didn't want one. But since meeting you I cannot think of being with anyone else. And when I am in your company I am the happiest I have been in a very long time."

He squeezed her hand, hugged her to him, and kissed her deeply. He then grabbed the backpack and indicated that they should go. They crawled to the steps so no one would see them through the arrow slits. Then they turned their flashlights back on and made their way downstairs. They proceeded back to the first room. Lucien cut a short length of rope, tied it to the door handle as before, and let it fall through the floor opening to the room below. If they had to return at least they would be able to get up and out of the lower room. Lucien lowered himself into the room below. Chante tossed down their things as before and then swung down, once again, into Lucien's arms.

"I could get used to this," smiled Chante.

They carefully made their way back into the tunnel, being twice as careful as before, hoping the odds were still in their favor for remaining safe. This time no rope was laid behind them, as it would not matter, since they would be going well past its end, anyway. Who knows what lay ahead, they may need a rope yet. Within ten minutes they found themselves at the same point when the rope had ended last time. They flashed their lights ahead. The ground actually looked drier. The wooden beams above and to the sides looked more intact. In fact, the wooden beams had changed in their appearance. Lucien shined his light above them for a thorough view.

"Look at this beam. It is definitely newer and not of the older style at all. These beams are not fifteen centimeters square like in the tunnel by the fort at the beginning of this tunnel. These are more like seven centimeters square. Either they changed the type of wood they were using, or this portion of the tunnel was completed by different people at a later date."

Chante found a small chip of wood on the ground as before, wrapped it in tissue, and added that to her case with the other one. "With this fragment we will have a sample of both types of wood."

They once again made their way forward. The going took longer than they expected, but choosing each footstep was even more imperative since they were no longer laying down rope. The incline came to a stop, was flat for several yards and then began to decline. Lucien had Chante stop and he backed up to the highest point. He once again looked at his altimeter and checked the elevation, writing both down in his small notebook from his chest pocket. They stood with their flashlights looking down into the slope. It was gentle so they continued. Five minutes later Lucien paused again.

"Do you smell that?"

Chante sniffed at the air. "Yes, it smells fresh. I think it might be sea air."

"I think you're right." Five minutes later, the path leveled out and they were now stepping through a mixture of soil and sand. Soon it became all sand instead of dirt, and the beams above them were gone and solid rock took their place. A few yards more and they could distinctly hear the surf meeting the shore, its rushing sound hitting rocks and echoing into the tunnel. A few more yards, a sharp turn to the left, and the tunnel opened up into a cave, maybe forty feet wide. The white surf met the shore about fifteen yards out. They walked to the edge of the water and they could just barely see past the opening of the cave through a sliver of sky with sparkling stars glimmering at the horizon. Lucien looked back and saw that the opening to the tunnel was well hidden due to the last turn of the wall. Clever, he thought, and then the realization hit him.

"We've made it!" said Lucien.

"Yes, but to where?" Chante implored.

Lucien did his best to calculate in his head where they must have come out.

"We are below the cliffs, and I have a feeling I know where. There is a sharp cut into the cliff north of the old German fort. Nearer to Miradou we have a zip line that goes from the top of the hill and it ends at a platform to the west of the fort. As many times as I have walked that area and even run along the cliff path I have never noticed anything from above. It must be quite hidden and recessed under the cliff."

They made their way down to the edge of the sand and rock where the water was lapping into the cave. Chante and Lucien saw the problem at the same time. They both stared out at the entrance.

"Okay," said Lucien, "we are out of the tunnel, but the water comes into the cave pretty far. It is almost closed off." He was stating the obvious, as there was a good twenty feet of water that was surging in from the rocky entrance. They shined their flashlights around both sides of the cave's opening. Lucien's light caught the dullness of a few flat stones. "There does appear to be a path of slightly flattened rocks on the left side. We might be able to go along those rocks and then swim to the opening against the surf. However, we will be too wet to climb the rocks out of the cave, and we still have to find a path going up the cliff. In the darkness that would not only be difficult but dangerous."

Chante did not seem too keen on that plan. "We may need to wait for low tide. Let's check the tide table on your phone and see when the next low tide is. I didn't bring my phone. I was afraid if it went off at the wrong time, it would be heard. If we were to get partway out and the tide came in, we could get into trouble."

"Good thinking." He pulled out his phone and did a search for the area's tidal readings. "It shows that the tide is rising and will be at its height at 1:30 am."

"And when is the tide next at its lowest?" asked Chante.

"Not until dawn, about 7:10. If we had tried to leave as I wanted, we would have gotten caught with more water coming in and the entrance would be closed off. It looks like we may just have to wait it out."

"And," added Chante, "the moon is waning and not very bright. We would not have enough natural light. We would have to use our flashlights and that means one less hand on any grip when climbing out and up the cliff."

They backed away from the water, turned around, and decided they would need to find a higher flat area to rest and wait. Their lights searched the area where they had emerged from the tunnel and along the back of the rocky wall. Lucien stopped and pointed to a dark spot to their left.

"Chante, shine your light where I am pointing." When she did, they noticed a tall spiked stone that cast a long dark shadow behind it.

*　　　　*　　　　*

That night Alericn was getting very nervous. He had watched Chante and Lucien go back into the chateau that afternoon while he sat at a café waiting for them to come out. Time ticked by, and when 5:00 came and the castle closed, he had not seen them exit. Where could they be? He supposed that they must have left within those three minutes he had gone to the men's room, but he wondered. He went and had dinner at home and decided he would check on Lucien at his house later. When he didn't see the lights on at Lucien's place or Chante's apartment, and both of their cars were still at each place, he grew more and more curious. Perhaps they walked somewhere locally and were having dinner. He did a cursory walk through town but did not see them. Finally he gave up and went home.

Chapter 14

When Chante and Lucien got closer to the large pointed stone and walked around it, they realized they were looking into another tunnel.

"This is incredible!" he said. "First, we didn't know that any tunnels existed; now we find several! By the look of this one it is entirely possible that this is the oldest, and may have been used for smuggling goods in or out of the country."

Chante stepped ahead of him to enter, but he grabbed her arm. "Wait. This tunnel has no doubt been here a long time and has also been exposed to sea air and water. It could be even less stable than the one we just came out of."

"You're right. Now that I am feeling so grateful for being out of a musty tunnel, I'm not sure why I am so anxious to go right back into one."

"On the other hand," added Lucien, "We have about twelve hours to wait until we can leave, so we might as well go exploring. Only this time we are using the rope." He opened his backpack for the rope and tied it around the tall stone. Then he gathered up the rest into his hands, and this time he laid the rope down with Chante right behind him.

Similar to the end of the tunnel from which they had just emerged, this tunnel was carved out of rock and the base was full of stones and sand, but it was smaller, more twisted and irregular, and it began to ascend. As it did, the stone gave way to sand and soil, but no lumber supported its sides or ceiling. They had gone about thirty feet or so when a gaping hole appeared in the ground before them and they abruptly came to a stop. Lucien put out his arm to keep Chante from moving forward. They could see that the tunnel continued on the other side, but why would the floor have fallen in, and where did the tunnel go on the other side?

"It looks like we've come as far as we can. For some reason the floor seems to have collapsed, but collapsed into what I wonder?" They turned their flashlight beams down into the hole. The path had fallen into a recess about a yard wide and six feet down. It was not possible to see anything beyond the darkness.

As Lucien shined his light down, Chante's light spanned the sides of the tunnel they were in and that's when she saw it. "Lucien, look. There is a vertical scratch mark on this ceiling stone. I think this mark is here for a reason. Could this hole be here on purpose? I think I am going tunnel happy. My excitement is beginning to build again. What do you want to do?"

"I'm not sure. It does not look very safe, but then, nothing we have done this evening has been very safe. And I think if I don't explore it I will find myself wondering why there is a hole here. It's too far under the hillside to have water reach this far in from the sea. I suppose it is possible that water may have soaked down into the ground from above, softened the layers of soil, and caused a hollow and subsequent drop, but the walls seem pretty dry. Looking down, it looks like there are some straight cuts in this nearest wall. I think you are right that it was marked on purpose. But for what, a hiding space for smugglers?" He paused, "Oh hell, why not? We've come this far, we've got a rope and we have plenty of time." He looked at Chante and smiled. She returned his look with a similar smile of her own.

Lucien tossed in the rest of the rope, which was much more than he would probably need. This time he went into his backpack and pulled out the garden trowel. "I would have preferred a shovel, but that would have looked pretty obvious walking into the castle, so I guess this small trowel will actually come to some use after all." He looked at Chante teasingly, "I got it just in case I need to dig myself out of a mountain." The smallness of the tool and the immenseness of such a task made them both laugh.

"Seriously Lucien, what happens if you get into trouble?"

"We'll deal with that, if it happens." Then he tucked the trowel inside his jacket, grabbed hold of the rope, and jumped down on top of the pile of sand and soil just a few feet down. He inspected the lower wall nearest to Chante and began to clear the dirt away to one side. She shined her light down so he could see better what he was doing.

"Yes," he replied. "The wall is cut down symmetrically. This was handmade." Then he moved around the fallen mound and shined his light along the edges. "Chante, there is another tunnel running off to the south." Before he knew it Chante's excitement got the better of her and she jumped down onto the pile right behind him. Lucien was surprised to see her suddenly appear.

"Sorry, Lucien. I'm not going to let you have all the fun. We are in this together."

"All right, but as before, the rope goes out behind us with slack, and you need to step exactly where I step." She nodded in agreement.

The walls were as narrow as the tunnel above, but the ceiling was lower. Lucien found himself ducking more so his head would not touch the stone above him. The soil was darker here and more compact. They did not need to go very far. Within just six yards the tunnel ended and opened on the right into a side room of about eight by eight feet. When their lights scanned the room what they saw made them take a big breath.

"*Magnifique!*" said Lucien, and they stepped into the small enclosure.

"Wow, is right," said Chante.

"I can't believe it. An old chest, still here?" They looked at each other and then back at the chest.

Chante was giggling. "What do you think, old pirate treasure?" Then the realist in her struck. "I can't imagine that anything is still in it."

Lucien agreed. "Any gold, I'm sure, is long gone. Thrown in a sack because the chest was probably too heavy to move. Still, the workmanship is impressive. It must be French, look at the metal."

Chante and Lucien kneeled down in front of it, and ran their flashlights over its top and sides. It was about two by four feet and two feet deep. It was made of dark wood, but at least half of the wood was reinforced with one-and-one-half-inch wide ornate iron straps. They came over the rounded top of the lid and met with others coming from underneath and up the front, with each metal band ending in the shape of a fleur-de-lis. The metal ran across the top, sides, edges, and especially around the top four corners, which were wider and more ornate. It was raised up off the ground on three wooden legs about one foot high with two-by-six-inch planks that came down from each corner of the box. The back right wooden leg was broken off and splintered and that seemed to be why the trunk was leaning against the back wall of the cave. The wood was dark brown, close to the color of the dark loam and stone that it stood upon. The metal bands were black from age, and a mold or dark moss was growing at the base of the wooden planked legs resting on the soil.

Lucien lovingly ran his hand along the metal across the top and around each rounded corner. Just watching him stroke the chest excited Chante. "Well, you might as well open it and get it over with."

Lucien laughed, but did move to the opposite end of the chest. "It actually looks like it would be quite heavy to open." Winking at Chante in the near darkness he added, "of course if I had some help, we could get inside it sooner." They both put down their flashlights so that the beams faced the chest.

Chante immediately readjusted her position around the left side of the chest to better grasp the lid and Lucien bent down. He looked at Chante. "Ready?"

All of a sudden she said, "Wait! What if it is full of gold? Is this chest the property of the military base, the town, the finders—that's us—or do you think this is some prank set up here for local diving clients?"

"Chante! Can we just open it and then talk about that later?"

She released a deep breath and then they simultaneously lifted the heavy lid and let it come to rest against the back of the cave wall. It was heavy, and the rusted hinges creaked loudly. They grabbed their flashlights and looked inside. There was a dark cloth wrapped around something. Lucien handed his flashlight to Chante. He lifted out the bundle and slowly unwrapped the cloth. Inside was another wooden box, but it was made from a lighter colored wood, and was more finely made.

Lucien sat and rested the box upon his stretched-out legs. Chante examined it closely and saw that it was similar in design to a very old Secretary's desk drawer, but this had a wooden lid made to fit over the top. It was about fourteen by sixteen inches and five inches deep. It had a simple swing latch on the front.

Lucien angled the box toward Chante. "I'll hold it and you open it." Chante handed back Lucien's flashlight, while the light from hers was firmly fixed on the box latch. She was beaming widely with anticipation. Slowly she drew her hand forward to the small catch in front. She rocked the small hook to the side, and then lifted up the wooden lid.

There was a brief moment when their expressions of expectation were replaced by looks of puzzlement, for inside were no gold coins, but an old dark leather satchel. It was ornately tooled with fleur-de-lis and edged with a scrolled vine design that went across the top, around the side edges and along the bottom edge of the front and back of the bag. It felt fairly light and was about three inches thick. An overleaf of leather was folded over the top and hung down the front of the bag. A strange looking seal kept it locked with an iron ring coming up from the bag through the cover. Lucien carefully set the wooden box on an angle on top of the corner of the chest to more closely examine the leather bag. Chante sat down and then carefully placed it into her lap.

Lucien ran his fingers across the leather. "The leather feels very stiff, but looks surprisingly intact despite its probable age."

Chante also could not help but run her fingers across the beautiful tooling. "How old do you think it is?"

"I'm not sure, but the bag is undoubtedly French. If I had to guess it must be from the Middle Ages, making it at least five hundred years old, maybe older. Getting secured inside a box, inside a chest, in a dry cave, kept it in pretty good condition."

"Lucien, we cannot open this here. I'm sure whatever was placed inside of it must be still there as the lock is still intact, but we need to move it to good light and a clean surface, wear gloves, and hope nothing contaminates it until we can get that seal open."

"You're right, that's obvious. It would be criminal to try and open it here under these conditions. I suggest that we place it back into the smaller box to help preserve it until we can get it out of here."

"What do you think it holds?" she asked.

"It looks like a military communication satchel. But what it is doing here in this obscure cave is a mystery. How it has survived all this time and stayed concealed is perhaps a bigger mystery."

Lucien held the box open and Chante carefully placed the satchel back inside it. She closed the wooden lid and rocked the hook back into place. Lucien opened his backpack, took out all the items they had stuffed into it and carefully fitted the box into the backpack with their hats protecting the edges. It was too large to fit completely, but with the same old cloth covering the top edge of the box, he was able to use the two buckles of the backpack to hold it in securely. They stuffed the other items into Chante's large bag, but she placed the trowel in her pocket. Chante helped Lucien carefully put the backpack over his right shoulder, and Lucien gathered up the rope. They returned to the sunken pile of dirt, but he stopped to examine the soil more carefully.

"This soil seems fairly soft and freshly fallen." They shined their lights onto the soil. "Look how much lighter in color the soil appears here than it was where we came from. I think this must have fallen sometime recently. Otherwise it would be the same as the soil in this lower tunnel."

Chante agreed, "But it looks like we are the first ones here, since there were no footprints when we arrived." That puzzled Lucien even more. Only a human would have been heavy enough to make it collapse. It was if it had been blown clean. Lucien helped Chante up the rope to the tunnel above, carefully handed the backpack up to her and then he got out. He reorganized his load and they followed the rope back to the sea cave.

Chante checked her watch. It was almost 8:00 pm. There was still a long wait ahead of them. They searched around the back of the cave for the flattest surface on which they could stretch out. Chante excused herself to finally find some relief from the coffee she had drunk in what seemed like hours ago, and Lucien did the same. Then they settled down in the dry sand between two large rocks where they could watch the surf. The roof of the cave came down fairly far, but they could see a dark sliver of the sky and some stars. Looking out to sea they noticed a bobbing yellow light in the distance. It must have been a passing boat, which appeared just as bright at the stars above. Lucien rested the backpack securely next to them on a rock to keep it as dry as possible. Chante curled up next to Lucien and he put his arm around her, as it was getting a bit cool with the night. With each passing minute the cave was closing up and darkness would soon surround them.

"I am so excited," she said, "I doubt very much whether I will be able to sleep at all. I can't believe there are so many tunnels in this hillside. I can't believe we actually found something. Even if everything in that satchel has crumbled away, the bag, the box, and the chest are extraordinary!" She looked up at Lucien, "And I can't believe what a great date this has turned out to be!"

Lucien laughed. "A date? It has been more of an amazing adventure, but now I have ten times more questions than I had before. Why haven't the tunnels been discovered before? Who dug these tunnels? The tunnels look different. Did the Romans, the Spanish, the French, or pirates originally dig the tunnels, or are they older? Why doesn't the fort have records of these tunnels, especially since the builders of the fort must have known about at least that one tunnel in the fort's basement? They must have seen the other end when they built and cemented in the river's channel. Whoever closed off that northwest tower must have known about the tunnels leading away from the tower. How could the diving teams that have continually explored these coastlines not known about the cave and discovered these tunnels? And because so much of this seems pretty damn obvious, that means that at least one person must know about the tunnels, and if so why are they keeping them a secret? Who could know about them? Why would they conceal their location? And if they knew, how could this small tunnel with an ancient chest not have been discovered long before now?"

Chante smiled at him. "You do have a lot of questions. Now for the questions that I have: Where should we open the satchel? How are we going to get the satchel open without tearing the leather? How old is the satchel? What is so important inside of it that someone had so very carefully sequestered it away? Who should we tell about the satchel? What should we do with whatever is inside the satchel? Do we contact the nearest museum, the police, an archeologist, or a historian? Do we place your father at risk by telling him? Do you want to tell Alerion? And how can I not write about this incredible adventure and our discovery?"

Lucien smiled at her. "When I see this much excitement in your face and these many questions on your lips even by this unromantic glow of a flashlight, I can only marvel at you once again. Chante, I am very excited about our finds, but I want you to know that even before we entered that tower tonight, I knew you were someone very special."

That stopped her questions. He pulled her into his arms and that was when she answered him with a long and intense kiss. Lucien reached down and turned off their flashlights.

An interlude of time later, they lay in each other's arms, patiently watching the narrow strip of stars disappear with the tide coming in. Chante set her watch alarm to go off at 7:00 am, as that should give them enough dawn light to guide them out of the cave. Then they curled up next to each other and fell asleep.

Chapter 15

When Chante's watch alarm went off it made them both jump. They sat up and looked out of the cave toward the morning sky. The water was pounding at the rocks and there was a much larger gap revealing a dawning glow beginning to light up the distant horizon. They got up and Lucien went to explore the cave's entrance. With the help of his flashlight, he found the steppingstones leading to the water's edge, and he could see the stones leading out of the cave to the left as he had seen the night before. The tide had made its remarkable transition from high to low, revealing with each minute more, daylight and the way out.

He returned to Chante and they carefully packed up their belongings. Lucien led the way, Chante stepping where he had just been. As the dawn had only just begun, Lucien still needed to use his flashlight to lead them out safely. The stones were still wet so they took each step with great care. As they approached the edge of the cave, the water still slapped at their feet, so they were extra careful to balance with every step. After they rounded the lip of the left side of the cave, Lucien looked up to the cliff to see which way to go. Tumbling rocks, shrubbery, and a very high and steep cliff made it look challenging, but with all they had been through there had to be a way up and out. They rounded the rocky entrance getting a little splashed, but avoided slipping. The only mishap was that the trowel fell out of Chante's jacket pocket. Lucien told her to leave it. They both wanted out and away as soon as possible.

Lucien had to swing his flashlight back and forth to find a path through the underbrush, as it was quite rocky and the shrubbery was thick. There was barely a rabbit's trace of a trail, but he managed to wind up between some barberry bushes and sea buckthorn. They took a breath at a small flat area just behind a scraggly alder. Within a few minutes a thin line of light appeared on the horizon. The trail was rocky and several times small rocks moved under their feet and fell down the side of the hill. At one point Chante slipped but Lucien grabbed her just in time. At last, Lucien could see the outline of the top of the cliff above. They rested at another somewhat flat area and watched, as the sky grew lighter. They were just thirty feet from the top of the cliff but the trail came to a halt against the base of the vertical cliff face. Lucien looked back to see if there was another way up, but he could not see anywhere else to climb. Chante was a little lower than he was when she looked up to see why he had stopped.

"What's wrong? Why are you stopping?"

"I can't see where to go. The cliff goes straight up."

Chante gave the ridge a long look. "I do see a post up there. I'm not sure what it is or if it is strong enough, but if you can throw a rope over it we may be able to use it as an anchor to climb." Lucien stepped back down to where Chante was to see what she was looking at.

"Oh, I know what that is. It's a kilometer-hiking marker. There's a hiking trail along the cliffs. That makes a pretty far throw, but I think I can do it. It might take me a few tries, though. He slipped off the backpack and carefully handed it to Chante. She held it while he removed the rope. He made many knots along the rope to make it easier to climb, and then made a large loop at the end of the rope. Lucien made his way back to where he had stood a minute before, higher up. The dawn was growing brighter, which would help. Not knowing where to throw the loop because he could not actually see the mark was a challenge, but he was determined. He tried several times to get the loop over the marker, but he couldn't get the rope to go where he wanted it to. Chante helped by letting him know how close he came each time and which way to aim his next throw. One time when he pulled the rope back it caught on a bush and stuck, so he had to flip the rope until it dislodged. Finally, on the eleventh try, the rope went perfectly around the marker and held fast.

Now the light was beginning to come onto the top of the hillside. He put all of his weight on the rope and it held. Chante helped him put on the backpack, again, and then he had Chante pull the rope tight. He climbed steadily up the rope and onto the cliff above. Then Chante secured her bag across her shoulders. He told her to secure the rope around herself and hold on. He secured his footing at the base of the cement marker and pulled her up. At last she reached the top of the cliff safely, and both caught their breath as the bright morning sun hit them full in the face.

*   *   *

A diving boat was anchored off the shore of the cliffs. An early morning cup of coffee sat steaming in the recessed box next to the steering, and the rounded view of binocular lenses bobbed with the boat as they scanned the waterline. Then a sparkle at the top of the cliff caught his attention. Two figures could be seen. A glint off of the back buckle of the man's backpack revealed what the viewer never expected. The size and shape told him that the secret had been discovered. How in the hell had that happened? He'd trolled this coastline for more than a week knowing that the spot was somewhere nearby. He chose to wait out the night to be ready for the lowest tide to better spot the cave opening. Beaux had completely misled him, but there were only so many places the cave could be. When both figures at the top of the cliff began to walk to the south, the boatman put the binoculars down, tossed his coffee over the side, started his engine, and quickly headed for Collioure's small port. He was madder than hell!

*   *   *

As Lucien led the way along the cliff, Chante looked around. "Where are we?"

"I know exactly where we are." he pointed south. "See that squared off outline on that ridge? That is the old German fort. We are not far at all from Collioure. Follow me."

He led her away from the cliff and around the sunken German fort. Before they knew it they were walking through a large parking lot. They walked out of the entrance and wound their way along the curving road that led all the way down into Collioure. They walked past the library and back to her apartment. It took them a good twenty minutes to get there. The only person they saw was Madame Charlene on her way to open the bakery, but she did not see them as they were still a long way from approaching that end of town. Soon they were walking up the stairs to Chante's apartment. They went in and carefully laid their loads on her dining table. Chante was careful to take out the two slivers of wood that she had wrapped in tissue and placed them next to the box.

Chante took a quick shower while Lucien made coffee, and then she made breakfast while he showered. She did not have any clean slacks that would fit him, but she was able to offer a man's tee shirt. It was a little tight across the shoulders, but otherwise it fit.

They sat silently at the small balcony table sipping their coffee and eating eggs and toast. They hadn't realized how hungry they were until they smelled the brewed coffee. They kept looking back inside to the box resting on the indoor dining table.

"Okay Lucien, now what? Shall I run through all of my questions again?"

"I don't think that will be necessary Chante. I thought about it in the shower, and I think we should call my father and ask him what the best plan of action might be. He'll want to see what we found. Plus he'll know what to do."

"Well it's not even 8:30. Will he be up this early?"

"I don't think so. It is Sunday. We'll try in a couple of hours." Then Lucien saw the sunlight on her hair and could smell the sweet scent of soap on her. He leaned toward her and smiled, "I think we should celebrate our nocturnal adventure and rescue, and take a morning nap."

She smiled as they rose. Lucien closed the French doors and led her into her bedroom.

It was 11:00 when Lucien stirred himself to rise. He quickly got dressed and walked back into the dining room to make his call.

"Hello, Papa. Good morning. Are you well?" He asked as he starred at the box on the table. "Listen, something important has come up and Chante and I need to see you again. Are you free today?" Chante poked her head out of the bedroom to listen. "At 1:00?" Chante nodded yes and he replied. "Yes, that's good. Thank you. We will see you then," and he hung up. Chante emerged in a blue robe and came and sat on the couch.

"Chante, do you have a larger bag that we can transport the box and satchel in? It is not very well-hidden in the backpack, and I think I would like it secured better."

Chante went back into the bedroom, looked through her closet and removed a small suitcase she had brought thinking it might work.

"How's this?"

"Perfect," he responded. "Do you mind if we use a large cloth or towel to wrap the box in to keep it from moving about in the suitcase?" Chante went to the bathroom and brought back a large white bath towel. "Yes, that will work well." He wrapped the towel around the box and carefully nestled it into the small suitcase.

Chante got dressed and they left her apartment. By noon they were on their way with a brief stop at Lucien's apartment so he could change his clothes.

Just as Lucien emerged from his apartment he saw Alerion across the street walking by. His back was turned and he was walking away. Lucien was about to call to say hi, but then he didn't want to draw attention to what he was doing or where he was going. Still it seemed strange. Alerion's apartment was several blocks away. He wondered why he would be on his block. Maybe he had been checking on him?

Half an hour later Chante and Lucien pulled up in front of his father's home. Lucien carefully took the suitcase out and greeted his father on the front steps.

"Lucien, are you two planning to stay the night?"

He hugged his father and kissed his cheeks, "No, Papa."

Chante greeted Gervais and they went into the house.

"To what do I owe this visit so soon after our last? I am not complaining, mind you, but to see my son and his beautiful Chante again, I am very pleased."

"We have something to show you, Papa."

They settled on the couch and Gervais sat in his easy chair. He leaned forward as he had before. Chante wondered if he had back pain which was relieved by leaning forward, or if he was slightly hard of hearing and leaning forward helped him to be closer to the speaker. In truth, it was a habit Gervais had learned with his students. If he leaned forward in his chair, he appeared to be truly interested. Now he did it as a matter of habit, though in this instance he was very curious as to what these two were up to. He kept looking at the suitcase.

Lucien began. "Papa, Chante and I have had quite an adventure since the last time we saw you." He told him all that they had done, the tunnels they had explored, and about the chest with the box containing the satchel. With each new detail his father edged closer and closer to the edge of his chair. When Lucien at last gestured to the case before them, Gervais leaned back and stared at them, floored.

"*Mon dieu!* My son, I am in shock. You both could have come to great harm, yet you sit before me with such a story." He stared at the case again. "And you say you have not opened it as yet? It remains still intact?"

"Yes, Papa. Do you think we should try to open it? Should we contact any authorities? It is obviously very old. What should we do?"

Gervais considered the questions. "I would normally suggest that we go to a laboratory at the university to open it, but such a discovery would be most difficult to keep from my fellow professors, to say nothing of the talk that might be generated by the students. No, it is best that we keep it between us for now, and prepare a space here. I suggest we open it, but also document the process. We will need to properly prepare a clean room. There may be nothing in the satchel, in which case there will be little to report. But if there is something of significance we will need to deal with it in quite a different manner."

"What would we need to prepare such a space?" asked Chante.

"I will draw up a list. If you can find everything that we need today we can begin to work on it tonight. If not, then we'll wait until everything can be assembled."

Lucien took the small notepad from his chest pocket and handed it to his father. "Write up your list and I will go out immediately."

The list consisted of a dozen white cotton gloves, a low-watt light bulb, small wooden tongs, acid-free paper, several transparent archival envelopes, a 2" deep archival box, large tweezers, a large roll of clear plastic sheeting, and a ultra-violet light.

"The only thing you do not need to get is a large magnifying glass. I have that. Oh, and get a large roll of wide masking tape."

Chante was intrigued. "How do you know what to get?"

"Ah, my dear, as a historian I have sometimes needed to handle old archives. I just learned a few things along the way." Then he turned to his son. "Lucien, if you don't mind, I will keep Chante here to help me prepare the space for us to work in. You will find a photography supply on the main boulevard for some of these items, and a hardware store should have the rest."

Lucien gave a nod to Chante, grabbed her keys, and went out the door. Then Gervais showed Chante to a back room that he used for storing old furniture and boxes. They moved as much as they could, lining up the boxes along one side of the hallway. They set up a large dining table in the center of the room, directly under the overhead light fixture. They dusted the room and mopped the floor. It took Lucien almost two hours to find everything they needed. He also stopped to buy some roasted chicken, salad and drinks so no time would be needed to cook.

When he returned, they got to work completing the preparations. First, they brought a standing lamp in from the living room, wiped it down, and put a low-light bulb into it. Then they fitted the overhead fixture with the ultraviolet light. Third, they taped a piece of heavy black material over the window and then taped a sheet of plastic over the window frame. They also covered the table with a sheet of plastic. Gervais found a large kitchen tray, which he scrubbed, and then had Chante cut a piece of plastic to fit its surface. On this she laid the tongs, tweezers, magnifying glass, and gloves. To one end of the table they stacked the acid free paper, archival envelopes, and box. Gervais looked everything over, remembered one more thing, and briefly left the room. He returned with two small adhesive bandages.

"What are those for?" asked Chante.

"Chante, put on a pair of gloves and firmly hold up the tweezers from the base. Tweezers are fairly sharp. This allows us to handle old paper or parchment without putting holes in it, and they are already sanitized. It's not perfect, but it will certainly work." Gervais also put on a pair of white gloves. He unwrapped one bandage and folded it over one end of the tweezer points, curling the adhesive edges around the tweezer post. Then he opened the second adhesive and covered the second sharp point in the same way. Lucien and Chante were glad that they had come to the right person. "Okay, let's take a short break, eat some dinner, and then get to work."

Lucien was hungry on two levels. He realized they had not had lunch, and he was also hungry to know what was in the satchel. Chante could hardly eat even though she was hungry. The anticipation was driving her to distraction. Gervais lit into the roasted chicken as if he had not had breakfast or lunch and ate very quickly. Then they removed their shoes, put on fresh white gloves, and looked at each other to make sure they were ready for the endeavor.

Chapter 16

Lucien carried the suitcase into the room and set it on the floor next to the table. He opened it, lifted out the box, and unwrapped the towel from around it. Ceremoniously he placed the box in the center of the table. They all stood around it like three surgeons about to open the patient of the century. Gervais took a digital picture from all angles, set the camera down, and inspected the box closely with the magnifying glass for several minutes.

Chante could not hold back. "It looks like a French Secretary's drawer to me."

"Yes, there are similarities, but that is what is peculiar. Lucien, describe the chest you found it in."

"The chest was made of very dark worn wood and it had elaborate blackened iron bars around it that ended in the shape of a fleur-de-lis. It stood on wide wooden legs about a third of a meter high. The wood was dry except for the base of the feet. The feet were also well worn. In fact, one wooden leg was missing so the chest was leaning against the wall. We got the feeling that the tunnel had caved in recently, maybe in the last year, as the chest seemed fairly protected from the elements, in spite of being close to the sea."

"From that description the chest sounds like it was most likely a hutch chest, because decorative ironwork and reinforced metal straps were relatively common, which puts it around the 1300s. I'm not an expert on furniture, but as far as I know wooden drawers of this nature did not have lids. It has to have been custom made. I need to point out one very important fact: the Secretary's desk was not invented until well into the mid-1400s, and even the French *ecritoire* desk was not built until the mid-1600s. I believe this small box predates both. This is an internal drawer from a hutch chest that has had a lid fitted to it. As for its country of origin, when chests were being constructed they were generally made of oak in England, poplar and pine in Germany, and walnut in France. It sounds like it might be made of walnut, which turns dark with age." He paused in admiration. "Now, let us open the box."

Lucien stepped forward and did the honors. When the lid was opened Gervais took more pictures to show the satchel's placement within. Gervais had Chante cut a piece of plastic and set it on the end of the table. Then Lucien lifted out the satchel. Chante took the box and covered it with the plastic. Then folded the plastic underneath it, so as little dust as possible would settle on to it.

The satchel now lay before them. Gervais took more pictures, especially close-ups of the locking mechanism. Then he picked up the magnifying glass and looked at the satchel carefully. "Once again, it appears to be French."

"I thought that it looked similar to a military communication satchel," said Lucien. "The tooled leather work is particularly well-done."

Gervais had to agree. "It is beautifully rendered, but I am actually surprised about that. Normally military satchels were much plainer than this. This leather tooling is elaborate, and one can hardly ignore the fleur-de-lis on it. I think this satchel conveyed messages from either royalty or a very wealthy and important individual."

"But look at the seal," said Chante. "That's what I find even more significant. We couldn't really see what it was in the darkness, but now that we have good light, it's circular with writing."

"You are absolutely right, my dear. I believe it is. I think this dates somewhere from the late 1300s to early 1400s. It has some writing around it, but I can't tell what it is." Gervais used his magnifying glass and got very close. "As I thought, it looks to be Latin, but the words are indistinguishable." He put the magnifying glass down. "This type of seal was in common use at the time. It is simply a miracle that the wire that was threaded through the loop and then sealed with lead is still intact. In fact, had you not told me where you found it I would have thought it was a fake."

"A fake?" asked Lucien. "Surely not."

"Son, I said 'if'. This looks authentic."

"But how do we get past it and see what is inside?" asked Chante.

"Patience my dear," added Gervais. "Let me take pictures and then we will discuss that." Dutifully he picked up his camera once again. He took an overall shot of its placement, then several close-up shots at all angles of the lead seal.

Now Lucien was at odds. "Okay, what do you propose? Should we cut around the leather to keep the seal intact or cut the wire?"

"I don't think cutting the leather underneath is the answer, as it would surely do more damage, so the answer is to cut the wire, but carefully and in the right place."

"And where is that?" asked Lucien.

"In order to prove that the cut was not hidden under the loop we will cut it along the side. Son, please get my wire cutters from my tool box over there," and pointed to his toolbox in the corner, covered with plastic. Lucien took off his gloves momentarily and pushed things around until he found the tool. Chante sanitized the cutters, and handed them to Gervais, who contemplated exactly where to cut.

Chante quipped, "This rather does feel like an operating table." Gervais made his cut midway between the loop and the lead seal. He carefully put the cutters down next to the satchel, picked up his camera to record the placement of the tool, and then a close up of the cut. He carefully unthreaded the wire, removed the seal, set it down next to the satchel, and took another close-up to show that there was only one cut in the wire loop.

"Chante, open one of the transparent archival envelopes for me, if you please. I want to handle this as little as possible." She did so and Gervais very slowly and carefully placed the seal into the envelope. She put the envelope on the end of the table with the wooden box.

Gervais paused. "Now comes the hard part, as the leather is fairly stiff, having been in the same position for hundreds of years. It could easily crack. At this point we will need to employ something I've heard will work, but have never tried."

"Papa, what are you suggesting?"

"A friend of mine has horses, and after years of using and restoring old leather saddles that sometimes curl, he uses a combination of a hairdryer and leather conditioner."

"But won't the hairdryer just dry the leather out even more?" asked Chante.

"The heat is used to open up the pores of the hide, and then the conditioner gets into the pores and makes it more flexible. I'm not suggesting that we open the satchel all the way back and flatten it, only to open it just enough so that we can get into the bag and pull out whatever is inside."

"And where would we find a hair dryer in a bachelor's home?" asked Chante.

"Believe it or not I also like to do a little woodworking as a hobby, and I use wood glues. I bought a small hairdryer to speed the drying time. Son, would you please go to the back porch and open the box marked 'woodworking tools' and find the dryer. Chante, please go to the kitchen and find my leather shoe conditioning cream under the sink, then go to the bathroom and bring a dozen ear swabs from the cabinet."

They both went off to fetch the items and then rushed back and placed them on the table. Gervais plugged in the hair dryer and held it in his hand.

"The trick to this is to heat the leather, but not to make it too hot to the touch. The problem is I'm wearing gloves and might not be able to feel how hot the leather gets, so we are going to be methodical about this and do it by the clock."

Gervais turned over his wrist and showed it to Lucien. "Lucien take my watch, which is old-fashioned I know, but it actually has a sweeping second hand." Lucien did so and held on to it. "I'm going to heat the outside of the satchel at the top where it curves over and you will let me know every time ten seconds go by. I'm going to fan the heat over the satchel's top curve, let it cool for ten seconds and then repeat the process for a total of one minute. Then Chante, I want you to squirt some of the leather conditioner onto a small surface. Use a small clean plate from the dishwasher and dip a swab into the conditioner and then hand it to me. I will probably need several, along with a clean white cotton glove to spread it evenly and wipe off any excess. We can't get the leather too hot and we should not add too much conditioner to the leather, only enough to soak in. So let's see if we can coordinate our process and get this bag open in one piece."

Chante returned with a small plate and the swabs. Gervais turned on the hairdryer. He looked at Lucien and said, "Begin".

He slowly moved the heat from the dryer back and forth for the first timing, then held it up for the wait, and repeated it three times. He turned off the dryer and handed it to Lucien. Chante handed him the first swab and readied another. The conditioner immediately soaked in. He did it again and wiped it all along the top. The leather drank up the conditioner quickly and he asked for a third swab. Then he took his white glove and gently stroked the top to make sure any extra oil was removed. They all stared at the bag. It seemed like they were trying to bring a patient back to life.

"Okay, the first part is done. Now for the hardest part."

"That wasn't it?" asked Chante.

Gervais chuckled. "No, now we need to see if we can lift the top without it cracking and do the same thing on the inside at the top, where we cannot see the leather."

Chante beat Lucien to the question. "How are you going to do that?"

"Not me my dear. My hands are too big. You will do it." Chante's eyes got big and immediately she became hesitant. "You saw how I did it. Lucien will hold the top open a couple of inches so I can use the hair dryer on the inside. It might work better if you forget the swabs and just place some leather conditioner on your gloved fingertips and work it into the leather that way. Begin with a fresh pair of gloves."

Chante removed the first set of gloves and put on some fresh ones. Gervais made sure three of her fingers were evenly coated and then signaled for Lucien to lift the front flap a small amount. They began again with the timing of the dryer. When a minute had passed, Gervais nodded for her to slip her hand in and proceed.

"Begin in the middle and gently go one way, then return to the center and go the other way."

Once she had done so, she removed her hand and said she needed a touch more conditioner. Gervais added some to her fingers, which had now taken on a slightly orange tinge from the old leather. This time she began at the edges and worked toward the center. When she was done, she used her other gloved hand to spread it evenly and then wipe it clean. She withdrew her hands and held them up as though she had just finished a messy operation.

"Lucien, keep hold of the flap," and Gervais and Chante changed gloves again. "Okay son, now while it is still a bit warm carefully lift the flap a little higher and I am going to reach in and gently see what we find. Don't lift it too high or the leather will crack regardless of all we have gone through."

Chante held the sides of the satchel and slowly Lucien lifted the front flap. Gervais stretched his fingertips into the opening and reached inside. As soon as Gervais could get his fingertips just hooked around the inside of the pouch he could feel some kind of stiffened edges. Chante and Lucien were holding their breath.

"It feels like sheets of paper. Lucien, lift the flap just a little higher and I think I will be able to curl the contents over the top and pull them out."

Lucien was still concerned. "Are you sure it won't tear the paper?"

Gervais smiled. "I don't think so, I said it feels like paper, but I don't think it is." Gervais placed his index fingers of both hands underneath the sheets and his middle fingers on top of the sheets, pinched his fingers together, and carefully rolled the top of the sheets over the inner edge of the leather. He slowly pulled them out and laid them on the table. He took up the large tweezers with their ends wrapped in adhesive bandages and separated them, revealing two sheets.

They stared at the yellowed sheets before them.

"It's parchment," said Chante.

"No, Chante, this is velum, from calves' skin. See how thick and sturdy it is?"

Lucien could no longer contain himself. "But what is it? Who wrote it? And why was it in that chest? It must be of some importance."

All three bent down to try and read the small fine penmanship, but it was Gervais who had the answer. "I would have expected French, or maybe even Middle French, but this looks like Old French, which was used by the feudal elite."

"How old does that make it?" asked Chante.

"Well, vulgar Latin was the base of the language before the 9th century. Old French was the Gallo-Romance dialect spoken by the Anglo-Normans, meaning that it was spoken in England, parts of southern Italy, and even in the Crusader states in Antioch and Jerusalem from the 9th to the 14th centuries. Middle French didn't begin to be spoken until after that, when it became known as *langues d'oil* or in the southern regions as the *langues d'oc* or Occitan. It is also possible that there is a Catalan influence, owing to where it was found."

Lucien carefully scrutinized the two sheets. "I see some French words, but there are different endings, different spellings and words I've never seen. Plus, some of the ink is faded and hard to read."

Gervais pointed to the bottom of the second sheet. "One thing is for sure, we have a date. I believe that says 1307."

All three stared at the date and then at each other. Chante looked at Gervais. "I know that date is significant."

"Yes, very much so. That was the year Philip IV charged the Templars with heresy and had them arrested.

We need to get this translated as soon as we can, and as quietly as possible."

"Papa, do you know someone who can do that?"

"Yes, there is a professor in the linguistics department at the university who is familiar with ancient languages, but I dare not take the vellum itself to him."

Chante had an idea. "What if you took photos of both pages and then uploaded them to your computer and e-mailed them to him? That way he doesn't know what they are printed on, or their true provenance. You could say that one of your students discovered the sheets in an old book. You believe they are a hoax, but are curious about a translation."

"Maybe, that is a bit tenuous. It might work. In the meantime, we can have the slivers of wood sent to a lab and get the dates for them. Of course it will only reveal when the tree was felled, but that should be close enough."

"But," asked Lucien, "what do we do with the real papers, or rather the vellum, the satchel, the seal, and the box?"

"The less they are moved, the better to preserve them. I will take the pictures of the vellum now, then we will leave them right here on this table. Cover everything with plastic, and lock the door. No one knows we have them."

Chante and Lucien nodded their agreement. Gervais picked up his camera and carefully photographed each page. When done he placed each sheet of vellum into an individual, clear archival envelope, and placed both of them into the archival box. Then they turned off the lights and exited, locking the door.

"Thank you for all of your help, Papa, but now I have made you part of our . . . well, I don't know what to call what we've done? Because of my incessant curiosity, I've brought you both into something that may become a problem for all of us. I broke into the trapdoor at the fort and destroyed government property, and we trespassed where we were not supposed to at the castle. But I don't think having possession of the obviously deserted box, satchel and papers is a crime. Is it?"

Gervais could only shake his head slowly in disagreement. "Lucien, I'm afraid that it is. There are antiquities laws, which say that items found on federal land belong to the government. You did say that the cave was below Fort Miradou, right? Then they could claim the findings belong to them."

"It was actually more north of old Fort Carré," added Lucien, "but I don't know how far along the coast the military owns land."

"But," added Chante, "what if the finds were donated to a museum before the government found out? Would the military try to take away something that important which the public has the right to know about and a museum is already in possession of?"

"Probably," answered Gervais, "the government or the department of antiquities could still go to the museum and simply take the papers."

Lucien was a little crestfallen. "Then it has all been for naught. Not only do we not get to share whatever it is we've found with the world, we can't tell anyone about it."

"I didn't say that," returned Gervais. "We could actually announce the findings to the world via a top newspaper release and negotiate with the Louvre or any other museum of our choice to have them on permanent display. But you are both jumping ahead. We don't even know what the papers say or who wrote them. They could simply be old papers that mean little or nothing now. Don't tell anyone anything, not even Alerion. Let me get some answers for you, have the wood pieces analyzed, and

I will get back to you just as soon as I have heard anything."

They agreed, talking long into the night about the possibilities, and due to the late hour, they decided to stay the night and leave early the next morning.

Chapter 17

On Monday morning, Lucien went to his office and realized he had a lot more work to do than he thought. In just a couple of weeks he had to prepare for the Journalist and Reporter's Abbreviated Field Combat Encounter. The attendees needed files begun, histories reviewed, accommodations assigned, and field exercises developed since last year's event. Also, every year something new was to be added to enrich the experience and allow some change for those who had previously attended and were looking for something different and more exciting than the year before. It taxed his brain, so he decided to get Alerion's input. While he was at it, he wanted to make a few inquiries of a different nature with him.

Lucien saw Alerion coming down the hall about fifteen minutes later and called him in. Alerion had a worried look upon his face, but he tried to hide it with a half-hearted smile. Alerion saluted and Lucien responded.

"Good morning, Alerion. Have a seat. I'd like to talk to you about some things coming up."

Lucien noticed that Alerion dropped his shoulders with noticeable relief. "Yes, sir. How can I help you?"

"As you know, our annual Journalist and Reporter's Abbreviated Field Combat Encounter is coming up and I'm going to need some help with its organization. You were here for the last one and even participated to some extent, so you know what was organized. This year I would like for you to help me organize it, and the first thing we need to do is to prepare the files for each attendee."

"Yes, sir, no problem. Glad to help."

"We also need to up the bar on last year's events. Last year we took them out on the rubber skiffs and did some practice rescues. Can you think of something we might be able to add this year that they might enjoy, but also challenge them?"

Alerion thought about it for a few moments. He was thinking. *"Yeah, we could drop them into the basement tunnel and teach them survival methods in old mines,"* but said, "How about having them go down the zip line? I can think of a couple possibilities that they may have to use in the field, such as getting across jungle terrain, or from a burning building."

Lucien's face lit up. "That's a great idea!" That surprising compliment made Alerion genuinely smile. "Aside from those things, would you please set up their room assignments? I've got the roster of who is coming. We'll need to put together a dossier on people to record their needs, specialties, and limitations. After the event we offer field recommendations, so we will want to know who to watch."

"Yes, sir, I'm happy to assist, sir."

Now that Lucien had warmed him up, he tiptoed into the next subject.

"I noticed you coming in a bit tardy. Was your weekend that good?" he smiled.

"It was just an ordinary weekend, sir," but he could tell that Lucien wanted something more of an excuse for his tardiness. "The colonel wanted to see me in his office this morning."

"Oh really, what about?" Lucien watched Alerion's facial muscles twitch.

"Nothing much, sir. He just wanted to ask how the work on the files in the new storage room was going."

"Really?" Lucien leaned forward in a pressing manner. "Did he ask about anything in particular?"

"No sir, just in general," but Lucien could see the small lines around his mouth grow taut.

"Have you found anything of interest? And, more specifically on the topic that you and I discussed before?"

"No, sir. They are pretty much boxes full of paperwork having to do with past personnel from dozens of years past. It's been pretty boring actually."

Lucien decided to approach things in a different way and leaned back in his chair.

"I saw you this weekend. I was sitting in a café on the quay with Chante and I was about to invite you over, but you seemed to be in a hurry. You kept looking behind you. Were you looking for someone?" And he decided to lighten up the inquisition a bit. "Were you tracking a pretty girl?"

Alerion's eyes opened just a little wider than normal and he shifted his weight, trying to laugh it off.

"Yes, sir. I was watching this woman on the beach. I was just about to approach her when she got up and left, and I lost her in the crowd. I thought I was behind her, but then I lost track of her and looked to see if I had passed her. She must have slipped into a shop. She was a pretty blond from Italy with such a lovely smile and laugh. I was fairly charmed."

Lucien felt the story was a fabrication, but he learned all he needed to know for now. For the first time since he had known Alerion, for almost four years, he sensed a lie, and an odd feeling of mistrust came over him.

"Well, if you find her again and it works out, maybe the four of us could have some dinner together. I still want you to meet Chante."

Alerion nodded nervously. "Yes, sir, will that be all?"

"For now. Thank you, Alerion. Carry on." Alerion saluted and quickly turned and walked out of the office, leaving a frown upon Lucien's face. For now there was nothing to do but wait. Wait for Alerion to find any architectural plans, wait for a translation of the papers, wait to see what they might do depending upon those findings, and wait for the next time he could be with Chante. Waiting was perhaps the hardest thing that a soldier can do. No wonder it takes nerves of steel, and his nerves were getting tested. The one thing completely wonderful in his life was how he was feeling about Chante. So he launched into his needed paperwork and put all other thoughts aside.

By the end of the day he and Alerion had set up preliminary files for the field encounter attendees, and he decided to spend some time with Alerion in the storage room to help him out. They made small talk and it seemed to help Alerion become more at ease. Lucien could also see for himself what the files held. Alerion was right. Most of it was perfunctory business, but he was happy to see that Alerion was quite capable and concise with his organizing and getting the information onto his laptop for transferring to official files. It really helped to smooth things over between them. It put Alerion back at ease and very grateful for the assistance and the company. Lucien also let Alerion know that he was taking a late lunch the next day with Chante at Valmy Park, and that they also had possible dinner plans. Since they had already put together the plan for the encounter coming up, he felt he could take off the next afternoon.

Alerion was very happy to hear that the outing was away from Collioure and had nothing to do with their past escapade. Maybe this relationship was the perfect thing to keep Lucien occupied. He understood the desire, but at the same time he was taking time away when he should be working.

Later that afternoon Lucien made sure his office door was closed and then he called his father to check in with him.

"Hello, son. I was just going to call you."

"What's new, Papa?"

"I told you, son, it would take a while to get any information back, but I'll tell you where we are in the process. I found out that the nearest accelerator mass spectrometer that tests for radiocarbon 14 isotopes is in Gif-sur-Yvette, a commune in the southwestern suburbs of Paris. I got a referral from one of my associate professors at Perpignan to speak with someone about the process and I finally got a call back this morning. Here is what I found out. It's a good thing that you got two slivers of wood, as the dating process is easier to interpret when two or more objects are found at the same site. However, I was told that the dating they can give us, may only be accurate to within 10 to 80 years."

"Hmm, that testing may or may not help us determine the age, but how long would it take to get the results?"

"The test itself takes only about an hour, but because their lab is the only one in France with this specialized testing, and because there is a lot of archeological work being done throughout France, it will take several weeks before they can test the samples, and it costs about €100 per piece. Do you want me to ship the pieces to them?"

"The price isn't too bad, though on first thought it is rather expensive for slivers of wood that may not be accurately dated, but it's the time it may take to get the results that is disappointing."

"I know, son. Just let me know and I will carefully package and ship them. I will split the cost with you. I want to know their age almost as much as you do."

"Okay, let me think about it today and I'll let you know. Were you able to check special collections for Vauban's work on mines and tunnel warfare?"

"Yes, I checked first thing this morning, but there was nothing. Sorry, son."

"Then what about the letter and its translation?"

"The letter. You know, Old French took on words from the other Romance languages of the time, such as Celtic, Italian, and German. Of course, there were many local dialects being spoken at the time these papers were written. The langue d'oc version in the south included the dialects of Provence, Auvergne, Gascony, and Languedoc. There are also many grammatical characteristics that have to be contended with… "

"Papa, please spare me the history lecture. Have you found someone to do the translation?"

"Oh, sorry son. No need to ask anyone else. Your father is very resourceful. You know, it is a good thing that I was a top student in Latin in school, because Old French is derived from it. I've been working on the letter myself, but I need another day and night to finish the translation. I should have it done by Wednesday. Can you and Chante come over that evening? I will have it all ready for you."

"Sounds great, but what is it? Who wrote it?"

"I don't think we should talk about it on the phone. When you come over, you and Chante can read every translated word, at least *almost* every translated word. There are still some I am not clear on yet, but I'm getting close."

"Then we will see you Wednesday night by 7:00. We will bring dinner."

"Great, son. See you then."

Lucien hung up and was so excited he decided to call Chante.

"Chante, good morning. How are you today?"

"Hello Lucien. I'm feeling great, excited and nervous, but happy."

"That about sums it up for me, too. I've got some news from Papa."

"You seem very excited. So... what is it?"

"The wood samples have to be sent to Paris and the results could take up to a month to get back, but as for the papers, he is translating them himself and will have them ready for us to read Wednesday night!"

"Lucien, that's wonderful! I'm so excited. Did he tell you anything about them?"

"No, but it must be big. He didn't want to talk about it over the phone." Then Lucien changed the subject. "Listen, I've got an idea that might help us pass the time. Tomorrow is Tuesday and I'm thinking about taking a late lunch at 2:00 and spending the afternoon with you. In all your time here have you ever gone to Chateau Valmy in Argelès-sur-mer?"

"I know there is a vineyard and restaurant there, and I've seen the castle every time we pass it on the road into Collioure, but I've never been there, as I heard the hotel is very exclusive and their restaurant rather pricey, but excellent."

"Ah, then you've never been to their park?"

"No, is it nice?"

"Yes, it is beautiful. The park is part of the hotel grounds, but it is free and open to the public during the day. It has a myriad of paths that weave across the hillside and at the top one gets a great view of the entire Roussillon plain. It makes a great place to walk and relax."

"That sounds wonderful. Shall I pack a picnic?"

"Yes, that would be great. Can I pick you up tomorrow at the car park by the carousel?"

"Yes, okay. Will I see you tonight?"

"I'm going to need to work late, so let's save up our desire to see each other until tomorrow. Is that okay with you?"

"Yes, of course Lucien. I will see you then."

They hung up and Lucien went back to work to make up for the hours he would be gone the next day.

Tuesday's sunrise was tinged with pink and reds, but cleared to a lovely sunny day with only a few wispy clouds, typical for October. She watched the smile on Lucien's face as he drove. His crisp blue shirt matched the sparkle in his blue eyes. She was once again struck by how handsome he was, with his slightly wavy dark hair and gently pointed chin. Today she wore green slacks, a light green blouse, and her black flat shoes to walk the park paths.

Valmy was only ten minutes from Collioure, so the drive was quick. They drove up the long driveway, past the vineyard and its wine tasting room, and turned off to the left into a wide gravel parking lot below the hotel. They climbed the white stone stairs to the park entrance and entered through the gate to the right of a long visitors' building. Just inside the gate, the chateau stood dramatically to their right. Its white ornate façade rose like a fairy-tale castle with its red-tiled roof and soaring spire chimneys. It had a large terrace that faced the park with a wide grassy lawn; and there, centered like a jewel in the middle of a green velvet dress, was a large central fountain dancing in the sunlight. The wide manicured lawn gently sloped up a hill that rose between the house and the foothills beyond.

Lucien carried the food. "I like the new picnic basket."

"I like it too. I figured if we are going to go on more picnics we should have a real picnic basket instead of plastic bags."

"Let's go for a little walk before we eat."

They linked arms, crossed the emerald green expanse, and began to stroll up the far dirt path, which sloped gently up the hill in an easterly direction. Along the way they stopped at a small open wooden hut that had pictures and descriptions of the birds found in the area. They read signposts with the names of the trees and plants, paused at a small green pond with croaking frogs, and enjoyed many artistic stone statues and pillars dotting the hillside. Finally, near the top of the hill they came to a white stone terrace that looked over the park. Lucien set the basket down on a stone bench and led Chante to the edge of the stone balustrade. The hillside trailed down from their right to their left with more paths and statues. A creek ran down the hillside, spilling over rocky falls, to rest in small pools below. Tall pine, sprawling beech, and majestic oak trees graced the hillside coming down to the lawn, which met with the fairy-story white castle to the left. Over and past the park into the northern distance, the Roussillon plain stretched far and wide. One could see even past Perpignan. It was one of the best views of the entire area she had ever seen.

Several other couples were roaming the pathways and crossing the grass. As Chante was looking out across the vast plain, Lucien noticed far below that a man was looking straight up at them. He briefly studied the man, who was wearing a heavy dark blue fisherman's jacket and a Breton mariner's cap. When the man saw that Lucien was returning the look, his head turned quickly and he walked briskly away. Perhaps he was just another park enthusiast intent on reaching the lookout that they occupied.

"This is incredible," exclaimed Chante. "You can see so far; to the coast to the east, the Pyrenees in the west, and well beyond to the north, more than what I could ever have imagined. It is truly remarkable."

Lucien held her close. "Do you know anything about the castle?"

"No, nothing, but it is so beautiful," she replied.

"A lawyer named Jules Pams in 1888 married a rich heiress and they built their home on 80 hectares. He became the Minister of Agriculture in the early 1900s and decided to build gardens on his land as a showcase. He was well known for his vineyards and he sold wine to the wealthy throughout Europe, even to Russia. Eventually a man named Victor Peix, who made his money from distilleries, purchased the property and built new wine cellars. In 1997 his grandson, Bernard Carbonnell, refurbished the entire property, including the winery and turned the castle into a luxury hotel. It has only five rooms, which can be booked for a lavish stay, but I understand that each of them is magnificent. The entire property is a marvel to behold, and the park is free for all to enjoy."

On the terrace was a tiled table where they sat and ate their lunch. It was hard for Chante to take her eyes off of the view, and it was hard for Lucien to take his eyes off of Chante, but now and then he cast a glance around them looking for the same man who had looked up at them, but didn't see him. When lunch was finished, Lucien led her further around the hillside. They went past rose gardens and palms to a view over the hillside facing the eastern coastline, and eventually wound their way down, following the creek, back to the beautiful expansive lawn. It had been a lovely park with fantastic views and Chante was very glad she had been able to share it with Lucien.

Chapter 18

Lucien and Chante exited the garden and returned to the parking lot, but then Lucien led her to a fenced area on the right. There, they were able to look down to a lower leveled area where three donkeys were penned and munching on barley straw. There were also two peacocks that pranced through the yard. Lucien glanced at his watch and realized that they had only five minutes to go. He guided her to an open gate to the right. Other people had also gathered and were now entering.

"What's in here?" asked Chante.

"You'll soon see because we are going in. Have you ever seen eagles up close, held a falcon, pet a parrot, fed an owl, or watched storks build a nest?"

Chante turned to him in surprise. "No!"

Lucien smiled, "Well you just might today."

Lucien purchased the tickets and they walked down wooden steps to a wide grassy area. To the left were large cages filled with different birds and to the right were bleachers where people were already gathering and waiting for the show to begin. Lucien picked their seats just two rows up in the center, just as a falconer approached the audience and welcomed everyone. In his gloved hand he held a large red-footed falcon. He shared a short history of falconry, talked about the different birds at the sanctuary, and introduced his assistants. As he spoke, beautiful birds of many kinds were brought out of their cages and allowed to fly back and forth in front of the audience to a handler on the opposite side of the field.

Each bird was treated with food as it flew from one side to the other, swooping in front of Chante and Lucien, within arm's reach. They could feel the swooshing of the air from each bird's wings, as the birds raced past their faces. The birds soared by with sleek shiny bodies and the light glinted off their sharp eyes. The birds also made shrill wild calls. It was an amazing feeling to be so close to these huge soaring birds.

Near the end of the show, after eagles, hawks, buzzards, parrots, and kites had sailed before them, the falconer asked for volunteers from the audience. Did anyone want to feed an owl? At first no one raised a hand, but then Lucien was surprised when Chante stood and said she would like to. The trainer had her come down off the bleachers and stand before the crowd. He put a falconer's glove on her hand, and then gave her a small dead pink mouse to hold in the gloved hand. She didn't even flinch when the dead mouse was handed to her. The handler whistled, and from the other side of the park a gorgeous white owl flew in a circle above their heads and then dove almost straight down, swooping within a hair's breadth of her hand and successfully plucking the mouse right from her hold. Chante beamed with delight and giggled like a child, she was so excited to be that close to one of her favorite birds.

At nearly 4:00 Lucien sent a text to Alerion to let him know that he would not be returning that day as it was already getting late. He would be in early the next morning. That gave Lucien the chance to spend more time with Chante. After the experience of watching her with the birds there was no way he wanted to end the day away from her. He had seen the delight of a happy child within the woman. It made his heartbeat stronger and a wide smile remain on his face.

When the show was over they visited the cages below, as there were so many more birds to look at. Only a fraction of the birds on the property had been in the show. Many more were open to view, talk to, and watch their fun antics. They took their time to enjoy every large and airy cage. They read about the type of bird and its territory, and they called the name of each bird listed on each cage's label. Then they walked up steps above the bleachers to another level and visited even more birds there.

They stood spell bound, as they looked up. On top of one of the largest birdcages two huge white storks stood next to a giant nest they had constructed. Chante and Lucien watched as the larger of the two birds threw back its head and pointed its long beak to the sky. Then it began to chatter its mandibles, producing a rising and falling rattling sound, like two bamboo-sticks clacking together. The sound was so resonant and unique that it was hard for Chante and Lucien to tear away. One of the trainers said that the pair had held that nest for eleven years and in this past season they had hatched five eggs. Chante could not take her eyes off of them. The birds preened each other and rubbed their long beaks against each other's cheeks. It was obvious that the two birds had been paired for some time, and seemed very much attached to each other.

Chante realized that they had been gone a long time and asked if they had to get back. Lucien told her that he was free for the evening and that if she were willing, he would like to treat her to dinner at La Table de Valmy. She was thrilled and the light in her face became even brighter. He loved making her happy. They walked around and visited with the birds for a little longer, then walked to the chateau. As they were crossing the parking lot, Lucien saw the back of a man's head with the same blue cap on, sitting in an old grey Renault. Lucien steered Chante quickly away to the chateau.

They found a great place to sit with a view on the restaurant's lovely outdoor patio. They ordered drinks and watched the Roussillon plain turn golden as the sun was setting, and then to lavender as the light faded.

A waiter lit a hurricane lamp at their table as dusk approached, and then returned with menus for them to look at. A few minutes later they ordered. They decided to try two appetizers. She had the cod with sautéed Toulouges red onions, a specialty of the area. And Lucien had the Jabugo ham wrapped around melon. For their main courses, Chante stayed with fish and had the hake au gratin with olives, tomato comfit, and eggplant caviar; and Lucien had the planked veal with Roussillon peas and potatoes. They were too full to eat the cheese course, but after a break with some more wine, they opted to share a dessert, and had the praline heart with soft dark chocolate.

The evening was pleasant and relaxing, and their glowing smiles held their eyes to each other. Few people were dining that evening so the waiter catered to them. He lit an outdoor fireplace and let them be to themselves. Perhaps not so surprisingly, with the level of comfort the two of them had reached, there were silent and loving moments between them as they held hands. When the bill was paid and they stood to go, Lucien led her to the edge of the flagstone patio to peer at the broad valley below. He encircled her waist and she laid her head against his shoulder. She had never felt so happy.

"Lucien, I have had the most fantastic day. Thank you so much. What a change from what we went through just two days ago!" They laughed thinking about their trek in the underground tunnel, finding the chest, climbing up the cliff, and getting the satchel open to find mysterious papers.

"I'm not sure I would have ever done it alone. It was you that really stirred me to pursue the answers to my inquisitiveness. You actually had the foresight to pack a dinner for us, and be with me through the entire ordeal." He turned, still holding her around the waist. "I don't think you realize this, but you have taught me something very important. You've shown me a part of myself that I didn't even know existed. The very sight of you has made me a different man."

"Ah yes," she responded, "a man who is willing to break the law and risk his life and limbs to answer those questions!" He laughed at that, and it helped him come to terms with his feelings.

"Chante, after having gotten to know your adventurous spirit on our explorations together, I don't have any doubts now about how I feel, and I can only hope that you feel at least a fraction of what I do. I love you, Chante. I love the smell of you, the touch of you, your beautiful face, how you think, your thoughtfulness, and your wonderful humor. I love you!"

Chante was speechless. She had a feeling that the evening was heading this way because she was feeling it too, but to at last hear the words from his lips was better than any view, any swooping bird, any wine, or exquisite platter of food. Those were the words that sent her soaring.

"Chante, are you okay?"

"I'm sorry, Lucien. It's just that you took my breath away. After such an amazing couple of weeks, I've come to find that I feel the same way. I love you, too. I never expected this. I never thought I could remember what it was like to be in love again, or to be told that someone loves me. And now, here you are."

"Here we are." They kissed with elation, with sweetness, with the light of the stars brightening the sky above them."

Later that evening they lay in each other's arms at her apartment, wondering what the world would hold for them in the future. Lucien wanted to stay, but felt he had better get in to work extra early the next day, to make up for the time he had spent away. After a fond departure, Lucien left her apartment, and on his way home ran many possibilities through his head. He was as certain about their relationship, as he was uncertain about what finding the papers would do to their lives.

The weather seemed to be changing. A wind had picked up and he could smell that rain was on the way. He turned up his collar and dug his hands into his pockets. A block before the Mairie his eyes caught the brief sight of a man on a side street lighting a cigarette. The man was leaning on a wall next to the cemetery. For the moment that the light was on the man's face, he saw that he was looking above and beyond Lucien. It was the same man he had seen earlier at the park! By then Lucien had crossed the street and passed him, but something made him look back and up to see what had held the man's focus. Lucien noticed that a small light was on upstairs in the insurance company, but that was all.

Could it have been a coincidence that it was the same man he had seen earlier that day? Lucien knew that the man had not attended the bird show, because he had searched the crowd looking for him. Maybe he was just a lone tourist, discovering the local sites during the day, and needing a smoke that night? What did seem strange was that it was late, and with the threatening weather it was more likely that a tourist would be tucked into his hotel room. He wanted to dismiss it, but his soldier's sensibilities told him otherwise. He hurried his pace, and when he got to his apartment he made sure his door was secured and his windows locked. Although it was rare for him to lock his door when home, it was something Chante had gotten in the habit of doing while living in Los Angeles. At least he knew she would be safe.

The wind got stronger as the night wore on and it began to rain sometime late that night. The wind made Lucien's window rattle and then he heard the rain falling.

That night Chante had another dream. At first she thought she was back in a tunnel, but then she realized she was in a long dark hallway, walking very quietly and slowly. The next thing she knew she was having a hard time breathing. Chante awoke with a start, panting. She realized her room was stuffy with all the windows closed up. Then she heard the wind and the rain and realized it must have been the storm. She got a glass of water and went back to sleep.

*   *   *

Just after midnight, on the hillside above Collioure, a man in a dark hood walked up to a large house. He picked the lock of a large wooden door to a beautiful home at the end of a cul-de-sac, which had an incredible view of the Collioure harbor far below. When the lock clicked, he swung the door open and then turned and quickly closed the door. He walked to the alarm box and punched in the code to turn it off. He knew there was no one in the luxury furnished home. He turned on his small flashlight and made his way past a modern low white leather couch, a beautiful ivory carved tusk on a glass side table, and a set of silver collectible snuffboxes on a display shelf. He jogged up the wide oak staircase to the upper level and found the master bedroom.

His flashlight scanned the walls of the room. There it was, on the wall opposite the bed, "Boats at Collioure" by André Derain. He wasn't particularly fond of twentieth century fauvism, but he knew it would sell for at least a million Euros, enough to carry him for several years. Until earlier that year it had hung at the Metropolitan Museum of Art in New York, but he had gotten word from his contact that it had been brought back to France by a private buyer, who was obviously not presently enjoying it. The homeowner was probably off somewhere buying more art for his collection. What was the use of having something if you weren't there to enjoy it? But then, the burglar could not give a damn anyway. His contact and buyer in Monaco would quickly take it off his hands.

He took a long round carry case off his shoulder and laid it on the carpeted floor. Then he removed the painting from the wall, turned it over, and also laid it on the floor. From his pocket he removed the tools he needed to open the backing and dislodge the canvas from the wooden frame. Then he popped the staples from the canvas frame and rolled up the painting. He slid it into the carry case and slung the case back over his shoulder. He jogged down the stairs, reset the alarm, and closed the door silently behind him. He had been in and out in less than seven minutes.

Chapter 19

On Wednesday morning Collioure had the look and feel of a winter's day. The streets were wet and the sky was still filled with dark grey clouds. Lucien arrived at the fort early. When Alerion got in Lucien asked how he was doing. Alerion reported that still nothing had shown up in the storage records and asked how his date with Chante had gone at Valmy. Lucien was all smiles and told him about the beautiful park and the aviary show, which Alerion had never seen. It sounded good. Maybe he would check it out one day, though he was more interested in going to a wine tasting there. They busied themselves all day working on the files for the encounter. Lucien mentioned that he was going to Chante's that night for dinner. If Alerion had planned to surreptitiously follow him, he might not if he knew where Lucien was headed. And if it was going to rain, he doubted that Alerion would even be tempted. Then again, he wasn't as worried about Alerion following them as he was about the stranger.

After work, Lucien stopped at his apartment to change his clothes and get his car. The cold wind hit his face as he left his apartment and walked to his vehicle. Dark clouds were again mounting for another night of rain. Lucien pulled up his collar and on the way carefully scanned the street to see if he was being followed. He did not see Alerion or the man from Valmy Park, but he was on high alert. Many people were on the street hurrying home, and many looked suspicious due to their own raised collars, but his excitement kept his mind occupied. He was feeling like a boy waiting for presents and he was pretty sure this feeling would remain until he could get to his father's and find out what the papers said.

Chante met Lucien at her door with a fond greeting. "Hello, my love!"

Those words took him by surprise. He was not used to being called sweetheart names by anyone but his mother, so many years before. All of his past girlfriends had called him only by his name. It was something new and he liked it. His surprised reaction quickly left him. He held and kissed Chante, then they locked the door and left.

When Lucien had left the fort for the day, Alerion had been downstairs working in the storage room. Lucien had been so intent on leaving as soon as he could that he didn't stop in or text good night to Alerion. When Alerion finally came upstairs and saw that Lucien had already left, he felt relatively certain that Lucien would be seeking warm companionship that night at Chante's. Still, he had to be sure. He walked to the other end of town, but scowled as the cold wind was biting at his neck and face. He wanted to go home to a nice glass of wine, but now that he knew where she lived, he walked behind Chante's apartment to confirm their presence. Looking up, he could see that no lights were on in her apartment, and her car was still parked in the parking lot. Maybe they went out to eat instead, but somewhere in the back of his mind, he had a feeling it was more than that. On his way home he stopped at Lucien's apartment and saw that his car was gone. They were out somewhere, but suddenly he didn't care. He really did not like following Lucien under the colonel's orders. He was only half-heartedly following them, because he felt he was compromising his friendship with Lucien by doing so.

The wind was still blowing and periodically showers splashed the windshield, as Lucien drove them to his father's house. He told Chante that he would have his father send in the wood slivers to be tested. They might as well garner as much information as they could. By the time they stopped to pick up some dinner, the darkening sky had turned black.

They finally arrived, parked the car, and walked to the front door just as the rain began to fall. But something was wrong. The porch light was not on and his father had not come out to meet them. When Lucien knocked there was no answer, and when he tried the front door handle it was unlocked. Lucien put up his hand to keep Chante back. He slowly opened the door into the living room, but the room was dark. He paused to listen, but heard nothing, except the pelting rain. Panic gripped him and he swung the door open and called out.

"Papa! Papa, where are you?" Nothing. He cautioned Chante to stay where she was on the porch as he eased himself past the front door. He knew the house well enough to find his way in the dark, plus with the streetlight shining in a bit he could see the edges of the furniture. Chante could not hold herself back so she entered silently behind him and pulled the front door closed to keep out the moisture. They tiptoed down the darkened hall, but then Chante grabbed onto his arm and he felt her freeze and gasp for air. He grabbed her arm and held her.

Her panic was infectious and Lucien had to call out. "Papa, are you here?" From further down the hall they heard a groan. Lucien reached for the hall light and flicked it on. His father was lying face down on the floor midway down the hall. They rushed to him, and as Lucien turned him over he emitted more groans. Lucien put his arm around his father's back and sat him up. As Gervais' eyes got used to the light and he realized his son and Chante were there, he slowly came to.

Lucien held him while Chante ran to the bathroom, wet a washcloth, and brought it to them. She gave it to Lucien to wipe his face while she ran to the kitchen for a glass of water. When Gervais could keep his eyes open, Lucien began with the questions. "Papa, are you okay? Are you in pain? What happened?"

After Gervais took a sip of water and nodded that he was better, he began. "I had just gotten back from my errands about 5:00. I was on my way down the hall when someone pummeled me on my back. It must have knocked the breath out of me, and then I was hit over the head. What time is it now? How long have I been out?"

Chante looked at her watch, "It's nearly 7:00."

Lucien looked down the hall to the clean room where their treasures were. The door stood open. "Oh no!" Lucien got up, ran to the room and stood at the door. He flicked on the switch and looked at the table. "It's gone!" A knot of disappointment built up in his stomach. He turned to Chante and his father, his face suddenly drained of color and repeated, "It's all gone. Taken."

Gervais raised his hand to quiet him. "Son, please help me get up. I need some fresh air. Lucien, Chante, please help me."

They supported him to the back door and out to the covered porch. The sky was still dark and the rain was coming down, now more lightly. The back patio light was on, throwing light across the fenced yard so they could see that there was no one there but themselves. They guided him to his porch chair and Gervais eased into it. They waited for him to catch his breath, but then he spoke in hushed tones. "Don't worry, I saved the papers."

Lucien was confused. "What do you mean? Where are they?"

Gervais held up his finger to his mouth. "Son, I think we should play it safe. There might be listening devices in the house. When I finished the translation late last night, I knew I had to protect the original and the translation. I left the wooden box and the satchel on the table, but I took the papers to my bank this afternoon. I got a safe deposit box and put the archival box with the papers in it. Then I went to the university for a few hours. When I got home, whoever it was surprised me, but they only got the wooden box and the satchel. Not the papers."

Chante and Lucien heaved a sigh of relief, but then Chante remembered, "What about the slivers of wood and the lead seal, where are they?" Lucien went back into the room and carefully looked around.

When he came back he reported. "They're gone too."

Gervais suddenly looked very pale in the light. Lucien was concerned more for his father, and he asked him again, how he was feeling. Was he dizzy or in pain?

"I'm okay, son. My back aches and I think I'm going to have a good lump on my head, but I think I'm okay." Suddenly, he looked with great concern at Lucien and Chante. "Somebody has been following you. Someone knew you had found something. Someone knew we had those things here. Who knew any of this? You didn't tell anyone, did you?"

Both Chante and Lucien confirmed that they had told no one, that they had not even spoken about it among themselves for fear that someone would overhear them.

"But someone knew about it, Lucien. *Someone* knew!"

Lucien thought about what he had seen in the last week. "I've something to tell both of you. For more than a week, I have gotten the feeling that someone was following me. Chante, I saw someone watching us at the Chateau Valmy gardens. I didn't say anything because I did not want to spoil the beautiful day we had together.

Then last night I saw the same man again. He was downtown and I saw him light a cigarette. The man quickly shook out his match, but I know he was not standing in the darkness just to get some fresh air at 11:00 pm with a storm looming."

Chante had a pained look on her face. "I wish you had said something to me and had stayed the night."

"Had I done that, I would not have had my suspicions confirmed. Someone knows what we are doing and has definitely been following us."

"But who, Lucien?" asked Chante.

"I find it hard to believe, and I cannot be certain, but this man is not the only one. I think Alerion is also following us. But I just cannot believe that Alerion would do this to you, Papa. I know that he is a trained soldier and capable, but honestly I don't think he would raise his hand against you, for what? For something he knows nothing about? No, that does not make any sense. I think it is the stranger. "

But it was Gervais who finally asked the big question.

"But what should we do about all of this? If we go to the police and they come out here, they will want a description of what was stolen. If we say it was an ancient box with a early 14th century leather satchel, they will want to know where it came from, what was in it, and why someone would want to steal it. If we don't say anything, we could still be dealing with someone wanting to break in here again and further search for the papers."

"Wait," added Lucien, "we don't know if whoever did this actually knows if there was anything in the satchel. Since they did not find anything here, even with the element of surprise, they may think that the satchel was empty all along." He looked up at his father and then placed a hand on his arm. "Thank goodness you had the brilliant idea of putting the papers into a safe deposit box. Whatever made you think of doing that?"

"Son, you haven't asked the most important question of the evening."

Lucien looked concerned, "What?"

"What the papers said. It was because of what I translated that I knew I had to make sure they were kept safe." All of a sudden that very question dawned on both Chante and Lucien and they leaned in to hear what he would say.

Gervais began. "It is a secret letter addressed to Pope Clement V from Jacques de Molay, the last grand master of the Templars. It is obvious that the communication never made it to the Pope. The satchel was disguised in a wooden case, or it would have been seen for what it was. It must have been clandestinely handed over to a private messenger, who might have gone through the same tunnel that you went through from the chateau. They probably left it in the trunk thinking they would be back when it was safer to relay the satchel to the Pope, perhaps by boat, since the items were in a cave at the shore." Gervais took Lucien's arm. "Or, someone purposely concealed it there so the Pope would not receive it." Then Gervais got a chill. "Son, let's go back inside, but we cannot talk about anything until we are sure that we are not being listened to. We will write notes if we need to discuss it."

Chante was feeling like she needed to take care of both men. "I'm going to get our dinner ready and then we will make a plan." The two men nodded.

Gervais felt well enough to make it to the kitchen table. Chante got their dinner together while Lucien carefully looked through the kitchen, hall, clean room, and living room. He looked inside lights, behind and around the bookcases, around his father's bedroom, under tables, and in the phone receiver for any type of listening device, but found nothing. They had a nearly silent dinner of chicken Florentine crepes and a goat cheese salad. The wine they had brought to celebrate with remained on the counter, because Chante cautioned Gervais against having any alcohol in case he had a concussion. Even though the house seemed clear, they were hesitant to say anything. While they were sitting, sipping some coffee, Gervais motioned to Chante to reach for the drawer behind her at the kitchen counter and pointed to a paper and pen inside the drawer. She got them out and they both watched as Gervais wrote something down.

Aloud, he said, "Please, can you both stay the night? I would feel a lot safer if you did." Then he showed them the note: *"Tomorrow morning we will go to the bank and you can read the translation."* Lucien and Chante nodded.

"Of course, Papa. We'll stay. I'm going to call Alerion now, tell him that you've fallen, and that I am staying with you." He picked up his phone and made the call. Alerion answered at the first ring.

"Hello, Lucien, what's up?"

"Alerion, I'm afraid I won't be in tomorrow morning. My father has had a nasty spill. I'm with him now, but I need to take him to the doctor tomorrow morning."

"Oh no, is he okay?" The concern in his voice seemed genuine, and Alerion now knew where they had gone.

"He seems to be okay, but he hit his head and I think I should stay with him tonight and make sure he is okay through the night."

"Yes, of course. No problem. I'll let the colonel know, if he asks."

"Thank you Alerion. I should be back by midday."

"Okay, see you then." And they rang off.

Lucien looked at his father. "He seemed genuinely surprised and concerned."

"Then we have an even greater mystery on our hands, son. Tomorrow we can talk about it more, but I think for now I need to lie down and get some rest."

Lucien helped Gervais to his room and into bed. Chante finished up the dishes and then Lucien once more made up the foldout couch in the living room. He made sure to check underneath and around the couch bed for a listening devise in case he had missed something on his first search, but all was clear.

*   *   *

Late that night a dark figure with a duffle bag over his shoulder trudged slowly along the lane past the old cemetery with its high cement walls. He walked as close to the wall as he could in the darker shadows. Weeks before, it had been a brighter byway when a streetlight had lit up the opposite side of the street. He had made quick work of that and so far the bulb had not been replaced. He had accomplished a lot that day and he was tired. His dampened cap sat low on his head, as it had just begun to lightly rain again. He made his way past the first large square pillar that supported the heavy wrought-iron gated entry of the cemetery. He glanced through the bars into the shadowy recesses of the enclosed tombs within, and then quickly made his way further down the street. Near the end of the road he ducked into a small entry and found his way into a back alley.

He was angry as well. He kept a mental score of where he stood, one loss and one gain, when he had hoped to have two gains. At least the week had not been a complete loss. He'd have to work harder to achieve his ultimate goal. He reached his destination and paused. His teeth were clenched as he stood in the cold, listening. His eyes swept the area, but no one, not even a wandering dog or stray cat, was around on this winter-like night. He set his load down quietly, reached into his pocket, and found the key he needed. He unlocked the tall door and carefully placed his bundles inside. Then he quietly shut the door, relocked it, and slinked back into the alley. He'd hoped to be on his way out of town that night, but due to circumstances that he had not counted on, it would have to be later in the week. He skirted the back streets, and made his way to the small dock at the far edge of town.

Chapter 20

The next morning Gervais had a black and blue mark on his right shoulder blade, and his head had a rounded bump, but otherwise he felt okay. While he was getting ready, Chante and Lucien made up the couch bed and tidied up the living room, but they were not keen to speak about what had happened or what they were about to do. They left as soon as they could and went out for food. Chante thought Gervais should go to a doctor, but Gervais refused. Instead, he instructed Lucien where to go for breakfast. When they were settled inside and had ordered, they discussed how anyone could have known what they had and what they were doing, but came up blank.

"Papa, after we go to the bank let's go to an electronics shop nearby. I want to buy a bug detector. When we get back to your house, I will scan the entire house just to make sure there are none."

"Thank you, son. That's a good idea. That will make me feel safer. Then you should do the same at both of your apartments and at your office."

Lucien had not thought of doing so at his office, but his father was right. If there were a listening devise in his office, then he would know who was most likely to have put it there, despite his genuine reaction over the phone.

All three had pretty good appetites, but they ate quickly looking at their watches, wanting to get to the bank as soon as it was open. The Société Générale Bank was nearby. After adding Lucien's signature to the paperwork for the box and obtaining his key, they were shown into the vault where the safe deposit boxes were held. With the bank agent now out of the room, Gervais opened the flat metal lid, took out the archival box and lifted out the papers. He laid them side-by-side, and laid the typed translation down last. He cautioned them not to speak out loud as they were on a bank camera, but had them read the translation to themselves. It read:

His Holiness Pope Clement V
Supreme Pontific of the Holy Roman Church
Avignon, France

Your Holiness,

It is the day of our Lord March 14, 1307.

I congratulate you on your consecration as Pope. You may recall that we met at the home of Cardinal Presbyter Stephanus of St. Ciriacus in 1303 in Rome, at the conclave held there. I found you to be a truly pious man, devoted to the works of our Lord, and a great teacher. I hope that this letter finds you in good health.

Circumstances have caused me to contact you secretly. I have just returned from the Fortress at Limassol on Cyprus where we stood with Amaury of Lusignan, and succeeded in ousting his brother King Henry II from that land. Word reached our outpost that allegations against our Order had been presented to King Philip IV by Esquin de Floyran, but they are false. As we were in battle and could not leave, many Brethren of our Order were detained until things had come to a rest. We have now returned to France and have recently arrived at our commandery at Mas Déu.

The Commander here, Ramon Saguàrdia, has informed me that further allegations have been heard coming from the Royal Court. This seems hard to believe, since our Order secured for the King additional lands, loaned him a substantial amount of money to finance the Flemish war, and then defended him at the insurrection in Paris. I have the gravest of feelings that at any time we will be called to court to personally answer to these allegations.

King Phillip is a mighty man with much power, but Holy Father, our Order remains faithful and seeks continued protection under the wing of the Holy Roman Church. We stand ready to continue to serve in the name of our Lord. It has become necessary that I now appeal to your Holiness with a plea for support for the Order before this goes any further. I therefore, seek an audience with your Holiness, so that you may be able to hear me out first hand. I implore your Holiness to listen to my words on this matter, so when you hear further accusations you will know them to be falsehoods.

The allegations are heresy, denying Christ, spitting on the cross, obscene kisses, carnal relations among the men, and praying to idols. I can assure you that none of these are true. Christ is our Savior. Neither I, nor any of my fellow brethren, would ever deny him. As the cross is the symbol of the church, neither my fellow brethren nor I would ever dishonor the cross. No kisses abhorrent have been placed upon another, but only humble pressings upon the hem of Holy men of the cloth. As the Lord has proclaimed relations between men unclean, neither I, nor any of my fellow brethren would ever do so. None have had a part of performing it or enduring it, and have never heard of any Knight Templar engaging in this sin. It is against our precepts and any Knight found to have done so would be turned away from our Order. And last, no idols of false gods have been recognized or adored by us. As God is my witness, I swear my statements to be true, and beg your Holiness to support the Order when his Highness King Phillip calls upon you to answer for our work.

It is with fervent prayer that this appeal reaches you at Avignon in a timely manner, and that I may relay and swear before you in my person that what I say is true.

Your humble servant,

In the name of the Lord, Amen

Jacques de Molay
Grand Master of the Order of the Temple
Mas Déu Commandery

When they both had finished the letter and looked up at Gervais, their eyes were wide with surprise, but Gervais held up his hand to keep them silent. Then Gervais repacked the documents and the translation, called the bank agent back to join his key with the one he had to lock away the metal box. They exited the bank and got in the car. Both Lucien and Chante exploded with exclamations and questions. Chante let Lucien speak first.

"This letter is incredible! How important is this document? What should we do with it? What does this letter mean to our history?"

Gervais smiled. "We know it was written in March of 1307 and that the Pope did not receive this letter. However, we do know that sometime later that same year, Molay and many of his knights were summoned to the Pope in Avignon. What they did not know is that King Phillip was also on his way and arrived just after the knights. The Pope became accusatory and demanded testimony from the Templar leaders to respond to the charges, no doubt at the king's insistence. Whether it was simply part of the king's plan all along to get the knights there, we don't know. However, I'm sure Molay quickly realized that even if his March letter had arrived it had been ignored. It must have become pretty obvious very quickly that the Pope had now changed sides. You see, what Molay did not know at the time was that Clement V had reversed the earlier Papal bull issued by the previous Pope, Boniface the VIII, which kept the state and the church separate. Once Clement V was elected, King Phillip applied pressure so that the previous Papal bull would be reversed. The change allowed the king supremacy over the church and any secular ruler. In effect, the Pope had become powerless. From then on, it was only a matter of time before the arrests began. Later that same year, on Friday, October 13, the word went out to have all Templars arrested, and then the hearings and trials began."

Chante was shaking her head, "So it was a trap all along."

"I'm afraid so," added Gervais, "and some believe that is why Friday the 13th is considered unlucky to this day. Under the laws of heresy one important loophole existed. It meant that the king would no longer be liable for repayment of the vast loan that the Templars had made to him, and he could abscond with all the rich land holdings and the treasury of the Templars that had been amassed in every country where they had organized within the Order.

"While the hearings continued, it was only a year later, in August of 1308, that Pope Clement V tried to have the leaders of the Order acquitted. The only way he could do that was to have them make statements of innocence and then grant them absolution. The knights could not again travel to the Pope in Avignon, because they were in a weakened state from repeated torture. Instead, the Pope sent three Cardinals to them in Chinon to conduct interrogations, with several notaries witnessing and writing down the proceedings. For four days, Jacques de Molay, Grandmaster of the Order, Raymbaud de Caron, Preceptor of the commanderies in Outremer, Hugo de Pérraud, Preceptor of France, Geoffroy de Gonneville, Preceptor of Aquitania and Poitou, and Geoffroy de Charney, Preceptor of Normandy, were interrogated. Each said that they were innocent of the charges brought before them. Each swore that they had told the truth, and asked for forgiveness and mercy. Each was then given absolution, absolved in the eyes of the Lord, and restored to the unity of the church, but in word only. The written record of this came to be known as the Chinon Parchment. King Phillip ignored their testimony, and despite the fact that the Pope suspended some of the proceedings, many of the Templars that could be found, were condemned and burned, and in 1312 the Order was officially disbanded."

Lucien continued the story. "On March 18, 1314, after Jacques de Molay and Geoffroi de Charney had been held prisoner for five and half years, the day came when they were to be killed. They were taken to the far end of the Ile de la Cite on the Seine River in Paris to be burned at the stake. It is said that before the flames were ignited at their feet, Molay prophesized that within a year the King and the Pope would both be dead, and they were. Pope Clement V died one month later from cancer, and King Philip died of a stroke that November."

"History finally corrected itself when in 2001," added Gervais, "a researcher of historical handwriting discovered the Chinon Parchment misfiled in the Vatican's secret library. For nearly 700 years the Templars had been thought of as wayward and thieving Christian monks, but they had been wrongfully accused. With the Chinon Parchment brought to light, the allegations were found to be false and the cover-up was discovered, so the Vatican reversed its original findings and announced that all had been forgiven."

They were quiet for a moment, and then Lucien spoke. "So, if the letter was written in March the previous year and the Chinon parchment was written in August the following year, is that significant?"

"Anything that old, and still in excellent condition, is exceptionally valuable. The fact that it is written in Molay's own hand to a Pope, and that it predates the Chinon parchment, probably even more so. Historically, it brings to light more knowledge about the times than we knew before, and that is what gives it the most value in my opinion."

Chante was exasperated. "It just goes to show how quickly allegiances can switch, politics can be bartered, and history can be changed."

"The questions that arise now," asked Gervais, "are what to do with what we know? How to deal with the forces that seem to want to stop us, and what do we hope for as an outcome?"

"Well, I certainly don't want any of us to go to jail," answered Lucien.

Chante looked at Gervais, "I would like to see this letter in a museum so all can appreciate the situation that Molay and the Templars were in during that time."

Gervais did offer something. "I know that if you can prove where the papers came from, that would lend additional substantiation that you are telling the truth. If you don't say anything about digging up the floor at the fort, and there is no evidence that you trespassed under the chateau, then your chances of avoiding prosecution become much better. All you have to do is decide what to say when asked how you found the chest."

Chante gave Lucien a worried look. "But that would mean going back to the chateau, sneaking through the exposition door again, removing the tethered rope from the door that helped us get into the tunnel below, putting the metal plate back into place, and securing those two doors shut."

Lucien smiled. "That can be done. While we are at it, we can get more slivers of wood from the tunnels, take a picture of the chest, get a sliver of wood from it, and have each piece of wood tested. I get the feeling whoever took the box, lead seal, satchel, and pieces of wood, doesn't know where they came from. We know no one else was in that cave tunnel because there were no footprints and the box and satchel were still intact."

Gervais added, "I wouldn't be so sure about that, but once you've done those things, I suggest you write to the curatorial department of the Louvre or the museum you want to get the letter into and make an appointment to show them your findings. And I know you are not going to like this, but when you have done all of that, I suggest you go to the police and tell them the story of how you decided to explore the cliffs and discovered the cave and its contents."

Neither Lucien nor Chante liked the list of things to do, especially the last. They would need to discuss it to decide what and when to accomplish it all, to keep their stories straight, and to make sure they were not getting followed. In the meantime, they went to the hardware store and got additional locks for Gervais' front and back doors, and went to a specialty electronics store to buy a bug detector. Then they returned to the house and Lucien scanned every square inch, but did not find any bugs. He also installed the additional locks. Chante cleared the clean room, removed all of the used plastic, put it into a large trash bag, and set it on the back porch. Lucien then moved all of the boxes in the hall back into the extra room. It was 11:30 by the time he had finished, but now feeling much safer, Gervais told them to go. He promised to keep his cell phone on him in case any trouble developed, and that they would talk later.

Chapter 21

On the way back to Collioure, Lucien and Chante, once again, discussed how it was possible that they had been followed, and how anyone could have learned that they had anything of interest. Maybe someone overheard them at the café where they had discussed their plans to enter the tower and then followed them. It was also possible that they had been overheard talking about what they had found at her apartment, or on the phone. Or maybe the man in the shadows near the Mairie had followed them and overheard them. The last possibility, which Lucien hoped above all others was not true, was that Alerion had followed them, and fearing for his job, had reported them to the colonel or the authorities. If that was the case, it was only a matter of time before one of those parties approached them.

They also discussed how they would get back into the cave and to the chest. By the time they returned to the apartment they knew what they had to do, and were ready to set their plan in motion. When they reached Chante's apartment, Lucien ran the bug detector all around her apartment and even out on the balcony. He found nothing. Now, with time running out, he had to get back to his apartment, drop off his car, change his clothes, and get back to the fort. He would check for listening devices at his office and his apartment later.

The cold wind had scattered the clouds. Patches of puddles remained in the streets and people still wore their coats. In the meantime, the work on his desk had piled up.

The last thing he could do was fall behind in his duties. When he arrived, he popped into Alerion's office. Alerion had a stack of folders on his desk and was deep in concentration at his computer. When he saw Lucien he stood and saluted.

"Sir, how is your father doing? Is he all right?" The concern on his face was obvious.

"Much better. He hurt his back falling, and he has a lump on his head, but he's doing better."

"How did he fall?"

"He was going through some old boxes in his house and had piled them up in the hallway. Then he accidently fell over them. I've moved the boxes back, and he needs to take it easy for a couple of days, but he'll be okay."

"Thank goodness for that." Then Alerion shifted his attention to the files on his desk. "I've been busy, as you can see. The files are prepped for each attendee for the ACE project." Just between them, Alerion had taken to abbreviating the Journalist and Reporter's Abbreviated Field Combat Encounter to the Abbreviated Combat Encounter, to the ACE project, because it saved time and breath. Lucien saw the pile of files and was impressed.

"I can see that. You have been busy." They continued to discuss the encounter, what was left to do, and about several of the individuals that would be attending. They also discussed possibilities for who would be the best reporter to focus on for promoting the entire program. All seemed well with Alerion, and as the afternoon wore on, Lucien was feeling more confident that Alerion had nothing to do with his father's incident. At 4:00 Alerion said he was heading downstairs to continue organizing the storage space, and Lucien was happy to hear that he had not forgotten the additional task that Lucien wanted him to work on.

This gave Lucien a chance to run the bug detector in his office. He did not find anything planted there, but was still concerned about the safety of Chante and his father. That put an extra crease of worry to his brow and added stress to his stomach. This reminded him that he had not taken time to eat lunch, so he went to the commissary and grabbed a sandwich. There were few people in the cafeteria-like room, so he gave his father a call. Gervais was fine. He had taken the rest of the day off from the university, saying that he had fallen and hurt his head, and he was told to take the rest of the week off. He would be back to the university the following Monday. He had already called his department to have another professor cover his class for the next day. Lucien was glad about that and realized that his father was a lot smarter than he sometimes gave him credit for.

Later, as he was standing outside of his office and about to lock up, Alerion came bounding down the hall with excitement in his eyes.

"Lucien, I need to show you something. Follow me back downstairs."

The look in Alerion's eyes was infectious. Lucien finished locking his office door and nodded to Alerion to lead on. He knew that Alerion could not have texted him as the walls were so thick in the basement, that a signal was not possible. They reached the storage room, looking ahead to make sure that Rousseau and Duran had left their new office. Officers were not prone to staying later than they needed to. Who could blame them, especially Rousseau and Duran, who had been allocated to an office without windows? Alerion led Lucien to the far side of the new storeroom and a stack of boxes that he had been going through. The same small card table was now set up with Alerion's computer as he was constantly transferring information to digital files. He had to transport it back and forth from his office daily, but it was the best way to accomplish the needed documentation.

"I went into shock when I found this old file, and I do mean OLD, mistakenly placed into this box of newer information on maneuvers from the '70s." The label on the manila folder said *Articles Déplacés Ecclésiale Stockage* (items moved to Ecclesial Storage). "That was not what caught my eye. It is what I saw when I opened the file with only this one sheet of paper in it. I could not believe it. It is dated May 11, 1940. That is one day after the Germans invaded France."

He lifted the single sheet of typed yellowing paper from the file and handed it to Lucien. It had on it a list of items that had been previously stored somewhere else, but its file name implied that whatever the list was, had been moved to the church for safekeeping. They looked at the paper together. It was comprised of a short list of numbers followed by letters with no other accompanying information. Whatever the list was meant to represent, most likely due to the date, was never meant to reach German hands. But Lucien was puzzled.

"The church? But why would anything be moved there?"

"Maybe the items had been kept at the chateau, but thinking that the Germans would soon be here and possibly occupying it, the owners thought it best to move them. I have always thought that the church was holy ground meant only for ecclesiastical things, but maybe it also served as a secret storage area for important documents during the war? I've been in that church several times in the last couple of years, but I can't think where there would be any storage areas except maybe the vestry. The high altar and all the chapels are open to view. Surely the Germans would have gone through that church from top to bottom searching for anything of interest, but they may have been focusing on more expensive religious artifacts to finance their war." Alerion looked at Lucien for a response, but then he saw that look once more come over Lucien's face. "Oh no, you're not going to go rummaging through the church in the dead of night are you?"

"No, Alerion. I'm sure I can just ask the parish priest about anything that was stored in the church during the war and see what he says. Were there any other files like this in that box?"

Alerion immediately got a relieved look on his face, "No, there wasn't, I looked." Then another thought came to him. "I'm probably going to hate myself for asking this, but when was the old lighthouse turned bell tower closed off? Weren't people allowed at one time to climb the tower?"

"Alerion, that bell tower hasn't been accessible to the public since it was built in the late 1600s as far as I know. Besides, bay water has been washing against that tower for centuries. No telling how stable it really is, and I'm sure it would be way too moist inside to store anything in, especially of paper." Although, he had to admit the idea did intrigue him. That might be the perfect place to secretly store odd items, in an airtight container that no one might get to but the priests of the church.

"Yes, but there *is* a working clock in what we now call the 'clock tower.' I wonder who services it?"

"Good question, and I know just the person to ask."

Alerion gave him a dubious look. "You are not going to get your girlfriend to ask for you, are you?"

"I was actually thinking of just going to the tourist office and asking myself." Although he was also thinking that any person writing about their travels in the historic town might like to know the answer to that, and Chante could easily ask. But he responded to Alerion with, "Okay, let me take a picture of this paper with my phone and then you can record and file it away. Thank you very much for bringing it to my attention." Then he thought he had better add, "Although, I'm not sure it will be of any use, it is interesting. If you find anything else like this, please let me know."

Alerion nodded and Lucien took the picture. Then they set the file aside and left, locking the door behind them.

That evening Lucien stopped at his apartment and checked for electronic bugs, but found none. Then he changed and went for dinner at Chante's. Afterward they walked up to their lookout at the gazebo, where they first had kissed. The storm had passed, but it was cool. He told her about the file that Alerion had found in the storage room and that he had not found any bugs in his apartment or at his office. That meant the person who had broken into his father's home was not with the police or the military, or was not a professional spy. But whom did that leave? They finalized their plans, which they would put into action right away. It would be another late night.

He walked Chante back to her apartment, making sure that she locked her door, and he went home. By 10:30 he had gathered what he would need. He turned his lights out by 11:00 and then waited another half hour, just in case. He scanned the streets for anyone that might be watching and then he put on his backpack, left out the back entrance of the apartment complex, and took a long walk. No one was around in the nippy air, but if someone had been watching his window, they would have thought he had retired. At least that was what he was hoping for. Twenty minutes later he was where he wanted to be.

He tied off his rope, shimmied down the cliff and only needed to wait a half hour before the next low tide was occurring. It wasn't the lowest the tide would get, but it would have to do. At least this time he was better prepared with the right boots and a headlamp so both of his hands could be free. He got somewhat wet, but he made his way into the small sunken hole using a second rope and found the chest just as they had left it. He managed to easily snap off a small piece of wood splinter from the back leg that was broken. He placed it in a plastic bag and then into a hard plastic container for safekeeping. He took close up pictures of the chest as well. He then went back up the rope and was back to his apartment by 2:00 am. When Lucien had safely returned to his apartment, he sent Chante a text letting her know he was back. She had been nervously waiting to hear from him, and when she had, she could finally sleep in peace.

The next day was Friday, so he went to Banyuls-sur-mer for some supplies during his lunch break. He found exactly what he needed for less than 100 Euros and packed it into his backpack. He let Chante know that all was ready. On his way back he made a quick stop at the Mairie. He was surprised that Moniqua remembered his name. Lucien asked him if he knew when the old lighthouse had become a bell tower for the church, but Moniqua had no idea. No one had ever asked him that. He said he would try to find out, but Lucien said not to bother. Lucien also walked up and down the streets of the town to locate above ground where they had been the weekend before, below ground. When he located the same altitude and direction, he found himself near the top of the hill in front of a residential home. He looked at the front door and to his surprise saw a white and red tile above the door in the shape of a Templar cross. It had to be a coincidence. How could it be anything else? He wondered who lived there.

On Saturday he and Chante went back to the chateau. Today he was dressed in his fatigues. Chante in comparison had dressed down in grey slacks and a heavy jacket, and wore the backpack. The weather was definitely changing to the cool of the year. The sun was out, but a breeze kept the air chilly. When they got to the northwest display room they waited until no one was walking through, and then Lucien unlocked the door with his pick, once again. Chante slid past the door and descended the steps. He was not sure about this part of the plan that Chante had come up with. He was every bit surprised when he found out that she knew how to handle a torch kit and weld. It seems she had been the only one in her high school to get into the normally all-boys welding class. And because she really wanted to learn and the boys took the class just to goof off, she got the only A+ in the class. She was full of surprises. All he had to do was stand in his uniform in front of the door looking like he was simply a guard for the art in the room. All the while he kept the door slightly ajar to keep it from locking again. If for some reason he felt he had to close it, he was the one who could pick it open again.

Chante shimmied down the rope and got another sliver of the wood from a beam just inside the tunnel, wrapped it in a plastic bag and then placed it in a hard plastic container. She could not help but remember how she had romantically swung down and into Lucien's arms the last time they were in this room. Then she pulled herself up and removed the rope. To close the metal over the hole, Chante used the rope around the door handle and wound it around the sheet metal. It took all of her strength to pull it back, but she managed to lever it back into place. Then she undid the rope and packed it away. Chante stepped back into the corridor and closed the door. She pulled out the torch kit and welded the hinges of both doors closed. While the welds on the hinges were still hot she pressed some of the rust and dirt that lay on the ground onto the hinges. Chante was surprised at how authentically old and rusted the doors looked when she had finished.

There was still a hole in the lock of the second door, but with a small piece of metal that she had brought, she was able to weld it over the locking mechanism. She had to use a water bottle to pour water over the torch nozzle to rapidly cool it down so she could pack it away. The rope cushioned the bottom of the bag and the welding gear rested on top. With the backpack all packed, she exited the door at the base of the stairs. It took all her strength to pull that door closed, but she finally managed. Lucien could hear the door scraping across the floor so he knew she was on her way up. Thankfully, no one was in the room to hear it and no one had entered that looked suspicious. She had taken less than fifteen minutes for the entire operation.

She lightly tapped on the gallery door behind him and he opened the door to let her out. She was beaming with her accomplishment and how well the plan had worked, though she had had her doubts as to whether she was going to be able to move that metal plate. They walked around the courtyard of the chateau once more as tourists might do, took some pictures, and then exited the castle. It wasn't until they had a drink in a bar on the far side of town that Chante realized her hands were a little shaky from the task. Lucien was very proud of her and could not stop looking at her and admiring her spunk.

That night they packed up the wood splinters for Paris, composed a letter, and enclosed a check. Lucien also sent an email to the lab explaining that a package was getting mailed on Monday with payment and asked for a quick test and response. Pleading probably wouldn't work, but it never hurts to ask, especially if it was a special request from the military, even though he did not have that authority.

Early Sunday morning they put their second plan into action. First, they had an early coffee and croissant and then walked toward the church of Notre-Dame-des-Anges. Near the church they stopped at a bench and huddled together for warmth, as it was downright cold that day. Not only was it cold, there was some morning fog that had drifted inside the harbor. They wore warm jackets and wool hats, but they also carried white cotton gloves in their pockets. Lucien began by describing some of the background that he had recently discovered on the church, while they waited for the priest to unlock the doors. They had about ten minutes before the 9:00 o'clock opening.

"The building that we see today is probably the third church built on the site. We don't know when the first one was built, but there was most likely some kind of place of worship here, ever since there were people living in the area. There may have been a church here as early as the first century, especially since the town had a port that was growing in importance and receiving merchants from all over the Mediterranean. No doubt, people were thankful that trade was happening and needed a place of worship. The Moors were here in the 700s, so there may also have been a mosque built. We know that Alphonse, the count-king of Catalonia and Aragon in 1172, inherited the Roussillon area. Under his administration the castle and town began to seriously grow, so it's likely that a Christian church was established certainly by then.

"When Collioure came under the Aragon crown's administration, an influx of money and land traffic increased the town's importance. Alphonse's son Peter, inherited next, married the heiress Maria of Montpellier, and they lived in the castle for several years. There is a story about the importance of the territory in 1205. It seems that Peter gifted the Roussillon area, which he controlled, to his bride, and in exchange he expected to receive from her the wealth of Montpellier. When she refused to sign the agreement, he threatened her and the people of Montpellier. Reluctantly, she gave in to protect her people, but she was not heard of again. Perhaps it is a coincidence that the church was then named the Saint Marie Church."

Chante could not help but interrupt, "Wow, you have been reading up on its history. You got all this at the library?"

"No, online actually. I also inquired at the tour office about the tower, but the guy didn't know when it was built. It is amazing though, that there does seem to be more information on the church than on the chateau."

Lucien looked around to see if anyone was watching them. Lucien did not see anyone in particular, but the streets were starting to gather early risers: some tourists, waiters from the cafés, and shopkeepers were opening their stores. Lucien wanted to be the first ones in the church. While they waited, Lucien continued the history lesson.

"With the growth of trade at its port, and the need to have the town grow economically, the crown of Aragon granted an exemption from taxes to its inhabitants. That definitely helped the town to grow, and naturally with growth came problems and the need to control them. There were various authorities the populace had to abide by, so Count Peter appointed a chief bailiff who would oversee all local laws so no one else could interfere. Kind of like a local sheriff. Peter also established a market for trade every Tuesday and an annual fair to further promote commerce. The market is still held, but it is now on Wednesdays and Sundays, and there are several different fairs throughout the year. Along with improving commerce, Peter also created a trade monopoly. He took control of how travelers moved in the region. Instead of an overland route through the foothills of the Pyrenees, travelers were discouraged from crossing more westerly routes and obligated to pass instead, along the eastern coast through Collioure. So the town needed a place of worship to accommodate these extra travelers.

"Due to the increase of traffic, local commerce, population, and incoming port trade, it was also necessary to increase the area's military structure. The Templars were already present, so they helped build up the fortifications to the castle. In 1208 Peter granted to the Templars a parcel of land inside the walls of the castle, and another outside the walls between the castle and the sea. By then, the Templar housing had been integrated with the castle. That was when the Bishop of Elne also granted the Templars the care of the church with its income, and the following year, Pope Innocent III confirmed their holdings. The Templars may also have helped build the church.

"Now we jump ahead in time. When Vauban arrived around 1659, he had additional structures started to fortify the castle and the town. That's when he added the bastions, reinforced the old fort structure, and upgraded Fort Saint Elme. In building the walls and the fort on the hill, as Papa explained, Vauban had his man Hillaire move the townspeople and clear their old town buildings so he could completely restructure and enhance the fort where Fort Miradou is now. He also had the old church leveled to expand the Chateau's defenses. The people complained about having to move, but they were even more upset about losing their church. After the fortifications were completed, the people were able to resettle and rebuild their church on the same spot where the old one had been, and this time they attached it to the lighthouse tower. That occurred sometime between 1684 and 1691. The famous Catalan artist, Joseph Sunyar, designed the nine Baroque altarpieces and the three-story high triptych in the church that we are going to see. In 1810 the pink dome was added to the tower and the lighthouse became a bell and clock tower."

"I always wondered why tourists weren't allowed in the tower. It would normally seem like the perfect tourist attraction. Isn't it safe any longer?"

"Hopefully, we will be able to find out."

"You did pack the rope, right?" asked Chante.

"These days I would not leave home without it." He smiled that wide grin that caused Chante's heart to swell with love for him. Finally at 9:05 the priest arrived. He unlocked the front doors, went inside to turn on some lights, and then left again to go back home for his second cup of morning coffee and the paper. There was no morning service as in the off-season Mass was only celebrated in the early evening.

Lucien and Chante got up from their bench and meandered over to the church, nonchalantly, hand-in-hand.

Chapter 22

Lucien and Chante entered the church. Its wide arched door swung in easily, but certainly not quietly. They entered and walked up the center aisle between the long wooden benches that divided the room. It was fairly dark, lit only by some electric lights on the pillars, but there was also a lighted candle at each chapel. The candles helped to alleviate the gloomy feel of the expansive room and added a spark of warmth to the otherwise chilly space.

Chante had not been in the church since she first arrived five years ago. She appreciated good art, but icons were not of particular interest to her so she was never drawn back into the church. Lucien went right up to the front of the high altar and dug into his pocket for a one-euro coin. He inserted it into the light box to the left side of the main dais, and the entire front altar lit up and began to glow. Elaborate flourishes of gold gilt covered nearly every surface. The high altar was a concave curve that reached all the way to the ceiling and was divided into four lateral sections, one rising above the other.

On top of the dais of three steps from the church's wooden floor, a large oblong wooden altar was covered with a white embroidered cloth. Large candles in rounded brass stands rose at each end. Shining brass vases stood on pedestals to either side, but they were now empty. Later in the day they would be filled with fresh flowers before the evening service. Behind the altar, a façade of four-foot high golden painted arches and panels lined the base of the wall. On the next level up were two sets of statues on either side of the central stature of Mary rising to heaven. On the far left was Saint James the Major, holding a scallop shell, and then Saint Paul with a bald forehead, holding a sword. On the other side of Mary was Saint Andrew on a cross in the shape of an X. The fourth was Saint John the Evangelist with a book and chalice.

On the level above these figures were four more figures. On the far left was Saint Bartholomew with a knife, then Saint James the Minor with a bludgeon and palm frond. On the other side was Saint Philip with a sword, and Saint Matthew with a sword and book. On the next level up were five figures. On the left was Saint Thomas with an architect's square. Next to him was Saint Jude with a book. On the opposite side was Saint Simon, also with a book, and Saint Matthias with an axe. In the center was Saint Peter with his right arm holding up the papal cross. Then four more statues were squeezed in at the top, called Hope, Charity, Justice and Faith. Four large paintings were mounted between the saints on the second and third levels. On the higher level the two paintings were of local historical interest and showed two stone towers. Centrally topping this elegant Baroque-styled display was an artistic sun's rays, representing God.

Lucien pointed up. "Notice the two pictures of the towers. One represents the ancient pillar that used to stand on the hill where the fort is now, and the other represents the tower at Elme."

"Ah, now I know. There's a stone in the pavement outside the church also with these two towers. I always wondered what they represented. The entire altar is so beautiful."

"Look a little closer at the tower paintings. What do you see?"

"Hmm. Oh, I see. There are doorways cut into each painting. Why is that? It seems strange to do that to a painting."

"Yes, it does. Perhaps we will be able to find out, why?" Lucien moved to the chapel on the right. "Now come over here before the lights go out because we only have a two-minute window."

To the right was a lovely little chapel with each Saint's picture beautifully framed in white and gilded in gold.

"What is this chapel?" asked Chante.

"Saint Dominic and Saint Catherine are shown the Holy Rosary by the Virgin. There are also pictures depicting the Annunciation, the visitation, Christ's birth, his Presentation to the Temple, and the Assumption. It is this chapel that the priest enters to climb the twelve wooden stairs to the pulpit."

The stairs rose up and stood between this and the next chapel. Within this corner chapel against the front wall was a more modern wooden cabinet and behind it and to the right of it hung a rich burgundy velvet curtain. It was behind this curtain that Lucien imagined was a door, which would lead to the back of the high altar and eventually to the bell tower.

Just as they reached the curtain, the lights on the high altar went out. Lucien already had his hand on his flashlight and switched it on. Chante turned hers on too. Behind the curtain was a narrow wooden door that was locked. They both put on the cotton gloves they had left over from the box and satchel operation. Lucien handed Chante his flashlight to free his hands while he reached into his pocket and took out his lock-picking tools. He was quick. It took only one minute to hear the lock click, and with a push the door swung open.

They stood in a small wooden alcove and directed the beams upward to reveal narrow wooden stairs rising to a second floor. Lucien pulled the door behind him almost to a close, so they could exit when ready. He did not want them to be locked in like they had been at the castle. It was dark, as no windows from the outside were on this portion of the church wall. It was also quite chilly, so Chante was glad she was wearing a jacket. The stairs creaked with every step. They were obviously quite old. Lucien hoped that they could not be heard by anyone entering the church. At the top of the stairs was a six-by-six foot landing. Just as they reached the top of the stairs they heard the front door of the church open and then shut.

They froze where they stood and immediately turned off their flashlights and waited. They did not hear anyone approach the high altar, but they did hear a coin drop in the high altar light box. Then they noticed to their immediate left, thin slivers of light coming through the back of the high altar. It had to be where those cuts were around the two tower paintings. They stood there waiting for the two minutes to be up and the light to go off again. Lucien held Chante's arm while waiting in the darkness. Both focused on listening for the sound of someone walking in the church. A few minutes later they heard the sound of the front door closing.

They turned their flashlights back on and shined them on the back of the high altar. Wooden planking lay all along the back of the high altar in a narrow hallway about a yard wide. To its right was a plaster wall rising to an open-beamed ceiling with the roof structure showing. Another wall stood perpendicular to the first and went to the rear of the building about ten feet back. In the center of that wall they found the outline of a door with a small wooden handle. Lucien gently pushed on it and it swung in with a small creak. It opened into a long narrow room with lockers lining the left side.

"Jackpot," whispered Chante.

They shined their flashlights back and forth along the floor. To their right they saw the base of another door. They made a note to check it out later.

"That has to be the way to the clock tower," whispered Lucien, "but I'll bet what we need to find is somewhere in these lockers."

There were eight six-foot tall old military metal cabinets, all dark gray and completely covered in dust. Instead of a padlock usually found on lockers such as these, each had been fitted with a small rim cylinder built into the doors. Lucien checked the first one and it was locked. He once again went into his jacket for his picks. He turned to Chante after he got the first one open.

Chante was already grabbing the handle to open the first cabinet. "Now, what are we looking for?"

Lucien withdrew his phone from the inside pocket of his jacket. He opened it to the picture he had taken of the page Alerion had found in the storage file.

The first cabinet did not have any files that matched the list. They were plainly marked with church business and carefully stapled together. These pages were worn, with white order lists and yellow invoice sheets dating from 1950 through 1959. The second cabinet had the same from 1960 to 1971. Apparently fewer orders were made.

"These just seem to be old business files. But I might need to open all the lockers to be sure. This could take a while."

The third cabinet had files dating from 1972 to 1985. Even fewer items had been ordered. The fourth one had files dating from 1986 to 2000. It seems church business was waning, and here these type of files came to an end. Perhaps the priest had the newer files at his home. In the fifth cabinet were files of baptisms, confirmations, weddings, and funerals of church members listed by each year they had been performed. They began in 1949 and continued into the sixth cabinet. Chante and Lucien were becoming frustrated.

"Do you ever get the feeling that if one just worked backwards, from the bottom of the pile instead of the top, that one might find what they want sooner?"

In the seventh cabinet were letters posted between the various church priests and other parish ministers located throughout France, but none seemed to bear a date earlier than 1949 or had any numbers or letters that matched the list. In the eighth and last cabinet, Lucien found something more interesting. It contained what he could only imagine to be copies of the 300 sermons written by Saint Vincent Ferrier in Catalan, and his treatise on spiritual life. But there was nothing in these files that had number and letter headings.

Lucien looked at his watch. It had taken them about forty-five minutes to go through the eight file cabinets and they had not found what they were looking for.

"Okay, there's only one place left to look and that's in the tower." So they carefully fitted the files back into the last cabinet as they had found them, and Lucien did his best to trip the tumblers back, to a locking position.

They turned to the door on the wall behind them. It was locked, of course. This lock however was not a key lock, but a standard combination padlock that uses a three-digit numerical combination with 39 ticks.

"Uh-oh, this is one type of lock that a set of pin and tumbler lock picks cannot open. In this case they are useless."

Chante stood there feeling rather helpless and shaking her head. "I don't see how we will be able to open this without the right combination, because I heard once that there are over 64,000 possible numbered combinations to a 39 digit master lock."

"Not necessarily. There is a way to reduce that number greatly."

"What do you mean? How do you do that?"

Lucien took the small notepad and pen from his chest pocket and handed them to Chante. "I'm going to show you. I've got very sensitive fingers. I think I can handle this."

"Yes you do." Chante smiled and Lucien returned the smile.

"No, really. Your job is to hold the light on the lock and then to write down the numbers that I tell you."

"You're kidding me, right? We could be here all day."

"I guarantee you that it will take less than fifteen minutes."

"Wow, I wish I had known this trick in school. I was forever forgetting my locker combination." She took the paper and pen and focused the beam of light on the lock.

Lucien took the lock in hand and turned the dial a few times to see how it felt. Then he turned it to zero and then to three, pulled the clamp hard and moved the dial left and then to the right only a small amount. It seemed to click between 1 and 2. "Okay, here's the first number. Write down 1.5. Then Lucien slowly continued around the dial and felt thirteen more clicks that produced thirteen more numbers. Some were a whole number and some were a half number, until he got back to zero.

"Now cross out all of the half numbers and tell me what you get."

Chante did so and then read the remaining numbers to him. "We are left with 4, 14, 15, 24, and 34."

Lucien smiled. "Okay, now take away all the numbers that have the same last digit. That is, all the ones with a four and we are left with 15. That's going to be the third number in the combination. We just eliminated 22,000 tries. That was the easy part, now let's continue. We will now take that number and divide it by four."

"Okay, but that doesn't divide equally. It divides into three with three left over."

"No that's good. What we want is the remainder, which is the number three. So now we begin with three and add four to each number around the dial until we get to 39, the last number on the lock. So the first one is three plus four, which is seven, four more is eleven, and so forth. Now write them all down."

Chante did and came up with 7, 11, 15, 19, 23, 27, 31, 35 and 39.

"Good, then one of those is the possible first number. Now we need to find the second number. There's a little formula for this. We have to change the first number. So if it had been a zero it now becomes 2. If it had been a 1 it becomes 3, if it was a 2 it becomes zero, but since our remainder was a 3, we change it to 1. So here we go. One plus three equals four. Now continue and write them all down."

Chante did and came up with 4, 8, 12, 16, 20, 24, 28, 32, and 36.

"Great, so our first number is one of the numbers from the first list, the second number is one from our second list, and the last number is 15. So that cuts your 64,000 possibilities down to less than 100 combinations."

"That's amazing! But does it work?"

"Let's see. Start calling out the combinations and I'll try each combination. Cross out the ones that don't work. One is sure to be it."

They did so, but it still was no small task and took a while. On their 39th try they hit the right combination with 23-16-15. The lock opened easily and they both turned, beaming at each other. Lucien slipped off the lock, hung it on the latch and opened the door.

They shined their flashlights in and could see a small platform with building stones on the inside wall of stairs. They wound up to the left and down to the right, but which way to go?

"I see some light above so I'm willing to bet that's the way the person goes who needs to adjust the clock. I doubt we go down as with each level down the moistness from the water outside increases. So let's go up and see what we can find." Lucien carefully closed the door behind them.

The steps were very narrow so they had to go up single file. At one complete turn of the stair they came to a small platform and on the left wall was the back of the clock. It was much larger than they expected, being this close to it. An odd-looking type of key hung to the left, presumably for adjusting the time. The stairs continued, so they wound around another complete circle and came to a larger platform with windows that looked out over the bay, the town, and two points to sea. They were sealed with glass and recessed into the room, most likely so that wind and rain could not come in and ruin the mechanism of the clock a floor below. There was one more turn of the stairs and they found themselves on a wooden platform that spanned the room with four smaller recessed windows evenly spaced around the tower. Above them was an open network of wooden crossbeams that held the upper red brick cap securely in place. There was no possible place for storage of any kind.

"I don't understand." Lucien shook his head. "I would have thought for sure that the records would be kept up here."

Chante felt a little more realistic. "Lucien, it is very possible that the records were moved again and are no longer in the church. However, we have one more possibility, down."

"You're right, we might as well check it out."

They slowly descended, holding on to the cold stones of the wall as they went, past the door they had originally entered, and continued to descend. Two spiral circles down they came to another locked wooden door, which had a metal bar across it held by two metal loops, and a sign that read, "Danger. Do not enter."

Lucien was not surprised. "I don't know about you, but I have never run across so many locked doors in my life. I'm getting rather tired of them."

"I think that is the point. It deters thieves."

"You're right of course. At least this is a lock that can be picked, but that sign is rather disheartening. Although one thing puzzles me, if the base of the tower is so dangerous, then it is unlikely that anything is stored there. We'll have to be extremely careful. The floor could be weak."

Chante smiled, "We have to check it out anyway, to eliminate all possibilities."

The bar across the door only looked to be a deterrent. It easily slipped out to one side, and they leaned it up against the wall. One more time, Lucien pulled out his lock picks and went to work. He had used his lock picks more times in the last two weeks than he had in his entire life, and he was hoping it would be close to his last. They had served of late as the handiest tools that he owned, that and rope.

The lock was a little rusty, but he had not brought another can of de-rust, so it took longer than he wanted, but the pins eventually tumbled in a line and the lock opened. They entered a small dark round room that had a solid floor. It appeared to be made of steel and sheet metal, and had iron bars across the structure. Lucien was surprised to see this much metal, but it also made sense. Some reinforcement of the tower must have been necessary or the tower would have fallen long ago. At least the mystery of how the tower had been stabilized was now known.

Chante and Lucien saw another door on the opposite side of the room. They looked at each other in surprise and carefully walked over to it. There was no lock, just a wooden handle that they pulled open. Lucien made a mental calculation.

"I think we are headed back into a lower part of the church, only accessed from the tower."

They entered a small passage, and after six feet, descended stone steps to the left. It opened into a long narrow room, running the length of the building, right below the room with the metal cabinets. Their flashlights shone along the floor of the long empty space, heavy with dust, and at the far end they saw a large covered mound.

Chapter 23

By the time Chante and Lucien reached the end of the long church hall, the mound looked larger than they expected. A huge carpet was folded over it, and it was covering something of substantial size. The dust on the floor and on the carpet was thick. It was obvious that no one had been in this room for a good many years. Chante told Lucien to stand back as she was going to dust off the top of the carpet to see what they were looking at. She took off her wool cap and began to beat the carpet briskly. Lucien took refuge, turning away from the flying dust. Then they both stood back and waited for the remaining particles to settle, their flashlights shining through a dusty universe.

When most of it had settled Lucien gave the carpet a closer look with his flashlight and once again whispered, fearing that his voice might be heard now that the church proper was just on the other side of the wall. "It looks like a Turkish carpet."

Chante came closer, cast her eye over the design and felt the nap. She saw the knots on the underside in a corner piece and whispered back. "It looks Turkish because that's the style, but I believe it is French."

Together they lifted a fold and another to partially open it up.

"Look at all these baskets of flowers on a dark blue background. There are deep borders, and this looks to be a partial mythological scene going to the other side. I would truly be shocked if it was, but it looks like a Pierre-Josse Perrot.

Lucien had an appreciation for art history, but could not place the name. Chante could tell by his silence.

"Perrot was a famous carpet designer in the 1800s known for his Savonnerie, manufactured Persian-looking carpets. He made them for Louis XIV, with more than a hundred masterpieces. There are several in the Louvre."

"I imagine his works were hard to get and they had great value, even in his own time. Someone obviously hid it away in here so the Germans would not take it. Chante, do you think you can help me slide the carpet on to the floor so we can see what is hiding underneath it?"

Chante gave him a bright smile. "Please, let's."

They set their flashlights along the floor and then each took a corner of the carpet and heaved it with great effort. Eventually it slid to one side, revealing a hefty dark leather and iron trunk with a heavy clasp.

"Another trunk? This is crazy, though it doesn't look nearly as old as the one in the cave, but still, it must have been here for a long time if we are to judge by the amount of dust in this room."

"Lucien, this has to be what we are looking for. Let's open it."

Chante moved to the side and grasped the trunk lid with both hands. Lucien followed and took the other side. It felt like déjà vu opening another trunk. This one was also stiff and heavy, but because it had been protected from the elements, opened rather silently. Inside were two small metal cabinets with a metal handle on top of each. They looked positively dwarfed in the huge hollow of the chest.

Lucien lifted them out and set them on the floor next to the trunk. Rocking the front lever of both boxes, he opened the lids to reveal old files of papers. At once he saw that they were identified with numbers and letters.

"At last!"

Lucien once again turned on his phone and scrolled to the list with all the numbers and letters. It began with 118-1VD, and followed with 001-1050RAR, 1012-1163-CC, 1209-1229-CA, 1100-1207RT, 1184-1230-IEIP, 1262-1343-RM, 1344-RA, 1493-ESP, 1642-1659-RF, and 1668-V-H, among others.

Lucien opened up the first file folder. It had coordinates, maps, and sectioned topographical displays. At last he saw the wording "Via Domitia". It was hard to keep his voice to a whisper with his excitement.

"This is a file of maps of the Via Domitia, built by the Romans. This is incredible! There is documentation here on the road from Italy down through southern France and into Spain." Then he looked at the file name and nodded. "Oh, I get it. The file name is 118-1VD. The road was begun in 118 BCE and finished in 1 CE, and the VD is Via Domitia. So the numbers are years and the letters are abbreviations for the subject."

Lucien took out the next file. It was marked 001-005RAR. When he opened it, there were sketches of Roman plaques and scrolls with Latin writing, along with pages of text in French identifying the translations as *Redaction Agricole Romaine*, or Roman Agricultural writing, which was what the RAR stood for.

"This is a description of how the ancient Romans farmed. They use the ancient term *iugerum*, which is about 2/3rds of an acre or a quarter of a hectare. Here is a list of vineyards and these are property deeds of ancient vintners."

Lucien went to reach for the next file and then they both heard it: a heavy "thwak" on the floor above them.

They froze. Someone was above them where they had just been.

Lucien whispered close to Chante's ear. "Let's get these files into the backpack and we will look at them later. Then we return the metal cabinets to the chest. We need to get out of here."

Chante looked at him with her eyes wide. "We won't be able to move the carpet back to the way it was. It's too heavy. And if we go back the same way we came we will run into whomever it is. Knowing what happened to your father I'd rather not do that."

"We'll look for another way out," Lucien assured her.

They worked as quickly and as quietly as they could without talking. They got all the files into the backpack and carefully placed the metal file canisters back into the trunk. Then they moved to either side of the trunk and carefully, as quietly as possible, let the trunk close back into place. The space was already greatly altered due to the amount of dust that had been moved and imprinted upon. They would not be able to hide the fact that someone had been there, but they did the best that they could. Chante was concerned about their footprints, so she decided to further sacrifice her wool cap and with her foot used it as a dust mop to weave back and forth across the floor, erasing their prints.

While she was doing that, Lucien shined his flashlight along the back of the church wall, searching for any exit. At the end where they had entered the long room, he found a square cutout in the wood in the wall. It was only two feet high and wide, but it was intriguing. He wondered what it was for or where it might lead. He lightly pressed the top of the panel and it swung in and up. Lucien shined his flashlight and looked inside. Then he turned and smiled at Chante. He was once again thankful for their good luck in getting out of crazy situations. By then Chante had mopped the dust all the way to the entry stairs, then made her way to Lucien.

"Here," he said, "this seems to be a way back into the church. I think it might actually have been a priest's hole. In case there was trouble, the priest could hide in here."

Lucien shined his light inside to see the curve of the back of the altar at its base. They had found an alternate exit from behind the altar, on the side opposite from where they had entered. It was then that Lucien saw a cut in the interior wall to the right, with a wooden handle. As long as it could hide them, even briefly, they would be out of harm's way. And if it actually went somewhere, that somewhere begged for investigation. He crawled in and Chante followed him. He told her to close the panel behind her and she did. Lucien crawled to the right, pulled on the wooden handle and shined his light in. The answer was simple, elegant, and very welcoming. He crawled through the hole, moved something aside, and stepped on to a soft carpet. Chante followed and inhaled with a small surprise.

They had just entered the vestry behind a clothes rack. Priest's robes were hanging on hangers and hooks. A mirror and bench were there for the priest to change into ecclesiastical attire. A wooden wardrobe stood against one wall and in it various robes hung over wide-padded hangers, covered in clear plastic bags. These robes were apparently worn on special occasions. The room was also obviously used for storage, as some broken wooden picture frames were leaning against a wall, and a wash bucket and mop stood in one corner. They scanned the small room and found the special door used by the priest to walk out on to the dais. They both placed their ears to the door. If they opened the door at the wrong time, they would be caught exiting this private chamber. They waited a minute more, heard nothing, and then carefully edged the door open. Lucien saw all was clear, so he grabbed Chante's hand. They quickly walked out and quietly shut the door behind them. Then they stepped off the dais and tiptoed off to the right, to the next chapel, the Altar of the Blessed Sacrament, which shared the wall with the vestry. They nearly ran all the way down the side aisle to the back of the church. They opened and shut the large church door behind them quietly, welcoming in a deep breath of clear cold sea air.

Lucien looked at his watch. It was 10:50 am. They carefully scanned the scant crowd outside, but did not notice anyone looking suspicious or following them. It was a quick walk back to Chante's apartment. When they arrived, Lucien opened the backpack and pulled out the bundle of files on to the dining table. The files were five inches deep. He laid them out in order, because he had now figured out what the sequence was. He picked up the first file again and studied the map with its coordinates and pictures of the ancient Roman Via Domitia. The file also included a probable route that Heracles had taken, something he was surprised to see, due to the mythical nature of his adventures; and there was a map of the route of Hannibal's trudge from Hispania to Italy.

All Lucien could remember from his studies was that the road was named after the Roman Proconsul, Gnaeus Domitius Ahenobarbus, which was where the name Domitia came from. Chante turned on her computer and they learned more about this famous road, following a brief Internet search.

They read further about the junction of the Via Domitia and the Via Augusta at the Trophy of Pompey, located just twenty minutes from Collioure. There were also remains of Roman bridges, which they were surprised to learn no longer existed due to German bombing, but here were photographs from when the bridges still stood. The file went on and contained a list of survey and archeological teams that had worked in different areas along the road. A list of items found at different sites was listed, including where they were housed, whether at a museum, university exhibit, or storage facility. But no date after 1941 was listed.

He handed the file to Chante, who was reading more on the road, and he picked up the next file marked 001-1050RAR. This was about ancient Roman farming. There were several pages with a list of vineyards by owner's name, listing total amount of hectares and production yields through the years. Several copies of various property deeds in Collioure were included, such as the Dominican Church, the previous fort, the church of Angels, four large local landowners, and the fishing cooperative. The file also included sketches of Roman plaques and scrolls with Catalan writing that had once been attached to local buildings. He thought he recognized the building in one black and white photograph, but he knew that a plaque no longer was on that wall. So these files were like little time capsules of information showing how things had been prior to the war. Perhaps they had been taken so that if the building was bombed, they would have a picture to go by for rebuilding purposes. He supposed that some ruler at the Chateau Royal demanded that an accurate historical record be kept, like how a family collects photos in an album, and digital photos on phones and computers.

He handed that file on to Chante and picked up the next one, which had on its file tab 1012-1163-CC. When he opened it he realized that the CC must have stood for Crusade de Cathar. Chante remembered some of their history from the book she had checked out of the library.

She shared her recent knowledge with the aptitude of a star pupil.

"The Cathars were a Christian dualist movement believing in the idea of two principles, one good and the other evil. They called themselves *Bons Hommes* or 'Good Men'. To them, an evil god had created the world of sin and it inhabited the human body. They considered themselves cursed and could not be resurrected until salvation was achieved through a ritual called the *consolamentum*." Then she turned to Lucien, "Do you think that is where the Hermitage de Consolation got its name?" He wasn't sure.

There were also descriptions of other religious groups that influenced the Cathars, from the Marcionites to the Manichaeans, the Bogomists to the Paulicians, and the Christian Gnostics. These religious groups had largely dualist beliefs, also believing in good versus evil. A timeline of Cathar history was also included. From their first known place of residence in Limousin, France in 1012, to a list of all the councils, and the Catholic churches that condemned them. There was also a list of the burnings in Toulouse, Charoux, Cologne, Goslar, Liège, Reims, Tours, Lombez, Vézelay, Béziers, Montpellier, Troyes, and Montségur, among others.

One paper with a subtitle of 1208, gave information on Pope Innocent IIIs Cathar Crusade. Arnaud Amaury, a Cistercian Abbot from the Abbey of Cîteaux, was then in command. At the time, thousands of Crusaders had joined the ranks for a reserved seat in heaven, and to be rewarded with whatever available plunders might come their way. Consequently, Béziers and Carcassonne were sacked. Chante also remembered the famous saying from one of Amaury's men, when he asked how to tell a Cathar from a Catholic in the fight? Amaury replied, "Kill them all, the

Lord will recognize His own." Over 7,000 people, from the very young to the very old, were massacred.

The next file was labeled 1209-1229-CA. When he opened this file Lucien realized that CA stood for *Croisade Albigeoise*. Among its maps of troop movements, a list of attacked strongholds, and the crusades timeline, was a copy of the famous historical chronicles about the Albigensian Crusade by Peter of Vau de Cernay (1212-1218). He was known to be Catholic, but wrote more objectively about Cathar beliefs. There was also a copy of the *Song of the Cathar Wars* by William of Tudele (1213). Information online let them know that William's description is one of the three main and most complete narrative sources on the wars against the Albigensians.

Lucien again passed this file on to Chante for review. The following file was labeled 1100-1207RT. When he opened the file the first word he recognized was "Templier" for Templars, and a map of how their residence sat within the Castle Royal. The RT stood for *Résidence des Templiers*. There was a list of local land holdings of the Templars, naming several wineries, commanderies, and forts. He scanned the list to see what might be close, and saw that there were dozens of sites within fifty miles. One that caught his eye was Mas Déu, which they had already explored.

The next file was labeled 1184-1230-IEIP. It appeared to be historical documentation on the Episcopal and Papal Inquisitions. It documented the process called *accusatio*, in which one person accuses another of a crime, and an *inquisitio*, who judges the case. Several cases were outlined with dates, but they were copied from an earlier document. Then there was a list of dates of the different inquisitions with notes to see other files for the 15th and 16th century inquisitions. He looked ahead and sure enough, there was a file labeled IM (*Inquisition Medieval*),

IESP (*Inquisition de Espania*) at the end of the 14th century, and IP (*Inquisition Portuguese*) in the mid-1500s. It also included a page on inquisitorial procedures, adding that a Grand Inquisitor headed each inquisition after 1200. There were also files on the Protestant Reformation, the Catholic Counter-Reformation, and the witch trials through the mid 1800s. What was chilling was the list of Grand Inquisitors from 1483 to 1820.

There were files labeled 1262-1343-RM (*Roi de Majorca*), which contained information on the Kings of Majorca when those rulers were at the chateau. There was another labeled 1344-RA for when the King of Aragon was ruling. There was a file that read 1493-ESP, which had to be when Collioure was part of Spain. Another file had on it 1642-1659-RF, which appeared to be when the French took up residence at the chateau. The next one was labeled 1668-V-H when Vauban had his builder, Hillaire, carry out his building plans all over southern France. Lucien knew this was when Fort Elmo and the fort on Cape Bear were built. It was this file that captured Lucien's attention. Was there any mention of tunnels? He scanned carefully through this file searching for anything that would give him architectural information above and below the ground. Nearing the end of the file he came to a sheet that caught him by surprise.

"Chante, look at this! It's a geographical sketch of the chateau façade and the defense wall that once linked the chateau to the fort. Look, below. Don't those horizontal partially shaded lines look like tunnels?" No key identified what they were looking at, but because of their unique knowledge they knew what they were.

Chante put down the file she was reading and with her finger traced one of the lines from the fort to the chateau.

"That must be the tunnel that you and Alerion found. Look how it goes right across the river to the northwest tower. And, here is one that goes right through the old town and out to that edge of the coast. That's the one we found that went to the flooded room. "

"Yes, but look at all these other short lines. There is even one that goes to the church. But some don't lead anywhere. What in the world are they for? I see six other short lines, but they don't seem to link with anything, or so it appears on this map."

"Maybe these smaller spaces were for storage of goods, ammunition depots, or simply wine cellars." Chante could not help but shake her head in wonder. "This means that these tunnels have been here for at least 400 years! How could they possibly have lasted?"

Lucien smiled and readily agreed. "I know! I've gained a new reverence for those old wooden beams. I'm guessing that the results from the wooden slivers that we sent in for testing should confirm this dating. I think the tunnels have lasted because they were mostly sealed up. Moisture is a destroyer, as we saw with the rusted doors and what it does to metal locks and hinges, but when little moisture is present there is better preservation. In the tunnel that ended at the sea there was a great deal of sand on the ground. That sand probably pulled the moisture in like a wick. I'm sure the wood also absorbed some moisture, but the ground got most of it. Remember how worn away the feet of the chest were? We need to get these files into the safe deposit at the bank."

Chante agreed and added, "And with this additional history that we've found it means that I now have a rich historical tapestry from which to write a solid article on the history of the Chateau!"

Lucien turned to Chante. "As soon as we finish with the bank tomorrow, I want to go back to the church and get into the back of it again. I need to close and lock several doors."

It was nearly midnight by the time they had both gone through all the files several times and discussed them. Their heads were spinning with the information. It was almost too much to take in. They felt they needed sleep to let it all settle.

Chapter 24

That same Sunday morning, Alerion was up early and inside the Brasserie de la Marine at the end of the quay for a cup of coffee and croissant. Once he had seen the light on at Chante's the evening before, he knew where they would be for the night. He was growing tired of the escapade anyway. It was depressing. He wanted to end it. It had been two weeks and it was obvious that Lucien was spending all of his free time with his new girlfriend. He hadn't noticed anything peculiar, unusual, or suspicious, aside from the fact that they had gone into the Chateau twice, as far as he was aware. Clearly, Chante and Lucien were getting on in their relationship. He had to laugh at how Lucien had said, 'but you will like her when you meet her.' He had seen more of her than he cared to, and had less personal time with Lucien in their off hours than he wanted to admit.

Alerion thought about their friendship. He first met Lucien when they attended the commando kick-training course at the fort, four years before. Then, Lucien had recently become a sergeant. Alerion had fallen in love with the area and a year later he applied for a post at the fort in Collioure. Since he had met Lucien and worked with him, he had come to find him a good-hearted man, if not a bit sad. The loss of his mother at an early age had left Lucien feeling at a disadvantage around women. He was too self-conscious. Alerion knew that Lucien had experienced a distinct lack of female company because of it. None of the relationships with women whom Lucien had met in

Collioure had developed into anything beyond acquaintance. Lucien had also shared his feelings of worry about his father. Now, with Gervais' latest fall, Lucien was probably worried even more.

It had also become obvious to Alerion that Lucien was experiencing a growing restlessness. He could see that Lucien was dedicated, but military service just did not seem to suit his character. Alerion saw the adventurer in Lucien, but not the soldier persona that usually comes with the job. Lucien was a quick thinker, and quite capable of pulling more than his own weight. Even though Lucien was his superior, they had become good friends, and Alerion felt comfortable talking with him. Lucien had respectfully supported him through two or three misadventures with women, and in storms around the colonel. Lucien could be a real taskmaster, but he also pushed him to accomplish more, and he knew it would only make him a better soldier and person. Alerion was almost five years younger, but they enjoyed their time together, especially over a good glass of wine. A true brotherly kinship had formed between them of the type that sometimes can form between soldiers, and Alerion was thankful for it. It made his life at the fort more enjoyable.

Thinking about Lucien in the military made him think about his own life. Alerion was glad that he was not on active maneuvers. He had done some overseas work, as every soldier had to mission out at one time or another, but it suited him to be stationed here in this beautiful village, with beautiful women coming in every high season, and his mother only an hour away. However, aside from odd jobs in his early twenties, he had done nothing with his life but work for the military. He enjoyed it, but like Lucien, he was not keen on fighting. Collioure was a great place to work and live. This area, surrounded by vineyards, had so appealed to him that he had become a real wine aficionado. Someday he would do something with the money he had inherited from his father. Perhaps one day he would buy some land and grow grapes. But for now he was stationed here and the work was interesting enough.

It was stressful for him to think of Lucien as a target to watch and report on. The colonel obviously wanted him watched for some reason, though he had not shared why. But it seemed a prudent procedure for a French soldier being courted by an overly attentive American woman. "Swallows," or female agents, had to be guarded against. The colonel also knew something was up in the basement. Instead of acting as an agent keeping an eye on his best friend, Alerion had come to think of himself more as a protecting angel. But who would watch over him?

Thinking of this reminded him that lately he was experiencing the odd feeling that he was being followed himself. It was only a subtle sensation at the back of the collar that told him something was up, but he didn't know what it could be. He wondered if the colonel was having *him* followed. He had not seen anyone specifically shadowing him, but he could feel eyes upon him. He would be walking through town at night and then someone would quickly turn their head away, pull down the brim on their hat, duck into a shop, or walk off in a different direction to blend into a crowd. Or maybe it was his own guilty conscious for actually agreeing to follow his friend and superior. It seemed so odd to being doing so. The colonel definitely had his suspicions about something, but he wasn't letting him in on it. It seemed more precautionary, than anything else.

Enlisted men generally did not become pals with their superiors, but he and Lucien seemed to be the exception. The recent experience in the tunnel, the cave-in and his resultant rescue, then concealing their explorations, had all been more stressful than he expected. Alerion knew full well that because of their friendship, Lucien had been able to con him into breaking into the trapdoor and that made him an accomplice. He had fully cooperated too, by buying tools and surreptitiously smuggling them into the fort. They had trespassed and damaged private property, hidden the evidence, and then lied about it all. But there was no way he was telling the colonel anything about *that* escapade.

He was thinking that on Monday he would tell Lucien about the colonel's orders to follow him, and that he wasn't going to do it anymore. He would say that his cover was blown because Lucien had caught him. He was pretty sure there was no danger, and he'd seen nothing that appeared to be a problem. Lucien was simply a man courting a woman and was obviously in love. All Alerion had with Lucien was friendship, and that was worth holding on to. He wanted to be honest with him. He had not said anything to the colonel about finding that file of numbers and letters in the storage room. Besides, he didn't find it until late Friday afternoon and the colonel had already left for the day. On Monday he would ask to be removed from the job of following Lucien, since he was just acting like a man in love. Frenchmen have a special camaraderie when it comes to understanding the pursuit and trial of gaining a woman's trust and love. The colonel would surely understand. Besides, the ACE program was less than a week away and would keep Lucien busy.

Staring out to sea on this gray foggy day, he began to wonder what he should do differently in the future. Then he spied Lucien and Chante at the end of the bay near the church sitting on a bench with their backs to him. He had not considered that Lucien would have such an early rendezvous with her. He couldn't see much of her as she had on a woolen hat, which partially hid her face, but he knew it was Chante. Then he watched them get up and walk to the church. Alerion immediately got a gut feeling and stood up, knowing what had happened. Lucien had turned right around and told Chante about the file he had found with the numbered and lettered listings! It had been way too much of a coincidence to visit the church so soon. He watched them casually stroll to the entrance of the church, where Lucien opened the door for her. To anyone watching, they looked like every other couple visiting the church on a Sunday morning, but he knew they had a specific objective.

As long as they were in the church he would know where they were. As long as he was sitting here he could claim that he was following his assignment. But now he was a little angry with Lucien. He ordered another coffee. A half hour went by and they did not emerge. A middle-aged woman went in with an arm full of flowers and came out five minutes later. Now he was perplexed. Perhaps they had found something. He kept looking at his watch. Another ten minutes went by and still they had not come out. A part of him was beginning to worry. What if they had gotten caught where they shouldn't be, or fallen down in the tower? What was taking them so long? After they had been in the church for forty-five minutes he could not stand it any longer. He got up, paid the bill, quickly ran to the WC and then walked quickly to the church.

He entered the church and scanned the partially darkened room, but did not see Chante or Lucien, or anyone else for that matter. It was eerily silent inside. Because it was a fairly gloomy morning the high windows were little help for light. The electric sconces on the pillars were on, and he noticed that the priest must have lit a candle at each chapel. It was Sunday, so visitors would come and light more candles to brightened the darker chapels. Only when a tourist placed a euro into each chapel's box did the church grow warmer with the artificial light.

Alerion walked slowly up the middle aisle and looked to the chapels on either side, but did not see them. He knew Chante and Lucien had to be in there somewhere, as he had not seen them come out. He was about to actually start looking more closely into each chapel and behind every curtain, when the church doors opened at the back of the room and someone walked in. He quickly sat down in the front row on the left side. He didn't want to get caught looking behind curtains where he should not be. After a few moments he rose and walked to the left, past the high altar to the eighth chapel next to the vestry. He paused, then moved at a slow pace to the ninth and tenth chapels, as if he were a tourist slowly looking at the art, and then skipped the last two to leave.

When he reached the back of the room and stepped through the entry, he pretended to leave by opening the door, but then turned to look back toward the front. He would simply wait for this one person to leave. When he looked in to see where the person was, he saw a man wearing a dark blue coat and a mariner's cap. Something seemed very suspicious about his movements. The man was looking very carefully into each chapel with a less than religious manner about him. He was definitely searching for something, lifting altar cloths and pulling back curtains. Alerion was going to wait until this person had left and then go back into the church, but to see someone do exactly what he was about to do was unnerving. At that point the front doors swung open and an older couple came in. He took the opportunity to exit. He went past them quickly. The sound of the door must have surprised the man inside, for he stopped searching and pretended to be interested in a chapel.

Alerion briskly walked out past the nearby café. He decided to slip into a ceramics shop and made his way toward the back of the interior. He made a pretext of examining colorful tiles, which gave him an excellent view of the church and the walkway along the bay. He held up one painted tile, and then another, waiting for the searcher to leave the church and walk by. A lot was going through his mind. Was this stranger following Chante and Lucien, or was the stranger following him? This could confirm that strange feeling he had been experiencing. The stranger was obviously searching for something. Could this man have known about the list that he had only just discovered and shown to Lucien? Could Chante be in partnership with this man, telling him about something hidden at the church? Had she played Lucien all along in the search for treasure, with a partner on the side?

Lucien, why did you have to go digging around at the fort? Why couldn't you just do your job? Who is this woman you have lost yourself to? Now Alerion wasn't sure he trusted her. Things did seem to have moved quickly for them. Who knows how much Lucien had told her? What Alerion was now sure of, is that Lucien had told her about the list of files in the church. That sparkle in Lucien's eyes when he had discovered the tunnel under the fort had started it all. Lucien had tried to hide it when the list appeared, but Alerion knew that gleam was of the same caliber. Hopefully, Alerion was wrong about Chante and she would prove to be a good influence and keep Lucien out of trouble. But who was this man that was trailing them, or him, and why?

He picked up the same tile with a leafy green color on it for the fifth time, as he was beginning to like it, but then he saw the man with the dark coat walk quickly by, his head sunken into his thick collared jacket and a wool scarf high up over his chin. Alerion put down the tile, stepped closer to the front of the shop, and watched the man walk around the curve of the boardwalk and disappear between two buildings. Alerion then quickly walked back to the church. The previous couple was just coming out when Alerion went in. He figured that Lucien and Chante had now been in the church for over an hour. Where could they be? Could they have passed him? He didn't think so, but he had lost track of them before.

Alerion hurried down the far right aisle to the only corner where he could imagine stairs might lead up to the tower. He pulled back the burgundy curtain on the far wall and saw the door slightly ajar. He thought to himself, 'you're slipping, Lucien. You should have shut and relocked the door behind you.' Or had the stranger opened it and then got scared away when the last couple had entered? Alerion opened up his phone and used the light to take him up the stairs. He got nearly to the top of the squeaky stairs when he heard the front door of the church open again. Then he realized that *he* had no way to lock the door below him, and even now with every step the squeak of the old wooden steps might be heard. So he froze. At first he was thinking it was probably just a tourist, but then what if it was the man in the coat doubling back? He should have waited longer at the ceramics shop. This was not the sort of thing he was trained for. He was not a spy, he was a paper pusher; sometimes a 'go fetch' private with some special skills, but this was not one of them.

After about a minute he was surprised when he heard a lot of chatter at the entrance to the church. A tour group had arrived and was being escorted by a guide. The guide began leading the group down the center aisle and describing the chapels to either side. Now he was confused. Had someone entered when the door opened previously? Did they leave when the tour group arrived, or were they now hiding in the church? The guide would not normally speak aloud unless the church appeared empty. It was obvious that the group was getting the full tour treatment. This might take a while.

While Alerion waited on the stairs, he did not know that in another part of the church, Chante and Lucien were descending to the lower floor of the tower. Finally, the group made its way to the high altar and made such a clatter, taking pictures and making comments that Alerion used their noise to hide the squeak of the stairs and made it to the top. Within a few more minutes the group had made its way around the church. In that time, Alerion found the door in the wall and went in to find the long line of lockers. Had Lucien seen these? He walked to the end of the row of the lockers and then the light on his phone went out. Rather than stroke it back on, he decided to stand in the dark and listen to see if he could hear where Lucien and Chante might have gone. What he did hear made him freeze against the wall. It was definitely the one sound he wished he had not heard, and that was the squeak of the stairs that he had just ascended. There was nowhere for him to go except to stand still against the wall, partially hidden behind the end of the row of lockers, in the dark.

Within a few seconds, he heard footsteps at the top of the stairs and coming down the hallway, but no light was visible. He had left the second door open. He heard the man quickly approaching under the cover of complete darkness. The stranger must have come directly toward him because it was all over in less than three seconds. He struck Alerion's head with a hard blow, and his body bent forward and hit the floor with a heavy thud. This is what Chante and Lucien heard on the floor below. The assailant took off his night-vision headgear, laid it down, and turned on his flashlight. He grabbed Alerion's arms and lifted him to a sitting position, leaning him against the last locker and the wall. He went through Alerion's pockets, pulled out his phone and turned it off. He removed Alerion's watch and put both in his own pocket. He tied Alerion's hands behind him to the metal feet of the last locker and tied a cloth over Alerion's mouth and around the back of his neck. Then he covered Alerion's head with a black hood so that when he awoke he would not be able to see who his assailant was.

When the perpetrator had finished, he refocused his light on the bank of file cabinets along the wall. There would be plenty of time to search each one and to question the soldier later. For now, there was nothing to do but explore while the church was open, and then come back later before the evening service with the one tool he needed. With Alerion's body secured, the stranger stood up and found the tower door conveniently unlocked. He went up to the top of the tower and then descended down, to find the lower door also unlocked. He walked the long narrow hall until he came to the trunk. He opened the trunk, found the inner metal files empty and cursed every saint in the church, on the other side of the wall. Then he swore an oath to Saint Erasmus, the Patron Saint of Sailors. He would soon get his hands on what he wanted, regardless of the obstacles.

Chapter 25

Alerion slowly came out of his unconscious state to find his head was throbbing painfully. What had happened? Where was he? He opened his eyes and only saw black. Then he felt the cloth tied against his mouth, the restriction in his arms, and the cold floor beneath him. He was feeling dizzy and that seemed to bring on some nausea. After some confused and panicked moments he forced himself to calm his breathing. Getting sick would definitely worsen his situation. He began to breathe slowly and then recalled what had happened before he was attacked. Now it was dead quiet in the room. He did his best to wriggle as much as he could to determine whether he could move, but he had been bound tightly. After some time he grew exhausted, his head hurt too much and there was a ringing in his ears, so he gave up. Someone would surely be back for him. For some time, he drifted in and out of a haze.

At one point he heard a door open and shut. Then he heard the Mass begin with the usual pomp of music and oration. Now he knew what time it was. It had to be about 5 o'clock, the hour when the Mass began in the fall and winter. Alerion wondered if he could yell with a cloth in his mouth, and he tried to do so. What he did not know was that his assailant sat nearby, waiting silently. When Alerion began to call out, despite the restriction around his mouth, the man hit him hard against the side of his head, which threw his head against the wall. He passed out again. No one would have heard him anyway over the music during the service. The man next to him waited, but he did not need to wait long. There were only fifteen attendees for Mass, and the ceremony was over by 5:45. At 6:10 the priest left and locked the front door of the church.

Sometime later, a high-pitched buzzing noise brought Alerion back to consciousness. His brain finally discerned a pattern to the noise: the sound of drilling, a shuffling of papers, the closing of a metal cabinet, and more drilling. He figured the noise must be attracting attention and someone would come. Lucien or someone would hear it. The man placed the drill bit into the locking mechanism on the next file's lock, filling the space with the sound of grinding metal. No one except the two occupants of the room could hear it. The church was closed, music played at the local café at dinnertime, and they were heavily bricked in, deep within the back walls of the church. No one outside could hear the noise.

Alerion lost count of the times the man drilled, but could tell the work was getting closer by the vibrations in the metal at his back. With every drilling, the ringing in his ears increased. At last he could see a small bit of light on floor through his head covering. The man picked up the drill and leaned into the lock on the last locker. The vibration set Alerion's teeth on edge. Who was this man? What did he want? Didn't he know that if Lucien had found the information it would no longer be here? The man shuffled more papers and slammed the last file at his back. The man paused and noticed Alerion's head move.

The stranger bent down and growled into his ear, "You are awake. Good. I've got some questions for you."

The man stood up to stare down at the black cloth covered head below him. He removed the covering from Alerion's head and undid the cloth at his mouth. Alerion stretched the edges of his mouth to bring his lips back to their normal shape. He realized that he was very thirsty.

He asked for water and the man gave him a drink from his small bottle of rum. This made Alerion choke, and each cough made his head hurt more. He looked up at the man before him, but his upper body was still in darkness. A flashlight lay to the side with its beam facing him, almost blinding him with its brightness. Then the low voice began again.

"Why are you following that man and woman?"

Alerion heard the question, but his head hurt and he wasn't sure he heard the question right. "Ser-geant Rey - nard?" he slurred, asking.

The voice came nearer his ear. "What did this Reynard find and where is it?"

Alerion was unsure what he meant. All he could think was that the "it" he was referring to must be the files from the list of letters and numbers. The man kicked him, which brought Alerion partially around. All Alerion could say was "Wha-at?" What do you wa-ant?" He heard himself slur and wondered why.

The man bent down on his haunches and considered his words. The voice was a growl, deep and menacing, asking where were the contents of the chest in the cave?

The tenor of his words hit Alerion's eardrum like a sledgehammer, and he actually began to imagine the weight of a sledgehammer on his head. He was baffled now more than ever. What chest? What cave? Had Lucien actually found something in some chest nearby? The man before him must not have found Lucien or Chante with the papers. Where were they?

After Alerion did not answer, the man slapped his left cheek. Several moments went by. All Alerion could do was moan. A second lump was forming on the back of his head and combined with the first one, the two were beginning to feel like a second head. The pain running from temple to temple was fierce and he could feel a trail of blood drip down the back of his neck. He tried hard to stay conscious. He heard sounds and they formed words, but the words did not make any sense. All he could do was listen. He heard in his head: Who are you? What do you want with me? What papers, what chest? But his words were garbled. His brain was spinning. Slowly his mind refocused. The man began again.

"How do you know Reynard? What's your connection with him?"

Alerion considered the question. Providing some information might prevent another violent response. His mouth was finally able to form some words, but they were slow. "We work to-geth-er. I'm his ass-is-tant."

"Why are you following him?" the stranger rasped.

"I'm keep-ing an eye on him."

The man considered the response and seemed to be thinking.

"Lean forward. I'm going to untie you from the lockers, but no sudden movements. I've got a knife so don't try anything." Not that Alerion had any strength left in him to do anything anyway. He was just this side of conscious. The man untied Alerion from the lockers and pulled Alerion's arms in front of him and retied the two wrists together. "Get to your feet."

Alerion was thankful to be released from the locker and he steadied himself against the wall. His shoulders ached, and his wrists stung with the sudden rush of blood to his hands, though it was only momentary. The man picked up his things on the floor and packed his bag. Alerion saw the drill and a pair of night-vision goggles. *That's* how he had approached him so quickly. Then the man slung the bag over his left shoulder. He grabbed Alerion by his left arm, pulled him up, and began to force him to move. Alerion was becoming more conscious now that the blood was flowing through his body.

"Where are you tak-ing me?" Why was it hard for him to speak?

"I'm getting you out of here and to a safe place." The man tried to assure him.

Alerion was now baffled. Who was this guy and what was he going to do with him? As they descended the stairs, the creaking of the steps was even louder than he remembered. The man had to actually support him. He was unsteady on his own. They got through the door at the base of the stairs and the burgundy curtain. He walked him to the back of the church. The church door was locked on the outside to keep anyone from entering, but a simple pushing of the door from the inside would open it. It was a safety measure that had been implemented several years back due to another church in France that had been locked with a couple inside. A fire had broken out from a fallen candle, but when they went to leave they were locked in and they burned with the church. Since then, all churches had this safety measure imposed.

The man opened the front door of the church and peered out. The restaurant closest to the church was nearly deserted, though music was playing. One couple was sitting at an outdoor table. A candle on the table lit up their faces, but they were mostly facing the water and the church was over their left shoulder. The man stepped back inside the church. He turned toward Alerion and wrapped the black cloth that had been over his head now over Alerion's bound wrists.

"We are going to walk out of the church and around the right side to the beach. We are two old friends out for an evening stroll. I'm going to have a knife at your side so don't try to yell or get away."

The man unsheathed a knife from his belt and showed it to him. Alerion took in a quick breath at the reality of its jagged wide blade and point. The man grabbed Alerion's right arm tightly. With the man's right hand gripping the knife he put it into Alerion's right pocket, the blade's point pressing against Alerion's side. Then the stranger opened the front door again, he gave a quick look, and pushed Alerion out, tucking up close to him.

Alerion was gaining some coordination from his disorientation. While in the church he would not have been able to walk on his own without leaning on the stranger. Now he was gaining his land legs and the night's cool air was reviving him. They quickly rounded the backside of the church, saw no one, and walked to the boardwalk away from town. He was leading Alerion down toward the water. Walking through the sand made their gait sluggish so the point of the knife came through the fabric and poked him more than once. Alerion did his best to keep that point away. At the end of the beach there was a small rowboat. When they reached it his abductor stopped.

"Now we are going to take a little ride. If you try to yell I will simply stab you. If you keep quiet you'll live. Now get in!"

Alerion grabbed the edge of the wooden hull with both of his hands and swung a leg in, and then the other. He sat on the boarded seat. The man tied Alerion's wrists to a metal loop on a locker between Alerion's legs. The stranger pushed the boat out into the water and then jumped in the boat. There was very little light at this end of the bay. The café at the end was closed this time of the year in the late season. For the first time, Alerion got a good frontal look at his abductor with the flash of the lighthouse lamp every few seconds. In those few moments he could see that the man's face was sun and wind-weathered. He had deep crow's feet beside his dark eyes, and his shoulders were broad beneath his heavy seaman's coat. He also wore heavy dark serge pants and worn out short black boots. His hair was black and unkempt, and the dark blue Mariner's cap was worn low on his forehead.

The stranger placed his knife on the seat beside him. It was enough of a deterrent to keep Alerion silent. The man began to row out of the bay and past the lighthouse. The bobbing boat made Alerion queasy again, but as they got past the swells the boat evened out. They were heading out around the corner of the headland to the south. Five minutes later he saw a boat tied up to a private dock. The boat was a Portofino 40. This type of boat was a more practical cruiser, ideally suited for coastal exploring, and it could be fast when not loaded down. His sea-faring host secured the rowboat to the cruiser with several floats between them. He untied Alerion's hands from the metal box below him and then loosened the rope around Alerion's wrists allowing a space between his hands. He wasn't sure why at first, but then he saw it was so he could grab each wrung of the boat's ladder. The man climbed the ladder and then turned around and growled at Alerion.

"Get out!"

Alerion looked up at the ladder and realized he was helpless to do anything but follow directions, at least for now. His head was in too much pain for immediate action. He was able to climb the ladder only by using as much concentration as he could. It was either that or fall overboard. He grabbed each wrung of the ladder with difficulty. The ladder rungs were wet, and the rowboat was bobbing. When he got to the top, the stranger flicked on the interior lights and pushed Alerion down three steps and into the open hatch. He pushed him further into a low bunk and told him to lie down. He tied his hands loosely to the brass fitting at the head of the bed and tied his feet loosely to the bottom bar. The man brought him a bucket and a cup of water.

"Here's some water and the bucket is to piss in, but you're not moving from this bed, at least for now."

"What are you going to do with me?" Alerion asked. Finally his slurring had ceased.

"I'm holding you for ransom, of course."

"But Sergeant Reynard doesn't have any money to pay for me."

"I don't need money, I just need what he found in that trunk."

"What trunk are you talking about? I don't know about any trunk."

"No matter, Reynard knows perfectly well what I mean and that's all you need to know." Then he went topside to secure the rowboat and have a smoke.

Alerion looked around him. The cabin was enclosed on three sides, giving the boat fair protection from the weather. Although he gauged the boat to be fairly new, it was a mess inside. It was obvious that the man was living onboard. The small galley had a fridge, cupboards, a convertible table that folded down, the bunk he was on, and inset shelving along both sides that held books, maps, and for lack of a better word, junk, pushed into every crevice. The pilot's steering was at the other end and set higher for better forward vision.

The bunk he was in was small, but had two blankets. It wasn't until he saw the blankets that he realized two things: he was cold, and he had to pee. He used the bucket and then tried to cover himself as best he could with the blankets. A short time later the man tossed to him some bread and cheese. He ate it without thinking. He had only had two cups of coffee and a croissant that morning. The very act of chewing though, made his head hurt even more. After two hours of feeling sorry for himself the feeling turned to anger at Lucien and Chante, which transferred to anger toward this man, and then he was exhausted. He turned on his side so the bumps on his head were not pressing against the pillow, and finally he fell asleep from exhaustion.

Sometime during the night he had a dream. He was in a tunnel, his feet were being held down, and he was being buried alive. The colonel's face was looking down at him angrily. He awoke from the dream cold and stiff. He readjusted the blankets. His head was still hurting, but the sharpness of the pain had eased. He was thirsty so he was glad he had some water. He detected no movement around him and did not hear any breathing so he figured the stranger was sleeping topside. He sat up and dug into his pockets for his watch and phone. Both were gone. He noticed that a wire had been added to one of his legs and twisted into the chain on the bed, which held it in place. Even if he was able to chew off the rope, which would take days to accomplish, he couldn't bite through wire. He was still feeling weak and ended up falling back into a restless dream state, back into a dark place.

Chapter 26

Early Monday morning Lucien went back to his apartment and changed into his fatigues. He placed the package with the wood splinters into his car trunk so he could get them to the post office during his lunch break. He arrived at the fort a few minutes early. When Alerion had not arrived by 9:30, Lucien called his cell. There was no answer so he left a message. That was odd. Alerion had always shown up for duty. If he were going to be late he would call him directly. Lucien called Alerion's landline in case he was sick at home. No answer, but he left another message. Lucien then went to his desk and looked at the pile of folders for the coming event. Maybe Alerion was detained for some reason, had not charged his phone, and was at a café getting coffee. He would wait a bit longer. Lucien went through the files and made a list of what still needed to be done. When another hour had gone by he decided to call his father, but all was well with him.

After that, Lucien was continually troubled at each passing minute with no word from Alerion. The colonel's secretary had also called and left several messages for Private Bellamy on his desk answering machine, his cell, and his home. Lucien had planned to pick up Chante and go to the bank, but with Alerion missing he changed his plans. When it came time for lunch, Lucien raced to Port Vendres to ship the wooden splinters, and return the welding tank. On the way back he stopped at Alerion's apartment, but he did not answer and the door was locked.

He went back to the office hoping Alerion had showed. He had not. It was time to go to the colonel, and he did. Lucien expressed his genuine concern for Alerion. It was not like him to just disappear. He was curious about one thing. He told the colonel that he thought that he had seen Alerion following him around town and wondered if the colonel knew about this.

Colonel Grosvenor took a deep breath and came around the outside of his desk to be closer to Lucien. His jowls puffed air and then he relented.

"Actually sergeant, I asked Private Bellamy to keep an eye on you. You seemed to be focused on things other than your job. He was growing very concerned about you and so was I. He told me he wasn't sure he trusted your girlfriend. The duty chief said that for two weeks you worked very late and you left looking dirty and exhausted. That seemed odd for just moving boxes. The carpet people were told there was a drain in the storage room and a plate had covered the floor, yet you never spoke to me about that problem. I know that you've walked around the chateau several times, though I can't for the life of me think why you should suddenly be so interested. I know you have a new girlfriend, but I find it hard to believe that a veteran soldier like you would fall prey to an American pretty face. You've taken extra time off, although I know your father had a spill and you had to take care of him, but something else is going on. So what is it, and what is your fascination with Vauban?"

Lucien was taken aback. He had no idea the colonel had been having him watched that closely.

"You are as well-informed as ever, sir. I can assure you colonel, there is nothing going on. I had a feeling that Alerion was following me on a couple of occasions. The woman I am dating is Chante Morgan. She is doing historical research and that's why she wanted to go to the

Chateau several times. I was helping her with research on Vauban. The storage room floor had the look of a foundation crack, so I just reinforced the floor. I didn't want to bother you with problems that I could easily handle. However, I believe someone else has been following Mademoiselle Morgan and myself, besides Private Bellamy. A man was watching us last week at Valmy Park and a few nights ago I got a glimpse of the same man in town. Now Alerion has disappeared. I think something has happened to him."

The colonel squinted his eyes, which meant he was analyzing the situation. He decided to disregard all of the rest and stick to the problem at hand. "I'm not pleased that you have both attracted the attention of someone questionable, but you are right. It is not like Private Bellamy to not call in. He was supposed to report to me first thing this morning, and he did not show or call."

Lucien looked at the colonel and thanked him for being honest, and added. "Do you think we should go to the police?"

"He has only been missing for a few hours. The police won't begin any search until 24 hours have passed, but I will have Privates Rousseau and Duran begin searching for him right away. Where do you suggest I have them begin looking? Where have you been that he might have gone? Where did you last see him?"

Lucien had not seen Alerion since last Friday at work. Alerion had been working in the storage room going through the files. He thought about all of the places that he and Chante had been and wondered what to tell the colonel.

"I'm dating Mademoiselle Morgan so we've gone to many places where Alerion could have followed us. I've even introduced her to my father. Perhaps Alerion's apartment manager can check his rooms to make sure he is not inside. There may also be some kind of clue there as to where he might have gone. Maybe his mother took ill suddenly and he departed in a hurry to go to her? She lives just outside of Carcassonne. Maybe he's had an accident or is hurt somewhere?"

"I can assure you, sergeant, we will do our best to find him. If he does not report in by tomorrow morning, you will go to the police and report him missing. In the meantime, if Private Bellamy does show up, we must let each other know."

Lucien left for Chante's at the end of the day even more shaken. Alerion had still not answered his texts or calls. Had Alerion been followed by the same strange man that had been following them? Had the man followed him and Chante to his father's house? Was it the same man that attacked his father? If the man knew where his father lived and knew he had the contents of the chest, why did he wait three days to break in? How did he know what they had been carrying? Had the man heard he and Chante talk about their find? The box had been transported in a backpack or a suitcase, completely innocuous vehicles for carrying it in public. Lucien raced back in his memory for anything he could have said that anyone could have overheard. He battled with his brain to remember.

It had been early morning when he and Chante had climbed out of the cave and up the cliff. They had gone straight to Chante's apartment and on the way had seen only the baker. Between them they had not spoken along the street at all. When they had reached her apartment they piled the items on her dining table. He did remember saying to Chante that he should call his father because "he'll want to see what they had found, and he would know what to do." That was at 8:00 in the morning. They had eaten and gone back to bed until almost 11:00. He knew what had happened during part of that time as he was actively involved, but while he'd slept for the remaining time, how would he know? He remembered reaching his father by phone when they had gotten up, but he knew that he had not said anything to his father about what they had found. All their immediate questions about what to do had been asked at the cave. In fact, he remembered telling Chante that she did not have to repeat her questions at the apartment. That's when he remembered. He had asked Chante if she had a large bag to transport the box and satchel in, and something about securing it. So he had spoken aloud those words, but the French doors had been closed and there were no listening devices found. He was puzzled.

He bent his head and closed his eyes trying to picture the apartment from that morning. He remembered Chante picking up both of their plates after breakfast and going to the kitchen. He had picked up their coffee cups and moved them inside to the dining table. And the one thing he did not remember doing, which might have been his mistake with a false sense of security, was immediately closing the balcony doors. Anyone that might have followed them from town could have followed them to the apartment, climbed the olive hill beyond the French doors, and hidden themselves behind the trees and bushes. They might have been able to both hear and look straight into the apartment. They didn't need a listening devise. They only needed one good pair of ears and eyes or binoculars. Who in the hell would be interested in what they had found? Certainly not the owner of the chest, he was dead and long gone. If it had been the military they would have come and gone with a small, organized tactical group. It had not been police or they would have made themselves known long before now. No, it was a loner, or two at most. Perhaps someone at a distance had hired the man to watch them? Only someone that knew what they possessed would go to such trouble. Someone was desperate to get a hold of the contents of the satchel, and he knew why — for the money — but who?

By the time he'd left the office and arrived at Chante's, Lucien was growing distraught. It had dawned on him that if someone had been watching from the hillside they might have seen the document files in the apartment. If they had, that would have left Chante in a most vulnerable position all day. Had he placed Chante in danger? When he arrived downstairs at her building, he flew up the stairs two steps at a time. When he arrived, and she did not immediately answer when he knocked, his heart hit the doormat. But then she called from the other side. Lucien? His heart was back in his chest. She let him in and he held her tighter than he had ever done so before. He broke and went past her to make sure the French doors were closed and locked. They were, and he returned.

Chante closed and relocked the front door. Lucien had not seen anyone follow him over. He had to quickly ask. "Are you okay? Did you hear or see anyone today? Are the papers okay? "

"Everything is fine. It's been very quiet. The papers are still here. I've been tucked up reading and cooking all day. I thought we were going to the bank today, but you didn't call. I figured you got too busy at the fort."

"I'm glad you are okay and the papers are still safe, but we need to move those files to the bank vault first thing tomorrow morning."

Chante was looking at him with concern now. "I know. We will. Are you okay? What happened today? Something's happened."

"I'm very worried about Alerion. He never showed up for work today and he is not answering any of his phone messages. He's never done that." Chante could see the furrows of worry on his face. "If Alerion does not show up for work tomorrow morning, the colonel wants me to officially report him missing to the police. Also, I had a heart-to-heart talk with the colonel. He admitted to having Alerion follow us. My own assistant! It's hard to believe he would agree to do such a thing, but the colonel can be quite persuasive. Maybe he didn't trust you or me about something. He asked me questions about why we had gone to the chateau so many times, and about my interest in Vauban."

"What did you tell him?"

"Nothing about where we were not supposed to be."

"How many times did you say we went to the chateau?"

"I didn't say, but covered for us by saying that you were writing an article on the chateau. But now that I think about it, I did say that I had introduced you to my father."

"You did? Oh dear. I guess it is just a matter of time."

"Time until what?"

"Until they get to your father and question him. Will he know what to say? What about the files he must have on his computer? There must be inquiries with the testing lab, his searches for Latin translations and medieval manuscripts. And then what happens when they get down on their list to all the places we've been, including the church? Do you think they will be able to tell that we opened locked doors and lockers? Do you think they will go into the tower and then to the lower level at the back of the church and find the empty files in the chest?" Chante's blood pressure was rising and now Lucien needed to calm her.

"It depends upon how thoroughly they search. I honestly don't think anyone has been where we were for many years. Though I am very glad that we got those papers before anyone else did!"

Chante was not so sure about that, but Lucien got lost in thought. He turned his head toward the darkness outside the French doors. In his mind's eye he saw Alerion's face, how he rolled his eyes and the diligence with which he performed his work. He also recalled a look of frustration on Alerion's face, not wanting to get caught with the trapdoor in the fort. He remembered the look of fear on Alerion's face when he got trapped in the cave-in. There was also the worry he showed when he thought the colonel had found out about the tunnel. Damn it! Where was he? He and Chante had to be prepared for a possible visitation that night. He was not leaving her alone.

"I'd better call Papa to let him know what's going on, and warn him that the police may be around to question him tomorrow." He had already pulled out his phone and was dialing. "Hello Papa, it's me. Are you okay?"

"Yes son, nothing has changed since you called earlier. What's new with you?"

"A lot. Today the colonel told me that he had asked Alerion to keep an eye on Chante and me, but we cannot be sure where he has followed us. Then Alerion did not show up for work today. He's not at home and is not answering his phone. Due to the fact that we now believe there is a third party following us, the colonel has two men searching for Alerion. If Alerion does not show by tomorrow morning, I am to go to the police and report him as missing and then they will look for him, too.

"The second thing is that the colonel asked where we had been that Alerion might have followed us to, and I mentioned that I had introduced Chante to you. You could get a call or be visited by the colonel's men. If the police come into it, they could also interview you. Of course I didn't mention everywhere we had been.

"I also think it might be a good idea if you remove all information from your computer that might have anything to do with what we found. You may want to clear all online searches and move all the pictures you took on a thumb drive to the safe deposit box.

"And one more thing. While Alerion was organizing some old files of fort records in the storeroom, he found a strange file. It had a list of items that we believe were moved from the chateau to the church the day after the Germans invaded France in 1941. It was only one sheet of paper and on it was a list of numbers and letters, but it got me thinking. So Chante and I, believe it or not, went to the church and got into an upstairs chamber behind the altar and tower. We found another chest with the very papers that the list referred to. We now have those papers here, and we looked through them all last night. They appear to be historical files on the area, a veritable time capsule of the local knowledge of the time. Tomorrow we need to get these papers into the safe deposit box, as well. Tomorrow is Tuesday. Can we pick you up by 8:45, so we can take everything in tomorrow morning when the bank opens? Will that work for you?"

"Yes, son, that's fine. In the meantime, I want to let you know that I placed all the plastic from that black trash bag out with the trash, and it was picked up today."

"Oh, I hadn't thought of that. Good."

"I will go through my computer tonight, offload the information and clear my files and file history. I'm so sorry to hear about Alerion, though. I hope he turns up soon."

"We do too. See you tomorrow morning."

"Good night, son." And they hung up.

Chante had been standing nearby, watching him. When he hung up he took Chante into his arms and saw her concerned face.

"Chante, I am so sorry that I have gotten you into this mess. You must think I am absolutely crazy. Here I convince you to break into a national tourist site, trudge through tunnels, sleep in a cave, climb a cliff, weld doors closed, then break into a church and steal papers. Believe me, I have never done anything like this before in my life, and I never will again! I've been a 'follow the rules and don't upset the status quo' guy all my life. I've been on assignment and had to do some challenging things, but this is not a military assignment. Maybe my life was getting to be so boring I needed to create a mystery for myself. I don't know. Then I met you and adventure just seemed to be calling. But now Alerion is missing. I never realized how good a friend he is to me. I think I've been taking him too much for granted and probably pushing him too hard. I feel terrible. I know there is not much I can say to you, except I am very sorry and I will make sure to protect you."

Lucien's apology calmed Chante. She smoothed a small curl of hair that had fallen on his forehead and was partially covering his furrowed brow. She cupped his right cheek with her hand and smiled.

"My love, let's be clear about this. I wanted to get into the chateau. I wanted to go through that tunnel. Yes, it was chilly in the cave, but I loved being there with you and making love in the dark with the pounding surf. The cliff hike was not as bad as you make it out to be, and it was my idea to weld those doors closed, not yours. I fully admit that I've gotten caught up in this mystery, maybe as much as you have. There is also a part of me that is disappointment with Christian theology. Breaking into the back of the church was also a protest, in my own small way. Getting behind that altar made it feel as though I had pulled down a huge curtain and found out that the great OZ was not what he seemed. Behind all that gold is nothing but dust and secrets. Besides, no one probably knows those papers were there, anyway. We can always turn the papers over to a historical society. And if we do, then we will have done our small part to bring some history back into the light, adding one more piece to an old puzzle. I know that we will find Alerion. I know we will."

Lucien considered her long statement. "We still broke into the church and stole those papers."

"But if no one knows that they were there and cannot claim them, how is that stealing?"

"I'm not sure, but getting past locked rooms and trespassing are illegal. I'm thinking I should go back to the church tomorrow to lock the tower door and make sure the door downstairs in the chapel is locked again."

"And when are you going to be able to do that?"

"I don't know, but as soon as I can."

"Okay, but tonight we need to talk about what we will say to the police if Alerion does not come back. And before we launch into that we need to eat." And with that she got up and went to the kitchen to complete the last preparations for their dinner. Chante had made a cassoulet with a salad, and a blackberry tart for dessert. As soon as the last bite was eaten, they cleared the dishes and held on to each other on the couch, discussing what to say and what not to say.

Chapter 27

When Alerion had not arrived on Tuesday morning by 9:30, the colonel picked up his phone and dialed the cell number of his friend, Chief Souveterre of the police. They had known each other for several years. They even played cards together on occasion.

"Raoul, it's Émile."

"Good morning, Émile. How are you?"

"Concerned. I'm sending over Staff Sergeant Lucien Reynard this morning to talk to someone in your office."

"Okay, what's up?"

"He'll need to fill out a missing person's report with you. "

"Lose one of your men, Émile? How did you manage to do that?"

"I can assure you Raoul, the missing person had help, but it wasn't from me. He is Private First Class Alerion Bellamy and we suspect foul play. I've already put two of my men on it as he is military, but I'm going to need your help. Can you spare some men to help us search? He was last seen at the fort where I have already launched a search, but we haven't found him. He could be anywhere in or out of town. Perhaps Sergeant Reynard can help you decide where to start searching.

"Raoul, I had Bellamy keeping an eye on Reynard. I had gotten the feeling that Reynard was up to something and Bellamy might have discovered what it is. But I find it hard to believe that one may have turned against the other. They work together and are good friends. However, a third party has shown some interest in them, as well. A man has been spotted trailing them, and Bellamy may have gotten in the way. See what you can get from Reynard and follow up on any leads, will you?"

The chief considered the request. "Of course, Émile. We haven't had a missing person for several of years. Not since Monsieur Dousset passed out drunk for two days in a neighbor's vineyard *chibotte*. We are stretched a little tight right now. I have an investigation going on for a robbery that was reported yesterday, and just a few minutes ago I received a report that a body washed up on the beach at Port Vendres after this last storm. We are getting an I.D. now. I may need to take care of your problem myself, but I think we can accommodate you. I'll check in with my men on any suspicious characters in the area."

"Thanks, Raoul. Keep me in touch with what happens." And they signed off.

*   *   *

Lucien had a troubled night of sleep. He had dreamed of Alerion lying helpless somewhere. By 8:00 the next morning he and Chante were off to his father's house and all three were in the bank by 9:05. Gervais was excited to take a look at the files they had found. As a history professor it was like feeding a hungry man. The more he read, the more he wanted to digest, but Lucien very much wanted to get back to Collioure as soon as possible, and Gervais would have the opportunity to come back to the bank later.

Halfway back to Collioure, Lucien got a call from the colonel saying that Alerion had still not turned up. He told him to go directly to the Collioure police station and file the missing person's report.

When he got off the phone, Lucien let Chante know what transpired, and they decided to go to the police together. When they arrived in Collioure they made their way to a yellow building with blue shutters that blended in with the local architecture. One would not know it was a police station unless one noticed the police going in and out from time to time. He wasn't sure with whom he should speak, but an officer greeted him. Lucien gave the man his name and said that he needed to report a missing person. The officer was young with short-trimmed brown hair and hazel eyes. His nametag read Officer Gene Fernand. He had them wait in an interview room, but soon the door opened and Chief Souveterre entered. Officer Fernand closed the door behind them and then stood nearby with an open notebook to take notes.

"Bonjour." He extended his hand and shook the hands of Lucien and Chante. "I'm Chief Raoul Souveterre. Colonel Grosvenor called and said you want to report a missing person. He seems very concerned. I hope you will be able to cooperate fully so that we can find Private Bellamy quickly."

Chief Souveterre was an impressive man. He was tall, trim, and had short wavy dark hair that was graying at each temple and sideburn. His eyebrows were softly angled over light brown eyes, and his nose was sharp. He sported a thin oilman's moustache with a bushy center thinning to the edges, over natural lips. He wore a crisp white shirt, a dark tie, a dark blue suit jacket, dark blue slacks, and very shiny black shoes.

Lucien and Chante introduced themselves and the interview began at 10:20 am. The chief leaned across the table, studying their faces, and then wasted no time in opening up the questioning while the officer took notes. Where had they last seen Private First Class Alerion Bellamy? *At the fort.* How did Lucien know him? *They'd met four years ago at a previous training course. Bellamy applied to work in Collioure, and ended up becoming his assistant.* To the best of his knowledge, did Bellamy have any enemies?

No. Was there any reason why he might leave town? *He has a mother living east of Carcassonne. Perhaps he went there?* He worked with the private the closest. Did he get the feeling that Bellamy was having financial or emotional troubles? *No!* They needed a picture of him, and were on their way to his apartment to search it. Then the harder questions came. What had Private Bellamy been doing that might bring him into harm? Was there something going on that the police should know about? What did he think had happened to him? What had Lucien and Bellamy been doing for the last couple of weeks? Had Private Bellamy been doing anything particular in his work that would attract attention? Had Private Bellamy met anyone of interest of late?

Lucien had been trained in interrogation techniques, so why was he feeling a little awkward? He thought about his and Alerion's tunnel experience, but he honestly did not think there was anything there to see or find. So what, an old tunnel that went nowhere? He did not think that any military personnel could interpret something heinous about that discovery. If anything, he was helping to cover it up. He informed the chief that he and Private Bellamy had been working on a project in the fort's basement to create a large office for new personnel, assigned by the colonel himself. Aside from Alerion possibly straining his back by moving boxes, of which he never complained, he didn't know how he could have come to any harm. He had only just learned that the colonel had asked Alerion to keep an eye on him and was making reports.

The chief then addressed his questions to Chante.

"Madame Morgan, I understand you have recently moved to Collioure. You have an apartment in town?"

"It's Miss now, Chief Souveterre. I'm divorced. And yes, I have a one-bedroom apartment located behind the Dominican Winery, just west of the windmill."

"What was your business before you moved here?"

"I helped run a photography studio with my ex-husband in Los Angeles, and I am a writer."

"From what I can find of your published articles you write about travel and history. Are you working on an article right now Mademoiselle Morgan?" The chief's eyes smiled across at her with amused interest.

"I thought I would write an article on the historical changes that the Chateau Royal has gone through, a sort of overview of those changes through the ages, but I'm finding some of its history rather illusive."

"That's all very well, but I would like to read a preview of that article before you publish it. You wouldn't mind, would you? Please consider me your first stage of approval. We are rather particular on how our town is portrayed."

Chante was surprised to hear his cautioning tone. "Yes, of course. I would be honored if you would give it first perusal."

The chief went on to ask more questions. Why was she in Collioure? When did she arrive? How long would she be staying? How had she and Sergeant Reynard met, and where had they been visiting in the last few weeks?

Chante responded in a calm manner to each of his questions. Then they both recalled most of the places that they had visited while dating. They named the two restaurants they had gone to for dinner. They had gone to the chateau a couple of times for some historical research for the article she was writing; they had visited Camp Monastir; they went to the Banyuls-sur-mer Grape Harvest Festival; and to Chateau Valmy Park and the aviary show. They disclosed that they had proclaimed their love for each other and that Lucien had introduced her to his father. They had even gone to church together! Lucien knew that if one disclosed very personal information, it would appear that they were opening up and sharing what they knew. They decided to use this ploy before they got to the station.

Lucien also added that in the midst of conducting their courtship, Lucien had noticed that someone besides Private Bellamy had been following them. He had seen someone he didn't know watching them at the Valmy gardens.

"Describe the man in the park for me as best you can."

Lucien had only seen him at a distance, and only momentarily, before the man had ducked his head under his cap and scuttled away. "He wore a longish dark blue jacket with a hood and a dark mariner's cap on his head. He had dark eyes and hair."

"Did you see him Mademoiselle Morgan?" She had not.

"I saw him again in the Valmy parking lot and later that night downtown, leaning against the wall of the cemetery smoking a cigarette. The light had only momentarily showed his face, but I recognized him as being the same man. The only thing that I could see was that he had a dark complexion, either from the sun or by heredity." Any other features he could not remember.

The chief asked, "And when was this?"

"It was the night the storm blew into town. I had been at Chante's until almost 2300. I was walking home along the west side of Rue de la République, and past the street to the cemetery."

The chief listened closely, tilted his head at this last bit of information, and asked, "In one word, how would you best describe the man you saw?"

Lucien thought about it for about three seconds and then said, "Swarthy, but not in an attractive way, more scruffy."

The chief stood up and partially walked the room, thinking about his description. He was interrupted by a knock on the door. It opened and he was handed a message. He read it and then looked straight at Lucien, who was looking proper in his working fatigues, though a little too calm for the chief's liking.

"Have you ever come into contact with a man named Beaux Falchan?"

"Falchan?" Lucien ran that around in his head. It did have a familiar ring to it, and then he remembered him. "Yes sir, he runs the local diving company."

"When did you last see him?"

Lucien was surprised by the question. "Quite honestly, I don't know. I'm sure I've seen him walking about town and taking his boat out with his diving clients, but I don't think I've seen him for several months, sometime during the summer season is my best guess."

The chief sat holding the message he had received. "He *did* run the local diving company. His body washed up on the beaches of Port Vendres this morning. We didn't even know he was missing. One of his diving buddies alerted us when he didn't show for a diving trip. Then, his friend confirmed the body's identification a few minutes ago. We are trying to reach his wife, who seems to be out of town. We believe the man you described as following you, ran the local diving company before Falchan. Several years ago we believed they were working together stealing from diving clients. We could never really link Falchan to the thefts and there was only circumstantial evidence against him, but we believe it was his partner doing the dirty work. However, no goods were discovered at their homes, the diving boat, or the dock, so instead of a case coming to court, the old diving owner was told to get out of town and to stay away. It was believed that without his influence, Falchan would set his life straight and keep only to his diving business. That seemed to hold for a couple of years. However, over the last year we have had a rise in thefts, so we now believe that they may have been working together again, and the outcast may have done away with Falchan, but we don't know why."

At this point the chief looked from Lucien to Chante. "If it is the same man, the funny thing about this thief, is he wouldn't be interested in you unless you had something he wanted. Do you have something of value that a thief might like to have? Do you think that Private Bellamy had anything of value worth stealing?"

Lucien hesitated, which was unlike him, but he had never been in this kind of situation before. He was very sorry, he replied, he didn't know anything about the dead man, except to know that he ran the diving club in town, but that was it. He'd never even spoken to him. As for anything this thief might want, he had nothing of value except a few old French stamps his father had given him, but their value was still inconsequential, even to a collector, and he didn't think Bellamy had anything of particular value.

The chief asked for a description of Alerion and all the details needed for them to begin a search. Then the chief stood, thanked them for the information, and asked them for phone numbers where they could be reached. He instructed that if either of them saw the same man again to let him know immediately. He told Lucien to go back to work and Chante to return home, and the police would contact them when they found Private Bellamy. They were told not to leave the area and he would have someone watch Chante in case the man tried to follow or approach her. He explained that he was short-handed, but trusted Reynard, a trained soldier, to be on his guard.

Lucien escorted Chante home. On the way, Chante told him not to go back to the church, as now they would be watched. He agreed. There was nothing he could do now but wait and see. He went back to work, but he was nearly useless at his desk. His imagination ran wild with possibilities, and the lies he had told to protect what they had found weighed heavily on him. Lucien let the colonel know about their meeting with Chief Souveterre. The colonel's men, so far had found nothing except one shopkeeper who had seen Alerion in his ceramics shop on Sunday morning, and thought he had headed toward the church. The colonel let Souveterre know.

If Alerion had reported to work, he would have helped Lucien with the final preparations for the ACE week, as it was only a couple of days away. Now with Alerion gone, there was even more for Lucien to complete. At least it kept his mind and hands busy.

At 4:00 that afternoon the chief called Lucien and Chante back to the police station. He had new information. Anxious and hopeful, Chante and Lucien returned to the same interview room and waited for the news. The chief and Officer Fernand entered and sat down across from them.

"At approximately 3:00 this afternoon we got a call from the parish priest at the Notre Dame church. He found an internal door that is normally locked to be open and thought someone had broken in. When we did a search we found that lockers upstairs behind the high altar had been broken into. There also was blood found against one wall." Lucien rose to his feet.

"Any sign of Private Bellamy?"

"No, but it could well be his blood that we found. We are waiting for confirmation from military records."

Chante pulled Lucien to sit down again, and took his hand to comfort him.

"However, now I have more questions for you," began the chief. "Why do you think that Private Bellamy was being followed, and why do you think his life may have been threatened?"

Lucien's brows were in a deep furrow, but he looked directly at the chief to answer. "We didn't know that he was being followed and we don't know why, either."

"I think you might, but you are not saying. We have forensics at the church collecting prints and evidence. There's a lot of disturbed dust, and hopefully it will tell us enough about who was there and what happened. The lockers had each been drilled into and their locking mechanisms destroyed. At this time it does not look as though anything has been taken from those files, but someone was awfully curious and thorough. We followed the footprints to the tower door, which was also found unlocked, and downstairs we discovered another unlocked door. It led to a floor underneath the first that can only be reached through the tower. Two small metal file boxes were found empty in a chest and the dust was greatly disturbed there as well. Someone had tried to cover some foot tracks. The parish priest did not even know that there was a lower story at the back of the church, let alone an expensive carpet, a chest, or hidden file boxes. He had only been in the tower once when he first came to Collioure three years ago, when the clock mechanic had showed him the mechanism. You said you went to church. Was it that church and when did you go there?"

Then it dawned on Lucien that Alerion might have followed them that day.

"We did go to that church this past Sunday morning."

"And what exactly did you do there?" Souveterre raised one eyebrow and cocked his head forward.

Chante looked at Lucien and he carefully chose his words. "We were visiting the church as tourists.

Mademoiselle Morgan had not been in the church for several years and wanted to see it again. We spent a good amount of time in the church examining the main altar and side altars, but I can assure you that we did not drill any holes into any metal cabinets. I don't even own a drill. We would never deface church property. We never saw Private Bellamy before we entered the church, during the time we were there, or after we left."

"We'll see what the evidence shows and we will be able to tell if you are lying or not. You are aware that we have a camera that scans the beach. If you are lying we will know. Is there anything else you would care to share with me at this time? I would hate to catch you in a lie, being one of our trusted military personnel. Colonel Grosvenor would not be too pleased, either." Lucien was silent while his heart and mind were racing. He said nothing.

"Very well then," replied Souveterre. "You may go for now, but as soon as all of the evidence from the scene has been examined, I feel I will probably be seeing you again. Do not leave town. Is that understood?"

Lucien and Chante agreed, thanked the chief for the information, and hoped the police would find Private Bellamy soon. Chante was pale and nervous. An officer came to drive her home. Lucien was angry that anyone would hurt Alerion, and he was feeling very guilty, as this whole thing was entirely his fault. He told Chante that he was going back to the fort briefly to report to the colonel, and then he would see her within the hour.

Chapter 28

When Chante and Lucien left the police station, chief Souveterre made a call.

"Hello Alexis, Raoul here. When you've closed the Mairie come to the station. I want to speak with you."

Alexis agreed, but he was anxious about the meeting. When he arrived a half hour later, the chief waved him into his office and told him to close the door. Alexis stood before him, but it was obvious that he was nervous as his eyes darted about the room. What Souveterre did not see, were Alexis's fingers shaking, hidden behind his back. The chief stood and looked down at him.

"I want to talk to you about your position at the Mairie. You are my cousin's son, my second cousin, but don't think for one moment because we are related that I will cut you any slack. I gave you that job at the Mairie so you could help support your parents. I also gave you the assignment with extra pay so you could keep an eye out for strangers and any possible crimes being committed in town. Yet within the last year you have only reported one problem, that kid who was stealing at the central market. But in the last year there have been four reported robberies, and you knew nothing about them. Now I know it might be a long shot that you might know anything, but there has been nothing else from you. Can you explain why I am not getting the cooperation from you that I was hoping for?"

Alexis spread his arms and lifted his shoulders in a gesture of innocence. "I am sorry Raoul. I'm still getting to know all the townspeople. Many are still strangers to me. I assure you that in time I will get to know everyone and be able to better know who lives here and who is a stranger. Please cousin, I like this work and I need the job."

The chief looked down at the files on his desk and despite how he really felt about the young relation in front of him, he needed his help now more than ever.

"I need your help, Alexis. Two days ago a very expensive painting was stolen from a home up the hill. I need you to keep your eyes open, especially now in low season, for any strange person or unusual activity. The person may be long gone by now, but while you are standing behind that desk doing nothing, keep an eye out that window!"

"Yes, Raoul, I promise, I swear." But the chief was not finished.

"That's not all. We now have a missing person, a soldier from the fort that has disappeared. I'll have a picture of the man soon so you will know what he looks like. Maybe he just ran off with a girl, or maybe he has been kidnapped. You are positioned on a main corner in the center of town. You are my eyes and ears and I pay you extra to work for me in that capacity. I need you to keep a close watch, and I expect you to earn that money. Is that clear?"

"Yes, sir, but I assure you I know nothing about those things. It's the slow season so there simply aren't that many people coming into town. With the cold and wind everyone is bundled up and everyone looks suspicious. There have been no new businesses opened in the last three months. No new licenses have been issued since summer. Who would do so after the high season anyway?"

Souveterre considered his statement, and what Alexis had said was true. He owed it to Alexis' father and mother to give him a second chance. Alexis' father could not work due to an accident that crippled his legs, so Raoul needed to give Alexis some leeway. As Alexis already seemed so nervous, he decided not to say anything about the dead body. Local gossip would get the word around soon enough.

"All right. Be especially vigilant, Alexis."

"Yes, sir, I will do my best, sir."

Alexis was about to turn and go, but then he remembered something. "Wait, there was a soldier from the fort, who was unhappy that we did not have the historical information about the town and the fort in our archives that he was wanting. I think his name was Reynard." The chief's attention was raised.

The chief smiled. "Sergeant Reynard? Is that so? And why did he say he needed this information?"

"He said it was for an information packet he was writing for some journalists coming to the fort for a training of some kind."

"Ah yes, I know about that. That's legit, but that is the kind of information I am looking for. So step up your game Alexis, or it will be your first and last year at that post."

Alexis was cowering. He was obviously scared.

"Yes, sir. I will, sir." He backed out of the office and nearly ran into the doorframe when he turned on his way out. Alexis hurried down the street to his own apartment, located off the Rue de Jardin. He wondered how long this arrangement would work. His nerves were beginning to get to him. He opened a kitchen cabinet and grabbed the expensive bottle of Cognac he had gotten used to enjoying. He chugged a gulp right from the bottle and collapsed onto his new couch. He looked around the room and saw the new television, CD player, amplifier, and speakers, and the small but expensive dining set and rug, and wondered how long his fortune would last.

He pulled out his phone, made a quick call, and then stuffed the phone back into his pocket.

*   *   *

Alerion's kidnapper was smiling. The timing was just right. He finished writing his letter, placed the paper into an envelope, sealed it and wrote a name on the front. He tucked the letter into his jacket pocket and went topside.

Alerion had just swallowed the second chunk of bread and slab of cheese he'd been given. His head was much clearer now and he was angry and frustrated. He already knew what the note must have said. His feet were still tied to the bed frame and his hands remained tied together at the wrists. If he only knew what the hell was going on and what this man wanted. Those files with numbers and letters must have been much more important than he realized, or maybe it was something else entirely. He didn't know. He just wanted this to end. Then he heard the man leave the cruiser, detach the rowboat, and leave.

*   *   *

Lucien returned to the fort and informed the colonel what had happened at the station. The colonel's men had not yet located Alerion, but said he would keep his men looking. Just as Lucien was leaving the fort the security guard stopped him at the exit.

"Sergeant Reynard, some kid just delivered this letter for you at the gate." Lucien thought that was strange, but he took it in hand, turned away from the guard, opened it and turned pale. It read:

I know you have what I want. Leave the contents of the satchel under the steps of the windmill tomorrow at midnight and I will release Private Bellamy. If the contents are not delivered or if you contact the police, he will be killed, and then your girlfriend is next.

Mixed feelings of fear for Alerion and Chante, and anger for whoever wrote the note, were seething inside of him. He was going to question the guard to find out what the youth looked like, but he knew it would not lead anywhere. The man had obviously paid a kid to do a simple job. When Lucien arrived at Chante's complex he nodded at her guard standing outside and then went up the steps to her door. Chante let him in, and within a few minutes he had shown her the note. Chante sank into the living room couch with a shocked look on her face.

"Oh no! Now what do we do? Go to the police anyway?"

"With everything we've lied about, and this man's threats to kill you and Alerion, I don't think we should."

"So you think we need to give him what he wants?"

"I think we should."

"This guy doesn't know what was in the satchel. We could give him literally anything old and he would think it was what we found in the cave. We could make copies of some of the files that we found at the church and when he picks them up we follow him back to where ever he is keeping Alerion and . . . "

"And what? Hit the guy over the head and walk away? I don't think that would work. Besides, the box and the satchel, which he already has, are obviously old French. The papers from the church are modern compared to those items. Even though they are pre-1941, they aren't medieval. One look and he would know we tried to trick him."

"I guess you are right. When I think about it, we are as guilty of theft as he would have been if he had gotten to the letter first. "

"Yes, but there is one big difference. We are not threatening someone's life, and we have not taken anyone hostage or demanded a ransom! Besides, what's to stop him from taking you or my father hostage next, or threatening my life until he gets what he wants?"

Chante took a deep breath and let out a sigh. "True, but how would the guy know, even if we did speak with the police? Though, somehow that doesn't sound like it would bode well for us after we explain why Alerion was taken. We would surely be forced to submit the letter to the police and probably be fined or jailed for trespassing, for withholding information, interfering with police business, and even for stealing a national treasure."

"I'm not sure we want to take the chance of telling the police. Right now I'm more concerned for Alerion's life."

"Lucien, it is quite possible that the police will turn up evidence that we did more than just visit the church. We may not have a choice in continuing to hide the truth."

"You heard what the chief said. Someone else was in the church after us. That person may well have covered our tracks. We know we did not drill into those lockers."

There was a silence between them as they came to the realization that their story might not hold up, and they tried to think of what to do. Chante put her arm around Lucien and then he pulled her to him. The comfort of each other's arms was all they had.

"Don't worry my love," assured Chante, "You'll think of something."

Lucien kissed her for that reassurance. Chante was hoping for something more than a kiss, if nothing else but to comfort him, but he was too upset to think of anything else. She could see he was exhausted, but he declined to rest, her offer of dinner, or even a glass of wine. At least Lucien was glad that Chante would be safe with an officer outside, so he decided to go home. He needed time to just sit and think it all through.

Very early the next morning, after too many hours of lost sleep, Lucien finally got an idea, but he had to check on something before he could see it implemented. It was a long shot, but it was the best he could come up with in so short a time. He had to go to work at the fort, despite the fact that his best friend was being held hostage, as the first of the journalists would be arriving that afternoon. Since Alerion was not available he would need to serve as the one who greeted them.

Before he could put his plan into operation, Chief Souveterre asked him and Chante to once again return to the police station. Panic quickly set in. Had the police found evidence incriminating them of lying, or did they have more information on Alerion? If they were arrested they could end up in jail, without being able to deliver the letter, and then Alerion might come to his end.

The officer assigned to Chante escorted her to the police station where Lucien was waiting. Once again, Officer Fernand showed them into the same interview room, and Souveterre followed and immediately began.

"Perhaps you will be surprised to learn that our forensic team worked all night to discover what the evidence collected yesterday would tell us." The chief opened a file folder and scanned the report before him. "It appears that the church chapel door leading upstairs behind the altar had its lock picked by a professional. Small scratches were detected below the lock. No fingerprints were found on or around the lockers. It is presumed that whoever broke into them wore gloves. All we found were metal shavings below each lock that had been drilled. And the blood found in the church has been confirmed as Private Bellamy's." Chante winced, but Lucien was not surprised.

The chief continued. "Marks in the dust on the floor showed a mixture of several shoe prints. We know that one set must be Private Bellamy's, but three sets lead into the tower and then back into the rear of a lower floor of the church. The door leading from the tower to the lower room had also been picked. In the lower room an old carpet had been moved aside and a trunk was found with a great deal of disturbance around it. Inside were two old metal file boxes, which were empty. Again, no fingerprints were found. So our conclusion is that there were three men who broke into the building. Perhaps they followed Private Bellamy into the church. Perhaps he challenged them, or saw them break into the lower church door in their search for something. To keep Bellamy quiet they probably knocked him around and then bound and gagged him, or someone would have heard him calling. They must have waited until the church was closed to do the drilling into the lockers. Then they searched the church and obviously found something in the boxes in the trunk downstairs and took it. What is surprising to me is, if they got what they were looking for, then why take Private Bellamy hostage, unless he could identify them? As I told you earlier, the parish priest had no idea there was a trunk, let alone a lower room. We are conducting a round of inquiries throughout town, asking residents if they noticed anything out of the ordinary, or saw any strangers. Are you sure there is nothing that you two can tell us that would aid in the investigation?"

Chante looked at Lucien, he looked back at her, and then turned to the chief. "No sir, but please do your best to find him. He's a good friend and I am very worried for him. And sir, I need to go to Perpignan to see my father.

He fell and hurt himself and I need to make sure he is all right. May we please go to see him? We will come right back."

The chief eyed them both. Having lost his own father, with little connection to him in his last years, he knew the value of family. "Yes, that is fine, but come right back."

Chante and Lucien said goodbye and left. They walked to Lucien's apartment, got in his car, and drove to Perpignan. He called his father on the way and said they were coming and would explain things when they got there. It was just after 11:00 am. Lucien called the colonel and told him he had to check on his father, but that he would be back in plenty of time to meet the first four journalists that would be arriving by 4:30. He also requested a meeting with the colonel as soon as he returned to go over the week's plans for the incoming journalists. The colonel agreed and would expect him as soon as he returned.

When they reached Gervais' house, Lucien quickly informed him what had happened and showed him the note. Gervais agreed they had to get the letter. They went to the bank and got the archival box but not the translation. Then Lucien told Gervais and Chante his plan, hoping it could be put into place without too much difficulty. If things did *not* work out he might possibly end up in jail. They were to check with the colonel if they did not hear back from Lucien by the next morning. Gervais insisted on returning to town with them and would wait with Chante until they knew that Lucien was safe. The three of them drove back to Collioure. Lucien dropped Chante and Gervais off at her apartment and he returned to the fort.

As soon as Lucien arrived he went to see the colonel. The colonel ushered him in and Lucien shut the door behind him. He told him that he had not been fully honest about what he had told him, but still only gave a brief and limited sketch. He showed him the ransom note and explained that he could not contact the police, but that if the colonel would allow his plan to take place, they would be able to rescue Alerion, capture the man who had taken him, share the credit for the important find, and a few early journalists would be able to get a taste of undercover work in the bargain. Would the colonel allow him to go forward with his plan? At first the colonel was angry about the lies, but realized that the plan was a good one. He agreed, but only if he could add a few military personnel to the team for safety and backup.

At 4:45 the first four journalists arrived. They were shown their quarters, given dinner, and then called in to a special closed meeting, along with four soldiers, Lucien, and the colonel. The four journalists were eager to participate in a special maneuver before the rest of the members arrived. Each was paired with a trained soldier. At 8:00 pm the men had been given their assignments, outfitted with their gear, and by 9:00 they were ready to go.

Chapter 29

The windmill rested on a high knoll overlooking Collioure, just to the south of town. The eastern top of the hill facing the sea had been transformed into a park with walking paths among pine trees. Olive trees surrounded the western top of the hill, around the windmill. Six of the eight men surrounded the area in different places. Two were beyond the windmill, hidden in the brush among the trees on a slope that led to Fort Elme. On the hill's northern slope facing the town about halfway down was the lookout point where Chante and Lucien had shared some special moments. Two more men were hiding just off the path behind the gazebo. It was probable that the kidnapper would head this way, as a path led down to the closest road out of town heading south to the border. Two others were hiding near the gate that led to the west off of the hillside, near to the rear of Chante's apartment complex, but it also allowed a way out of town toward the highway. The fourth pair hid down in the town. They were sitting in a car as a relay team in case the man returned to town. The colonel sat near the winery, waiting with a headset, ready to direct the maneuver. The soldiers and reporters wore night vision goggles and were dressed in camouflage. By 11:00 pm all were in place, waiting for the appointed time.

At 11:30 Lucien made his way along the main path from the back of the Dominican winery up toward the windmill. At first it was only a dirt path with stone steps zigzagging up the remaining hillside to the top. On that side of the hill, the small grey-green leaves of the olive trees gently fluttered in the occasional light evening breeze, and their rough and dark divided trunks offered hiding places in the shadows. The only sound was the distant pounding of the surf. There was only a sliver of a moon and it was getting chilly again. At the top of the rise, a platform of cement and flagstones formed a base for the windmill. Lucien knew there was a team of men watching him not far away. He also had to believe that the stranger might be watching him, to make sure he was alone.

It had been quite a while since Lucien had visited the windmill and his memory of how it was laid out was a bit sketchy. For one, he could not remember if there was a hollow under the windmill stairs. He would have to figure that out when he got there. He knew the windmill dated from the medieval period; built sometime in the late 14th century for crushing olives for oil. In the early part of 21st century the then-crumbling windmill had been rebuilt and converted into a grain mill for demonstration purposes for the tourists. The mill took on the name of "Moulin de la Cortina," Moulin, meaning, "mill". The mill took its name after the hill, originally called La Courtine, meaning a curtain, as the hill was a curtain that separated the town from the rising mountain behind it.

When Lucien arrived at the windmill, its cloth sails were gently fluttering but the wind blades were not turning. The windmill was only turned on during the day in summer season. A stairway curved up on its left side, but Lucien went around to the front on the right side. That was where the main stairs rose to the entrance of the small round building that housed the authentically reproduced wooden gears. As he thought, those stairs rose in a curve going up, but there was no hollowed space below them. There was a brick seating area below the stones that met with the wall at the base of the windmill. Lucien placed the box there in a protected corner. With his task fulfilled he walked away, very much hoping that his plan would work. He returned the same way he had come up, exited the park in front of the winery, and walked back to where the colonel was waiting. It was now ten minutes to midnight. All teams were given word through their earpieces that the package was in place and pick up was expected at any time. Fifteen long minutes went by without any movement.

Finally, at five minutes after midnight, the two men high on the hill watched as a man in a dark coat made his way off the high trail from Fort Elme. They waited until he walked past and then whispered the sighting to the colonel and the other teams. Everyone was on high alert. Only the team at the west gate had a direct view of the mill stairs. The kidnapper reached the base of the mill, opened the box, looked at the contents, and then made his way back up the trail holding the package to his chest. When the man walked past the team hidden among the olive trees, they radioed that they were on the move. Slowly they advanced about one hundred yards behind the thief. Wispy grey clouds sometimes blocked the moon's thin crescent light, but the soldier and journalist kept the thief in sight.

The path was of dirt and fairly soft, so their footfalls were nearly silent. The only other sound was a night bird that periodically called out. The scent of soil, dusty olive trees, and now and then the smell of the sea drifted up the hill. The second team on the west side now made their way up a parallel path that went up to meet the Elme foot path, but they were a good hundred yards behind the first team. The team on the eastern side of the hill did the same, but they were even further behind. The fourth team in town was ordered to take their vehicle south out of town and wait for instructions.

The colonel and Lucien in his car, followed the soldier's vehicle. The first ground team rounded the top of a hillock, and when they looked down they could see a vehicle on a dirt road slowly driving away. It began to climb the hillside to the west, bumping over one of the rough vineyard roads that crisscrossed the rolling hills. The team radioed that the perpetrator was getting away and which way he was heading. The soldier in the first car was quite familiar with all the local roads and managed to quickly turn up the hill onto a side road that would eventually wind its way into the vineyards above.

The first and second ground teams began to jog up the hill in pursuit of the car. The direction that the kidnapper's car went was easy to follow as its headlights were on. If the first car that was following came up the hill and got too close, the kidnapper would see the car lights, know that he was being followed and either speed up, or worse, kill Private Bellamy and dump his body. They couldn't take that risk, so the ground teams were their best bet. The three journalists that were part of the three ground teams in pursuit were not in as good a shape as the soldiers they were with, but they did an admirable job of keeping up.

The kidnapper's car had to go slow as the vineyard roads were very narrow, rocky, and curved. Four minutes passed, and to the surprise of the first team jogging fast to catch up, they saw the car stop and then heard a car door slam. They were not sure what that meant, but that gave the team the window they needed to get even closer to the vehicle. Now the team in the car caught up driving slowly right behind the third ground team. The car did not need its headlights on as the soldier inside could see the ground team jogging in front of them with his night vision goggles. Lucien and the colonel's vehicle were behind the first car, also with their lights off.

Then, just as they rounded a curve in the road, the first ground team saw the kidnapper's car take off again. On the left was a small farmer's hut. There had to be a reason why the car had stopped, so the two men diverted from trailing the car and went into the hut. Lying on the ground was Alerion, out cold. The soldier felt for his pulse. He was alive.

"Colonel, Private Bellamy has been left in a vineyard hut. We've got him. He's alive, but he seems to be drugged. We'll stay here until he can be picked up, but we need a vehicle to follow the perpetrator's car in pursuit." The men untied Alerion's hands and feet and carried him out of the hut to wait for a car.

The second and third ground teams stepped to the side so that the car following them could turn on its lights and speed out to follow. Now with Lucien's car lights on, they headed for the hut. The soldier and journalist at the hut carried Alerion into Lucien's back seat. He was responding with moans, but he was alive.

The men in the first car radioed that they could see the perpetrator's vehicle and were in pursuit. The car was heading further up the hillside, but it turned south and traveled through the hills above Port Vendres. Then it headed east again toward the D914 highway to the coast. They were closing the gap between them, but the stranger must have seen the car following him and sped up. If he got on the highway he would be able to blend into traffic and within fifteen minutes could cross the border into Spain and disappear. Fortunately, because the hour was late, few vehicles were on the road and the car in pursuit took advantage of this and sped up as well.

Another soldier reported to the colonel "Sir, he's turned off. He is now on a small road heading down toward the water, just north of Port Vendres."

Since no other cars were on this road, and due to its speed, it had to be the kidnapper. The colonel and Lucien had just reached D914 but were still a few minutes away. Alerion was beginning to come to in the back seat due to the bumps and turns that the car was making on the rutted road getting off the hill, but his eyes remained closed and he was beginning slowly to react to brace himself.

Lucien heard him and called out, "Alerion, are you okay?" Alerion was slow to respond, but he did mumble that he was groggy, but okay.

Then the team in the first car radioed again. "Sir, we can see that the car has stopped and he is probably on the run. There is a small dock there, sir. We think he might have a boat."

"That's all I need to hear," responded the colonel, and he got on his phone to the coastguard in Banyuls-sur-mer. "This is Colonel Grosvenor. We are in pursuit on land but need a boat to intercept by sea. The perpetrator will most likely be heading south to the border in his boat, and traveling at top speed. We need that boat stopped and the man secured. He could be armed and dangerous. We must stop him before he goes into Spanish waters. We also have an injured man and could use some medical attention upon arrival. Call me back as soon as he has been spotted and apprehended."

The colonel rang off. "Quickly, to the Banyuls coast guard station."

Lucien wanted to take Alerion straight to the hospital, but now that he was coming around and seemed better, Lucien turned the car around and headed off again. "Should we have the men head back to the fort?"

"Hell, no. There's nothing like a capture at the end of a pursuit. Those journalists will be talking about this maneuver for years to come!" Then he turned on his headphone speaker. "Ground teams, call for vehicle pickup and all rendezvous at the Banyuls coast guard station. We'll see you there."

Less than four minutes later they were pulling into Banyuls-sur-mer. They turned off Avenue du Fontaule and headed to the water to the coast guard station. Just then the colonel got a call.

"We have spotted the boat and we are closing in."

The coast guard boat was much faster than the smaller loaded down cruiser. Within moments the coast guard spotlight was on the boat. They called out over the horn for the boat to stop and prepare to be boarded. The boat did not slow down so they had to come along broadside and shoot tow lines across to capture it. The small boat did not have a chance. Within two minutes the boat slowed and two guards held their guns on the man who was seen on board. Within moments they had boarded the cruiser and had the man in custody. One of the guards dislodged the lines, turned the cruiser around and followed the coast guard boat back to their station.

The colonel, Lucien, and all the teams were standing on the dock watching as the boats came in. Alerion had his head propped up watching with one eye through the bright lights at the dock.

When both boats were tied to the dock, Lucien turned to Alerion and asked if he was all right for the moment. The medics from the station had already checked him out, noting some dehydration, but going steady enough to hold for five minutes, before heading off to the hospital for a thorough check.

They all watched as the kidnapper was marched into the coast guard office. Then Lucien asked the colonel if he could board the kidnapper's boat and find the letter. The colonel had a coastguardsman accompany Lucien and they boarded the cruiser. Lucien found the package in the captain's map box and brought it back.

The colonel had spoken to the guardsmen and was making arrangements to have the man escorted to the Collioure police station. Then he turned to all the men on the pursuit teams and congratulated them on a job well done. They could now go back to the barracks at the fort and get a good night's sleep. There would be a meeting on the events the next morning at 9:00 am sharp. No one was to speak about the event to anyone or they would be arrested for interfering with police business. They had very few facts to go on anyway and no one wanted to risk their jobs by reporting the crime to their papers. The men agreed.

Lucien quickly returned to Alerion in the back of his car. A soldier had brought water and it helped stir him around. Slowly, Alerion was coming back. A few more minutes and his eyes focused more.

"Alerion, are you okay? Can you speak?"

"Lucien." Finally both eyes began to focus on Lucien's face.

"Yes, it's me. Are you okay? Are you hurt?"

"I feel groggy, like a hangover. What's going on?" He pulled his head up and began to look around. Several of the journalists were watching from outside the car. "Who are all these people? Where am I?"

"You're in Banyuls-sur-mer at the coast guard station. We've just apprehended the man who took you hostage. You've been drugged, but are coming out of it. The cold sea air should be helping. You'll feel better in a few minutes." Lucien waved the men back away from the car.

"Lucien, are you okay? I followed you into the church, but couldn't find you. He followed me in, and then hit me over the head. He held me captive on his boat."

"Don't try to talk too much right now. We are going to get you to the hospital to make sure you are okay. Just sit still. We'll be leaving shortly."

The colonel said he had paperwork to handle with the coast guard captain and would see Lucien the next day at the morning meeting, but wanted him to get Alerion to the hospital for a thorough once over. Each team was leaving the coast guard station and heading back to Collioure, except one vehicle that would return the colonel when he was ready.

The hospital was only ten minutes away. As soon as Lucien reached it, he had a nurse and doctor take Alerion in. When asked what had happened, he only told them that Private Bellamy had been the victim of a crime and had just been rescued by the coastguard. For now, Alerion needed medical attention. Alerion was gaining more clarity and by then was able to describe his injuries. He knew not to say anything else. The medical team wheeled him off to run tests and make him comfortable for the night.

Finally, Lucien was able to call Chante and Gervais and let them know what had happened. He had gotten Alerion checked into the hospital and was heading back to his apartment to sleep as he had next to no sleep the night before and had an early meeting with the rescue team at the fort.

Chante and Gervais had been on the edge of their seats waiting for his call for what seemed like hours. It was almost 2:00 in the morning. Once Lucien finished giving them a short rundown of what had happened, he added that he was still not sure what would happen with the colonel, or how much he was going to have to tell him, but he did have the letter in his possession. Lucien would let Chante and Gervais know as soon as he could, how things went in the morning. Chante had already made up the couch in the living room for Gervais. She wanted to see Lucien badly, but understood the situation. They would see Lucien tomorrow.

The next morning Lucien was at the hospital at 8:00 to check on Alerion. Upon arriving at the hospital the night before, Alerion had an MRI due to his head injuries. It was determined that Alerion had received a pretty bad concussion, but had recovered on his own. It was thought that the concussion might have been greater, but it was only the drug that had created the symptoms of a hangover. His ears were still ringing, though it had lessened, and the doctors thought his full hearing would come back, in time.

Lucien sat down next to Alerion, who was ordered to remain in bed until he had been officially released. Bandages were on his wrists, but his ankles fared better and were only bruised. It was his head that had suffered the most. Lucien sincerely apologized for everything that had happened to Alerion, taking all the blame, himself. He knew that Alerion was probably very angry with him, and he deserved it. He only hoped that someday Alerion would forgive him.

Alerion put a hand on Lucien's arm, "Lucien, my friend. I do forgive you. I don't believe that you or Chante had any idea that someone would find out about the record with the file numbers and letters, or that they had any value."

"Alerion, that's not what the man was after. He was after something else. A historical letter that Chante and I found elsewhere in a chest in a cave."

"A letter? What kind of letter causes that kind of harassment?"

"A letter written to the Pope in 1307 by the Grand Master of the Templars."

"What? Really? Is it authentic?"

"We believe it is, but it will still need to be authenticated."

"Wow, and here I was upset over a sheet of numbers. I thought you had told Chante about it and that you were going directly to the church to find the files."

"We did, but that is another story. Those files are no more than historical summations from before 1941. They are of historical benefit, but their value is most likely incidental compared to the letter."

"So this man thought you had hidden the letter at the church?"

"Quite possibly, but we had not. Gervais had actually taken the letter to a bank and placed it in a safe deposit box for safekeeping."

"So what am I supposed to say or not say to the colonel and the police?"

"You had better tell them as near to the truth as you know it. However, I see no reason to say anything about the tunnel under the fort, do you? It could get us both into more trouble than we want."

"Don't worry. And about the church?"

"That you found a paper while going through the files at the fort which indicated that files were taken to the church. Somehow this man found out about them and followed you to the church, but that's all you know. I'll be talking to the colonel this morning and figuring out with him how to handle the letter. For now, take some time to recuperate and I will see you later today."

"I went into the church because I saw you and Chante go in, but not come out. Where did you go?"

"We must have been leaving out the front while you were upstairs. We had no idea you were inside."

"But how did you get past me?"

"There was a priest's hole right through the back of the wall of the church high altar. We can tell you all about it later, but for now you need to rest and prepare what you are going to say to the colonel, and the police."

Lucien said goodbye and quickly turned, but just long enough to see a look of concern on Alerion's face. Lucien's shoulders were still carrying the guilt that wouldn't leave him.

Chapter 30

The four journalists from the night before were in the meeting room when Lucien entered the next morning. Shortly thereafter the colonel arrived. The soldiers that had been on detail the night before with the journalists, had already been debriefed a few minutes earlier. The colonel took the lead and got the meeting started.

"Good morning men. The rest of the attendees will be arriving today and your official encounter week begins tomorrow. However, for the four of you who were able to assist in the maneuver with us last night, I want to sincerely thank you for your willingness to step in. You performed very well and helped us catch the man that we needed. Private Bellamy is doing much better and will be released some time later today. You have Sergeant Reynard to thank for your evenings excitement, as it was his idea to give you first arrivals a taste of what it is like to work undercover in the field.

"The case has been turned over to the Collioure police, who are now in charge of the investigation. Aside from holding Private Bellamy hostage, the police believe that the perpetrator may also be guilty of other crimes, and are continuing their search for additional evidence. With regard to what you know and how you assisted, I'm going to ask the four of you not to share what happened last night with your fellow journalists, and more importantly not to write about the incident for publication until more of the case has come to light, and I say you can. We cannot jeopardize the case as we are still looking for accomplices who could be in the area. However, when the police chief says that the evidence has been secured, which will most likely be collected within the next 48-hours, you will have exclusive rights to report on the event with all the details outlined for you. Is that understood?" The four men looked at each other with excitement in their eyes and nodded. "That's all for now. You are free to enjoy the rest of the day until 1900 hours when we will meet for dinner in the mess hall with the rest of the journalists."

The four men from various newspapers throughout France smiled with the news that they had exclusivity. Lucien was fairly certain that they would not say anything or they would lose the advance story to their fellow journalists. They left the room and the colonel turned to Lucien.

"Sergeant Reynard, please join me in my office. We have a few things we need to discuss."

Lucien grabbed his briefcase and followed the colonel upstairs to his office. Chief Souveterre was waiting there for them. Lucien was surprised to see the chief there and now was a bit hesitant to share as much as he was hoping to with the colonel, but he would see how it went. After renewed greetings they all sat down.

"Perhaps," began the colonel, turning to Lucien, "you will begin by telling us what you found, where you found it, and how it has bearing on last night's events."

Lucien opened his briefcase, opened the archival box, and showed them the plastic archival slipcovers that contained the two pages of the letter.

"Mademoiselle Morgan and I found a coastal cave with a short tunnel that had caved in and revealed an old chest. In the chest we found a box with a satchel that contained this letter. Although we saw no one, we figure that this man saw us leave the cave and began to follow us to take it from us. He must have already known of its existence, as we were followed for days. In doing so he had to have also seen Private Bellamy follow Chante and me at the colonel's request. We had gone into the church that morning, but had left without Private Bellamy knowing. Because Bellamy thought we were still in the church, he followed us. The man pursued Bellamy thinking that we had hidden the letter in the church, but we had not. Or perhaps the kidnapper thought that Bellamy was a competitor for the letter. He must have surprised Bellamy and knocked him out. He probably discovered that Bellamy was actually my assistant and determined to hold Bellamy for ransom so that he could have what he wanted. Two days later he sent a ransom note to me, but threatened to kill Bellamy if I involved the police.

"Several days before, we had taken the letter to my father, who is a history professor in Perpignan. He translated it from Old French, and due to its possible value, deposited it into a safe deposit box at a local bank. What you see before you is that letter, written in 1307 by the Master of the Templars, Jacques de Molay, to Pope Clement V. It asks the pope for protection from King Philip IV and predates the Chinon Parchment by a year and a half. Its authenticity and value are yet to be determined, but this man was no doubt in the market to sell it to the highest bidder. Because of the threat to Bellamy's life, we used the letter as bait and then enlisted the colonel's help to recover both.

"Chante, my father, and I, would like to have the letter authenticated and if it is as it seems, then we would like to see it donated to a major museum as a national historic find, perhaps to the Musee de l'Histoire de France in Paris. Due to the colonel obliging me with the unusual maneuver that transpired last night, we would like to share this discovery with the colonel and the National Center for Commando Training. We would like to give due recognition to the Banyuls-sur-mer coast guard and the Collioure police for bringing the assailant to justice." At this, Lucien turned to the chief. "I sincerely apologize for keeping this information from you, but I believe that by applying pressure to this man you will be able to make a case of assault and kidnapping, and also most likely solve your theft and murder cases. I believe with those charges made, your department will receive national recognition in solving the case. I know you must have many questions and I will do my best to answer as many of them as I can." He stopped and looked at the colonel and the chief, waiting for their responses.

The colonel was impressed and smiled, but the chief was angry that Lucien and Chante had lied and withheld information from him. He fully intended to query Private Bellamy later that day and to interrogate his prisoner later that morning. He still needed to know who the co-conspirators were, and Morgan, Reynard, and the professor would need to be questioned further and give statements. The colonel tried to soften the chief's temper by having Lucien turn over the ransom letter, which would substantiate the reasons for the abduction and not contacting the police. Everything had worked out, had it not, asked the colonel? The chief was holding the man who had not only been robbing Collioure's citizens, but he also had the kidnapper and murderer. The chief grumbled his gratitude and then left the office, reminding Lucien that he expected him in his office as soon as his duties permitted. The chief and the colonel nodded their goodbyes.

After the chief left, Lucien turned to the colonel. "Colonel, I deeply owe you an apology for not coming to you immediately, but quite honestly I didn't know someone was after what we had, which had only quite accidently been found."

"So you came across it accidently? You will still have to tell me where it was found. I know that French law having to do with treasure troves allows the finder possession outright, but I think you know as well as I that normally a treasure belongs to the owner of the land on which, or under which, it is found. Was the cave under military land?"

"I cannot share that information at this time sir, because I sincerely don't know. However, just know that there is nothing else there of great value, and that we seek no financial gain from it. We only want the letter's historical significance confirmed and displayed for all to see as a part of our national heritage. We are willing to share the credit for the find and hope that will be ample thanks for not pressing charges against us for withholding information. It is possible that there may even be some financial remuneration from a museum and in that case the reward can be equally shared. What do you say, colonel? Can we make this work?"

The colonel puffed up his cheeks in thought and looked out his window. Clear sky helped him to clear his head to think. "Let's see what the police discover, and we will have the letter authenticated. If the chief releases you of blame and no charges are filed then you have yourself a deal."

Lucien let out a long held breath and reached to shake his hand. "Thank you, colonel. I, Chante, and my father really appreciate it."

The colonel finally eased and gave him a slight grin. "Now get back to work. The other journalists are arriving and if Bellamy is feeling back to his old self you two have a lot to do in the next week. But for now I want you to keep an eye on *him*. Make sure he remains safe and does not overdo it."

Lucien saluted, thanked him again, and was out the door. On the way back to his office, he called Chante and Gervais to let them know where things stood, but that it was not over yet. He let them know that the police would still be interviewing them, as the investigation was still ongoing, but at least Alerion was okay and hoped to be released later that day.

At the police station, Chief Souveterre began to interrogate whom he now knew to be Fiacare Gael Morcant. He was the man who had run the diving company before Beaux Falchan.

"Fiacare Morcant, you have been charged with trespassing, breaking and entering, assault, theft, and kidnapping, and it is very possible that soon we will also find evidence of grand theft and murder. We also believe that you have accomplices. This is not the first time you have sat across the table from me. Four years ago you and Falchan were accused of theft. At that time you were asked to leave town and never to return. Yet, here you are. Why are you back in Collioure?"

Morcant took a breath and crossed his arms. He was wearing a long-sleeved faded blue shirt, with the sleeves partially rolled up. His forearms were tanned and on the inside of his left forearm was an old anchor tattoo. Under this shirt, which was open two buttons down, he wore an old Breton shirt with blue stripes, but the shirt was so old that the white had turned to beige and the collar was frayed. He no longer had his coat or cap on, so his unkempt hair was looking stringy. His dark brown brooding eyes squinted and his heavy dark eyebrows furrowed with a scowl on his face. He wasn't answering.

"That's okay, we know why you are back. You are back to your old tricks. You probably talked Falchan into working with you again, and when he refused you killed him after extracting what you wanted to know. The question is what did he tell you?"

Morcant was still silent.

"The next thing we know is that you saw a soldier and his girlfriend coming out of a cave along the coast carrying something you wanted very badly. You began to trail them, but then realized that someone else was following them as well. Did this person also know what they had found, or did you believe that you had some competition?"

Morcant remained staring directly at the chief.

"So you and two other men followed Bellamy into the church because you believed that he knew where the couple stashed the goods. You beat him to get him to tell you where, but he didn't know or didn't say. You picked the lock to the door that went upstairs, and drilled into every locker. You didn't find what you were looking for, so you searched further in the church, picking open another door leading into the tower. You made your way to a downstairs room and found a chest under a rug with two file boxes. You took their contents, but it would seem that was not enough, and something of greater value was still being held from you. So you took your victim hostage and held him for ransom in order to get the special item you did want. Have I got that correct so far?"

During this description, Morcant slowly looked up and was surprised by what the chief said. At last he spoke.

"I did not pick any locks. I don't work with anyone and I did not kill anyone!"

"Is that so? Why should I believe you? Suppose you tell me what did happen."

At this Morcant was once again silent.

"Were you in the habit of hiding your valuables in a cave?" Again, the chief got no response.

"Okay, let's talk about the thefts that have been occurring over the last year. How would you know what to take and where to go? The items that have been reported stolen were the usual: paintings, jewels, silver, and gold caches, all insured."

At that moment there was the slightest wince that the chief could detect in Morcant's face. What had he just said that caused that reaction? The chief looked at his watch. He had three more interviews to conduct, and for now Morcant was not talking. He told the officer in attendance to take Morcant back to his cell and he would speak again with him later. Mademoiselle Morgan and Professor Reynard were expected shortly. He would get their stories and hope to learn more from them now that he knew Reynard had lied to him.

Chante and Gervais were in the front room waiting. Chante was conducted first to the interview room. The chief pulled the chair out for her to sit and sat across from her.

"Mademoiselle Morgan, now that I know you and Lucien have been lying to me, I'd like to hear what happened in your own words."

"I'm sorry Monsieur Souveterre. What is it you feel I've lied about that you want clarification on?"

"First of all, how did you find out about the cave and the chest?"

"We simply found the cave by accident. We were exploring the coast, found a cave with a short tunnel where a section of the floor had sunken in from age and that's when we found the chest. We opened the chest and found a box and in the box a satchel. We dared not open the contents until they could be examined in a more protected environment. So we removed the box with the satchel and its contents and took them to Lucien's father, professor Gervais Reynard, who we hoped would be able to help us."

"When you did discover what it was, what did you do?"

"Lucien's father placed the contents into a safe-deposit box."

"How did Private Bellamy find out about it?"

"He didn't. We didn't tell him."

"How do you suppose his abductor found out about you finding the cache?"

"The only thing we can think of is that he saw us leave the cave, but we never saw him or anyone else."

"What do you hope to gain from this letter?"

"We hope it can be authenticated and put on display in a good museum."

"You've been back and forth between the U.S. and France with your husband for several years. Did you ever have occasion to meet the deceased man, Monsieur Beaux Falchan, who ran the local diving company?"

"No sir, I don't believe so. My husband and I don't dive, so we would have never used his services."

"I believe you were here up to five years ago when you were still renting. You could easily have met the man who previously lived in Collioure, the man who abducted Private Bellamy."

"Chief Souveterre, I don't know the man who took Private Bellamy. Who is he?"

"His name is Fiacare Morcant. He ran the diving company before Falchan. Do you remember him from five years ago?"

"No, I don't think my husband or I met him, either. We don't dive."

"Are you sure, Mademoiselle Morgan? I think that it is entirely possible that you have been using the pretext of writing about the chateau when you are really interested in treasure hunting. You are working with Morcant and together you made up a scheme to pretend to fall in love with a local military man, who could much more easily than you, search local records for caves and tunnels where a treasure might be found. Morcant followed you and Sergeant Reynard to steal the treasure. Then you would end the romance with the sergeant and receive a percentage of its sale."

Chante was so shocked that the chief could think up such a crazy story that she couldn't speak. That the chief might believe such a thing made her grow angry at being accused of conspiracy. She stood quickly in anger.

"I can assure you, Chief Souveterre, I never met Falchan or Morcant, or ever conspired to steal anything in my life! I love Lucien Reynard very much and am shocked that you think anyone would stoop so low."

The chief stared at her bulging eyes and reddening face, and determined that she was telling the truth.

"Thank you, Mademoiselle Morgan. You may go."

Chante grabbed her purse and, still mad, quickly left the room. She came into the front lobby and sat down hard, staring straight ahead. Gervais was about to ask her what happened, when Officer Fernand asked Gervais to follow him. A few moments later Gervais entered the room and the chief greeted him, extending his hand in greeting.

"Bonjour, Professor Reynard. My name is Chief Raoul Souveterre. Won't you please sit down?"

Gervais sat in the same chair Chante had just left.

"Professor, when did you first find out that Mademoiselle Morgan and your son had found something?"

"About a week ago they called me saying they wanted some information on the local area. They came to my house and showed me what they had found."

"What did you think about that?"

"I was in shock that they had discovered something that no one else had found before, and of course greatly surprised at what the letter was."

"Did they tell you where they found it?"

"Only in the vaguest of terms. Along the coast in a cave."

"Did they open the box at your house?"

"Yes sir, we carefully opened it together and documented it."

"You did? Where is this documentation now?"

"In a safe deposit box in a bank in Perpignan."

The chief was actually glad to hear that. That meant it was legally obtainable. "Did you know what it was when the satchel was opened?"

"No sir, it took me a couple days to research a translation from Old French."

"What did you do then?"

"I took the letter and the translation to the bank and placed them into a safe deposit box."

"And then what happened?"

"The paperwork stayed there until we found out that Alerion was being held for ransom, and then we got the letter out of the bank so that Lucien could use it to free him."

"And that's all?"

"Yes, sir."

"Where are the box and satchel that contained the letter, which everyone keeps talking about?"

Gervais thought about that for a second. "Aren't they on the boat?"

"No, they are not. Why aren't those two things still in your possession? You did say you had them."

"We did, but my house was broken into two nights later and they were stolen. And before you ask, no, I did not report it. We could hardly report something missing for which we could not substantiate ownership or value."

Souveterre cocked his head slightly and nodded, thinking. So where are the box and satchel if they aren't at the professor's house? Then he thought of something else.

"Did you ever give your son some collectible stamps?"

"What? No."

The chief was slightly surprised. Perhaps he had forgotten. Then asked, "What do you hope will become of this letter?"

Gervais gazed straight into Souveterre's eyes. "I'm a professor of history, Chief Souveterre. I was fathered by the will to know, mothered by the desire to understand, and my cousin is archaeology. I was born a child of history, to learn of it, see it, and to hold proof if it in my hand. Discovery of the truth is the first objective. Do you not agree?"

"You did not answer my question."

Gervais smiled. "I hope we find that the letter is really what it seems, because being this close to truth, just as you want to be this close to your killer, is what we live for. This letter may shed a small ray of light upon our knowledge of the past. Even its most basic intrinsic value is worth being placed in a museum for the public to see for themselves."

"So you were not planning to sell it for money to one Fiacare Morcant?"

Gervais pulled back in shock and his face grew stern and reddened. "Who? Certainly not!"

Again, the chief examined his face and determined that he seemed to be telling the truth. "You may go, Professor Reynard."

Gervais abruptly and indignantly got up from his chair and walked out to the lobby to join Chante. She stood immediately when she saw him. He took her by the arm and quickly guided her out without saying anything, though his face spoke volumes. He grabbed her equally for balance caused by his anger, which was making him a bit shaky at every step. The very thought of working with a kidnapper! Chante could see he was as upset as she was and bade him go around the corner for some strong coffee before walking back to her place. She needed one, too.

The chief took a break and went back to his office. He called the hospital and inquired if Private Bellamy had been released yet and if so, would they please send him straight to his office. They said he was to be released shortly and would deliver the message.

Raoul sat and thought for a few minutes. There was something very true about what the Professor had said. It was tantalizing to be this close to the truth of several things: the local thefts, the history of the letter, the reason for the kidnapping, and how and why the murder had been conducted. He was also thinking about what the night's events with the colonel's maneuvers might have been like. He wished he had been on that hunt, but he also realized that it had been a military case to begin with and he had only been asked to assist. Now with Morcant being held by his department, it was his turn to take the reins. He thought about the conversation in the colonel's office that morning. Where were the box and the satchel? Where was the evidence of the robberies? How could he tie the murder directly to Morcant? He needed proof of those three things. He would have the apartments of the sergeant, his girlfriend, and the professor searched to eliminate them as holders of anything. He had his secretary secure search warrants for those three addresses. He knew nothing was at Bellamy's apartment, because they had already been through it searching for clues when he went missing.

Finding answers to these questions seemed very close. No harm in indulging in a reward to spur him on. He asked his secretary to get him his favorite lunch of a smoked Jambon de Lacaune and Gruyère sandwich, and some fresh coffee. He could tell it was going to be a long day before he had the answers he needed.

Chapter 31

By 2:00 Private Bellamy was released from the hospital. He went home to take a shower and to change into his uniform. Then he walked to the police station and asked for Chief Souveterre. He was expected and taken to the interview room. The chief soon entered and introduced himself.

"Bonjour. I'm not sure we have formally met, which can be considered a good thing. I'm Chief Raoul Souveterre. You are Private Alerion Garner Bellamy attached to Fort Miradou, are you not?" He extended his hand and Alerion shook it.

"I am, sir. How do you do?"

"Good. Please be seated, private. As you can imagine, I have quite a few questions for you. I hope you feel up to answering them. How are you feeling?"

"Much better, sir. I got hit on the head pretty hard and suffered a concussion, but aside from two head wounds that are healing, my wrists are a little raw from the ropes around them for two days and two nights."

"I am sorry private, but we'll get to that later. First, let's start at the beginning. "What is your relationship to Staff Sergeant Lucien Reynard?"

"We are both attached to Fort Miradou in a semi-permanent position, sir. Meaning, we could be transferred to any fort, but for now we are stationed here. We handle the paperwork for the incoming and outgoing soldiers at the fort. I serve as Staff Sergeant Reynard's assistant."

"And how long have you been working with Sergeant Reynard?"

"For almost two years, sir."

"What happened that caused the colonel to have you keep an eye on Sergeant Reynard?"

"I'm afraid that is my fault, sir. You see, I often relay information from our office to the colonel for Sergeant Reynard, so I come in contact with the colonel fairly often. In off-season, as it is now, I sometimes do double-duty and may, at the colonel's discretion, perform certain tasks of research or errands for him. It wasn't until we had completed setting up a joint office for two new officers attached to the fort, and Sergeant Reynard had started dating Mademoiselle Morgan, that I noticed a difference in Sergeant Reynard. He was beginning to take more time away from his work, and some of his time away was unexplained. When I told the colonel that Sergeant Reynard had met a woman and that I had my doubts about her, he asked me to keep an eye on them. Not a 24-hour surveillance, but as much as I could when away from work, I was to report back to him where they went and what they did."

"I see. Did you witness them involved in anything of a questionable legal nature?"

Alerion should have expected this question. He tried hard to keep the vision of the tunnel below the basement out of his mind, so he focused instead on his final analysis from his observations of Lucien and Chante, and gave the same summarized statement that he would be giving to the colonel later that day.

"Quite honestly sir, nothing of an illegal nature. He just seemed like a guy falling in love, taking as much time as he could to be with her and not thinking about much else. I'm afraid after I spent so much time with him in and out of the office for the last two years I was getting a little jealous of the time he was spending with her."

"You and Sergeant Reynard were spending time together outside of work? In what capacity?"

"Just as friends, sir. We enjoyed a good glass of wine together."

"Understood. Now tell me what happened on the day you were kidnapped."

"Yes, sir. It was on Sunday morning. I had walked to the end of the quay and was having a cup of coffee and watching the fog start to clear on the bay, when I saw Sergeant Reynard and Mademoiselle Morgan sitting on a bench near the church. I watched them walk into the church, but when they did not come out after forty-five minutes, I wondered what had happened to them. Curiosity got the better of me, so I went in."

"Pardon me for interrupting. Is it possible that they could have left and you simply did not see them come out?"

"Yes, I suppose it is possible. I did hurriedly run to the toilet before going to the church, so that must have been what happened, but I had to go see for myself."

"Go on."

Alerion thought about what he was going to say next. "So I entered the church. When I got to the high altar and I didn't see them in any of the side chapels, I began to think they had gotten out and that I had missed them."

"Excuse me, did you pick the lock in the church chapel?"

"NO, sir."

"Go on."

"It had been a while since I had been in the church, so I sat and admired the high altar. It was pretty quiet in there, but then someone came into the church. To be honest, I was about to start looking behind the curtains in the chapels, but I did not want to be seen doing so. Sometimes lovers do the craziest things in the craziest places. I imagined them in a fond embrace behind some curtains. So I got up and decided to wait at the back of the room until the visitor had left so I could appease my curiosity. What I saw greatly surprised me, because this person was doing exactly what I was about to do. He was hurriedly lifting each curtain and looking behind it. I'll admit it, sir. I got scared."

The chief interrupted again. "Did you get a good look at him?"

"No sir, his back was to me at the time, and the lighting was low." Alerion continued. "I quickly left the church and went and stood inside one of the local shops, so I could catch a better glimpse of this man when he left the church. I saw another couple walk into the church and that must have stopped the man from searching, for he soon left, walked by the shop I was in, and then disappeared down the sidewalk and between two buildings."

"So then you were able to get a better look at him. Please describe him for me."

"Yes, sir. He is the same man that kidnapped me, but at the time I only noticed that he was a man of medium height, wearing a dark navy seaman's coat and a dark navy mariner's cap low on his face. When he walked by his head was down so I could not see his facial features, but his hair was longish and dark. I could see it curl out from under his cap as he was walking away. He was also carrying a dark bag over his left shoulder."

"Thank you. But you say he was by himself? No one was with him?"

"He was by himself, sir."

"Okay, then what did you do?"

"Something was troubling me about his actions. When I saw him leave the bay walkway, I decided to go back into the church. The couple that had gone in earlier left the church as I arrived, so I could then take the opportunity to look behind curtains myself. I can't explain it, sir. I still felt that Lucien and Chante must be in there. That's when I found the unlocked door on the right side of the altar. I figured the man had picked it, but got scared off by the couple. I decided to explore. I had never known there was a door there and curiosity got the better of me. I used the light from my phone to see so I could climb the stairs. I got about two-thirds up the squeaky stairs when the church door opened again. But I knew that if I moved anyone in the church could hear me.

"Less than a minute later the front door of the church opened again and a small tour group entered. When they got to the front by the high altar and their talking got louder, I took the opportunity to use that noise to cover the squeak of the stairs and get to the top. I decided to wait until they left to continue exploring. When they did, I used my phone again to find another door open and walked to the end of some lockers against a wall. Then the light on my phone went out. Just as I was going to swipe it again to get my light back, I heard the same squeak of the stairs behind me, so I froze. I figured it was either church personnel or the same man who had followed me in before. In either case, I did not want to be discovered, so I hid behind the last locker. I knew whoever it was had reached the top of the stairs because I could hear them pause. Then very quickly the man approached me directly and hit me over the head. I don't know how long I was unconscious, but it must have been for a long time.

"I came to consciousness sometime later and realized that I was tied up, my mouth had been covered, and a cloth was over my head. I tried to wriggle free but my head hurt so badly that I must have passed out again. I woke when the Mass began because I could hear the music and that brought me to consciousness. I tried to call out, but then the man hit me again, and later sometime after Mass had ended, I came to when I heard the sound of a drill. I guessed that he was breaking into the lockers searching for something. He noticed that I had wakened and that's when he removed the cloth on my head and the one across my mouth. He asked me why I was following 'the couple,' so I figured that he didn't know their names. He asked me if I knew where they had hidden the items found in some trunk in a cave. He had me completely stumped there. I had no idea what he was talking about, which he didn't like. Then he untied me and forced me at knifepoint out of the church to his rowboat at the far side of the beach, and then to his boat. He tied my feet and my hands to the cabin bed frame. He did feed me, but it was minimal. I had a terrible headache and ringing in my ears for the next twenty-four hours."

"Did you know what he was up to?"

"Yes, sir. He told me he was using me as collateral to get what he wanted and I watched him write the ransom note."

"Did you ever see an old box or old leather satchel onboard?"

"No sir, but the boat was pretty much a wreck."

"Did you ever hear him on the phone with anyone?"

"Yes sir, I did, but it was very short. Someone did call, but all he responded with was 'What do you want?' and then 'Just do your job'. "

That was good news. Now Raoul had testimony that there was another man working with Morcant.

"Did you know exactly what he was bargaining you for?"

"No sir, I had no idea."

"What happened yesterday evening?"

"I think it was about 2200 when he finally fed me an omelet for dinner. We motored to somewhere south and then again at knifepoint he made me climb off the boat and onto a dock. We got into a car, which was right at the dock, but I didn't recognize where we were. There must have been something in the food or water, because I just couldn't keep my eyes open. I passed out in his car and the first thing I remember was a wild ride down the mountain, and then a lot of men staring at me at the coast guard station."

"Do you think you have ever met this man before?"

"No, sir."

"Do you know a man named Beaux Falchan?"

"No sir, who is he?"

"He used to run the local diving company, but he turned up dead yesterday on the beach at Port Vendres."

"I'm sorry to hear that, but what's he got to do with me, sir?"

"Nothing, but we have reason to believe that he was killed by the man who took you."

"Who is this man, sir?"

"His name is Fiacare Morcant. He owned the diving company before Falchan, and we have reason to believe that he has been stealing items from local homes, and selling the goods along the northern coast."

"What happens now, sir?"

"Morcant is being charged with trespassing, and your assault and kidnapping, but we would also like to find evidence of his thefts, and we need evidence to link him to the murder, so we can bring further charges."

"I wish I could help you further, sir, but that's all I know."

"What you have told me is enough. We will have your statement typed up and have you sign it in preparation for presenting the case. I understand you are about to launch another journalist's immersion week. Are you feeling up to it?"

"The doctor told me to take it easy for a couple of days and not to drink any alcohol. Aside from the bumps on my head, I'm feeling pretty good. I don't actually go on maneuvers with the journalists, sir. I just help Sergeant Reynard keep track of their paperwork."

"I know the colonel wants to speak with you, so you are free to go check in with him. I'll probably want you to come back soon to sign your statement. If you think of anything else that might help us in our investigation, please let me know."

"Yes, sir." Alerion rose, saluted, and left.

There was something in the back of Raoul's mind that he couldn't quite get at. Something was not adding up. No one was taking the blame for unlocking the church doors. No surprise there. Why would someone admit to breaking and entering? But, where were the box and satchel? Where had Morcant stashed the stolen property if it was not in his car or on his boat? It looked as if he lived on his boat, so it was unlikely that he paid for an apartment. Not in Collioure anyway, as surely he would not have taken a chance by listing his name as a resident. Besides that, where was the evidence for the murder? Where was the gun that killed Falchan? It was not found on Morcant's boat, though he could have tossed it overboard.

Where was that autopsy report? That bullet in Beaux Falchan should have been delivered to ballistics yesterday. Where was the ballistics report? He called the coroner's office and left another message. He wanted to interrogate Morcant again, but he would prefer to have more proof of his other dealings to address with him. He also wanted to speak with Sergeant Reynard again. He had a few choice words for him and needed some things cleared up.

For now, Raoul was waiting for Officer Fernand to type the three statements that they had so far, and statements from various people in town were beginning to come in. Officer Fernand soon knocked on his door and handed him Sergeant Reynard's statement. He related that he was still not able to reach Falchan's wife, and that the coroner's office was on the line.

Raoul picked up his phone. Monsier Derouen apologized for the delay and said he was sending the report right over, but could sum up his findings. Falchan had been shot with a pistol at close range, but he had been thrown into seawater while he was still alive, as there was seawater in his lungs. So officially it was death by drowning. Even if the man could have swum to shore with a bullet in his chest, he had lost a lot of blood and probably would not have made it. There were bruise marks around the body from some kind of binding. He also had contusions on his shoulders and head, probably from being tossed against the rocks during the storm.

The chief still needed that ballistics report. Then his secretary brought in Chante Morgan's statement. He set it aside so he could finish Reynard's statement first, but then ballistics was on the phone. The bullet taken from the body was from a .32 automatic pistol. However, without the gun, the bullet could have come from any of fifty different models. They still needed a weapon to match to the bullet. So for now, all Souveterre could do was charge Morcant with trespassing, assault, and kidnapping. This case obviously still had some way to go. He still needed proof of the thefts as well.

Raoul went back to Reynard's statement. He reread where he had seen Morcant on the night of the storm, lighting a cigarette on the street by the cemetery. That seemed like an odd place to be, in the center of town late at night. With the police station just two blocks away, that was downright ballsy. He decided to read through both reports very carefully.

Alerion arrived at the fort and went to the colonel's office.

"Private Bellamy reporting, sir."

"At ease, private. It's good to see you back on your feet. How are you feeling?"

"Like I told Chief Souveterre, I've still got lumps on my head, but nothing I can't handle, sir."

"Good man." The colonel looked down at his desk and then to Alerion with a father's concern. "Still, I'd prefer it if you did not participate in the exercises being conducted with the journalists. I know you did last year, but it is not part of the job. You had better just stick to the paperwork this year."

Alerion was touched by his kindness. "Yes, sir." He was feeling weakened, but more emotionally and psychologically than physically. He had thought a lot about his feelings while confined on that boat; about Alerion, Chante, the colonel, his work, his unremarkable past, and if he got through the experience alive, how he would change his life.

"You were going to report to me how your assignment was going following Sergeant Reynard, but I think we all know how that ended up. What I'd like to know are the facts that led up to that. Why don't you focus on writing your report for me today at your desk."

"Yes, sir."

"However, I do have some questions I would like you to answer for me, now. So let me start with this. During those two weeks did you see or hear anything that might seem like Sergeant Reynard was not fully performing his duties?"

"No, sir. He took some time off, but he worked late a few days, and he came in early a few times to make up for his time away."

"During that time, did you see or hear anything that led you to believe that Reynard was breaking any laws?"

Alerion was repeating in his mind, *not the tunnel, not the tunnel.*

"No, sir."

"During that time did you see him enter or exit any cave or tunnel?"

NOT THE TUNNEL, NOT THE TUNNEL!

"No, sir." Then a relatively new feeling came over him. "If you will forgive me sir, may I speak freely?"

"Go ahead, private."

"It's a small town, colonel. Sergeant Reynard and I have worked together closely in the last two years, with many different teams of men coming and going for their training. Reynard is a good man, a dedicated man. I can assure you colonel, he puts me to task, but he works harder and longer than most. When we do have time off we enjoy a glass of wine together. We talk a lot and debate many things about the world, and when the season is in we watch the ladies, sir. We are both still single. Life in the military does not leave a lot of room for other things. I had gotten used to his company. So when a woman came along... "

Raoul knew what he meant. It had been more than two weeks since he had found warmth in a partner's arms himself. "You missed your drinking buddy."

"And friend, sir."

The colonel's men were dedicated and they worked long hours when training groups were in progress. Fort Miradou was one of the more recently rebuilt military forts, in a beautiful part of the world, with a long and proud history. Many, including him, knew its advantages way out-numbered its disadvantages. But if Bellamy had been watching Reynard and Morgan, how could he not have seen or learned about them finding anything?

"Do you know about any caves or tunnels along the immediate coast?"

"No, sir."

"Were you surprised to find out what he had been up to without your knowledge? That is, finding a cave and something from a trunk?"

"Very much, sir. In fact, when this Morcant asked me where the items were that came from a chest in a cave, I had no idea what he was talking about."

"I assume that Reynard has told you about the letter he found?"

"Yes, sir, he has, but I knew nothing about it before and I still have not seen it."

"I'm sure you will soon, Private Bellamy. But for now it is being held until we are ready to move it. That's it for now. You may go."

Alerion saluted, turned, and closed the door behind him. He made his way to Lucien's office where he was hoping to speak with him, but Lucien was out with the immersion team. Disappointed, he went to his office, sat down, and began to type his report.

Chapter 32

Alexis peered out the window of the Mairie, watching the street. He'd kept a close watch as the day went by. There was little else to do in the off-season. He hadn't heard anything about what had happened the night before until he went to lunch around the corner. Ever since then he had grown more nervous as each hour went by. Talk about the events of last night and this morning had traveled the town quickly.

Jeanine, who owned the laundromat and had been cleaning the floors late last night, watched as the yellow coast guard vehicle pulled up in front of the police station across the street. To her amazement she watched Monsieur Morcant being pulled out of the vehicle wearing handcuffs. She remembered him living in the village years before. She told the hairdresser next door, Marcine, as soon as she arrived to open her shop. Georgine was one of the nurses on night duty at the hospital when Private Bellamy was brought in. When she got off her shift and arrived home a little after 8:00 the next morning, she ran into her landlady Bibi, who was walking her dog. They spoke, and when Bibi was getting her hair done an hour later, she heard more news from Marcine. Then they watched as the professor and Chante walked by, crossed the street, and went into the police station. The grocer's wife, Adèle, had been doing laundry at the laundromat before going in to work her shift. She had spoken with Jeanine at the laundromat, and then later, as she was walking to work, she watched a young man in uniform go into the police station. She told her husband, Didier, what she had seen and heard. Didier then finished with his shift at their small grocery, and walked to the café around the corner for lunch. He had a glass of wine with his friend Dominique, who ran the café. It was the same place that Chante had taken Gervais after coming out of the police station. Dominique was able to overhear some of their conversation, and was telling Didier about it when Alexis came in for lunch and joined in, listening to the two men. Morcant was back in town! What had he stolen this time? Did he have anything to do with the murder? Who were the old man and pretty woman in the cafe? What did they have to do with Morcant? They looked upset. Maybe Morcant stole something from them?

The two men repeated what the townspeople knew of Morcant. He was a seasoned thief and experienced con man. They spoke of him as if he were a modern day pirate. When Dominique had known him as a customer years before, he remembered a night when Morcant had gotten excessively drunk on rum and called himself "the French Robin." He didn't know what he had meant at the time, but when Morcant had been sent out of town on suspicion of stealing, he realized that the reference was to the famous character of Robin Hood. Then all three shook their heads in dismay and talked about a funeral for Beaux Falchan, most likely to be held the following Sunday.

After lunch, Alexis thought about closing the Mairie early and going home, but then he was also on a sort of duty assigned by the chief and didn't want to disregard the warning so soon after receiving it. Because of his key position, a lot more was expected of him than he had ever wanted. Every week that went by made him more and more nervous. It was a tenuous position in which he had placed himself. He'd hoped that the money would allow him a way out, but it had only gotten him in deeper.

Alexis' father had begged his cousin to give Alexis a job. Alexis had hidden behind the door, listening to his father speak with Raoul on the phone. After all, his father told him, Alexis did have experience in customer service while living in Marseille. He had worked for a clothing store and a Monoprix department store. Even at his young age of twenty-three, he had also worked in an insurance office, though he had only been a filing clerk. He had also been a security guard, though it had only been for four months. His father swore that his son was trustworthy, but he just couldn't hold a job for long. He got bored easily and as a teenager had problems with alcohol. His father told his cousin that Alexis needed to have an important job so that he could take pride in what he did. His father stressed the importance of Alexis needing to put down some roots outside of the crime-ridden streets of Marseille. What better way than to have a job in a small town working for a member of the family, whom his father greatly respected. In truth, his father just wanted his cousin to keep an eye on Alexis, and who better than the chief of police? As long as Alexis did his job he would be fine.

At 5:30 Alexis ran upstairs to the insurance office to make sure it was locked after the last person had left at 5:00. It was part of his duties as caretaker of the building. Then he walked home and had a large snifter of Cognac to calm his nerves.

*   *   *

Lucien finally had some time to himself late that afternoon, after the first day's orientation to the journalist encounter. He had gotten the men's sleeping quarters assigned, had them all sign consent forms, went over the schedule for the week, and answered an hour's worth of inquiries. Reporters were relentless with their never-ending questions. He had one bright moment when a journalist actually asked about the history of the fort in relation to the town. He was happy to give a description of some of the history he had discovered within the last few weeks. With that over, and a break before everyone was to meet for dinner at 1900 hours, he made his way to the police station to keep his promise to Souveterre.

The chief ushered Lucien into the same small room, followed by the ever-present Officer Fernand, who once again sat to take notes.

The chief decided to start off friendly. "How was the first day of the encounter?"

Lucien knew the friendly ploy, but went along with it. "Fine, sir. All the preliminaries are out of the way and tomorrow the real fun — at least for them — begins. Anything new on the case, sir?"

"Some. I still have some questions that need to be answered. I'm hoping you can help me with them."

"Of course, sir. In what way?"

"You can begin by telling me why you didn't go directly to Private Bellamy and ask him if he was following you, and why he was doing so?"

"I have a healthy respect for Private Bellamy, sir. I figured he was following me because he did not like the fact that I was spending more time with Mademoiselle Morgan, than I was with him. Had I confronted him he would have had to admit his own feelings. I figured in time he would meet her and see that she is genuinely a good person."

"If you knew you were being followed by a second man, why didn't you warn Private Bellamy of this other man?"

That was a good question. One he had not considered before. He had only had concern for Chante and himself, which now he admitted was selfish.

"I should have warned him. I know that now, sir, but it all happened so fast and I was never really certain that either he or another man were actually following us. I had only seen the other man briefly at the park. I figured the second time I saw him might have been a coincidence."

"All right, but if you and Bellamy were such close friends, why didn't you tell him about finding the chest in the cave?"

"Private Bellamy is a business-only kind of guy, sir. He is a great many other things, too: intuitive, loyal, resourceful, a hard worker, and honest, but he is not what I would consider adventurous. That's why he is a secretary and not actively pulling duty in a combat zone. Besides, I had found the cave with Mademoiselle Morgan and we decided to keep it to ourselves."

"Between you two and your father, that is."

"Yes, sir, we needed to know what the letter said."

"Then why did you lie to me and cover up finding the items in the cave?"

"To be quite honest, sir, I knew that you would seize the letter and hold up any investigation of its authenticity before we could get it recognized for what it is and get it into a museum."

"You are correct, but you withheld evidence in a kidnapping. You could be charged with obstructing justice."

"I understood that was a possibility sir, but in this case, I believe there is already enough evidence to charge Morcant with kidnapping without the letter. You have the ransom note, and you already know that it was due to the letter. Besides, I'm sure the colonel will make a copy of the letter available to you to be included in your case. If I understand the legalities correctly, its disclosure would not have resulted in another outcome, which is the only way it would be considered obstructing justice."

The chief had to admit he was right, but it perturbed him. He let that one go, but decided to try once again on another point.

"When did you come out of that sea cave?"

"It was quite early in the morning, sir. Just after dawn."

"And how did you end up there so early in the morning?"

Lucien had not counted on that coming up. "We had been up all night and decided, as lovers sometimes will, to do something unusual, so we went for a walk early when the tide was low."

"I see. Then tell me this. Neither Morcant nor Private Bellamy admitted to picking the locks at the church. That only leaves you Sergeant Reynard. Why did you lie about that?"

"Please, Monsieur Souveterre. Morcant is a kidnapper, why would you believe him?"

Souveterre still believed that one of them was lying, but of all the charges this was the least of them.

"I'd also like to know who you think was responsible for breaking into your father's house and stealing the box and satchel."

"So you know about that? Well, I think it must be obvious that Morcant is responsible."

"But the box and satchel were not found on his boat. Where are they?"

Lucien was genuinely surprised. "They weren't there? Then I have no idea. Maybe he stashed them somewhere else?"

Souveterre had already considered that, but where? Reynard had lied to him before. Perhaps he was keeping the box and satchel back, like he had the letter.

"To be sure, I am having your apartment, Mademoiselle Morgan's apartment, and your father's house, searched. I hope you don't mind," he said with a smile. "I have to eliminate the possibility that the three of you are lying to me about not having them. I'm sure you understand."

"That is fine, sir. I'm sure you will not find the box or satchel in any of our homes." Lucien was glad that he had returned the welding tank and torch back to the store when he went to mail the package with the wood splinters. His lock and pick were in his second set of fatigues hanging in his office and the rope was in the trunk of his car.

"We still have not found out where Morcant has hidden his stolen goods. Are you sure there was nothing else in that cave?"

"No, sir. The chest was old and battered and there was nothing else inside."

"I do have one more question. Why did you lie about not having anything of value? Your father had no idea about any stamps he had given you."

"It is true, sir, I did lie about that. I simply did not want to tell you about the letter for the same reason I have already given you."

The chief was not entirely pleased with his responses, but those were all the questions he had.

"Sir," asked Lucien taking advantage of the pause, "Were you able to get anything out of Morcant? Were you able to tie him to the murder?"

"Not yet, but we are working on that." He looked at Lucien's concerned face, his forward shoulders and open hands before him. He'd learned to read people a long time ago. Reynard was either an accomplished liar or he was being honest with him.

"All right, sergeant, you are free to go. We will have your statements combined and typed up, and made ready for your signature. Stay in town and I will call you when the statement is ready."

Lucien stood, thanked the chief, and saluted. Just as he reached the door, the chief stopped him.

"Sergeant, one more thing is puzzling me, and that is your statement about seeing Morcant that rainy night. It just seems strange to me that he would be in the center of town when he should not be seen in town at all. Did you notice anything else that perhaps seemed unusual?"

Lucien thought about that evening and tried to picture the man and where he was standing. Then it came to him. "Actually, yes, sir. Now that I think about it, I did notice something out of the ordinary. I saw that he was looking well over my head when I crossed the street. After I crossed, and he could not see me, I looked up and saw a light on upstairs in the insurance company above the Mairie. I didn't know that they worked that late."

The chief thought about that and wondered himself. "Thank you, Sergeant Reynard. Thank you very much." Lucien turned and left.

After Lucien was gone and the chief went back to his office, his secretary came in with the autopsy report, the ballistics report, and the thin evidence file, which now contained the ransom note. The autopsy and ballistic reports already confirmed the things he had been told on the phone. He called the colonel and requested a copy of the letter to add to the evidence file. The colonel said he would have it sent over the next morning.

Souveterre rifled through the files on his desk and picked up the files on the four unsolved thefts that had occurred in the last year. He was looking for any clue that might help. The owner of the famous painting stolen in the last theft had software on his phone that let him know whenever the front door of his home was opened when he was away. That night he had been asleep in Paris at a hotel with his wife. In her statement she said she always complained of his phone dinging from missed calls in the middle of the night, so she told her husband to turn the phone off. When he turned it on the next morning, he saw that there had been an entry into their house the night before, but that it had been reset a few minutes later, which confused him. His wife reminded him that no one besides them had their alarm code. The alarm had been turned off within a few minutes, so the system must be at fault. As the next few minutes ticked by the husband became more suspicious, so he called the alarm company to see if their computers had shown an entry. They confirmed an official entry at 12:07 and a reset at 12:14 am. He and his wife packed their bags, cancelled their plans, and within twenty minutes were headed back to Collioure. When they got home and saw that the painting was missing and frame was on the floor, they called the police and left word at the insurance company.

Raoul looked again at the date on which Lucien had seen Morcant in the street. It was the same night the robbery had taken place. A glimmer of an idea was coming to him. He called his secretary and two of his officers into his office to let them know his next plan. The search team had just finished conducting their searches of the professor, Mademoiselle Morgan, and Sergeant Reynard's homes, when the chief reached them. Neither the box nor the satchel had been found, or any other incriminating evidence.

The chief smiled. It was now time to get aggressive. He called the local judge and requested another search warrant. The judge was on his way to dinner, but would have the warrant sent to the chief's office first thing the next morning. If Raoul was wrong he could always apologize, but if he was right it might just answer all of his remaining questions.

He was sure that Morcant was probably sitting in his cell, smugly thinking that no more evidence for any other crime had turned up. The punishment for kidnapping in France carried a term of only ten years imprisonment. With good behavior he could be out sooner. Souveterre had planned to interrogate Morcant again, but if he could gather more evidence before that, he would love to see Morcant get a good many more years.

That night he went through the statements from Sergeant Reynard, Professor Reynard, Mademoiselle Morgan, Private Bellamy, and Morcant, to think about what his next move would be. The search warrant arrived at 8:30 the next morning. He assembled his men and they made their way to the apartment complex past the cemetery. He knocked on Alexis' door just as Alexis was about to leave for work at the Mairie. The look on his face was one of shock.

"Raoul, what are you doing here?"

"I think you know why, Alexis. We have a warrant to search your premises. Please stand aside." Alexis' face turned pale as he was handed the warrant and two officers brushed by him and went inside. "I'll watch him," he told his officers. Raoul had already thought about what he would say to his cousin's son, but he withheld saying a word until his men could finish. Only four minutes later, after both officers had turned the apartment inside out, they returned to say they had not found anything.

"Then it is a good thing we included your storage space in the warrant. Where are the keys to your storage, Alexis?"

"I, I don't use the storage, but the key is here." He went over to a nearby bureau, opened a drawer, and pulled out a single key. Raoul took the key from Alexis and instructed the men where to look.

Each apartment had a separate storage area in the carport that lined the back of the apartment complex. All they had to do was match the space with the apartment number. They all walked to the space together. The closet-like storage measured four feet wide, three feet deep, and six feet high. Once the tall wooden doors were unlocked it became immediately clear that they would find what they were looking for. The storage contained multiple sacks piled on the floor in different shapes, and against one corner was a long mailing tube. Each officer took a bag and opened it up. In one bag were three books of a coin collection. In another were two small paintings in ornate gold frames. In a third was a box full of high-end jewelry. A fourth bag toward the back held the box and satchel from the cave, and the tube revealed the rolled up stolen painting. The chief had mixed emotions. He now had evidence of the thefts, but where was the gun?

Alexis went into shock. "But none of this is mine! I don't even use this locker."

"Really?" asked Souveterre with a big smile. "Then who do you have using your storage?" Alexis turned bright red and stopped talking. "It greatly pains me Alexis, but you are under arrest for grand theft." Souveterre signaled one of the officers to take Alexis into custody, and the other to transport the contents of the storage locker to the station.

Raoul sincerely doubted that Alexis knew that the items were in the storage space, about as much as he was sure that Morcant had put everything there, and that Alexis would soon give up Morcant up for the thefts.

Chapter 33

When everything had been brought to the station, photographed, and tagged, Raoul waited impatiently for Alexis to be brought to the interrogation room. As soon as Alexis was seated, Raul began.

"Alexis, Alexis, it seems you just can't stay out of trouble. Did you know that you are probably looking at a good twenty years in prison?"

Alexis looked anxiously and nervously from Raoul to Officer Fernand, who hardly looked up from his writing everything down. Raoul and the officer had serious looks on their faces, but inside Raoul had mixed emotions. He was happy to get the thefts cleared up, but sad that his cousin's son was involved.

"Would you care to tell me how all of those stolen goods got into your storage locker?"

Alexis was dumbstruck and was beginning to sweat. He didn't know what to say, so he said nothing.

"Alexis, your parents are going to be very upset with you. Of course they may end up cursing me as well for not watching you more closely, but in the end I think they will thank me for saving your ass."

At that Alexis got a confused look on his face.

"You don't know what I'm talking about, do you?"

Alexis managed a barely audible, "No."

"Then let me explain this to you. You are going to give up Morcant so that we can pin several counts of grand theft, plus murder on him, where I believe they rightfully belong. Unless you would like to confess to theft and murder, would you?"

Alexis swallowed hard but did manage to reply. "No."

Raoul nodded his head in agreement and responded with the kindness of a concerned family member.

"I know you didn't, but you will need to tell me everything. If you don't, you will go to prison for a very long time and Morcant will get out of jail way before you do. If you do tell me everything and put the blame where we both know it belongs, then things will go a lot better for you. Let's start at the beginning, shall we? First, tell me how you met Morcant."

Alexis took a deep breath, looked up at the ceiling, looked down, and then back at someone from whom he knew he could elicit some sympathy. He was trapped and he knew it. Morcant was already in jail and all Alexis could think of was that he would be joining him shortly. The thought of being in jail for most of his life made him blanche.

"All right, all right. I'll tell you." He took another deep breath and then began. "I met Morcant almost five years ago in Marseille. I was working as a filing clerk for an insurance company there. It was an okay job, but I was not making very much money. One day I met him in a bar near the port. He made me an offer that seemed like the answer to my problem. You have to realize that I was desperate. Mama was working long hours as a seamstress for a horrid man that runs a clothes manufacturing company. And you know how protective papa is, even more so, since he sits home alone all the time due to his automobile accident. He told me all the time to make sure I was staying out of trouble. He yelled at me to do better, to work harder. He drove me crazy. When they were together they fought a lot. I needed to get away from both of them and I needed to make more money so I could. When Morcant found out that I worked for an insurance company, he offered me a way out.

"What I had to do was simple. When filing the insurance papers, all I had to do was look in the file, read what was getting insured, write down the address, and note any security measures mentioned in the paperwork. Morcant took care of the rest. He wanted only specific things, and he waited for some time after I gave him the information before he stole the items. This was so the insurance company wouldn't get suspicious. He told me that he watched the house he planned to rob. He had some kind of electronic device that he would leave near the front door, which recorded the alarm code so he would know what to punch in when he got into the house. He paid me in cash for the information. Soon I was able to get my own place.

"One day an employee of the insurance company caught me reading one of the files. I dismissed it, saying that I was just curious and would not do it again. Two weeks later, when I noticed that the same woman was watching me, I decided that it was time to leave the job. Morcant was furious and he told me to get another job as an insurance clerk immediately. I tried, but my previous employer would not give me a recommendation, so I had to borrow money from mama to pay my rent. Soon after that she showed up at my apartment to bring me some food. I could tell that she got suspicious when she found some expensive items in my bedroom and an expensive bottle of cognac in the kitchen cupboard. I tried to explain away the silver candlesticks she had seen, by saying that a girlfriend of mine had asked me to store them while she was away because she didn't trust her ex-roommate; and that the alcohol had been a holiday gift from the company

I had worked for. But I don't think she believed me, and she told papa."

Alexis took a break and paused. Souveterre could not help but comment.

"That conversation about you was probably the first thing they agreed on in a long time. They called me several times asking me for help to get you out of Marseille. The only reason I was able to take you on is because the man who was running the Mairie put in his notice to leave. Now go on, what happened then?"

"When you finally told my parents that I was coming to work for you, I told Morcant that my parents had gotten me another job. I was leaving town and going to Collioure. I didn't know it then, but when he heard that, I'm sure he was surprised. Only after I moved here did I hear of his past history from others who remembered him. I don't think he really cared where I was going until I told him what I had been hired to do."

"You mean, working in a building that had another insurance company?"

"Yes, he saw his chance to not only continue running the same scam, but also for revenge for being told to leave Collioure. So when I moved here, he moved his operations back to Collioure. I was thrilled with the amount of money I was receiving for working at the Mairie and acting as the building security officer, along with the extra money from you and the cash from Morcant. I made more than I ever thought possible. And just so you know, I do send my parents money every month. Having the keys to the insurance office was a plus for my work with Morcant. All I had to do was get into the office after it closed and look through the files for the information that he wanted.

"Since he lived on his boat and had not established residency, he was not officially living in Collioure and was not listed as a resident. He almost never walked in town in case someone might recognize him. When he did, he wore a cap low over his head and walked the back streets late at night. Besides, he liked living on his boat. It offered him a vehicle for a quick getaway and the means to travel up and down the coast so that he could more easily transport and deliver the stolen goods."

"But now Morcant has been caught and is sitting in jail."

"I really did not expect that. He was always so careful, and such a professional, not stealing too often or too much, and often a great deal of time would elapse between me giving him the information and him taking the items. Besides, the items were insured. The insurance company would pay out. He told me that if he ever were caught, he would not say anything about me. He instructed me to do the same. Several times he threatened me on the subject. When I heard that he got arrested, I admit, I was relieved that he could no longer threaten me. Another part of me was also relieved that I wouldn't need to keep lying to you. Still, I knew I would miss the money and things like good Cognac. I also had a feeling that if there were enough evidence against him, he would blame me anyway. I also worried because he had my number on his phone. You must not have found his phone, because I waited all afternoon and evening after you arrested him, thinking he would either give me up, or you would find my number on his phone, but you didn't come to find me so I figured he stuck to the plan."

"I think he probably threw his phone overboard just before the coastguard stopped his boat, when he tried to run to the Spanish border. I'm sure he would not want his contacts on that phone compromised. He probably never even gave you a second thought, Alexis. So how did the things he stole end up in your storage?"

"I can only guess. When I moved in I had next to nothing. I certainly had nothing extra that needed to be put into that storage area. He must have stolen my key and made a copy. He *had* been in my apartment. I knew he had a car that he parked out of town. He wanted to park it in my carport, but I was too afraid he would keep stolen things in it and I would be blamed if he was caught, so I begged him not to. In the end he decided it was better not to park the car there either, but nearer his boat. But I swear, I did not know anything was in my storage."

"I think I believe you, but the question is, will a judge believe you? Now, to the murder."

"Please sir, I was shocked to hear that Beaux was murdered."

"So you knew him?"

"Yes, sir. I often sent clients to him and he brought advertising for his diving tours into the travel bureau. We may even have sat at the same table at the cafes."

"Did you call Morcant after I spoke with you last time?"

"Yes, and I told him that you said there had been a kidnapping and asked me if I had seen any strangers in town."

"What did he say to that?"

"He just told me to do my job and hung up."

"We have a witness who places Morcant across from the Mairie before midnight on the night of the last robbery. He says that he saw a light on upstairs in the insurance office. That was you, wasn't it?"

"Yes, sir. Normally Morcant would not come to town or anywhere near the Mairie. I had let him know about the painting weeks before, but I was not able to give him the valuation amount. He needed to know so he could set his own price. The first time that I was searching, an agent came back into the insurance building for something she had forgotten and interrupted me. I heard her coming up the stairs and quickly returned the paperwork to the files. I told the woman I had come in to shut a window that had been left open. So later, Morcant came to my house and made me get the information right away. He said he needed to get the painting that night, because the owners had finally left on holiday."

"And he did, not more than an hour later. I suppose he also had you find another address for him, the address of Sergeant Reynard's father?"

"Yes, but it took me a couple days to get that information to him."

Raoul realized that's why there was a delay from the time Morcant saw Reynard take the box from the cave, until he was able to rob the professor's house of the box and satchel.

Tears began to well up in Alexis' eyes as he asked, "What happens now?"

"Now you go to a jail cell and wait until you are transferred to Perpignan, where you will stay until the case comes to court. I'll have to evaluate the charges against you now that I have your confession and you have implicated Morcant as the thief. All that is missing is evidence that he killed Falchan."

"Will you be telling my parents what happened?"

"Yes, but I promise to put you in the best light that I can, stressing that he threatened you. You will still have to go to prison, but it won't be for kidnapping or murder. "

"Thank you."

The chief ended the interrogation and signaled Officer Fernand to take him back to his cell.

When Alexis was gone, Souveterre went back to his office. All he needed was that damned gun. Where in the hell was it? Maybe Morcant had tossed the gun out of the boat when he'd tossed the phone? If so, he would need other evidence to link Morcant to the murder. When he had a moment he called the insurance company and let them know what had happened, but that the painting had to be photographed before it was returned to its owners. It was an important piece of the evidence puzzle.

There was one more thing he felt he needed to do, just to cover all possibilities. There was one more place he needed to look. Souveterre borrowed the key to the Mairie that had been turned in when Alexis was taken into custody, and asked one of his officers to go with him. Since the Mairie was already under police protection, he didn't need a search warrant. He found the keys to the filing room, the bathroom, and the computer room. He had the officer search in those places, while he thoroughly searched the front office. He was about to go upstairs to the insurance office, when he heard his officer call him from the filing room downstairs, saying that he had found the gun. It was in the very back of a file cabinet, in a paper bag. Souveterre carefully removed the gun and looked at it. It was a late 1960's Le Français pistol, and he knew what kind of bullets it shot.

They relocked the office and returned to the police station. Souveterre had the gun immediately sent to ballistics to match the bullet, and checked for possible fingerprints. He doubted any fingerprints would show, but he was going to follow procedure to the letter. There was only one thing that perplexed him. Why would Alexis have the gun if Morcant had killed Falchan? Morcant probably stashed it there to implicate Alexis, as he had with the stolen goods in Alexis's locker. Morcant had been cunning and careful.

Two hours later he got a call from ballistics saying that indeed the fatal bullet had been fired from that gun, but no fingerprints were found. That was great, the bullet matched, but that information still did not tie the weapon to Morcant. Souveterre decided to have another chat with him.

Morcant was brought back into the interrogation room. They sat as they had before and once again Morcant just crossed his arms in front of himself and leaned back away from the table. Souveterre knew he was going to enjoy this next discussion.

"I've given you some time to stew in your cell. Have you decided to come clean and confess your crimes? Cooperation goes a long way, you know."

Morcant had not changed his attitude.

"I've nothing more to say."

"Really? Well what would you say to the fact that we found a pile of stolen goods in Alexis Moniqua's carport storage?"

"Then I would say that he's your thief."

"Actually, he had no idea that the storage locker was even being used. He came to town with very little and had no reason to use it. He doesn't even have a car so he didn't need the carport space. Not surprisingly, I had an officer take all the keys that we found on you, and had him check each one to see if any of your keys matched Alexis' storage key. Sure enough, one did. You had the means, and because you moved around at night and could easily access it, you had the opportunity. There is no way that Alexis had enough know-how or the guts to break into any home. Plus, we found a set of lock picks, and the tools you needed to extract the canvas from that very expensive painting that was recently stolen."

"That doesn't mean I took it. That was Alexis's storage locker. He's not as innocent as you think."

"Oh, I know that. He just gave me a full confession. He explained how he got the information to you from the insurance company, and then you picked the time to complete the job later. With a boat docked at a different town along the coast, and an old car that you paid cash for, you could easily get around on your own. We found the receipt for the purchase of the auto in your glove box, dated just under a year ago. A tax preparer would applaud you for keeping your receipt. The timing seems to fit perfectly with the first of four robberies that took place within the last year, the first one occurring just a week after the purchase of the vehicle."

Morcant said nothing, but his eyes squinted in anger at hearing about Moniqua's confession.

"I think there is now enough evidence to pin at least three counts of grand theft on you, if not more. Congratulations, you just added at least another ten years on to your sentence. But don't fret. Alexis will be in prison right along with you. Now that we've cleared all that up, let's move on to the murder. We found your gun and forensics has matched the bullet found in Falchan to the gun. We're only one step away from adding at least twenty more years on to your sentence. You must have hid it at the Mairie where no one would think to look."

With this news Morcant unlocked his arms, grabbed the edge of the table and stared directly at Souveterre.

"And I'm telling you I did NOT kill Falchan! I don't even own a gun."

"Really? It seems to me that Falchan, who used to be your partner, showed you where a coastal cave was so you could help him sell whatever was in there, for a huge profit. Then as soon as he showed you where the cave was, you shot him and dumped him into the sea."

Now Morcant leaned forward toward the chief with anger in his eyes.

"No! That's not what happened."

"Then why don't you tell me what really happened."

Morcant stewed and clenched his fists. His face tensed and he took a deep breath.

"All I know is that I had to follow Reynard and his girlfriend, but I couldn't be seen following them during the day in town, so I lost track of them for a couple of days. Then while I was watching her apartment, I overheard Reynard speaking to his father about working on some kind of translation."

"So that's when you got Alexis to find out where his father lived, and that's when you took the box and satchel."

Morcant continued. "A few days later I camped out near her apartment again and saw them leave early the next morning and walk to town. I had to walk the long way around town so I wasn't spotted. I hid between some buildings and then I happened to see the younger soldier go into the church. I knew he had been following them because I had seen him doing so twice, so I assumed that he was following them into the church. Since the translation of whatever it was had to have been something old and valuable, I thought they were hiding it in there. I didn't want him to get to it first, so I followed him in. Then he left, and Reynard and the girl were nowhere to be found, so I left. I thought I had been mistaken."

"But then you watched Private Bellamy go back into the church, and figured that he went in to retrieve the letter?"

"That's when I started to look harder for it and discovered an open door that led upstairs, so I went up."

"You must have had on your night-vision goggles to find Bellamy so soon, because he said he was in the dark and you came directly at him, plus the fact that we found them on your boat. I'm curious though, how did you know to bring the goggles if you didn't know that you were going to need them?"

Morcant grunted and sat back again.

"I just happened to have them. A habit left over from my service days."

"Right, and you just happened to have them in your duffle bag! You were obviously transferring them from the locker to your boat. So then you left Bellamy tied up and went to get the drill, which we found on your boat, so you could get into the lockers. You thought the papers were hidden there, but you had to wait until Mass was over to make noise. Then maybe Alexis joined you and you both went searching the tower and the lower floor for the papers."

"No, I never called Alexis."

"But you found a large trunk and took what was in the file boxes. Or since the papers that you wanted were still nowhere to be found, you got the idea to hold Bellamy hostage so that Reynard would have to give up the papers that had been in the satchel."

"No, I mean I found the trunk, but the file boxes in the trunk were empty. But I did not kill Falchan and you couldn't possibly have proof that I did."

Souveterre thought about that for a few moments. He was right. There was no proof right now that tied him to the murder. What would it take to do so? He had Morcant sent back to his cell.

Now that he knew Morcant was responsible for the thefts, he needed to match the found items with the theft reports for those past robberies. He spent the rest of the afternoon adding the pictures of the found goods to each file and writing up the reports about their recovery. Then one date surprised him. He went back to the different statements made by Lucien and Chante. When he found the same date and approximate time, which matched, he raised his eyebrows and a confused look came over his face. He looked up the tidal charts and then he made a call.

When he got off the phone, he knew he had him. Then Officer Fernand brought in a pile of reports.

When Raoul asked what the files were, Fernand replied that they were the statements taken from the town's residents. Raoul had almost forgotten about them, he was so busy with the interviews and the statements that he already had. He still had to go through all of them, just to make sure he had not missed anything. It would be another long night.

Chapter 34

At 9:00 the next morning, Souveterre called the colonel and asked for a meeting with the key people involved in the case. Even though it was Saturday, would the colonel mind if they all met at the fort? The colonel was happy to oblige and he let Alerion and Lucien know. Then Lucien told his father and Chante. They were all to meet at 11:00 in the visitor's reception room.

After Souveterre spent a long, cramped night at his desk in his office going through everything he had, especially the resident's statements, he now knew what had happened and was eager to share the news. The chief needed to stretch his legs and walk to the fort. The skies were clear, the cold weather had abated, and today the sun was out. At last the taste of truth was on his tongue.

When he arrived at the fort, the front desk officer told him that the rest of his party was waiting in the visitors lounge just down the hall. The clerk said he would let the colonel know that he had arrived. Souveterre walked down the hall and entered a white-walled room with large windows facing east. The light flooded the room and shined off the long-leafed plants that lined the wall at the base of the windows. Alerion, Chante, Lucien, and Gervais were all seated on beige-cushioned chairs at a conference table, waiting. The colonel appeared at the door, said his hellos and stood next to his friend. Souveterre nodded in greeting to the group.

"Thank you for coming. I thought I would share with you the results of our investigation. The cases of the kidnapping, the thefts, and the murder have now been solved." Everyone in the room sat up straighter with broadening smiles and congratulations. He looked especially from Lucien to Chante to Gervais.

"First, I want to apologize for the accusatory tones in your interviews. I find the process often effective in discerning truth from lies. I also apologize for conducting searches of your living quarters, but I had to eliminate each of you as complicit in hiding any evidence. At the time, the box, satchel, and gun were still missing, and they were key pieces of evidence. But you were not the only ones that had your homes searched. I also got a warrant to search the apartment and storage area of Alexis Moniqua."

Surprise mixed with confusion showed on their faces. They looked at one another questioningly, but Alerion, who was least in the know, was the one who asked.

"Sir, who is Alexis Moniqua?"

Chante also spoke up. "And how did you come to suspect him?"

"That's right, private, you were otherwise detained, and the rest of you may never have met him. He is, or was, the young man who ran the offices at the Mairie and Tourist Bureau for the last year."

Lucien remembered. "I met him. I spoke with him twice at the Mairie."

"I didn't suspect him until I reread your statement, Sergeant Reynard. You said that you saw Morcant looking up above the Mairie that rainy night, and mentioned that you saw a light on in the insurance office window. That's when I began to suspect Moniqua. I had a warrant issued to search his apartment. I knew his apartment complex had storage lockers in their carports, so the locker was included in the search. That's when we found the cache of stolen goods, including the box and satchel that your letter was in. Monique swore that he had no idea that those items were in the locker, and that he had never used that storage. It was obvious that Morcant had taken advantage of that fact, had stolen Moniqua's storage key, and then used the storage to hide his stash, unbeknownst to Moniqua. In case Morcant was caught, the items would be in Moniqua's possession, and Morcant would not be held directly accountable. Under threat of having several charges drawn against Moniqua for grand theft, Moniqua confessed that they had been working together.

"It seems that he and Morcant had been in business together for several years, first in Marseille where Moniqua was raised, and then in Collioure. Moniqua was also the security officer for the building and he had keys to the insurance company upstairs. That made it easy for him to enter when no one was there and search through their files for new policies. He would relay information to Morcant about any resident who had taken out insurance policies on art collections, jewels, and other items of value. He told Morcant what items were being insured, how much they were worth, the addresses of the homes, and details of the security measures protecting them. Morcant chose his time carefully, waited for the occupants to leave their homes, and then broke in and stole the insured items. He stored them in the storage space until he had a good amount, transferred them to his boat under cover of night, and then headed for northern ports to sell them. He was smart. He always waited a span of time after the policy had been taken out before performing the robberies, and took only those things he wanted. The insurance company, after a fruitless investigation, had no choice but to pay out on what had been insured. Later Moniqua received cash payoffs for his part in the crimes.

Lucien added, "So Morcant really was a modern-day pirate."

The chief nodded, "It seems so. And he used two people to help him in his endeavors. The first one was Beaux Falchan, with whom he had worked with when Morcant lived here years ago, and the second was Moniqua."

"And the murder of Falchan?" asked the colonel.

"That was more difficult to prove. I felt sure that Morcant was still working with Falchan. Why not have two locals working for him? Besides, Morcant and Falchan were both professional divers. I guessed that Falchan, had found the cave while on a diving trip and had seen the chest, but needed help removing its contents. So he enlisted Morcant to help him. I surmised that once Morcant knew where the cave was, he killed Falchan and threw him overboard so he could have the treasure all to himself.

"But," interrupted Chante, "when we found the box and the satchel in it, the seal had not been broken. Falchan would not have known what was inside."

"I think Falchan realized, like you and Lucien did, that no matter what was in the satchel it was valuable and needed to be opened in a more suitable place. He couldn't just tuck the satchel under his arm and risk getting whatever was inside wet by swimming back to his boat. So he looked for help."

The chief briefly paused to let that soak in, but then went on.

"When I got the confession from Moniqua saying that he had no idea his locker was being used to store the stolen goods, I believed him. I was a little blinded to the truth. You see Alexis Moniqua is the son of my cousin. I got him that job at the Mairie after his father begged me to get him out of Marseille and give him a job with some responsibility. So I did. Knowing that his parents had little money, I even paid him extra by reporting to me any suspicious activities in town, as a sort of undercover agent. The Mairie is so close to the central square that literally anyone coming into town, either driving or walking, goes by the Mairie. I'm sure he knows exactly who each of you are and where you live.

"But the gun that killed Falchan was not on the boat or with the stolen goods, and I still needed it to tie Morcant to the murder. I searched for the gun everywhere I could think, but I couldn't find it. I figured that Morcant simply threw it overboard with his cell phone before his boat was overtaken and he was captured. He had to get rid of his phone to protect the client contacts that were on it. With Alexis' confession, I realized he was not as innocent as I first thought, and that's when I had the Mairie searched. We found the gun hidden in a paper bag at the back of a file drawer in the basement. I sent the gun to ballistics, and the bullet found in Falchan's chest matched the gun. But there were no fingerprints on the gun, so even though I had the gun and knew it was the one that killed Falchan, I still could not tie it to Morcant.

"So I started over. I went back through all your statements, and that's when I found a few more clues. I already knew that Falchan and Morcant had once worked together and both were divers. So they already knew each other quite well and they knew the coast well. Since Falchan could not get the satchel away by sea, he needed someone to get it out by land. I thought that he probably made the mistake of telling Morcant about the cave and chest, hoping to get back in business with him after Morcant's return. Maybe he missed the money that he used to make with Morcant. Business together had to have been lucrative. Both had acquired fairly nice boats. It's more likely that he needed Morcant's contacts to sell whatever was in the chest. So Morcant shot Falchan and threw him overboard. Now that he knew where the cave was, he could just keep whatever was in the satchel for himself. Besides, he no longer needed Falchan, he had a much more lucrative relationship with Moniqua.

"There was only one thing wrong with that theory. The coroner said the body had been in the water for several weeks. That was well before you two found the cave. If Morcant knew exactly where the cave was, it would not have taken him all that time to get back to it. He would have gone back the very next day. I was puzzled by that time lag. It took me a sleepless night to discover why that would be.

"Then I wondered, could Falchan have told someone else about the cave? Perhaps he took that other person to the place along the coast to show him the cave, but for some reason ended up not showing the correct place. Maybe he had second thoughts? Maybe he was threatened? We may never know. So that person, who obviously did not know the coast well, had difficulty finding the place where the cave should be. That's when I thought of checking the tidal charts. The look of a coastline can dramatically change from a high tide to a low tide. Mademoiselle Morgan, in your statement you said you came out of the cave quite early in the morning, so I compared the timing. That person probably realized that he had to be in the area at the lowest tide for the best chance of seeing the entrance to any cave that might present itself. It must have taken him weeks, going back and forth along the cliffs in a boat, before he realized he would not be able to see the spot unless the tide was very low. He must have been sitting on his boat offshore, probably from the night before, waiting for low tide very early the next morning. Then you and Sergeant Reynard appeared on the shore with a large bundle, where he thought the cave was. That person must have been quite angry that you beat him to the treasure."

Chante remembered seeing the bobbing yellow light from a boat offshore that night. That had to have been whoever had seen them.

"Then, in your statement, Private Bellamy, you said that Morcant held you at knifepoint. I thought that was interesting. Why not at gunpoint if he had a gun? Morcant said that he didn't own a gun. I thought he was lying, but he was telling the truth.

"Next, since the stolen items had now been recovered, I was in the process of closing those theft case files, when I spotted something that got me thinking. Two of the robberies had occurred well before the murder, so there was no reason to connect the thefts to the murder. But two of them were much more recent. So I compared the dates and times of those thefts to the day you came out of the cave. Sure enough, the robbery of the coin collection had occurred early that morning at about the same time you were coming out of the cave. Morcant had been otherwise occupied, so he couldn't have been the one that had seen you.

"But, if it wasn't Morcant who saw us and knew where the cave was, who was it that killed Falchan?" asked Chante.

"It was the only person left who could have killed him, Moniqua."

"But how did that come about?" asked Lucien.

"I'm sure Moniqua had heard the story of how Falchan and Morcant had worked together years before, and gotten away with the many thefts. With Morcant back in town, Moniqua probably worried that he might make a lot less money, if not get cut out entirely, if Morcant went back to working with Falchan. When we asked around town if anyone had seen any strangers or if they had any information about Falchan, several townspeople mentioned that they had seen Falchan and Moniqua together in the last year. Even Dominique said he'd served the two a couple of times in his bar.

"My guess is that Moniqua befriended Falchan to keep an eye on him. It kept him close, so that if Morcant did contact Falchan for a job, he would probably learn about it. If that happened, all he had to do was wait for a good time to get him away from town and get rid of him, eliminating his competition. One of Falchan's diving buddies, the one who identified Falchan's body, even mentioned in his statement that he'd seen Falchan and Alexis go out on Falchan's diving boat several times in the last couple of months. It is not difficult to imagine that after so long a time, Falchan must have trusted Moniqua enough to share his discovery with his new close friend. Moniqua must have thought he hit the jackpot in hearing about the cave's treasure. Plus, Moniqua was younger than Morcant, and probably in better physical condition, so he could more easily climb down the cliff to the cave. Since Moniqua was not really familiar with the tides, it took him a while to figure out that he had to search at a time when the tides were especially low. Morcant would not have made that mistake. He knew that coastline well, but Moniqua did not want to tell Morcant where the cave was."

"So it was Moniqua who saw us exit the cave," added Lucien.

"Yes, and he had Morcant follow you to retrieve the treasure, because he had to work at the Mairie every day."

Now Alerion was catching on. "But why didn't anyone suspect Moniqua when Falchan went missing?"

"A couple things come into play here. One is that Falchan was not getting along with his wife, and Falchan's diving buddy made that comment. Two, it was the end of the season so Falchan's wife was out of town visiting her sister. That gave Falchan the opportunity to dive in places he would not ordinarily go with his diving clients. And that also gave Moniqua enough time to deal with Falchan. Three, after Falchan had shown Moniqua where the treasure was and Moniqua had killed him, Moniqua told the harbor master that Falchan had decided to join his wife and her family for a long-needed vacation, and that Moniqua had been given permission to use his boat while he was gone.

"When I read that statement by the harbor master, it seemed highly suspicious. After Moniqua dealt with Falchan's body, he pretended to be Falchan and sent extra money to Falchan's wife with a note telling her to spend more time with her sister. I'm sure he thought he would make more than enough money from the treasure to make up for it. She must have been happy to stay away longer on an extended vacation. Moniqua had already told Falchan's dive buddy that he thought Falchan was ready to skip town with a new lover. If Falchan's wife was to return and find her husband missing, everyone would assume that he had deserted his wife and run off with another woman. Falchan had taken plenty of female clients diving, and he was a flirt, so it was a perfectly plausible explanation.

"I'm sure Moniqua didn't expect Falchan's body to resurface and show up on a nearby beach. He must have panicked when he heard a body had been found. We could not reach Falchan's wife because she had left with her sister to go traveling elsewhere and did not tell anyone where they went. We left word at her sister's home to contact us immediately upon her return, and we finally heard back from her late yesterday afternoon. She was shocked by the news, of course. When I spoke to her on the phone she told me her side of the story. She's returning tonight for the funeral tomorrow. We helped her to prepare for the service.

"One more phone call provided information that tied the gun to Moniqua. I had to call his parents to let them know that he had been arrested for aiding and abetting a series of burglaries. While I was on the phone to my cousin the idea came to me. Did he own a pistol? He responded that he did, but it had disappeared a while back. He thought that kids must have broken into the house and taken it. But I had a pretty good idea who had taken it instead. When my cousin confirmed that it was a 1969 Le Français pistol from his old service days, I knew I could then tie the gun to his son."

Everyone was quite impressed by his recitation of the probable events.

The colonel was the first to speak. "I guess this means that you now have enough evidence to have both men prosecuted and bring your cases to a close."

"Yes. All I need is for the four of you to come to the station to sign your statements and then you are done. "

"So now," Lucien turned to the colonel, "can we release the information to the four reporters to whom we promised an exclusive?" The colonel nodded.

Then Souveterre stood, and the colonel extended his hand.

"Thank you, chief, for your excellent work!"

"Thank you, colonel for your cooperation, and for capturing Morcant. I'll let you know what happens." He saluted them all and left.

Lucien turned to Alerion, Chante, and Gervais. "Would the three of you mind waiting for me outside? I need to speak with the colonel alone." Then he turned to the colonel. "May I, sir?"

"Yes, sergeant, of course."

Chante, Alerion, and Gervais walked away down the hall, and the colonel turned to Lucien.

"What is it, sergeant?"

"Now that everything has been solved, you said that if the chief did not press any charges against us, you would consider my proposal. Would you be so kind as to have the letter authenticated and allow us to approach a museum for its inclusion?"

The colonel could not help but smile.

"I'm way ahead of you, sergeant. A copy of the letter was given to the chief, and pictures of the box and satchel were exchanged for those items in evidence. The three items, along with your father's documentation, were sent to Paris two days ago by military escort to be authenticated at the Musee de l'Histoire. I don't know exactly how long the authentication will take, even with the military requesting that they expedite the request, but we might expect a response soon."

Lucien could not believe his ears. Everything was falling into place. "Thank you so much colonel. I really appreciate everything you have done." They shook hands and saluted one another.

The colonel smiled, told him to have a good day, and then left the room. Lucien also left and quickly joined Alerion, Chante, and Gervais outside to tell them the good news.

The four of them walked to the station to sign their statements. Alerion went first, followed by Gervais, and then the chief asked for Chante and Lucien to come in together. He escorted them to his office and offered them a seat.

"I have both of your statements here for your signatures." He had them read through their statements and sign their names. When they had finished he played his last move.

"I do have one last piece of business that I need to discuss with you. I still have not solved the mysteries of the unlocked doors, the two extra sets of footprints in the church, and what happened to the papers that must have been in the file boxes in the trunk at the church. Now I might be able to overlook the illegal entry if the contents of those files were somehow to resurface and be anonymously donated to our local library. I'm sure the contents from those files would be dutifully protected, and the procurers of those papers would be most thankful if they were not charged with breaking and entering, or the theft of private property. Of course, I would also have to have their reassurance that nothing of this nature would ever happen again."

Lucien and Chante looked at each other, smiled, and turned back to Souveterre. Lucien answered for both of them.

"I'm sure the holders of those papers would be very thankful to learn of that generous offer, and the townspeople would be very interested to be able to read some amazing information on their local history."

The chief smiled and stood. "Then I think we understand each other." He extended his hand to shake both of theirs. "I'll keep in touch with the colonel and he can let you know what happens with the kidnapping, murder, and theft cases."

"Yes, sir. Thank you again, sir, very much." Lucien and Chante shook his hand again in reassurance, and then joined Alerion and Gervais in the front office.

Chapter 35

It was time to celebrate, so Chante invited everyone over for dinner that night. When Alerion arrived later that evening, the first thing he did was to apologize to Chante for even thinking that she might have anything to do with the plot. She told him there was no need to apologize, and before Lucien knew it, Chante and Alerion were seated on the couch discussing grape varieties and their favorite wines. He and Gervais sat on the balcony sipping at their glasses. Gervais smiled at his son.

"I hope this means that you two might think about having some adventures that don't involve tromping through tunnels, breaking and entering, or stealing private property."

Lucien laughed, "No, Papa. I've learned my lesson, but I do hope our adventures together become a permanent aspect of our relationship." He looked over at Chante and saw that she was radiantly happy. Alerion was all smiles and was being very gracious toward her. They seemed to have made friends quickly.

Lucien had wanted to take them all to dinner, but Chante insisted on cooking for the four of them. While they sipped their wine and Alerion had some sparkling water, they ate *pissaladière*, slices of bread with tomato sauce, onion, olives and anchovies, from a recipe in her new cookbook. Finally Chante called everyone to the table and Lucien offered up a toast.

"To good friends, good family, and love that keeps us going even in the darkest of hours." Then they drank and began to eat. For their main course, Chante had made quenelles of pike with lobster sauce.

Alerion also offered a toast thanking all three of them for showing him that exploring life is more important than any job and the everyday way of doing things. He explained that when he had been tied up and was lying helpless at the church and on the boat, he had given his life a lot of thought. He did, however, feel that he had had enough adventure for at least a while. Then he announced that he had some news. When he had turned in his report to the colonel, he had spoken with him further. He had thanked him for allowing Lucien to involve many of the colonel's resources in conducting his safe return, but he also wondered if the colonel would see him clear for an honorable discharge, as his concussion had caused some hearing loss, and he had decided to finally do something with the money he had inherited from his father. He wanted to get into viticulture, settle down, and make wine. He saw the shock in especially, Lucien's eyes.

"Don't worry, Lucien, I promised the colonel that I would wait until spring before leaving. Besides, I will be settling nearby and moving my mother to be with me. She needs some better care now that she is getting older, and I would like to spend more time with her while I can. Please be happy for me, as I have wanted this for a long time."

They were sorry to hear that Alerion's injuries had caused some hearing loss, but they congratulated him on finally realizing his dream and going for it. Chante then served mocha pots de crème for dessert. The espresso-flavored chocolate was the perfect ending to a great day. While they were eating dessert, Lucien got a call from the colonel. The colonel had just received a call saying that the letter appeared to be authentic. Would Lucien, Chante, and Gervais please make arrangements to come to the museum and speak with their acquisitions director? They cheered at the news and made another round of toasts.

That reminded Lucien about his agreement with Souveterre. He told Gervais to bring the remaining historical files from the bank to him on Monday, so they could be donated anonymously to the library as a special collection. Gervais agreed that was an excellent way to make sure the townspeople could appreciate even more of their local history. Then Chante turned to Gervais.

"I just realized that the seal and slivers taken from your house were not with the box and satchel. What do you think happened to them?"

"It's most likely that Morcant tossed them. They had no obvious value."

"And with the slivers of wood that we sent in to be analyzed, will their dating make any difference now?"

"I think that every bit of information we can piece together has its own importance. At least we will know how old the tunnels are."

Alerion could not help but ask. "What wooden slivers? What tunnels?"

Lucien chuckled. "I guess there are a few more things we need to tell you about, and we will, my dear friend."

Then Gervais could not help himself. "So Chante, are you going to write about the adventures we all went through?"

Chante gave that some thought. "While you and I were waiting those long hours for Alerion to be rescued, I made myself believe that everything would work out all right. Alerion would be saved, the murderer would get caught, and the letter would be real and get into a museum. If everything did work out, what would or could I write about? I can't really write about everything we did as an investigative article. That would call for facts and explanations that we cannot reveal. I certainly don't want to do a travel article on the tunnels of Collioure or it would make people want to come and dig all over the place. Now, with the historical information we found, I could do an article on the history of the chateau. And, I am toying with the idea of writing a book of fiction with a similar storyline, with the names changed of course. That way, I would be able to tell more than I could otherwise, and everyone who reads it would simply think of it as a good story."

Lucien smiled and reached out to affectionately cover her hand. "You know, that might just work. I hope you include at the end that everyone lives happily ever after."

She smiled warmly at him and covered his hand with her own. "Oh, I will. That's the best part."

Finally, after the dishes had been cleared, they shared more of the story about the tunnels. As the evening became late, Gervais began to look a bit tired. He was staying the night on the couch at Chante's so they could all go to the funeral for Beaux Falchan the next day. There was a service for him at the church at 11:00. On Monday Beaux's body was to be cremated and his ashes scattered at sea by his wife from his own boat. After that, she was selling the boat and going to live with her sister. At the same time on Monday, both Alexis Moniqua and Fiacare Morcant were going to be transferred to the larger police facility in Montpelier to await trial.

Alerion also got up to walk home. Lucien suggested that he and Chante walk Alerion part way, as Lucien was feeling the need for some fresh air. Alerion said good night to Gervais as he stretched out on the couch. Lucien and Chante would not be long.

The three of them walked downstairs and went to the back gate that led to the winery, where Alerion turned to say goodnight.

"Chante, Lucien, I want to thank you one more time for saving my life." Then he looked tenderly at Lucien and placed his hand on his shoulder. "That makes twice that you've saved me my friend! It looks like I owe you doubly. Maybe I can be of more service to you in the future. Perhaps a gift of a case of wine from my new vineyard will help." He reached forward and gave his friend a hug. "Anything my friend, just let me know," and he turned away and waved goodbye. A few steps later he turned and added, "Except going into any damn tunnels!"

Chante and Lucien laughed and watched him for a moment as he walked down the street. Then Lucien took Chante's hand and led her on the short walk up the stone steps once again to the gazebo lookout. They stood at the low stonewall and looked out over the lights of Collioure that sparkled along the beach walkway below them.

Lucien held Chante with his arm around her waist as they looked out over the lovely town with its stalwart castle, and beyond to the imposing fort high on the hill.

"Chante, I have not had a chance to really thank you for the part that you played in all of this." He turned toward her and held her with both arms.

"For which part?" she asked. "For egging you on to stay the night under the castle, for talking you into letting me weld the tunnel doors shut at the castle, or for lying along with you to the police?"

Lucien laughed at her. "You do have a way of cutting through my thoughts. Are all American women so outspoken?"

"I hope so, but then I just happen to be the one lucky American woman that got to meet you in this beautiful place and fall in love with you."

Lucien removed his arms from around her and took her hands into his. Chante looked up at his tanned face with the light of the moon upon it. The star-filled sky beyond seemed to wrap around his head and shoulders as a sparkling halo. She smiled when he made the next statement.

"Chante, I'm no angel, but I certainly don't intend to lead a boring life. In fact, I'm thinking of getting some additional training. The colonel has told me that with my experience at the fort, and the work on this case, I might start thinking of choosing a new direction. In my position, the most attractive arm of the service that appeals to me is the Departmental Gendarmerie and becoming a research detective. With my father a history professor, I guess some of his long-winded talks have finally had an effect on me. Historical crime seems to hold the most interest for me, but I also think there is a lot of present-day internal investigative work to be done with search and rescue operations, and especially with smuggling, so close to Spain and Italy. After some training, I could be looking at becoming a sergeant major in the near future.

"I guess what I'm trying to say is that without your interest in me, without you by my side, all that would mean less, unless I were to share the ride with you. Chante, I want you to remain a part of my life, and I a part of yours. Have you decided at all what you want to do? Are you going to stay here for a while, go live with your father in London, or go off searching for other tunnel enthusiasts around the world?"

"Oh Lucien, I have been thinking about that, and with everything we have been through, with how our love has remained constant through all of what has happened, I'm thinking I should go to London for a break... and I think you should come with me to meet my father. Then I see us settling here for a while, and after that let's see where the world takes us. Believe it or not, I've grown very fond of your father and tonight he let me know he has plans to write a new book and needs a research assistant. He asked me if I would be interested in the position. Now, I don't know if he is maneuvering to have me become a part of your family, or if he really likes me that much to work with..."

"He does, he likes you very much!"

"Then perhaps I might be of service to him. But to you, I'm hoping I can be more, much more."

"Are you saying what I think you are saying?"

Chante cast a look toward the view and smiled. "Far be it for me to lead you to any conclusion, staff sergeant. I'm sure you will make up your own mind when the time comes." She turned back to smile widely at him.

Lucien was beside himself with happiness and once again kissed her freckles and those soft warm cheeks, but then he paused.

"I will take your recommendation under serious consideration," he said, and at last kissed her with a strong embrace.

Chante's feelings about Collioure would never be the same, now that they had brought to light more than one secret, which the town had once concealed.

The adventures continue with
Chante, Lucien and Gervais in

The Murder of the Mystras Nun

About the Author

Lita-Luise Chappell is a versatile writer whose works encompass a broad spectrum from poetry to cookbooks, social commentary to short stories, and fairy tales to murder mysteries. With degrees in psychology she understands the range of human feeling and thinking, and with a doctorate in human sexuality, she is able to express the human desires that drive social behavior. After a lifetime of several different careers and world travels, she draws upon her knowledge and experience to entertain. One of her favorite places is the seaside village of Collioure.

For other books by this author go to
www.LitaChappell.com

33975877R00234

Printed in Great Britain
by Amazon